The Mule Soldiers

A Novel of the American Civil War

By

Blair Howard

ISBN-13: 978-1505549805

Foreword

The Mule Soldiers is the true story - fictionalized - of Streight's Raid into Northern Alabama, which took place from 19 April to 3 May 1863. A brigade of Federal infantry, led by Colonel Abel D. Streight, set out on a 220-mile ride to destroy the Western and Atlantic railroad at Rome, Georgia. The raid turned into a battle that continued for over fourteen days between Streight and Confederate General Nathan Bedford Forrest.

The most fascinating thing about the raid is that Streight's brigade of four infantry regiments was mounted on mules, a huge problem in itself. Not only did he have almost 1,500 stubborn and wily animals to contend with, few of his men had ever ridden a horse, let alone a mule. For Streight, it was a long and tortuous journey across Northern Alabama. For Forrest, it was one defeat after another at the hands of the very "able" Abel Streight, even though Forrest had the advantage of home territory and the sympathy and aid of the local populace.

They say that truth is stranger than fiction. This amazing story proves the point, for the end of the story is... well, unbelievable.

The cover photograph is courtesy of Donnie Nunne and Creative Commons (the Union soldier was the inspiration for Sergeant Major Ignatius O'Sullivan)

The Mule Soldiers

The Players

UNION:

Major General William S. Rosecrans: Commanding the Army of the Cumberland

Brigadier General James A. Garfield: Rosecrans' Chief of Staff

The Raiders:

Colonel Abel D. Streight: Provisional Brigade (The Mule Soldiers)

Colonel Gilbert Hathaway: Provisional Brigade - 73rd Indiana Infantry Regiment

Lieutenant Colonel James W. Sheets: Provisional Brigade - 51st Indiana Infantry Regiment

Lieutenant Colonel Robert Lawson: Provisional Brigade - 3rd Ohio Infantry

Lieutenant Colonel Andrew F. Rogers: Provisional Brigade -80th Illinois Infantry

Major James Vananda: Provisional Brigade -Chief of Artillery

Captain David D. Smith: Provisional Brigade - 1st Tennessee Cavalry

Assistant Surgeon Doctor W. Spencer: Provisional Brigade

Sergeant Major Ignatius O'Sullivan: Provisional Brigade - (Fictional Top Soldier)

Corporal Boone Coffin: Provisional Brigade - (Fictional aid to O'Sullivan)

Private Cullen Doyle: Provisional Brigade - (Fictional Wagon Master)

Private Andrew (Andy) McHugh: Provisional Brigade - (Fictional Mule Soldier)

Private Silas Cassell: Provisional Brigade - (Fictional Mule Soldier)

Support for Streight's Raid:

Brigadier General Grenville M. Dodge: Commanding Union Army, District of Corinth, Mississippi

Brigadier General Thomas W. Sweeney: 1st Brigade Union Army, District of Corinth

Captain George Spencer: Assistant Adjutant General, District of Corinth and Dodge's spy

CONFEDERATE:

General Braxton Bragg: Commanding the Army of Tennessee

Major General Earl Van Dorn: Commanding Cavalry, Army of Tennessee

Brigadier General Nathan Bedford Forrest: Forrest's Cavalry Division

Colonel George Dibrell: 8th Tennessee Cavalry, Forrest's Cavalry Division

Lieutenant Colonel W.S. McLemore: 4th Tennessee Cavalry, Forrest's Cavalry Division

Colonel Jacob Biffle: 9th Tennessee Cavalry, Forrest's Cavalry Division

Colonel William E. DeMoss: 10th Tennessee Cavalry, Forrest's Cavalry Division

Colonel James H. Edmondson: 11th Tennessee Cavalry, Forrest's Cavalry Division

Captain John Morton: Chief of Artillery, Forrest's Cavalry Division

Captain William Forrest: Chief of Scouts and General Forrest's Brother

Private Will Steiner: Scout - Forrest's Cavalry Division (Fictional)

Private Sam Corbett: Scout - Forrest's Cavalry Division (Fictional)

Private Isaac Boggs: Scout - Forrest's Cavalry Division (Fictional)

Colonel Phillip D. Roddey: Roddey's Cavalry Brigade

Civilians:

Emma Sansom - Native of Alabama

Author's Note - About the Maps:

I have included several maps to help you think your way around the battlefield. Unfortunately, due to the way Kindle formats images, and the type of reader you use, you may find them a little hard to view. That being so, I have uploaded large versions to my website. They are easily readable. You can find them here: http://bit.ly/1HuC52g

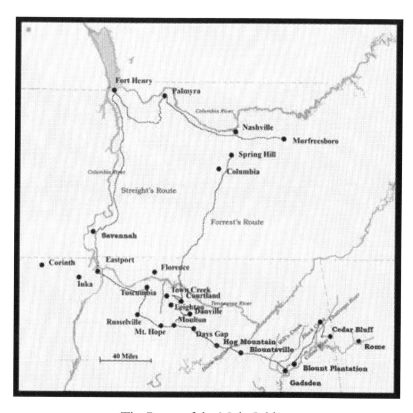

The Route of the Mule Soldiers

Contents

Chapter 1

Early Morning, March 5, 1863

Abel Streight lay in bed, staring up into the dark reaches of the ceiling, listening to his wife snoring gently beside him. It was past one o'clock in the morning; sleep did not come easily to Abel Streight these days. His mind was always busy, awash with memories of the past two years, of battles fought, won, and lost, a never-ending turmoil of the mind that constantly surged back and forth, to and fro, much like the ocean crashing endlessly upon the rocks of his imagination.

He rose from the bed, for the umpteenth time, and went to the outhouse to relieve himself, also for the umpteenth time, then went back to bed to stare again into the darkness. Lovina's gentle snoring bothered him not in the least.

This can't go on. I have to do something and quick. I shall go mad, if not. Congestion of the cerebellum. What the hell is that? Whatever it was, it had caused him to be removed from the duty roster in January and then sent home to rest and recover.

Abel Streight was a big man, always immaculately dressed and groomed, somewhat corpulent with a commanding personality. His large, square face was deeply tanned and heavily lined, his full beard neatly trimmed, and his top lip clean-shaven. He could be quick-tempered when the mood took him, often arrogant and demanding, but always fair and ready to listen to both sides of an argument or problem.

His childhood years were spent on the family farm in New York. At the age of thirty-one he moved from New York to Indianapolis, where he became a successful publisher until the outbreak of the Civil War halted his career. He had no formal military training whatsoever, but when war broke out, as a prominent citizen in Indianapolis, he was commissioned as a full colonel and given command of the 51st Indiana Volunteer Infantry Regiment.

Even though he lacked any military training, he was a competent battlefield commander, although for the first two years of the war he and his regiment had seen little action, much to his chagrin.

Abel Streight was frustrated, agitated, and quite upset with his lot. He was, so he thought, now fully recovered from that incomprehensible miasma that had laid him low. He needed to be back at the helm of his regiment, not sitting and idling away the hours, days, and weeks doing nothing in Murfreesboro.

General Rosecrans and his Federal Army of the Cumberland, of which the 51st was a part, had been, and in fact still was, *"regrouping"* after the Battle of Stones River, a bloody conflict that had taken place at the dawn of 1863. The number of casualties had been horrendous, more than 24,000 combined Union and Confederate. Although Abel Streight had not actually been wounded in the battle, he felt that he might as well have been. For more than a month, he had been confined to his bed. Then came the inevitable boredom of the household routine and a nagging wife; no, not really nagging, just an ever abiding insistence that he get off his backside and do something constructive. *Were those her words or mine? It really doesn't matter. She's right! Hurrah, hurrah, for Southern rights hurrah... damn, I can't get that stupid Rebel tune out of my head. I've had enough.* He sat up, turned to his wife and jabbed her in the side with his elbow.

"Lovina, wake up," he said, loudly.

Lovina groaned, muttered something incomprehensible, and then rolled over with her back toward him.

"Wake up. Wake up. Wake up." He shook her. He kept on shaking her until she responded.

"Oh my lord, what is it?" She turned over and pushed herself upright.

"We, that is I, need to do something," he said, agitated. "I am going mad. I am singing to myself in my head all the time, which would be all right, except that the tune is that damnable Bonnie Blue

Flag. It's intolerable. Intolerable, I tell you. We have to do something. I have to get out of here, do something. Anything."

She lay back on her elbows and looked up at him. "The Bonnie Blue Flag?" And then she laughed out loud. It was a tinkling laugh and derisive in its tone. "You really are going out of your mind. Go back to sleep. We'll talk about it in the morning." She rolled back over and stuffed a corner of the bed sheet into her mouth to stop laughing.

Lovina Streight was a good woman, a fine-looking woman, a colonel's lady in every sense of the word. She was inordinately proud of her husband, and fiercely protective of him. She also had an extraordinary sense of humor, and the thought of her somewhat straight-laced, officious Union colonel husband humming the Bonnie Blue Flag sent her vivid imagination into raptures. Try as she might, even with the pillow against her face, she could not completely smother her giggles.

"Oh for pity's sake, woman." Abel Streight was not at all amused, and he flung himself back down on his pillow, more frustrated and agitated than ever. *Hurrah, hurrah... oh for God's sake, please, please stop.*

They rose early, Abel and Lovina. It was a gray day, overcast with a hint of rain. Breakfast was its usual eggs and ham with scalding black coffee. They ate together in silence. When they had finished eating, they sat back in their chairs and looked at each other. It was one of those comfortable family moments when each seems to know what the other is thinking.

Lovina was tall, with a forceful personality, well thought of among the ladies of the senior officer class, and she was ambitious, almost to a fault. While she'd been lying in bed, she'd been thinking.

"So?" she asked, quietly.

"So?"

"Oh come on, Abel. Out with it. What's on your mind?"

"What's on my mind is this damnable boredom. I need to return to my men, but..."

"But what? So go."

"You don't understand, my dear. It's not the going, it's the being there. It's boring here, but there, oh my god. When the army's in quarters, there's even less for me to do than there is here. Everything is handled by my juniors. I sit. I smoke. I drink. I think. It's like sitting atop Mount Olympus with nothing to do other than stare down at all the little people and wondering how to get through the interminable day and then again the next, and the next. Oh, I shall have to return sooner or later, but...."

"Abel," she said. "Why don't you write to your friend, General Garfield, and ask for his advice?

Streight looked at his wife, seemed about to speak, and then simply shook his head.

"Why not?" she asked. "You are a good officer and a loyal and valiant one. You are well thought of in high circles. I know that from my own experience of such things. But you need more; you need that star on your shoulder. You need a little glory, something to set you apart. You must do something... something... well, something spectacular."

"Hah, and what might that be, do you think?"

She thought for a moment. "What about an independent command?"

He looked at her, incredulous. "You have no idea what you're talking about, woman. They don't give independent commands to infantrymen. And why me? Even if such a thing were possible, there are better qualified men than me."

"Oh, I doubt that," she said sincerely. "It is well known that it's not what you know but who you know. And General Garfield has just been appointed Chief of Staff to General Rosecrans. No, no, no, don't interrupt," she said as Streight opened his mouth to speak. "I haven't finished yet. I know you have been reading the newspapers, and I know you have read about the Confederate raiders that seem to be operating with impunity in the West. Why, my dear, can you not do the same?" She held up her hand as Streight again opened his mouth to speak.

"Hear me out. I read the other day that Confederate General Earl Van Dorn has been harrying General Grant like a rabid dog, and that General Forrest is operating unfettered from Memphis to Nashville. And then, in the east, Mosbey and Stuart are driving General Hooker to distraction. Is it not about time that our side took a little initiative?" She paused for breath.

Streight stared at her in open amazement.

"Think about it," she continued. "You have the rank, the enthusiasm, and you know the territory better than any."

Streight inclined his head, the corners of his mouth turned down as he nodded in agreement. "But, my dear, I say again: I am an infantry officer, not cavalry."

"I would think that would be something of an advantage. Have you not always told me that the horse is obsolete, more target than useful? True, a horse will get you where you need to be faster, but it eats ten times more than a man, and it is a rather large target for those spry Confederate sharpshooters."

Abel Streight was nodding, but something she had said had caught his attention. "Quiet a moment, if you don't mind, my dear. I need to think."

Lovina rose from the table and walked to the sideboard to refill her coffee cup. Streight sat at the table, tapping his fingers on the polished surface and staring at the clock on the mantelpiece. Then he rose and said, "Lovina, please clear the table. I'm going to fetch my maps."

She did as he asked and a moment later, he came back into the breakfast parlor with an armful of rolled maps. He sorted through them, found what he was looking for, and threw the rest onto the seat of a nearby chair. Lovina promptly retrieved them and returned them

15

to their former tidy roll. As she did so, her husband spread the chosen map out on the surface of the breakfast table. Then he stood for several minutes, staring at it. Lovina stood on the opposite side of the table, watching, but saying nothing; she knew better than to disturb her husband when he was deep in thought.

"Pencil, Lovina, please," he said, without looking up from the map, holding out a hand toward her.

Lovina pulled out a drawer in the sideboard, retrieved a pencil, and handed it to her husband. He took it from her, still not looking up from the map.

He hummed softly as he traced lines across the map. Lovina smiled as she recognized the tune, The Bonnie Blue Flag.

"That's it," he said. "Lovina, you're a genius. See here? Look, we are encamped here at Murfreesboro, yes?" He looked up at her.

Lovina looked to where he was pointing on the map and nodded.

"Good, now this here is the Tennessee border. Everything here is northern Alabama." He swept his fingers from one side of the map to the other. "And here, what do you think is here?"

"Why, Rome of course. It says so, right there on the map. I can read, Abel."

"Yes, yes, my dear, but what do you think this is?" Again, he pointed at the map.

Lovina was puzzled. She stared at the map, but could see nothing out of the ordinary. She shrugged her shoulders, shook her head slightly, continued to look puzzled, but said nothing.

"This, my dear," he said, with a flourish and obvious relish, "is the Western and Atlantic Railroad. It runs from Atlanta, through Rome and on into Chattanooga. If we could cut it and destroy it, we would disrupt Bragg's main line of supply from the south."

Slowly, she nodded in agreement.

"You said it yourself, Lovina. I do know that territory better than any other commander in the Union army, and I know the people. I have recruited men for the regiment all across the Northern Alabama territory."

"I always wondered about that, Abel. How is it possible to recruit Southerners to the Union cause?"

"That area, here," he pointed again to a spot on the map, "is solidly for the Union. Union sympathizers one and all; always have been, always will be. And that also means that we could count on local support to help. It can be done, Lovina, it can be done. Bring pen and paper. I must write at once to General Garfield."

And write he did:

Dear James,

I hope you will continue to favor me with your influence to convince the general to give me a suitable command for the purpose of penetrating the interior of the South. I am satisfied as I study the matter more carefully that I could do them more harm and our cause more good in a three-month campaign than I can, situated as I have been during this last year, in a whole lifetime.

Please consider this correspondence highly confidential and if you think it best for me to return at any time, telegraph me at my expense.

Detailed plans accompany this note.

I remain most truly your friend,

A.D. Streight

Chapter 2

March 20, 1863 - General Rosecrans' Headquarters, Murfreesboro, Tennessee

"General Rosecrans, sir." Brigadier General James Garfield, Chief of Staff of the Federal Army of the Cumberland waited at the door for the general to acknowledge him.

"Yes, Garfield, what is it?"

"Sir," Garfield said, stepping into the room. "I have a correspondence from Colonel Streight that I think you should see." He offered the general a small package of papers.

"Streight, of course. How is he? Down with some sort of ailment as I recall. Is he over it yet? Has he returned to duty? If so, I want to see him."

"He is much better, General, but as yet has not returned. He does, however, have an interesting proposal. And I must say, sir, I like what he proposes."

Rosecrans looked at the papers in his hand and nodded. "I will read what Colonel Streight has to say. Please leave me alone for," he drew an ornate pocked watch from his vest, cracked it open, noted the time, and then continued, "thirty minutes, no more. I have things to do, things that must be done."

Garfield saluted and left.

Rosecrans sighed, bit the tip from a new cigar, lighted it, drew deeply upon it, and then settled into a large, easy chair and began to read. The more he read, the more he was astounded.

"GENERAL GARFIELD," he shouted, not bothering to rise from the chair. "Get in here, now."

Garfield reentered the room, a slight smile on his lips.

"Have you read this? Do you have any idea what this man is proposing?"

"I have and I do, General. I think it could work."

"He's proposing to put two thousand infantry men on the backs of horses and parade them through northern Alabama, that's what he's proposing to do, some harebrained scheme to cut the Western and Atlantic at Rome, Georgia. Is the man suffering from brain damage? Is that why he was removed from the duty roster?"

Garfield knew Rosecrans well enough to be able to permit himself a small chuckle. "No, General. If you read on, I think you'll find that what he proposes has some merit. He knows the area well. He is an infantry commander - putting the men on horses, so he says, would turn them into a fast-moving strike force. He mentions that mounted infantry is something we already subscribe to and, in fact, cites a number of examples: John Wilder's brigade in particular. And there's no doubt that he knows Northern Alabama better than anyone else in this department. It all makes some sense."

"It might make sense, Garfield, barely, but have you considered that we just don't have animals enough to outfit such an expedition?"

Garfield hesitated for a moment, then took a deep breath and said, "Horses, no, General, but mules...."

Rosecrans almost came out of his seat. He glared at his chief of staff. "Have you gone mad, Garfield? Mules? That would make us the laughingstock of the Western Department, if not the entire Union."

Garfield smiled and shook his head. "I don't think so, sir. Streight is a good officer and a more than competent field commander. He knows infantry and knows the territory across Northern Alabama. I really think he could pull this off. But there's more...."

"Go on, General," Rosecrans drew deeply on his cigar, "tell me more."

"Well as you know, sir, General Grant has just authorized a like expedition from LaGrange to Newton Station in Mississippi to destroy the railroad there. If we authorized our own raid into Northern Alabama, each raid would, at least in theory, take some of the pressure off the other: the Confederate forces would be split. We might just pull off the double."

Rosecrans leaned back in his chair and continued to skim through the papers that represented Colonel Streight's outrageous proposal. Then, very slowly, he nodded.

"You may, indeed, be right, Garfield, but mules...." He visibly shuddered, regained his composure, and sat upright. "Send a telegraph to Colonel Streight. Have him report back here as soon as possible. I want to see the crazy S.O.B. as soon as he arrives. In the meantime, General Garfield, please look into the logistics of this thing. Let's find out if it's even possible. If it is, and if we're going to do it, let's get it right."

Garfield stood and saluted. "Of course, General." He turned and left Rosecrans puffing rapidly on his cigar and staring at Streight's proposal.

Chapter 3

March 28, 1863 - General Rosecrans' Headquarters, Murfreesboro, Tennessee

"Sit down, Colonel. You, too, General Garfield." General Rosecrans was not in the best of moods. "I, that is we, have been giving this idea of yours serious consideration. General Garfield has been trying to come up with the equipment you will need if I decide to approve it, and that's by no means certain. I tell you, sir, the more I consider it, the more harebrained it looks."

He put up his hand to stop Streight, who was about to speak. "On the other hand, the more I consider it, the more fascinating it becomes, and I do think it just might work. But, Colonel Streight, and this is a very large but, there's so much that could go wrong."

Again, he waved his hand as Streight opened his mouth to speak. "I know, I know, nothing will go wrong. Is that what you were going to say? Now, Abel, you and I and all creation know that it could, and indeed, it will. This is the Army, Colonel, and you above all others should know that if something can go wrong, it always damned well does. It's the way of things, Colonel. So, tell me why I should authorize this cockamamie scheme of yours."

Streight took a deep breath and said, "You should authorize it, sir, because it's the right thing to do. We need a victory, you need a victory, and General Grant needs a victory. I'm not saying this is the one, but I do think a weakened Confederate army to the east would at least provide you with a decided advantage, to say nothing of the boost in overall morale that would result.

"Not only that, General, the Confederate cavalry has been playing hell with our outposts, our lines of supply and communications. Van Dorn and Forrest have had unrestricted access to all points south, west and east. If nothing else, it would be a feather in your cap to give either one of them a bloody nose. I can do this, General. Just turn me loose, and I will destroy the Western and Atlantic at Rome and deny Bragg his supplies."

Rosecrans said nothing. He leaned back in his chair, stared at the chandelier that hung above the great table, and blew a series of tiny smoke rings up into the crystals.

Both Streight and Garfield remained silent, watching as the commanding general pondered the seemingly imponderable.

"Is it possible, James?" He looked at Garfield. "Can we really pull this off?"

"Yes, General, I think we can. From reports I've been receiving from the field, it seems there's little in the way of serious opposition. Speed is not of the essence, so if we use the rivers to transport the brigade south of the border, the trek across Northern Alabama should be quite uneventful provided that we operate under the strictest secrecy."

"You mentioned Van Dorn and Forrest; what of them?" Rosecrans asked.

"According to reports, both are operating out of Spring Hill, just south of here, more than ninety miles from Colonel Streight's planned route. And that's as the crow flies, General."

Rosecrans sighed, shook his head, and pondered some more. "I have serious reservations about the mules, gentlemen. Would it not be better to mount the men on horses?"

"Yes, General," Streight agreed. "It would indeed be better to mount the men on horses, but General Garfield has stated that he does not have horses to spare, so mules it must be."

Oh my God, Streight thought. *Mules! What have I done? What have I said? Heaven help me if I am wrong.*

"Be that as it may, General," Streight continued. "I know that territory. It's rough, wild, and mountainous. True, I did not have mules in mind when I put forth my plans for the expedition but, on reflection, I think mules would do very well under those conditions, better perhaps than horses."

Rosecrans looked hard at him, and then said with a sly smile, "And what of you and your officers, Colonel? Will you be riding donkeys, too?"

Rosecrans' mild sarcasm went right by Streight. "No, of course not, sir. I and my officers will ride horses, as is only fitting and proper."

Rosecrans grinned at Garfield who, sitting just to the right and rear of Streight, did see the irony of what Streight was proposing. He also grinned, though not for Streight to see.

"Colonel Streight, I have no doubt of your ability. You are a fine infantry commander and I can think of no one more qualified to lead a team of Mule Soldiers through Northern Alabama."

Garfield almost choked, but Streight did not seem to get it.

"Now then, Colonel," Rosecrans continued. "We'll take it to the next level. General Garfield, I assume you have beasts appropriated for the expedition."

Garfield nodded a little hesitantly.

"Then I propose you think about your own requirements, Colonel. I will not write the order until all is prepared and you are ready to move out. I will authorize a provisional brigade of four regiments, plus two companies of cavalry and a section of light artillery - two guns and ammunition should suffice. Do we have a date yet, gentlemen? And what are you going to do about training the men to ride these pesky critters?"

"Sooner rather than later, General," Streight said. "Two weeks from now, the 7th of April. We will have to train the men in the field, as we go."

Rosecrans looked at him. "You must be across the border and in Alabama by the 17th of April."

Streight looked at the commanding general askance, but Rosecrans made no comment.

"Go to it then, gentlemen," Rosecrans said, briskly, "but keep me informed every step of the way. And above all, this operation must remain a total secret. Understood? Good, then go about your business; we'll talk later.

Garfield and Streight rose, saluted, and left the room. Rosecrans stared after them, shaking his head.

Back in Garfield's office, the two old friends sat down together in front of the fireplace. There was no fire burning, but the room temperature was quite comfortable.

"Cigar, Colonel?" Garfield said, offering his open cigar case to Streight. "And I think a small drop of Scotch Whiskey might do us more than a little good. What do you say, Colonel? Will you take a drink?"

"I will, General; with a little water, if you please."

For several moments, the two officers sat and enjoyed their cigars. Then Streight said to Garfield, "I saw that look, James, when Rosecrans asked if you had the beasts. You don't, do you?"

"Well, Abel. That's not entirely true. I have managed to procure some nine hundred, or so, mules of one sort or another. Unfortunately, many of them are unbroken, and many more, maybe as many as a hundred, are probably too sick to be much use."

"Nine hundred," Streight said, thoughtfully. "We need more, James, at least double that number, maybe more."

Garfield nodded and drew deeply on his cigar. "The idea, Abel, is to forage for more animals as you make your way. I know, I know, but it's the best we can do. The commanding general has already placed an order for twelve thousand more animals and that has not been received well by the quartermaster general. He may not get any at all." He paused for a moment. "Have you given any thought as to the structure of your brigade?"

"I'll take my own regiment, of course, the 51st, and I thought perhaps the 3rd Ohio. They performed outstandingly in January."

24

Streight was referring to the Battle of Stones River. "Other than that, I would be happy to place myself in your hands."

Garfield nodded and tipped the ash from his cigar. "I think the 3rd Ohio is a good choice, and your own regiment, of course. I also think the 73rd Indiana and the 80th Illinois would serve you well. What do you think?"

"The 73rd would be an excellent choice. I know Gilbert Hathaway well, and he would have my every confidence. I know nothing of the 80th. Who commands? Do I know him?"

"Lieutenant Colonel Andrew Rogers. He's a good man."

"Rogers, yes, I've met him, once I think. And Colonel Bob Lawson of the 3rd, I also know quite well. How about the cavalry?"

"Well, we don't have many to spare, what with Forrest and Van Dorn being here, there, and everywhere, but I should be able to come up with something, I suppose. Have to. The commanding general has put his stamp on it, even though not officially. Leave that to me, also the artillery. I have just the man you need, if I can get him released. I'll draw up the papers and present them to the commanding general. By tomorrow, we should have an answer.

"Now, let's talk more about those bloody mules."

Streight and Garfield met again at noon the following day, March 29th.

"I have the commanding general's approval, at least in principle, for your provisional brigade. But this is all still absolutely confidential, and it must remain that way. Any chance of success you might have depends entirely upon the expedition remaining a total secret; the enemy *must not* learn of it until they are able to do little or nothing about it. Only myself, the commanding general, his adjutant, and yourself know of what we are planning. More will learn of it soon enough, but only as necessity dictates; the fewer that know the better. Understood, Colonel?"

Streight nodded and said nothing, listening intently.

"You will have the 51st, the 3rd, the 73rd and the 80th, as we discussed yesterday. You will also have two companies, I and K, of the 1st Alabama Cavalry commanded by Captain David Smith. As to artillery, you'll take two mountain howitzers and sufficient ammunition for an extended expedition; Major Vananda of the 3rd Ohio will command."

Streight leaned forward in his chair. "When are we to begin, General?"

Garfield shook his head. "That I do not yet know. General Rosecrans is still communicating with General Grant. We must be patient, Colonel. It's just a matter of time, a few days, perhaps."

But Abel Streight was not a patient man. In fact, he was a very impatient man, aggressive, restless, with a tendency toward rashness. He did not suffer fools lightly, and he was totally committed to the "cause." He hated bureaucracy and its inevitable delay in all things with a passion. Thus, when his long-time friend, General Garfield, suggested that he be "patient," Able Streight gritted his teeth, shook his head, but said nothing. Garfield might be his friend, but he brooked no argument when important matters were being discussed.

Garfield knew his friend only too well and could see by the look on his face that patient was the last thing that Streight was likely to be.

"Abel, there are larger issues at work here," he said, in an attempt to mollify the restless colonel. "Issues I am not at liberty to discuss, at least for now. Even though General Rosecrans has yet to write the order, he has assured me that the expedition is to go ahead, pending his conversations with General Grant. I suggest that you spend the next several days assembling your brigade and getting to know your regimental commanders. You also have a staff to assemble. You may not, however, discuss the nature of your expedition with anyone.

"Well now, time flies, and I have things yet to do." He stood and offered Streight his hand. "Good luck, Colonel. I will be in touch as soon as I know something."

The two men shook hands. Streight took a step backward, came to attention, saluted, then turned and left the room, closing the door behind him.

General Garfield stared at the closed door and sat down once more at his desk.

Chapter 4

April 7, 1863 - General Garfield's Office, Murfreesboro, Tennessee

"You are to leave with your command today, immediately, by train for Nashville," Garfield said to Abel Streight. "There you will pick up arms, ordnance, equipment, and half the animals you will need for the journey, some eight hundred mules, and horses enough for the officers. Your men will turn in their Springfield rifles in exchange for Smith carbines. You will then embark your brigade in its entirety onto steamboats for transportation to Palmyra, where you will disembark the brigade, leaving only a small escort on board for the trip upriver to Fort Henry. From Palmyra, you will march overland to Fort Henry, foraging for the rest of your animals as you go. Your quartermaster will be issued $3,000 to pay for your procurements in the field. By the time you reach Fort Henry, every member of your brigade should have a mount.

"At Fort Henry, you will again embark your brigade and head down river as far as Eastport, Mississippi, where you will meet with General Dodge. He will have with him four brigades of infantry and another of cavalry. Dodge has, or will have, instructions to provide a screen to divert the enemy from your true objective.

From there, you will travel quickly east to Rome, destroying as you progress any enemy assets you may encounter along the way. At Rome, you will destroy the Western and Atlantic Railroad and any factories and storage facilities you may find in the area. When you have achieved your objectives, you will return here via either North Georgia or Middle Tennessee.

"It is imperative, Colonel," Garfield continued, "that your mission remains secret. Only those senior officers with a need to know may be informed of your objectives. That need to know will be decided entirely by you, Colonel Streight. Is all understood?"

"It is, General."

"Good. Then I suggest you proceed immediately to your brigade. And may God be with you and guide you in your endeavors."

An hour later, Streight was at the railroad station with his escort and all four regimental commanders, watching as rank after rank of blue-clad soldiers boarded the cars. The process took almost two hours before all seventeen hundred men were aboard the train. When all were onboard, Streight and his staff boarded a private car in the rear. Only moments later, with a whistle and roar, the long train chugged out of the station, heading northwest to Nashville, a journey of some thirty-five miles that, with several stops along the way, would take about ninety minutes.

Streight and his four regimental commanders - Colonel Gilbert Hathaway of the 73rd, Lieutenant Colonel Robert (Bob) Lawson of the 3rd Ohio, Lieutenant Colonel James Sheets of the 51st Indiana (Streight's own regiment), and Lieutenant Colonel Andrew Rogers of the 80th Illinois - all settled back into the plush, luxuriously upholstered, seats and lighted cigars.

"Gentlemen," Streight began, when all were settled, "We don't have much time, so please pay close attention. What I am about to tell you is in the strictest confidence. Not a word must be repeated beyond this carriage; understood?"

All four men nodded their agreement and leaned forward to listen.

"We are going to mount the brigade and then strike deep into enemy territory." He paused and looked at each man in turn.

The four men looked at him, amazed. Colonel Hathaway smiled and leaned back against the upholstery. No one said a word.

"We are going to Rome, Georgia, to destroy the Western and Atlantic Railroad and any other facility that offers support to the Confederate cause." Again, he paused, and then continued, "We have a long and arduous journey ahead of us, gentlemen. The brigade is to be mounted; even so, it's not going to be easy. As you know, we are presently headed to Nashville. There we are to receive supplies: food, equipment, ordnance, ammunition, and... mules."

"*Mules?*" Colonel Lawson almost shouted. "Why in God's name mules? I am not riding any goddamn mule."

"Calm down, Colonel," Streight said, quietly. "Your horse, all of your horses, have been loaded and are proceeding with us to Nashville. All of the junior officers will be issued horses. The men... well, they will be assigned mules. We will, if all goes well, load the brigade onto steamboats and depart Nashville on the 10th."

"But why mules?" Sheets asked. "Why not horses?"

"It was felt, by others... and of course, myself, that mules would provide a more practical mode of transport. Where we are going, gentlemen, is rough country. I know, I have spent many months there, for reasons I am not going to go into here. Suffice it for me to say that mules are far better adapted to the cross-country conditions we will face. More than that, they tell me that a mule does not require as much food as a horse, which is also an important consideration."

Lawson shook his head. "Colonel Streight, far be it from me to cast a shadow on this enterprise, but have you considered that these are infantrymen? Most of my men, I know, and I'm sure most of the rest of the brigade, have never ridden a horse before, and we are going to ask them to spend weeks in the saddle upon one of the most ornery beasts God ever breathed life into."

"Be that as it may, Colonel, mules it will be, and the men must adapt quickly. This is not up for discussion. The decision was made by the commanding general with the full support of General Grant. I expect you, and your junior officers, to support the enterprise without question. Is that understood, gentlemen?"

All four colonels nodded, but had glum looks on their faces.

"Good, then let us get down to details. We will be in Nashville within the hour."

Chapter 5

April 9, 1863. Federal Encampment, Nashville

Sergeant Major Ignatius O'Sullivan of the 51st Indiana Infantry awoke well before reveille. As the top soldier, he had a tent to himself, a privilege he appreciated more and more as the years went by.

O'Sullivan, a transplanted Irishman, was a tall, heavy-set man: six feet two inches tall and 240 pounds of solid muscle. At forty years old, he was still in his prime: his black hair had not a hint of gray. He wore his hair long, just to the collar. His facial hair was limited to a huge mustache that swept away from his upper lip to join with even larger sideburns - a style made famous by Federal Major General Burnside – and his chin was clean-shaven. O'Sullivan was an impressive man by any standards and had the demeanor to match. He was a proud man and stood rigidly erect, his chest a great barrel, his arms knotted with muscles.

It was still dark when he left the tent and headed for the latrine to relieve himself. That necessary function completed, he walked over to the water pump. There he sluiced water over his head, reveling in the icy shower that made him gasp but injected new life into his still protesting body. A second sluicing, a shake of his head that sent his long hair whipping back and forth, a quick scrub with a remnant of a long defunct shirt, and he was ready to face the day. He already knew there would be much to do.

Sergeant Major O'Sullivan, still in his somewhat grubby undershirt, his suspenders hanging down around his legs, walked to one of the large tents that housed eight or more enlisted men. He lifted the flap and kicked the nearest pile of grubby blankets.

"Coffin, you piece of garbage. Get your lazy arse up. Get the fire started. I need coffee and be quick about it." He then turned and walked quickly back to his own tent to get dressed.

Corporal Boone Coffin raised himself onto his elbows, shook his head to clear it, and then crawled out from under the somewhat aromatic pile. Smelly or not, they kept the erstwhile Corporal Coffin warm at night.

Corporal Coffin was one of those soldiers who liked to keep a low profile. In fact his presence, at least among the officers of the 51st, was rarely noticed. Over the years, he had turned inconspicuous into an art form. He was a master of invisibility, an enterprising, unobtrusive scrounger, who had no master other than Sergeant Major Ignatius O'Sullivan. The sergeant major had long ago recognized the worth of the resourceful little corporal, and, while taking care of him, also took every advantage of him; it was a truly symbiotic relationship.

Coffin was a small man, just five feet eight inches tall and weighed less than 130 pounds. He was twenty-eight years old, his origins unknown, even to him. He wore his thin, receding hair long, shoulder length. His thin face was deeply tanned and clean-shaven, his eyes the color of burnt grass. His looks were deceptive. Coffin was an extremely intelligent man, resourceful, and a survivor of the first order.

Corporal Coffin did as he was asked, as he always did. He grabbed a huge tin coffee pot from behind the pile of blankets, went outside and stirred the embers of last night's fire. Showers of sparks whirled into the still dark sky as he added wood to the now glowing embers and watched until they burst into flames. Less than ten minutes later, he was at the flap of O'Sullivan's tent with a quart-size tin cup of steaming, black coffee. The coffee was so strong that Coffin himself was unable to drink it without watering it down. O'Sullivan, however, gulped a huge mouthful, swilled the scalding liquid around his mouth, swallowed it, smacked his lips and said, "Not bad, Coffin, not bad at all. Now, breakfast: bacon, eggs, fried bread, then get out of here and let me finish."

Coffin did as he was told. By now, the sun was just peaking over the hills to the east. It was going to be a beautiful day, weather wise, that is.

At eight o'clock that same morning, Colonel Able Streight sent an orderly to Sergeant Major O'Sullivan with orders to report to his field headquarters.

O'Sullivan arrived and was ushered into Streight's tent by his Aide-de-camp, Lieutenant Roach, to find him seated at a small, traveling desk.

"Ah, good, you're here, Sergeant Major," Streight said, returning O'Sullivan's salute, but remaining seated. "At ease, Sergeant Major. I want you to take the brigade to the stockyard to draw their animals."

"Animals, sir?"

"Yes, Sergeant Major, animals. Mules, to be precise."

O'Sullivan stared at Streight, open-mouthed, his jaw hanging. "Mules, Colonel?"

"Oh, come now, you heard what I said. Mules, mules. You do know what a mule is, don't you?"

"Yessir, but...."

Streight sighed, stood, turned, put his hand gently on O'Sullivan's shoulder, leaned in close and whispered in his ear, "Mules, Sergeant Major. We are about to become mounted infantry. The men will draw mules; all of the officers will ride horses. Now do you understand?"

"Oh, but I do indeed, sir," O'Sullivan said. His Irish brogue became more pronounced, the more agitated he became. "But mules, Corn'l sor. They are the most obnoxious animals God ever put on this earth, so they are."

"That's as it may be, Sergeant Major," Streight said, with a grin, "but mules it is, so let's have no more question about it. You'll take the brigade to the stockyard, and they will be provided with the best that the army has to offer... mules, that is."

An hour later, Sergeant Major Ignatius O'Sullivan, having halted the long column, was, along with Corporal Boone Coffin and Quartermaster Sergeant Ransom Morgan, leaning over the rail of the

33

corral, scrutinizing the milling pack of mules therein, almost nine hundred in all.

"Holy Mother save me," O'Sullivan said. "What a heathen-looking bunch they are. Why, some of 'em look half dead to me, and some don't look old enough to have been weaned. My, oh my, oh my. What in the world is this army coming to?"

It was a rhetorical question to which neither Coffin or Morgan replied. Morgan had already sized up the pack and found them, most of them, wanting.

"More'n half of 'em have never bin broke," Morgan said, shaking his head.

"Coffin," O'Sullivan said, out of the corner of his mouth, "I ain't ridin' one of them ornery beasts; go find me a horse. I'll make sure you get a nice ride."

"Sergeant Major, I ain't ridin' one of they critters either...."

"Oh, yes you are. Don't you worry none. I'll get you a good'n. But I needs me a horse. Off you go and find me one, and be quick about it."

O'Sullivan turned to face the waiting brigade. "Our good colonel, in his infinite wisdom, has decided that we are to be a mounted brigade, cavalry, if you please," he shouted. "And, as well you all know, that means we need something to ride and, me fine warriors, if you look to your left, you will see the animals upon which you will indeed ride."

O'Sullivan watched for the reaction, his eyes squinting as he surveyed the more than 1700 infantrymen.

"I heard that, Doyle," he said, marching swiftly along the right side of the column. "Would ya like to step out here and repeat it, so we can hear it one and all."

Doyle, a private of Irish extraction shook his head and stayed put.

"That was not a suggestion, you lanky son of a potato farmer. Get your arse out here and repeat what you just said."

Sergeant Major O'Sullivan was not a small man, but he was dwarfed by the gangling Private Doyle. Doyle, a long and skinny individual more than six feet five inches tall, stood head and shoulders above most of his peers. So out of place among his fellow infantrymen that it was inevitable that he would be singled out, for whatever reason, good or bad. Over the years, he had become hardened to such inconsideration, so he thought, and was not backward about making his feelings clear.

"I said, Sergeant Major, that I ain't gonna ride no goddam mule."

"And why not, pray tell?"

"Oh, come on, Sarge. There ain't one of them critters big enough. Me bloody legs would be trailin' the ground, so they would."

O'Sullivan looked him up and down, then looked over the rails at the animals corralled therein, and nodded in agreement. "Perhaps you're right, Doyle, me old son. Perhaps you're right. Get back in line. THE REST OF YOU, STEP FORWARD.

"COME ON NOW, QUICK ABOUT IT. There ain't no ugly ones, so step forward, smartly now. We don't expect you to marry 'em, just to ride 'em. You there, McHugh, step up to the rail. Pick you one out and go get it."

Private Andrew McHugh, though, was not having any of it. He remained at the back of the line of men.

"I said, step forward, McHugh."

Reluctantly, Andy McHugh pushed his way through the lines until he was standing against the rail.

"Now then, pick you one out. There's a good lad."

McHugh gazed at the seething mass of animals, shrugged his shoulders, and pointed to a stocky young colt standing just a little apart from the main pack, his ears twitching. "I'll do that one, Sarge."

"Go get him, son," O'Sullivan said, with a sly grin on his face.

Reluctantly, McHugh climbed the rail and pushed through the milling pack of long-eared hellions toward his ride of choice. For a

35

long moment, he looked at his newfound friend; the mule looked back, seemingly unimpressed with his new master.

McHugh, an average sort of man of Scottish descent was from Peru, Indiana. Twenty-nine years old and a little over five feet eleven inches tall, he wore his dark brown hair short, just above the collar, and kept it in place under a standard issue infantry kepi. He was clean-shaven, not really by choice, but because his facial hair was sparse and drew ridicule whenever he did try to grow it. He was a quiet sort of individual. Rarely did he have much to say about anything. He kept his mouth shut, his ears open, and spent his days concentrating on staying out of trouble. That, however, did not mean he went unnoticed, especially by Sergeant Major O'Sullivan, who recognized him for exactly what he was: a tenacious, inventive, and conscientious soldier who could be relied upon to the get the job done, no matter what that job might be. That he was still only a private was a mystery to his superiors in general and Sergeant Major O'Sullivan in particular. Thus, it was inevitable that he should be one of O'Sullivan's first choices to ride one of the noxious beasts that inhabited the corral.

Tentatively, McHugh walked around the rear of the mule until he was at its left side, reached out, took hold of the halter rope, and tried to lead the animal toward the rail, but the beast wouldn't move. McHugh tugged and pulled as the rest of the brigade cheered him on, but the animal would not budge.

"No, no, no. Oh no, McHugh," O'Sullivan shouted, loud enough for him to hear over the braying animals and laughing soldiers. "Up on his back. Up on his back."

"Come on. I cain't ride."

"Then there's no better time to learn than right now. Up on his back. Quickly now!"

McHugh looked at the mule; the mule looked at McHugh. *Is the bloody critter smiling at me?* He hesitated, stepped in close and, holding the halter rope with his left hand and a tuft of mane with his right, he swung his right leg up and over the mule's back. As he did so, the mule took a step forward and twisted its rump sideways and down McHugh went. He flipped over backward as he fell and landed flat on his back in a pile of manure. The mule walked a few steps, turned around, looked down at him, bared his teeth and brayed. The crowds of soldiers gathered at the rail did the same, hooting and hollering. Even O'Sullivan could not hold back a chuckle.

It was not so much that McHugh had ended up on his back, nor that he had fallen in a pile of muck, more it was the animal's attitude. Never had O'Sullivan seen such an evil look, or perhaps he had. *There had been that woman....* He shook his head to rid himself of the unpleasant thought.

"What are you laughing at?" he shouted at the rowdy crowd of soldiers. Your turn's acomin', so shut it. Do you hear?"

The noise at the rail died down; the noise within the corral did not.

McHugh scrambled to his feet, grabbed the rope, tried again, and down he went. After several more tries, all with the same results, McHugh finally stood close to the mule's head.

"Now, me fine friend," he whispered. "This is the way it's gonna be. You are gonna stand mighty still. I am gonna get up onto your back." Behind him, the brigade was silent, watching. "Now, Ignatius." *Yeah, I like that,* he thought, glancing sideways at the Sergeant Major. *From now on, Ignatius you will be.* "Now, Ignatius, I am going to be very gentle with you, and you are going to be very, very gentle with me. IF NOT, GODDAM IT," he shouted, "I'LL SHOOT YOUR SORRY ASS, SKIN YA, AND TURN YA INTO A BLOODY COAT AN' WEAR YA. GET IT?"

The mule flinched as McHugh shouted in his ear, then turned his head, put his nose close to McHugh's and snorted gently, showering his new master's face with a fine film of snot.

"Bloody hell; we need to do something about your breath," McHugh said, wiping his face with the sleeve of his tunic. "Now then, Iggy. Stand still."

Once again, tentatively, he grasped the halter and mane, swung his leg over the animal's rump and found himself seated, somewhat surprised at his apparent success.

Behind him, a great cheer arose from the watching soldiers.

The mule turned his head, looked at him, and snickered. *You are, you're bloody well laughing at me. All right then, so be it. Let's show 'em what we can do.*

Gently, he gave the mule a dig in the ribs with his heels. Obligingly, the mule moved off at a slow walk. McHugh, sitting very erect, as he'd seen the cavalrymen do, his right hand holding the rope, his left on his hip, walked him quietly around the perimeter of the corral.

Finally, McHugh and the mule now named Ignatius arrived at the corral gate, where McHugh gave the audience a deep bow, then grabbed his hat off his head and, with a whoop, flung it high into the air. Where it landed, he had no idea.

"Hey, y'all," he yelled, "I'm a cavalryman now."

Ignatius the mule nodded his head enthusiastically.

The crowd went wild. Without waiting for orders, more than a hundred soldiers vaulted the rails and began chasing the pack of now panicking mules around the corral.

"Hey, lookee here, I got me a pretty one," yelled Private Silas Cassell. "I think I'll call her Fanny."

"That ain't no Fanny," yelled another wag. "That there's a boy donkey, an' he's bin gelded."

"Ain't no donkey, neither," yelled Cassell, as he clambered aboard the "pretty one." "Iffen she's a he, why then I'll call her Abel, for the colonel."

"Colonel Abel will pull your guts, Cassell. You cain't go callin' the brigade commander a donkey."

"My Abel ain't no donkey, so I done said already. This is one fine lookin' ride. And, by God, I'd much ruther ride than walk. I think I'm in love. Yeehah!" And with that, the mule now known as Abel received a sharp kick in the ribs from the wildly excited Private Cassell.

Abel's head went down, his rump went up, his hind hooves shot backward and he deposited the erstwhile Private Cassell on the ground headfirst.

Dazed but undaunted, Cassell was up in a flash and, not wanting to lose the new love of his life, ran after the still wildly bucking animal. It was a match made in heaven; at least Cassell thought it was.

Sergeant Major O'Sullivan watched and listened to it all, shaking his head in disbelief. "Look after them for me, Sergeant Morgan. I have other things to attend to. I know you only have half of what we need, but see that they all get assigned. We will, so I've been told, be acquirin' more animals along the way. Oh, and see what you can do about finding that long leggety Private Doyle a mount. I'll be in my tent if you need me."

Chaos reigned over the corral for the next several hours.

It was almost four-thirty in the afternoon when Coffin arrived back at O'Sullivan's tent, outside of which was tied a very large, very powerful mule. Coffin was leading a very large, light chestnut horse with a wide white blaze down his forehead.

"Sergeant Major, sir. I have returned."

O'Sullivan slapped the tent flap aside as he ducked out through the opening. He looked at the horse, said nothing, and walked slowly around him. Then he looked at Coffin, then back at the horse, then again at Coffin.

"Coffin, you reprobate. That's a cavalry horse. Where in God's name did you get him? More to the point, how did you get him?"

"Best you don't ask that, Sergeant Major," Coffin said, looking down at his feet. "Let's just say I know someone and leave it at that."

"Is this likely to come back to haunt me, Coffin? Cause if it do, I'll bake your arse slowly over a low fire."

39

"No Sergeant Major." Again, Coffin looked down at his shoes. "Leastwise, I don't think so," he muttered, under his breath.

"You don't think so. What kind of a goddamn statement is that? If there's trouble for me, by the Almighty, there will be more trouble for you than you can handle. Got it?"

Coffin looked O'Sullivan slyly in the eye. "You want me to take him back where I got him, Sergeant Major?"

O'Sullivan looked at the horse, looked at Coffin, then again at the horse and shook his head. "No! Does he have a name?"

"I'm sure he does, Sergeant Major, but what it might be, I have no idea."

O'Sullivan nodded, and then looked sideways at the mule tied up next to the tent. "This," he said, with a nod of his head toward the mule, "is your new boon companion, no pun intended, Corporal. Ha, ha, ha."

Coffin looked at the mule and shuddered; the mule looked back at him with huge, soft brown eyes.

"Sergeant Major, I cain't ride no mule, and that's an exceedingly big one."

"And just the animal for you, so she is. She can carry you, your stuff, and most of mine, all at the same time. Treat her well. She may turn out to be the best friend you ever had."

Coffin gazed glumly at what he figured, at least among mules, must be a magnificent example of the genus. "What's her name?"

"As far as I know, Corporal, she has no name. Why don't you give her one?"

Coffin thought for a moment, then said, "I shall call her Phoebe."

Phoebe twitched her ears and turned her head to look at him, nodding.

"Seems like you have a winner, Coffin. Take her away now, and get to know her. Return here at, let's say, five o'clock. And," he glowered at Coffin, "I want to see you riding her."

Reluctantly, Coffin nodded and reached for the rope that secured the newly named Phoebe to the post. Phoebe snickered, nudged him under the arm, and allowed herself to be led away.

Sergeant Major Ignatius O'Sullivan watched them go, a huge grin on his face. "A match made in heaven, so it is," he said to himself.

Chapter 6

April 10, 1863 - Confederate General Forrest - Franklin, Tennessee

As Colonel Streight's soldiers were getting to know their new four-footed friends and readying themselves for the long journey ahead, some twenty-five miles to the south of Nashville, Confederate Major General Earl Van Dorn was leading two divisions of cavalry. One was commanded by Brigadier General William Jackson, the other by Brigadier General Nathan Bedford Forrest. Jackson's force numbered almost 1300, Forrest's, more than 2500. The target was Franklin, Tennessee. Van Dorn and Jackson were approaching Franklin by way of the Columbia Pike; Forrest was almost two miles away to the north on the Lewisburg Pike.

Forrest had been told by Major General Earl Van Dorn, Chief of Cavalry for General Braxton Bragg's Army of Tennessee, that the Federals had abandoned Franklin, which surprised Forrest more than a little because, along with Nashville and Murfreesboro, Franklin had long been an important base for the Federal Army of the Cumberland. It was not in General Rosecrans' nature to abandon such a strategically important section of the Federal defensive line. *Still, Van Dorn seems to know something I don't. And that, too, don't make sense. I have not heard a word of such, and my scouts are better than most. Still....* Forrest continued his musing as the column made its way slowly along the riverbank.

For almost three miles, the column stretched back along the road. The route closely followed that of the Harpeth River. Forrest, along with his second-in-command, Brigadier General Frank Armstrong, headed the column, behind Forrest was Sergeant Major Yancey Findel, and behind Findel came a bevy of the lesser officer ranks that made up Forrest's escort. The division was supported by a battery of six guns, two with Armstrong's regiment. The other four farther back in the column were commanded by Captain Sam Freeman.

The pace was leisurely. The column proceeded at the trot. Forrest was expecting no trouble until, just after noon, he heard the rattle of small arms fire away to the south, and then the dull BAM, BAM of two heavy guns less than two miles away to the northwest.

Forrest was surprised to hear the gunfire. Van Dorn's orders had been for him to enter the town first, now this....

On the Columbia Pike, Van Dorn's column had run into Federal pickets, and that he was not expecting. It seemed that Van Dorn's assessment of the defenses around Franklin were... wrong.

Far from being abandoned, the Federal commanding general at Franklin, Major General Gordon Grainger, had in fact been reinforced. His force included two full divisions under the commands of Generals Absalom Baird and Charles Gilbert - more than 6300 infantry - and they had been joined by the 1600 strong cavalry brigade of Major General David Stanley, now encamped four miles to the southeast of Franklin at Hughe's Mill on the north side of the river. Grainger could now field more than 8000 men, and he was expecting Van Dorn. For several days, he had been receiving reports from General Rosecrans in Murfreesboro that Van Dorn would attack on the 9th; those reports had been accurate and Grainger was ready.

Most of Grainger's troops were ensconced on the north side of the town on a bluff, in and around an unfinished fort. It was the ideal spot, with a clear field of fire in every direction.

Grainger had deployed the 40th Ohio, just 300 troopers commanded by Captain Charles Matchett, to the south of the town, with pickets guarding the approaches on the Columbia Pike.

The morning of the 9th had dawned clear and cool; the temperature was in the high fifties. By noon, the sun had risen and along with it the temperature. Both roads into Franklin were dry and dusty, and the haze raised by the hooves of the two advancing columns had reduced the visibility considerably.

On the southern edge of the town, facing the Columbia Pike, with the sun beating down upon them, Matchett and his regiment were waiting and watching. Only the twitter of the birds among the treetops disturbed the quiet of the early afternoon.

Less than a half mile away down the Pike, a single rifle shot rang out, and then another and another until it became a din, a single sustained roar. Then, out of the haze, a soldier appeared, running hard. By the time he reached Matchett, he could barely breathe, his face was beaded with sweat, and his clothes soaked through.

"They're coming, Captain," he gasped. "A whole passel of 'em, at least a couple o' thousand cavalry. The men are falling back."

But it wasn't the Federal pickets that appeared down the road, it was the 1st Mississippi Cavalry approaching at full gallop, hooves flying, and guns blazing.

"Hold fast, boys," Matchett shouted. "Fire on my command, then fall back in company order.... FIRE!"

The order to fire was barely heard as two 48-pound solid shots from the fort screamed overhead and then smashed down among the front ranks of the charging Confederate cavalry brigade.

As Van Dorn's column, headed by the 1st Mississippi Cavalry, cantered serenely toward the town, they ran slap into Matchett's pickets and, even though Van Dorn was expected, the pickets were taken by surprise. From several dozen places on either side of the road, all well hidden by tall grass, scrub, trees, and rocks, fifty Federal soldiers opened fire on the column.

From front to rear there was total confusion as startled horses and men surged first one way and then the other. Horses went down and men were thrown from their saddles and trampled beneath the flailing hooves. The chaos lasted no more than a minute or two. Officers and NCOs soon regained control and the melee subsided.

Riders were dispatched into the woods to search out and destroy the pickets, but they had melted away into the undergrowth.

"Sound the charge, Colonel," Van Dorn said to George Cosby, commanding Jackson's 1st Brigade. "Let's ferret them out."

As the sounds of the bugle rang out down the road, the leading regiment, the 1st Mississippi, pistols, and carbines in hand, took off toward Franklin at full gallop in column of fours. They had barely rounded the bend toward the outskirts of town when they heard the scream of incoming artillery fire from the fort above the town.

Fortunately, the heavy projectiles fired from two 4.8-inch James rifles were birdcage solid shots, not shells. Even so, the effect was devastating. The 48-pound iron missiles slammed into the ground among the charging horses, throwing up mountainous showers of hard-packed dirt and rocks, which inflicted horrendous wounds on both men and horses.

"Colonel, bring up the battery," Van Dorn said, calmly. "Set it up over there, by that house, and engage the fort."

"The range is extreme, General, 1400 or 1500 yards by my estimation, and all uphill at that," Colby said.

Van Dorn nodded. "Let's give it a try, Mr. Colby."

Swiftly, two twelve-pounder Napoleon guns were brought up, unlimbered, and ranged on the distant fort.

BAM... BAM!

The officers watched as the two Hotchkiss shells arched high into the air, only to fall short onto the slopes of the escarpment below the fort.

Seconds later, while the Confederate guns were in the process of reloading, two more forty-eight pound solid shots from the siege guns in the fort slammed into the hard-packed dirt only yards in front of the two Napoleons, showering the crews with dirt and rocks.

"Pull 'em out, Mr. Colby," Van Dorn shouted. "They have our range. No point in losing the guns."

High on the hill, on the unfinished walls of the fort, General Grainger was scanning the rapidly developing situation through his field glasses.

"General Baird," Grainger said. "That is Van Dorn to the south of the town, and there's another column approaching from the east, probably Forrest. Move your division across the river and engage Van Dorn.

"General Gilbert, move your division to Hughe's Mill in support of General Stanley. We are in no danger here."

At Hughe's Mill, however, Federal Major General David Stanley, an impatient man at the best of times, was already preparing for action. Like Forrest, he had heard the outbreak of gunfire to the south and was preparing to move out, without waiting for orders.

On the Lewisburg Road, General Forrest was readying his brigades to assault the town. Already, his two leading brigades, those of General Armstrong and Colonel Starnes, had already passed Hughe's Mill, though they couldn't see it for it was more than a mile away on a bend in the river to the north.

At the same time as Baird's division crossed the bridge within the town and slammed into Van Dorn, so Stanley crossed the Harpeth River via the ford to the northeast of Hughe's Mill. From there, it was a ride of a little more than a mile south to the Lewisburg Road.

Stanley had no idea where the enemy was; he was simply heading in the direction of the gunfire.

Stanley turned south and headed his division across country at the gallop. Minutes later, he burst out of the trees into a large clearing; the Lewisburg Road was one hundred yards ahead. So was the center of Forrest's column, which, due to its former leisurely pace, was now strung out along the road for almost four miles.

Right at the center of the Confederate column, Forrest's chief of artillery, Captain Sam Freeman, had already heard the noise of the approaching Federal cavalry and was in the process of unlimbering his guns when a hoard of troopers of the 4th U.S. Cavalry burst out of the trees.

Unfortunately for Freeman, the 4th was a veteran and experienced unit. They spotted Freeman's guns, now swinging around to face them and, without breaking stride, charged across the clearing yelling, whooping and firing as they went. Freeman's artillerists had no chance. The limber horses panicked and bolted, falling over one another and turning over the caissons. Freeman's men threw up their hands and surrendered.

On the south side of Franklin, Van Dorn soon found himself facing a full division of infantry as Baird's men poured across the bridge. Having been educated in all things military at West Point, Van Dorn was the consummate cavalry commander. His tactic was the Lightning strike: get in, do as much damage as possible, and get out. He was also well aware that a cavalryman on horseback presented a huge target and thus was no match for the modern infantryman, especially when that infantryman was armed with a rifled musket.

Baird's division numbered almost 3000, thus Van Dorn's twelve 1200 were vastly outnumbered. He was quickly driven from the field and back down the Columbia Pike.

Nathan Bedford Forrest was also well aware of the disadvantages of cavalry when faced with well-trained infantry and had long ago adapted his tactics. His philosophy was to use the horse to get where he wanted to go as quickly as possible, dismount his men, and then fight his troopers as infantry.

Taken by surprise as he was, however, Forrest, even though he outnumbered Stanley by more than two to one, found himself at a disadvantage. By now, he was on the outskirts of Franklin and attacking the town. With Van Dorn gone from the field, however, he found himself on his own facing five regiments of infantry and the heavy guns in the fort.

As was his strategy, Forrest had dismounted his leading brigades and they were fighting on foot when, suddenly to the rear, he heard the sustained roar of small arms fire.

"What the hell is that?" Forrest shouted at Armstrong, trying to be heard over the gunfire.

Armstrong turned in the saddle, looked back down the road, saw nothing other than the milling horses of the dismounted brigade and shook his head.

At that moment, a rider came galloping round the bend in the road. He pulled his horse to a sliding stop in front of the two generals and shouted, "Federal cavalry, General Forrest, a whole division by the looks of it."

"Where are they, Captain? Quickly now!"

"They hit the center of the column, General, to the rear of General Starnes brigade. Freeman's battery is taken and all are prisoners."

"Stanley, God damn him," Forrest growled. "I was wondering when he would turn up.

"General," he shouted at Armstrong. "Call off the attack. Get the men mounted. I want Stanley. If we make a quick run across country, we can get on his rear. I want my damn guns back."

Unbeknownst to Forrest, General Starnes, on hearing the ruckus to his rear, had turned his brigade around and was heading back down the road. Before he could reach Freeman's battery, however, he was hit by the rest of Stanley's cavalry and was quickly involved in a frantic running fight.

Starnes' brigade soon gained the upper hand and began driving Stanley back across the fields and through the woodland toward the ford at Hughe's Mill.

Captain James McIntyre of the 4th U.S. Cavalry was in charge of the prisoners taken in the attack on Freeman's battery. The Confederate prisoners were on foot, being hurried along at the run behind the retreating horse soldiers. Seeing that the Confederate prisoners were slowing him down, he released most of them, holding onto Captain Freeman and only a couple of dozen more, including one of Forrest's field surgeons, Dr. Skelton.

Freeman and Skelton were unable to keep up the fast pace, even though they were being goaded onward by their captors. They hadn't gone very far when one of McIntyre's troopers took matters into his own hands and shot Freeman dead. Dr. Skelton, too, was shot, but only through the hand as he tried to defend himself.

Leaving Freeman's body behind, but taking Skelton with them, and with almost all of Forrest's entire division on their heels, the entire 4th U.S. cavalry made for the ford and safety across the river.

Forrest and his escort arrived just as the tail end of Stanley's division was entering the ford and was too late to catch them. Forrest and his staff turned back to where Freeman's body lay. He dismounted, devastated.

He knelt beside the body, picked up Freeman's hand, felt for a pulse, shook his head when he discovered none, and said, in a low ominous voice, "God damn you, Stanley. This was a good man. You'll pay dearly for his death, I promise."

The battle was over. Van Dorn was on his way back to Spring Hill; Forrest would soon follow him. It was a Federal victory, though nothing to brag about and certainly nothing was gained.

Federal casualties numbered less than one hundred; the Confederate losses were a dozen or so more.

Franklin was the precursor to the running battle between Streight and Forrest that would range across more than 220 miles of Northern Alabama.

In Nashville, Colonel Streight and his Mule Soldiers were preparing to board the steamboats for Palmyra.

Chapter 7

April 10, 1863, 3p.m. Nashville Docks

Able Streight, along with Colonel James Sheets of the 51st, arrived at the docks in Nashville just before noon. Now they stood together on the upper deck of the *Hazel Dell* and watched as the brigade began to board the transports.

Even though it was Saturday afternoon, the docks were busy. Eight steam-driven transports - three side-wheelers, of which the *Hazel Dell* was one, and five stern-wheelers - were either tied up at the boardwalks or waiting in line. Most had arrived before dawn that morning, ready and waiting for the 1700 troopers of Colonel Abel Streight's brigade. They, along with 811 mules, 132 horses, two bronze mountain howitzers, assorted equipment and accoutrements of every shape and size, began arriving at the docks around three o'clock in the afternoon and started to board the riverboats for transport upriver to Palmyra. Chaos was an inadequate word with which to describe the utter confusion that descended upon the docks.

Overseeing this exercise in pandemonium, Sergeant Major Ignatius O'Sullivan, aided by the erstwhile Quartermaster Sergeant Ransom Morgan, and the diminutive Corporal Boone Coffin, grew more frustrated as the hours rolled by.

"Sergeant Major O'Sullivan," Streight called through cupped hands.

O'Sullivan looked up and shouted, "Sir?"

"Come up here, if you would, Sergeant Major."

O'Sullivan nodded, said something Streight could not hear to Morgan and Coffin, and climbed down from the saddle of his colossus of a horse.

A few minutes later, he was up on the upper deck of the *Hazel Dell,* standing beside Streight and Sheets, looking down on the chaos below.

"Your report, if you please, Sergeant Major," Streight said, his gaze never leaving the seething masses on the dock below.

"Well, sir, it's like this: that's a pretty poor lot of mules. Many of 'em have distemper; some seem to be malnourished and small. Some of 'em are not much more than, maybe, a year old and, Colonel, some have not yet been broken. They are, sir, a sorry lot, and so are the men, at least where the mules are concerned; ain't one of 'em can ride worth a durn, an' half of 'em have no mount at all."

"True, Sergeant Major, true, but they will have to do, the mules, that is, at least for now. But, when we disembark at Palmyra, you'll need to get them all ready, mules and men, and quickly. We will move out from Palmyra immediately and will have no time for play. You must make sure, Sergeant Major, that all of the animals are properly tended to. Those that need breaking must be broken as quickly as possible, and all of the men must be able to ride. 'Unable to ride' is not acceptable. I want the loading completed before nightfall. I want to be able to make away from here as soon as the gunboats, our escorts, arrive. Do I make myself clear, Sergeant Major?"

"That you do, sir."

"Very well, you may return to the dock. Dismissed."

O'Sullivan returned Streight's salute, spun on his heel, and trotted quickly down the steps and gangplank to the docks where Morgan and Coffin were doing their best to maintain order among the shifting mass of men and animals.

"Colonel," Sheets said, as they watched O'Sullivan walk down the gangplank and onto the dock. "Where exactly are we going and why?"

Streight shook his head and for a moment continued looking down at the chaos on the docks below. "I'm sorry, Colonel, I am not yet at liberty to give you the details. The success of our enterprise depends upon its secrecy. If the enemy gets wind of what we are about to do, the venture will be doomed before it's began. Suffice it to say that we are to drive a spear into the heart of the Confederacy. I will provide details when we are finally on these retched boats and away from here."

Sheets nodded then shook his head. "But mules, sir? And such sorry animals as these. I–"

"I know, Jim. But it is what it is. We must do the best we can with what we have, and I am confident that will be able to procure more, and better, animals between Palmyra and Fort Henry?"

"Fort Henry?"

"There, I have said too much. Please respect my confidence and keep our destination to yourself, Colonel."

Sheets merely nodded his agreement.

Little did Streight know that news of his departure from Murfreesboro had already reached the Confederate high command, and that he was being closely watched by enemy spies and patrols.

Normally, boarding a brigade of infantry onto transports was not a difficult task, especially an undermanned brigade as was Streight's. The problem that Saturday afternoon was the 800 plus mules, of which more than 500 were, indeed, unbroken. They, along with their 800 plus new masters, all of whom had no idea of what they were doing, or how to ride the unruly beasts, much less how to control them in the dimly lit and ceaselessly pitching holds of the transports, were in a constant state of unrest.

Panic among the mules was infectious. Animals bit and kicked each other and rider alike. By five o'clock that afternoon, no less than sixteen mules and riders had managed to fall off either the dock or gangplank into the water. All of the men survived, two of the mules did not. Those without rides were by now delighted still to be on foot.

Private Andrew Mc Hugh, having successfully boarded Ignatius on to the *Aurora* just after four o'clock that afternoon, was leaning on the rail of the upper deck watching the milling horde of soldiers and livestock on the dockside below. Andy was pleased with himself and even more pleased with his mule, Ignatius. Now his friend indeed, the one-time terror of the corral was behaving like a priest in a seminary. For some reason, Ignatius loved his new master, and Andy felt no less strongly about his new ride. When Silas Cassell joined him at the rail, the two had much to discuss.

Cassell was something of an enigma to his friends, his officers, and to Sergeant Major O'Sullivan. He was a man of opposites; one could never tell what he might be thinking. He was unreadable by those who didn't know him, and a mystery even to those who did. He was compliant, yet he could be hard-nosed, jolly and sad, often at the same time. He lived life ever on the lookout for the next opportunity to better himself, or the next threat to his person or well-being.

He was not a big man, just five feet nine inches tall, slim build, with a clean-shaven, angular narrow face that housed a pair of black eyes that glittered in the sunlight and a long, sharp nose that, together, gave him the appearance of a bird of prey. But that severe visage did not do him justice. He was actually a very caring individual, although he kept that side of himself to himself. His outward philosophy in life was to do exactly what was needed for him to get by with the least amount of effort. Like Coffin, he was the quintessential survivor. But that, too, belied the true Silas Cassell; he was, indeed, an enigma.

"So, what do you think, Andy?" Cassell said, leaning over the rail to view the ever-widening pandemonium below.

"'Bout what?"

"Well, where the hell are we going, for one thing, and what the hell for, and why on goddamn mules for a third?"

"Your guess, Silas, is as good as mine. The day the brass lets me in on their secrets... well, you know."

"So you have no idea what we're about then?"

"None whatever, but I can tell you this, it sure as hell ain't gonna be fun; downright dangerous, in fact, is what I would allow. One thing's for sure, I ain't lookin' forward to ridin' that pesky mule any distance, any distance at all, even though he seems to have pacified some."

"I heard you call him Ignatius. By God, y'all better not let O'Sullivan hear it."

"Awe hell, what's he gonna do? Shoot me in the ass? Hell, it will be so goddamn sore I won't feel nothin' anyway. And, did you note that there's no mule for the likes of him? Coffin managed to find him a goddamn horse."

"Stole him one, most likely," Cassell said.

"So how you doin' with your fine steed?" McHugh grinned at Silas as he said it. "You ain't no better off than me, and that's no lie."

Cassell drew himself up to his full height, all of five feet nine inches, and said proudly, "Me an' Able will do just fine."

"Yeah, well, you don't weigh but a hun'red pounds wet, so I can imagine you will. And, make no never mind 'bout me and Ignatius. If the Colonel ever gets wind of what you've named your beast, it'll be the stockade for you."

Cassell grinned sideways at him. "That would be 132 pounds, m'friend, an' old man Streight will never hear of it; at least I hopes he don't."

Together the two stood at the upper rail of the *Aurora* watching, chatting quietly, as the loading progressed and, as it did so, they were joined at the rail by more and more of their comrades.

Unruly though the mass was, all eight transports were loaded and ready to leave by nine-thirty that evening.

By nine o'clock, Streight had been joined by all four of his regimental commanders, Captain David Smith of the 1st Tennessee Cavalry, his chief of artillery, Major Vananda, and some twenty junior officers to boot. All were now settled in a large stateroom on the main deck of the *Hazel Dell*. Cigars had been passed around, strong drinks had been served, all were seated comfortably, and the conversation was lively.

On the lower decks of the transports, things were not quite so tranquil. Still, by ten o'clock, order of sorts had been achieved, and men, mules and horses were as comfortable as could be expected under the circumstances, which wasn't very. Without waiting for the expected escort of three gunboats, the order was given to cast off.

Thirty minutes later, with steam whistles blasting, vast clouds of black smoke billowing from the tall stacks, paddle wheels churning the water to white foam, the eight riverboats were cruising along, one behind the other, westward to Palmyra.

The fleet hadn't gone more than a dozen miles, however, when one of Confederate Colonel Tom Woodward's scouts spotted the billowing black smoke: the Mule Soldiers had been discovered.

Woodward sent a dispatch rider to report his discovery to General Van Dorn at Spring Hill but continued to follow at a distance, well out of sight of the Federal fleet. Late that same evening, the rider returned to Woodward with orders to continue to follow the fleet and keep Van Dorn appraised of the situation as it developed.

Chapter 8

April 11, 1863, Palmyra, Tennessee

The fleet docked at Palmyra just after eight o'clock that evening, the 11th of April. Even though reports had been arriving in Nashville daily about the Confederate attack on the town, they were ill prepared for what they now saw. Palmyra was in ruins and deserted, except for the fifty or so Federal soldiers on the docks awaiting the boats. Little was left of the once prosperous little community on the banks of the Cumberland. The houses and dockland buildings had been reduced to ashes, and in and under the waters around the docks lay the wrecks of four riverboats. The approaches into the docks were littered with obstacles - huge timbers, semi-submerged small boats, and large sections of dockland decking, barrels and crates of every shape and size, even dead animals - all of which had to be navigated with care. It was pouring down with rain, a cold, driving rain that quickly turned the thick wool uniforms of the Federal soldiers into heavy, soggy, tortuous rags that chaffed the skin and made life thoroughly unbearable. Had it not been for the rain, the town would still have been smoldering.

High up on the observation deck of the *Aurora*, Corporal Coffin, along with Privates Doyle (still without a ride), McHugh, and Cassell, huddled miserably under the canopy that covered a small part of the forward section of the deck. The rain, the destruction, the desolation, and the thoughts of what was about to befall them, all contributed to the overwhelming blanket of depression that descended upon them.

By nine o'clock, the first of the riverboats, the *Hazel Dell*, carrying not only soldiers, mules, and horses, but the entire command staff of the brigade, had docked and was unloading its personnel; the livestock would have to wait until morning.

By ten-thirty, the entire brigade had disembarked, tents had been pitched, pickets had been dispatched into the wilderness, but the livestock remained aboard the boats, restless and hungry. The muleskinners did what they could for them, but it was little enough, especially for the sick and suffering. As for the officers: they were comfortable enough, still aboard the *Hazel Dell*, warm and dry in their staterooms. The rank and file, not so much. True, they all were under cover inside their tents, but there was little comfort in that. The few who had a change of clothes changed into them. Those who did not lay down in their soggy garments to suffer in silence. Outside, the rain beat steadily down upon the canvas; water seeped in and turned the ground upon which the men had to sleep into a soggy quagmire of mud. In the picket lines, the men found what shelter they could beneath old-growth trees; the landscape was a wasteland, dark, desolate, and sodden. It was going to be a long night.

By first light the next morning, the 12th of April, the rain had stopped and most of the members of the brigade had risen from their soggy beds. Men were out and about, foraging. Fires had been lit, and the welcome aroma of strong coffee wafted through the encampment. Pickets were exchanged, officers bustled around, coffee mugs in hand, each one trying to look busy. Sergeant Major O'Sullivan and Corporal Coffin sat together in O'Sullivan's tent, the flap closed, and sipped steaming black liquid from tin mugs that had seen better days.

Theirs was a symbiotic relationship, O'Sullivan and Coffin. The two men could not have been more different: O'Sullivan tall and heavy set, Coffin diminutive and skinny as a rake, but each respected the other. Difference in rank aside, these two were as close as any two soldiers in the Union army. It was not exactly a friendship, more a mutual admiration for one another, and each was extremely protective of the other. O'Sullivan knew instinctively that Coffin had the superior intellect, and he respected it, drew upon it. Coffin also knew that he was by far more intelligent than his master, but he never showed it, to O'Sullivan or to anyone else. It was indeed a strange relationship, and one the two men kept strictly to themselves. When alone together, they were on a first-name basis; when in public, they adhered strictly to rank. It was a relationship mutually beneficial to them both, and they intended to keep it that way.

"Geeze, that's hot," O'Sullivan said, holding the tin cup away from his mouth and looking down at the steam rising from the liquid within. "How're you copin' with that mule?" he asked as he looked over the edge of the cup and sipped a noisy slurp.

"She still aboard the *Nashville,* but all right, I guess."

"You gonna be able to manage her?"

Coffin nodded and then took an equally noisy sip of his own coffee.

"And how are our supplies holdin' up?"

"Everythin's still aboard the boat, along with all the animals an' equipment."

"Not the brigade's supplies, you dolt. Our supplies, you know. Our stuff."

"Oh, that? We're good, Sergeant Major. Maybe could do with a little more of this good coffee and an extra slab o' bacon or two. How long we gonna be gone? How long's it have to last?"

"God only knows. I still ain't heard a word, an' that's unusual. Could be a couple o' weeks, could be months."

Coffin sipped and stared, then said, quietly, "So, what do you want me to do?"

O'Sullivan leaned back in his folding chair and stared at the lamp hanging from the tent pole, seemingly lost in thought. Then he looked at Coffin and said, "Make sure we have coffee, beans, bacon, lard, and whiskey enough for a month."

Coffin nodded his agreement.

"Do you think you could get a hold o' one o' them nine-shot revolvers?"

"You talkin' about a LeMat?"

"Yup, that's the one. It has a 20-gauge shotgun mounted below the regular barrel.

"That's a Reb weapon. Don't see too many o' them in this army. Still, I think I might be able to get a hold o' one, but it won't be cheap. Ammunition, though, would be a problem. The LeMat fires a 42-caliber ball; standard Union issue is 44 or 36-caliber."

"No matter. See what you can do. Boone, I have a bad feelin' about this trip. How much money we talkin' here?"

Coffin thought for minute, then said, "Ten, mebbe twelve bucks for the coffee an' stuff, an' another twenty-five for the gun."

O'Sullivan thought for a moment, then said, "Do it."

He rose from the chair, went to the small chest in which he kept his personal belongings, rooted around inside until he found the small, well-worked leather bag that Coffin had seen many times before. He loosened the drawstring that kept the bag closed, looked inside, and then withdrew a twenty-dollar gold piece, which he flipped to Coffin. The corporal deftly caught it, one-handed.

"Hold out your hand, Boone."

He did so, and O'Sullivan counted out ten silver dollars, and then looked into the bag at the now diminished number of coins within. "There's thirty," he said, looking Coffin squarely in the eye. "See what you can do with that. Go get us some more coffee. It ain't quite light yet, an' I need a waker up."

Coffin rose from the wooden crate upon which he had been sitting, wrapped the coins in a greasy rag, then pocketed them, picked up his cup, grabbed O'Sullivan's and left the tent, the flap closing behind him.

An hour later, O'Sullivan was at the dockside, watching as the first of the mules were about to be disembarked from the lower decks of the *Hazel Dell, Aurora,* and the *Nashville.* He was not impressed.

"ALL RIGHT, BOYS," he shouted at the milling mass of troops of Streight's brigade now gathered just beyond the limit of the dockland. "Those of you who were issued mounts, step forward. The rest of you report to the Quartermaster, Lieutenant Doughty. You'll find him awaitin' you beside the *Hazel Dell*. He will be givin' out the orders for the rest o' the day. And, by the skirts o' the Holy Virgin, you'd better be a list'nin' to him, or you'll have me to deal with. Get goin'.

"The rest of you, when your animal makes its appearance on the plank will step forward, grab its halter, and lead him away over that way, and there you will wait, PATIENTLY, until all are present and accounted for, man and mount both." O'Sullivan pointed vaguely toward the open ground beyond the docks to the east.

But it was not to be. The mules were much the worse for their overnight experience. They were excited, panicky, skittish, and braying loudly. The muleskinners were inexperienced and many of them were more than a little frightened of their long-eared charges. Thus, instead of the orderly train O'Sullivan was expecting, the gates were flung open and the ornery beasts charged down the rain-slick gangplanks like a herd of charging bulls, scattering soldiers left and right in their efforts to avoid being trampled. Before the first mule had made it off the gangplank and onto the dock, no less than six already rain-sodden soldiers had been bunted over the edge and were flailing about in the murky waters of the Cumberland, much to the delight of the non-mounted infantry already marching away to find the quartermaster.

And even before the first of the animals had descended the gangplank of the *Nashville*, O'Sullivan could see that they were indeed in sorry shape. Some were visibly sick; others, he could tell, had never been broken, and all were in a state of shock. Hard times were about to begin, so they were.

O'Sullivan stood on the edge of the dock, grasping the hairs at the sides of his head and snarled. Ignatius O'Sullivan was not a man easily moved, but the utter chaos unfolding before his very eyes enraged him.

The chaos was not confined only to the *Nashville*. The situation on board the *Aurora* was no better, worse aboard the *Hazel Dell,* where Streight and his retinue were making ready to disembark. Unfortunately for them and for the attendant riverboat crew, the good colonel was obliged to stay where he was and observe the pandemonium as it unfolded. Fortunately for all concerned, especially

Sergeant Major Ignatius O'Sullivan, the colonel well understood the situation and its origins, and was not unsympathetic, to beast or man.

"SERGEANT MAJOR," he shouted over the noise of the wildly braying mules. "Take your time. Get them under control and out of here as best you can. Then come and see me."

"Yes, sir," O'Sullivan shouted, inordinately grateful for his commanding officer's lenient outlook. "I will indeed, sir."

It took less than an hour to get all of the beasts off the boats, and the rest of the morning to drive, persuade, coax, and threaten them into some sort of order.

"Ah, Sergeant Major O'Sullivan." Streight met him at the door of the lounge on board the boat. "Come in, come in. At ease, Sergeant Major, there's no point in formality, at least not right now. How is everything going?"

"Well, Colonel... not so good, really, Sis. The animals are off the boats, and the men have them in hand, but we have forty-two dead, mules that is, from the distemper, and a couple o' dozen more too sick to walk, much less travel. And then... well, most of the rest are still to be broken. It's a dire, dire thing, sir."

Streight slowly nodded his head, seemingly lost in thought, then looked up. "How long will it take, Sergeant Major, to get them and the men ready to move out?"

Never one given to discretion or to hide the truth, O'Sullivan said, "Bloody hell, Colonel. I'm sure I have no idea. Two days, three, maybe, it depends. The men are not horsemen, sir, and those sad beasts will be the devil to break, if they don't break the men first."

"You have the rest of the day and tomorrow morning, Sergeant Major. Then, no matter the state of mule or man, we will leave this place and travel overland to Fort Henry. I cannot spare a single hour more than that; you must do the best you can with what you have.

"I sincerely hope we will have more mules and horses by the end of the day. Colonel Sheets is abroad foraging for animals among the local populace. With luck, we'll have a mount for everyone by midday tomorrow. Any questions or thoughts, Sergeant Major?"

O'Sullivan knew well enough when to keep his thoughts to himself, and so he did. "Er... no, sir. At least, not right now."

"Good. You may go and good luck, Sergeant Major."

O'Sullivan came smartly to attention, saluted, spun on his heel, and marched quickly out through the still open door. As he went down the stairs and through the lounge, he looked at the clock. It was five minutes after noon. He shook his head and broke into a trot. The next twenty-four hours were going to be.... *not fun, that's for sure.*

Early the following morning, well before dawn, O'Sullivan and Coffin were again sitting comfortably in the privacy of O'Sullivan's tent. The coffee was strong and scalding hot and, even though the rain continued to fall outside, both men were in a good mood, even optimistic.

"So," O'Sullivan said, leaning forward, his elbows on his knees, tin cup cradled in both hands just in front of his lips. "Did you get it?"

"No, at least not the LeMat."

O'Sullivan sat back in his chair. "Why the hell not?"

"Well, the gun I could have got. In fact, I could have got two of 'em, and cheap, too, but the ammunition... that I could not get. There just wasn't any to be had. Which is why they were so cheap. But I did get you these." He leaned around the back of the crate upon which he was sitting and dragged forth a large canvas bag. He pulled open the top of the bag, took out two large pistols and handed them to O'Sullivan, who laid down his cup on the dirt floor.

"Colt Army 1860," O'Sullivan said, holding one in each hand and nodding his head in appreciation. "Fine, fine pieces. Forty-fours, too. How much did you pay for them?"

"Eighteen bucks for both, including ammo and holsters. I... er, I called in a debt, so to speak."

"You mean you blackmailed some poor son of a bitch is what you mean. I know how you operate, Boone Coffin," O'Sullivan said with a sly smile. "God help me if ever I should step on your toes."

Coffin grinned at him. "No fear of that, Sergeant Major."

O'Sullivan hefted the two pistols. They were heavy, almost three pounds apiece, but they were finely balanced and he was not unfamiliar with the weapon. "Lovely, lovely. Lovely guns, so they are. Thank you, Coffin."

"There's more." Coffin reached once more into his bag and dragged out a massive sawed-down, double-barrel shotgun. "I remembered what you said about the shotgun built into the LeMat, and I thought you might appreciate this."

"What in the name of Mother Mary's skirts is that?

Coffin grinned. "It's a 10-guage Richards. It will stop a rinocapede."

"You mean rhinoceros," O'Sullivan said, taking the weapon from him and hefting it.

"Yeah, that."

"Bloody hell, Boone, it's a bloody cannon, so it is."

"An' I have buck and ball ammo for it, too." Coffin handed the bag containing the holsters and ammo to O'Sullivan.

"What about the rest of the supplies?" O'Sullivan asked, taking the bag from him and peering inside.

"All taken care of."

"An' how about that bloody mule? What was it you called her?"

"Phoebe, Sarge. And, well, she's big, mighty big, an' I ain't so big. But she's a good un, strong and fit. Where did you find her?"

O'Sullivan grinned slyly at Coffin. "You ain't the only one to engage in a little friendly persuasion. What time is it?"

Coffin reached into his tunic pocket and pulled forth a battered pocket watch and flipped it open. "Gettin' on for six-thirty."

"Time we was out and about, then, "O'Sullivan said, pitching the dregs from his cup onto the dirt floor. Then he strapped on the two holsters, slipped the two heavy Colts into them, butts facing forward, slipped into a heavy, black waterproof oilskin riding slicker that hung almost to his ankles, and jammed his timeworn, but well-loved Stetson onto his head.

"Take care of my stuff for me, Boone. I'll leave that bloody cannon with you for now at least. We'll be outa here by noon, at the latest, so be ready." And with that, he swept out of the tent, looking for all the world like some giant, predatory bird.

Coffin, drank the last of his coffee, then he, too, left the tent and made ready for the busy day he knew was about to begin.

By ten o'clock that morning, Colonel Sheets and the dismounted infantry had returned. The foraging had been somewhat successful, rendering some 370 mules - all of them fit, healthy, broken, and ready to ride - and 163 horses. This brought the grand total of available mounts to just over 1390; still not enough, but with a journey of more than sixty miles across country to Fort Henry, Sheets was confident that all would have mounts by the time they reached the fort.

By noon, with much shouting, pleading, and even bullying, the brigade was as ready to move as it ever was going to be.

Of the 1700 plus members of the brigade, more than 400 were still afoot. These were split into eight groups, one to each riverboat to defend against any and all Confederate raiders, and they were already steaming westward to Fort Henry, hooting and hollering at the remaining members of the now "mounted brigade" miserably assembled, sort of, in the open fields to the south of the town. Getting them saddled and mounted had been a fiasco all its own. The still mostly unbroken animals protested and did their best to avoid the saddle. Eventually all were saddled and mounted and with no little difficulty were moved slowly from the docks and into column of twos.

The rain continued unabated, and all except the officers and a few lucky NCOs who happened to own wet weather oilskin covers, O'Sullivan and Coffin among them, were soaked to the skin.

"Forward Ho!" The call began at the front of the almost three-mile long column, and was repeated, officer by officer, down the line to the end.

It started just behind the leading group. As the officers and NCOs moved off, and the first company of mule soldiers kicked their beasts to get them moving, a big gray mule decided he was having none of it. He brayed loudly, reared, jumped up, landed on his front hooves, shot his rear hooves backward, slamming into the chest of the next mule in line, and threw his rider headlong over his ears. Then he trampled him and made a mad dash across the field, reins flying, stirrups slapping his sides as he went.

"Go get him," someone shouted, and immediately three men kicked their animals and made to make chase. One spun like a top, ditching his rider; another simply lay down in the mud and nothing his rider could do would raise him up; the third, totally out of control, galloped down the line and back toward the dock from whence they had come.

Sergeant Major O'Sullivan, flanked by Corporal Coffin, was at his usual position at the head of the column just to the rear of Colonel Streight and his escort. Both were hunkered down in the saddle in the face of the driving rain, covered from head to toe in oil skin waterproofs, but the water still manage to infiltrate at the neck and seat no matter how they tried to prevent it.

Hearing the shout, O'Sullivan turned in the saddle and looked back down the column, just in time to see the big gray head out across the field at full gallop.

"God damn," he shouted. "Coffin, go catch that bloody mule."

"Me? Not in this life. That overgrown donkey is a killer, an' I ain't about to commit suicide.

The Sergeant Major scowled down at him, and then without a word, put heel to his horse's flank. With a yell and mighty splashing of hooves, he wheeled and sped off after the wayward mule.

O'Sullivan, not a cavalryman by any stretch of the imagination, was no mean horseman. In an instant, he felt a familiar surge of excitement as the great horse's muscles bunched beneath him and it surged forward, its stride widening as its speed increased. Within seconds, the horse had caught the fleeing mule, and without any instructions or guidance from O'Sullivan, put its shoulder to the panicked mule, and slowly began to turn him.

O'Sullivan was dumbfounded, as was the cadre of officers watching from the front of the column. It took but a few seconds for the horse to nudge the mule to a stop, then turn and stand in front of the heaving animal. All O'Sullivan had to do was reach down and grab the reins and, together, the trio trotted sedately back to the column, to much cheering and yelling.

"Well done, Sergeant Major," Streight called. "Where did you learn to ride like that?"

""Ah, well, Colonel, sir. It's like this..." But the colonel had turned his attention elsewhere and was no longer listening, much to O'Sullivan's relief.

"Where the hell did you get this bloody horse, Coffin?" O'Sullivan asked, leaning sideways in the saddle so that only the corporal could hear him.

Coffin grinned up at him from his perch on the not-so-small Phoebe. "Now don't I always make sure you have the best of everything, Sergeant Major?" And then he winked at O'Sullivan and turned his face to the driving rain, oblivious of the water running in torrents from the broad brim of his tired, but still serviceable hat. And, try as he might, O'Sullivan could pry not another word from the stoic corporal.

By the time the big gray mule had been returned to his master, chaos reigned once more. Dozens of mules, from the front of the

66

column all the way to the rear, were bucking and kicking, and their inexperienced riders could do nothing to stop it. Several headed for a nearby creek, and some lay down therein, leaving their riders splashing around in the icy water. Others managed simply to toss their new masters into the fast-running water and then head for the trees. A dozen or more took off across the fields, following the trail blazed by the now captive big gray, their riders hanging on for dear life. But, as everyone knows, a donkey's gallop is soon over, and that's no less true of a mule. Many slowed to a gentle walk, while others slid to a sudden halt, flinging their petrified cargos over their heads and down into the mud, to stand over them, braying like banshees.

One of the pack mules at the rear of the column, loaded down with a heavy load of ammunition boxes, was so frightened by the surrounding turmoil that he simply lay down in the mud and began braying loudly.

Private Andy McHugh, securely mounted on the mule Ignatius, held his breath and prayed. His prayer must have been answered, because Ignatius simply turned his head to look at him, snorted once, then turned again to face the front and stood waiting quietly.

Not so, the mule now called Abel. He flattened his ears and, with a huge leap, took off at lightning speed across the field in a huge circle with Private Cassell hanging on like some demented bulldog. Abel's circuit of the field ended almost where it began, but the animal was not done yet. Round and round he spun like a top, with Cassell hanging desperately on until, at last, the mule, tired and miserable and unable to unseat his rider, came to a sudden stop, at which point Cassell keeled slowly over sideways and out of the saddle to land on his back in the mud. Shaken up as he was, he was still hanging doggedly onto the reins, and grinning like a fool, inordinately proud of his own performance during his wild ride. His companions cheered wildly and waved their hats. Cassell took a deep bow, slapped Abel fondly on his withers, and climbed once more into the saddle.

It was more than an hour before order was finally restored to the column. Once more, Abel Streight gave the order to move out and, very slowly, and with much braying and snorting, the column began again, what everyone now knew was to be a long, long journey.

Chapter 9

April 14, 1863. Confederate Cavalry Headquarters - Spring Hill, Tennessee

Dispatch riders from Colonel Woodward, whose cavalry had now been tracking the progress of Streight's riverboats for four days, had been arriving at Major General Van Dorn's headquarters several times a day. Yet no one knew the purpose of Streight's mission, his ultimate destination, or even his name.

What Van Dorn did know was that to the west, in Corinth, Federal Brigadier General Grenville Dodge, commanding the District of Corinth, was preparing his force of more than six thousand infantry and cavalry for an expedition of his own. Knowing this, Van Dorn assumed that the unnamed brigade must be intending to join Dodge; either that or he was after Woodward. Without any specific intelligence, however, he was somewhat at a loss as to know exactly how to handle the situation.

Nathan Bedford Forrest was operating independently to the south from Fayetteville to Pulaski (he had left Spring Hill only the day before after attending the funeral of his artillery commander, Captain Freeman), while Van Dorn was operating west of Spring Hill. The only forces he had available to scout the southwest were a reduced brigade of cavalry located at Tuscumbia, Alabama, under the command of Colonel Phillip Roddey: three regiments of cavalry, a total of twelve hundred, more or less.

Van Dorn's thought that his only real option at this point was to sit tight and await developments. Thus, he sent riders to each of his field commanders with orders to deploy scouts in to the north and east, and to report immediately any new developments, either with Streight's force, or with Dodge's.

By noon the following day, reports from the field were already beginning to arrive on Van Dorn's desk. He quickly assimilated the new information and sent a rider immediately to General Braxton Bragg, along with a request for instruction as to how to proceed.

Chapter 10

April 15, 1863. Federal Encampment at Fort Henry

The journey across the peninsula between Palmyra and Fort Henry had been an arduous one.

The brigade had left Palmyra just before one o'clock in the afternoon on the 13th, in pouring rain. The going was slow, not just due to the state of the road, which was churned to mud by the long column of heavy beasts, wagons and artillery, but also by the inexperience of the now partially mounted infantry. While the state of the road covered by the head of the column was firm enough, by the time the first regiment, the 51st Indiana, had passed over it, the usually hard-packed dirt had been churned to sludge. And it only got worse. By two-thirty, the trailing elements were knee deep in thick, viscous mud that sucked and dragged hoof, foot, and wheel until the pace had slowed to less than a walk. By four o'clock, as one regiment became separated from another, the column stretched for more than four miles. When the column halted to make camp for the night, they had barely covered thirteen miles, just two and a half miles per hour and it was still raining.

On Tuesday the 14th, they did a little better. The rain had stopped, and the sun was shining. Wet and bedraggled as most of the men were, they awoke and rose to greet the day with enthusiasm. After all, they now were mounted infantry and abroad on what they all knew must be a great adventure. The column made some twenty miles before pitching camp at Bell's Old Iron Works on the banks of the Columbia River; they were now less than a dozen miles from their objective, Fort Henry.

They arrived at the fort the next day, the 15th, in the early afternoon. The foraging had gone well, and the available mules now numbered more than 1400. Even so, and with more than 200 horses, the brigade was still short mounts. Colonel Streight hoped to remedy the situation in the coming days.

Streight's plan had been to get the brigade back aboard the riverboats and on its way south to Mississippi that same day. Unfortunately, the boats did not arrive until midnight on the 15th, thus the plan was already off schedule.

Meanwhile in Corinth, the first elements of General Dodge's force had already left the city and were heading east to Eastport. Dodge's Federal cavalry brigade under the command of Colonel Florence Cornyn, comprised of five regiments, had left Corinth around mid-day on the 15th, just as the leading elements of Streight's brigade were arriving at Fort Henry.

Dodge himself was in something of a quandary. For three days, he had been expecting word from Streight that would provide him with a specific date and time for the Mule Soldiers' arrival at Eastport. No such word had yet arrived, and Dodge had no other option but to send word to Cornyn to halt his trek eastward and make camp until he received word from Dodge.

Cornyn established his camp some four miles to the west of Iuka, Mississippi and settled down to wait.

When Streight finally arrived at Fort Henry, his fleet had grown, almost exponentially. He had been joined by Brigadier General Alfred Ellet and his Marine Brigade consisting of two gunboats, a ram boat, and five transports, along with sufficient infantry and cavalry to support any action he might need to undertake. Ellet's mission was to escort Streight's fleet to Mississippi. Thus, he was now in overall command of all Federal fleet operations in Tennessee.

With the riverboats arriving so late in the day, it was decided to wait until morning before boarding the brigade. Just before dawn, the docks at Fort Henry turned into a hive of activity. It was not until mid-morning, however, that Streight learned from the local river pilot that, because of the water levels, the boats would be dock-bound for at least another day. Streight, already running behind schedule, was exasperated, but could do nothing about it.

By early evening the 16th, most of the now more than 1400 mules, and almost 200 horses had been loaded aboard the transports. Streight and his officers were all aboard the *Hazel Dell*, as were the members of Company A, 51st Indiana Regiment, including Sergeant Major O'Sullivan, Coffin, Doyle, Cassell, and McHugh. The rest of the regiment, along with some of the 72nd Indiana, was aboard the *Baldwin*, the remainder of the 72nd, the 3rd Ohio and the 80th Illinois were aboard the *Nashville*, *Ohio* and the *Aurora*. The supplies, equipment, and artillery were spread among the four remaining transports. And so, everyone, man, mule and horse, settled down for the night, and by ten o'clock, most of the men were in bed and the animals had had their nightly feed. The boats rocked gently against their moorings, and a new moon showed briefly through the scudding clouds, casting an ethereal glow over the river and the surrounding countryside. All was quiet.

Friday morning, the 17th, dawned bright and clear; it was going to be a beautiful day. Overnight, Ellet's flotilla had been joined by two more gunboats, bringing the fleet total to sixteen.

At five in the morning, the gunboat *Covington*, followed by the *Hazel Dell*, cast off and steamed calmly out onto the waters of the Cumberland, followed by the rest of the fleet in line astern.

High on the upper deck of the *Hazel Dell*, Sergeant Major O'Sullivan and Corporal Coffin, tin cups full of steaming coffee in hand, leaned with their backs to the rail, staring up at the billowing black smoke rising almost straight up from the twin stacks and listening to the water gurgling along the sides. Privates Cassell, Doyle, and McHugh were in a similar spot, with similar cups, just a few feet away toward the stern, but out of earshot. The great side wheels churned the river into white foam, driving the boat forward at a steady five knots. The rest of the fleet stretched out far behind.

O'Sullivan sipped the hot coffee, lost in thought.

"I'm going to call him Lightnin'," O'Sullivan said, without taking his gaze off the billowing smoke.

"Lightnin'?" Coffin said.

O'Sullivan nodded. "The bloody animal moves like nothin' in the world that I've ever ridden. Lightnin's a good name for him."

He sipped his coffee and continued watching the smoke.

Finally, after several moments, he glanced to his left and spotted the three privates talking among themselves.

"What are we goin' to do about Doyle, do you think?" he asked, not expecting an answer; nor did he get one. It was not Coffin's place to offer advice to the Top Soldier, although there were times when, unbeknownst to that same Top Soldier, he was able surreptitiously to steer him in almost any direction he so desired. This was not one of those times.

"I ain't seen the first animal that might suit that lanky mick." O'Sullivan thought for a moment, then said, "There are only two options as I see it. We could have him drive one of the wagons, I s'pose, or maybe we could persuade Major Vananda to take him on. Then he could ride one of them bloody great artillery horses."

Coffin almost choked into his coffee cup, but said nothing

"Well, we gotta do somthin', Boone. Cain't have the poor boy walk all the way to wherever it might be that we're agoin', that's for sure, so it is.

"DOYLE," he shouted. "Get your arse over here."

The big man looked down on his friends, shrugged his shoulders, and ambled over to where O'Sullivan and Coffin still leaned against the rail. He stood in front of them, silent, hands at his side, waiting.

"Doyle, I've bin thinkin'. How would you like to be an artillerist?"

Doyle tilted his head sideways and looked askance down at O'Sullivan, "Be a what, Sergeant Major?"

"Join the artillery, shoot them bloody great guns, ride one of them bloody great draft horses that drag 'em around."

Doyle slowly shook his head. "Er... I don't think so, Sergeant Major."

"Fine, then it's the wagon train for you. Go find Sergeant Morgan an' tell him I sent you. Tell him I said he was to make a wagon master out of you. Oh... my God. What am I thinkin'? Well, no matter. Go on, man. Go find the quartermaster sergeant an' tell him what I said."

Doyle opened his mouth to say something, thought better of it, turned and shambled away across the deck and down the stairs to the hold below the main deck.

"That, Boone," O'Sullivan said to Coffin, "is something I know I will live to regret."

Coffin merely nodded in agreement and sipped on his now rapidly cooling coffee.

"You're very quiet this fine mornin', Boone. What is it that's on your mind?"

"Tain't nothin'. I was just enjoyin' the peace an' quiet. We don't get too much of that these days, do we?"

O'Sullivan stared down into the dregs of his coffee as if he was contemplating the future. "Right you are, Boone. It's a rare day when we have little to do, an' I find myself out of sorts because of it, so I do. It's that feelin' of uncertainty I have, not knowin' where, what, or when, especially right this minute when nobody but his nibs seems to know the where. Where in God's name is the old bugger takin' us, I wonder?"

Coffin had no answer, so he gave none. Only the sounds of the water churning under the great wheels just a few feet away disturbed the tranquility of the early morning.

As the fleet made its way slowly downriver, the sun rose in the east and the ride became a decidedly pleasant one. With little to do aboard but relax, most of A Company were out on deck, lining the rails and watching the world go by. For now, at least, everyone was relaxed, even content.

Meanwhile, in the grand salon on the upper deck, Colonel Abel Streight had called his officers together for what amounted to a council of war, but it turned into a relatively informal question and answer session.

Officers present included Lt. Colonel James Sheets, commanding the 51st (Streight's own regiment); Major Ivan Walker, commanding the 73rd Indiana in the absence of Colonel Hathaway, who had not yet caught up with the brigade; Lt. Colonel Andrew Rogers of the 80th Illinois, and Lt Colonel Robert Lawson of the 3rd Ohio Infantry. Also, present was Major Vananda, his chief of artillery along with his cavalry commander, Captain Smith, and several company commanders of lesser rank, but with a need to know, at least in Streight's opinion.

The air in the salon was one of expectancy. Cigar smoke spiraled upward from every seat around the table, and from several other officers now leaning against the walls. Streight was at the head of the table, a large map spread out on the table before him. He rose from his seat to address the company.

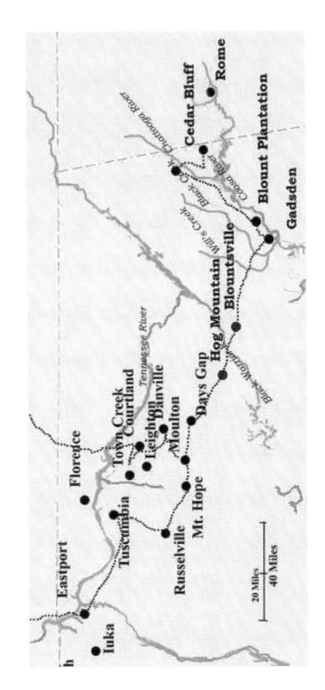

"Before I begin, does anyone need more coffee? No? Cigars, then?" Nobody did, and Streight nodded his head and cleared his throat. "Some of you already know what I am about to tell you. The rest of you are, I know, wondering about our mission, about the secrecy we've been forced to maintain. Well, secrecy no more, we are well on our way and, if the enemy doesn't know our objective at this point, there's little chance that they will learn of it in time to do anything about it.

"We, gentlemen, are going to strike deep into enemy territory and destroy their lines of supply and communication."

Streight paused and looked around the table, searching for reaction. The room was silent, every eye focused on the brigade commander.

"From here," he pointed to a spot on the map, "we will sail downriver to Savannah where we will stop over tomorrow night." All five senior officers leaned forward in their seats for a better view of the map, and the junior officers crowded in behind them.

"We will resume our voyage on the morning of the 19th and should reach Eastport, Mississippi, by mid-afternoon, where we will leave the boats and join with General Dodge.

"There are numerous Confederate cavalry brigades operating east of Mississippi, including Van Dorn, Roddey and, of course, Forrest. General Dodge is to provide a diversion, to draw attention away from us while we make our way cross country to Rome, Georgia." With a finger, he indicated on the map the rough direction of his intended route.

For a moment, all were silent as they gazed down at the map. There were several unhappy-looking faces among the gathered officers. Colonel Rogers was frowning and slowly shaking his head.

"That's some mighty rough country, Colonel," Rogers said, staring down at the map.

"Which is exactly why the commanding general insisted that the men should be mounted on mules; they are steady on the hoof and better suited to the terrain," Streight replied.

Rogers did not seem to be convinced, but he said nothing.

"You seem doubtful, Colonel."

"I don't know, Colonel Streight. I just don't know. Mules of good sound stock, perhaps, but that's not what we have here. And I have serious doubts that the men can manage the animals over such a lengthy trek. Few of them, as far as I know, have ever sat a saddle, and mules... well, we all know what cantankerous critters they can be. Not to mention the health of some of them, or lack of it, and the fact that most of them are unbroken."

"I have every confidence in the men, Colonel, especially those of the 51st. You, of course, know the men of the 80th better than I do, so there may well be some merit to what you say. Be that as it may," Streight continued, "We must make do, and do the best we can with what we have."

Crack! Crack!

One of the salon's great windows shattered, followed by the one opposite, as a Minnie ball tore through the room, barely missing Colonel Lawson's head.

"GET DOWN!" O'Sullivan shouted on the upper deck. "It's an ambush."

The officers in the salon hit the floor as did the dozens of soldiers lining the rails of the upper decks.

Some three hundred yards away, on the western shore of the river, undercover of the trees that lined the riverbank, a dismounted patrol of Woodward's Confederate cavalry opened a blistering volley of rifled-musket fire. The Minnie balls slammed, staccato-like into the wooden hull and cabin walls, sending knife-like shards of seasoned mahogany spinning across the decks and inflicting grievous wounds wherever they found a human target. Several soldiers suffered deep gashes to their face and arms. Two went down as the result of devastating wounds inflicted directly by 58-caliber Minnie balls.

None of Streight's soldiers, now flat on the upper decks, were armed, a situation that would be rectified within the hour.

Minutes later, BAM, BAM, BAM. Just ahead of the *Hazel Dell*, the gunboat *Covington* unleashed a hail of canister across the river. The gunboat's aim was a little high, and the two hundred plus canister balls did little harm to the snipers on the far shore, other than showering them with leaves and branches stripped away by the *Covington's* heavy guns.

Downriver, the other three gunboats were steaming quickly to join the *Covington*; the Confederate patrol melted away into the trees. This was the first contact the Federal fleet had had with Woodward's Confederate cavalry; it would not be the last.

In the salon, the officers had returned to the table, shaken, but otherwise unhurt. All were used to such minor skirmishes and were little affected by them.

"So," Streight said. "Comments, gentlemen?"

Had there been any before the Confederate attack, they were now forgotten.

"Very well, I suggest you get what rest you can between now and our arrival in Eastport. Before you do, however, please issue orders that no man is to be on deck unarmed."

Although the journey to Eastport was largely uneventful, Woodward's cavalry continued to shadow the fleet, often forging on ahead to take cover, fire on the fleet, and then melt away into the forests. They did little damage, other than to destroy the serenity of the sunshine cruise. Rarely did the gunboats even have time to range their weapons. When they did, targets were difficult to identify. The raiders picked their spots, made good use of the available cover, attacked like lightning, then disappeared into the woods.

The men on the decks of the transports had to be ever watchful and on their guard. The attacks, when they came, were never expected, though they were never totally unexpected either. Casualties on the boats were minimal. Before the fleet would reach Eastport, the brigade would suffer three killed and nine wounded, although two of those would eventually succumb to devastating gut wounds.

In Corinth, General Dodge was on edge, frustrated with the lack of communication between Streight and himself. For four days he had been waiting, and each day, almost hourly, he was receiving intelligence from Colonel Cornyn's cavalry patrols that the Confederate forces in Alabama were receiving reinforcements and now numbered more than 5000. Dodge, a cautious man by nature, grew ever more worried by this constant stream of adverse information. The more he received, the more pessimistic he became.

Colonel Cornyn, with two regiments of cavalry, more than 1600 troopers, was still encamped four miles to the west of Iuka, Mississippi. Dodge, himself, had for the past three days, had his infantrymen ready to move out at a moment's notice.

Dodge, though not a happy man, decided it was time to move. Thus, on the morning of the 16th, he gave orders for his troops to take the road east from Corinth to Eastport. Dodge, himself, with a small escort, rode out at noon to join Colonel Cornyn at Iuka.

To the east, the Confederate storm clouds were gathering.

Chapter 11

April 16, 1863. Confederate Headquarters, Tullahoma, Tennessee

Major General Earl Van Dorn had left Spring Hill at first light and arrived at General Bragg's headquarters just after noon. Upon his arrival, he requested an immediate interview with the commanding general of the Army of Tennessee. Bragg, however, was busy, and Van Dorn, never a patient man, was left cooling his heels for more than an hour in an outer office before being ushered into the general's presence.

"General Van Dorn," Bragg said, without looking up from the papers on his desk. "What are you doing here? Why are you not with your command?"

"There have been some major developments, General. I thought it best if I discussed them with you in person."

"Hmmm." Bragg still did not look at him, nor did he ask Van Dorn to sit, much to the cavalry commander's discomfort.

"Well, General... please continue."

Van Dorn waited no more. Without being asked, he sat in one of the two chairs facing Bragg's desk.

Bragg now looked at him, surprised at Van Dorn's temerity. Van Dorn was unconcerned. He was a man of supreme confidence. He had little respect for and was not in the least intimidated by his commanding general, considering him a cautious battlefield commander at best and an incompetent one at worst.

"General Bragg, Colonel Woodward has been watching a large force of enemy infantry that left Nashville by boat four days ago and is now steaming southward toward Mississippi. I have also received information that General Dodge has left Corinth and is now encamped west of Eastport. As yet, their purposes are unknown. It makes sense, however, to assume that the two forces intend to join and then advance either into Tennessee or Alabama. I am of the opinion that General Dodge's objective is Tuscumbia."

"What forces do we have in Tuscumbia?" Bragg asked, quietly.

"Colonel Roddey, with a single reduced brigade: 1200 men and two pieces of artillery. Dodge, without the infantry still on the boats, has, so reports suggest, slightly more than 6000."

"Hmmm, and what of General Forrest? Where is he?"

"General Forrest is operating west of Columbia with 2000 men."

"Have General Forrest return to Spring Hill and await further orders. You, too, General Van Dorn, should return to Spring Hill and await developments."

"Sir," Van Dorn began, not bothering to hide his exasperation, "I am of the opinion we should move immediately to reinforce Roddey at Tuscumbia. It makes no sense to allow the enemy to gain a foothold, and then have to drive him from it."

"General Van Dorn, I have little interest in your opinions, nor do I have very much concern for what General Dodge and a single, detached enemy division might be about. I have more concern for what General Rosecrans and his army in its entirety is planning. You, sir, must concern yourself with the day-to-day operations of your cavalry force.

"I do deem it necessary to stay abreast of what the force on the river is about. They could disembark anywhere, from Hamburg, to Savannah, Pittsburg Landing, Eastport, or anywhere in between. If that occurs, and all of your forces are in Alabama, how then are we to meet that threat? Please, use your head, General. You may leave, sir. Return to Spring Hill and there await developments. If the force now on the Columbia does indeed join Dodge at Eastport, you may then move sufficient forces to Tuscumbia to contain them."

Van Dorn, his teeth grinding, rose from his seat and, without saluting, spun on his heel and walked rapidly from the room, slamming the door behind him. Ten minutes later he was, with his escort, galloping back along the road toward Spring Hill, his temper barely in check.

Chapter 12

April 16, General Dodge's Field Headquarters, Iuka, Mississippi

Brigadier General Grenville M. Dodge, with his escort, arrived in Iuka in the late afternoon of April 16, ahead of the main body of his troops.

The thirty-two-year-old Dodge was more engineer than he was battlefield commander. He was conservative by nature, and of medium height and build, with a full set of facial hair and receding hairline. All of which made for a less than imposing figure. He was, however, a very astute and resourceful man.

When he met with Colonel Cornyn, his cavalry commander, late that afternoon he had two concerns, both of which bothered him immensely. First, he needed to know the strength of the enemy he knew he would soon encounter, and second, where in God's name was Colonel Streight?

The first was, so he thought, easy enough to answer. He would simply send scouts to Tuscumbia to assess the enemy's strength.

Thus it was that Captain George Spencer set out with a small escort on the road east to Tuscumbia. Spencer was an exceedingly resourceful man, more spy than scout, with a reputation for bringing home the goods. Unlike most scouts, Spencer had, almost without exception, been able to penetrate enemy lines, defenses and even camps, and escape with his body intact and the required information in hand. He was, in fact, General Dodge's go to man when things needed to happen quickly and this was one of those times.

Between them, the general and captain concocted a plan whereby Spencer would approach Tuscumbia under a flag of truce.

There had, over the past several months, been much confusion over the disposition of prisoners of war, on both sides. It was a dispute that, until now, had not been resolved. Spencer's mission, so he would tell the officer commanding the enemy forces in Tuscumbia, was to arrange for the exchange of prisoners, something that was indeed of interest to both sides. Thus, General Dodge prepared a dispatch to Confederate Colonel Roddey introducing Spencer and requesting that negotiations for the proposed exchange be opened forthwith.

Spencer left Iuka just after eight o'clock the following morning, the 17th. The thirty-two mile ride would take at least six hours; he did not expect to arrive at his destination much before three o'clock that afternoon.

As to the disposition of the elusive Colonel Streight and his mounted brigade of infantry, there was still no word, and Dodge was becoming more worried as each hour went by.

Some five miles to the west of Tuscumbia, his white flag fluttering, Spencer ran into a Confederate cavalry patrol. For several tense moments, the two small forces faced off on the dirt road.

"Advance and state your purpose," Confederate Captain Cole called. His troop held their weapons at the ready.

"Sergeant Grant," Spencer said to the bearer, "come with me. The rest of you remain here until I call for you."

Slowly, Spencer and Grant walked their horses forward along the dirt road until they were within ten yards of the Confederate patrol.

"State your name and purpose, Captain."

"Captain George Spencer, Assistant Adjutant General, Department of Mississippi, Major General Grenville Dodge commanding, with dispatches for Colonel Roddey regarding the exchange of prisoners. And whom do I have the honor to address?"

"Captain Cole, 4th Alabama Cavalry, at your service, Captain, and you are most welcome. I have friends who are presently prisoners in Corinth. If you will follow me, I will escort you to Colonel Roddey's field headquarters."

The two saluted each other, and Spencer returned to his escort. Cole deployed ten men to the rear of Spencer's small group, and the column set off along the road to Tuscumbia. They arrived on the outskirts of the town a little after five o'clock. They entered the city without being challenged but were stopped within a few hundred feet by a lieutenant in charge of the guard. He approached Cole close enough so that what he said would not be heard by the rest of the column.

"Captain Cole, sir," the lieutenant said, standing close to Cole's horse. "What the hell are you doing? These men should not be here, flag of truce or not. They should have been detained beyond the city limits. You know that."

Cole looked down at the lieutenant, somewhat embarrassed. "That's true enough, Lieutenant. My apologies.

"Captain Spencer," he said, turning in the saddle. "I am sorry, sir, but you must remain here until I have informed Colonel Roddey of your presence. If you hand me your dispatches, I will convey them to the colonel. It should take no longer than a moment or two."

Spencer nodded. He could tell there was no point in arguing. He handed the sealed package to Cole, who rode away into the city.

"The man's a spy, Captain," Roddey said to Cole as he read the dispatches. "Dodge knows we have no prisoners here. I paroled them all the first week of the month. Dodge is on the move, and he wants to know our strength."

Roddey thought for a moment, and then said. "All right, he want's information. We'll give him some. Here's what we'll do."

Roddey kept Spencer waiting for more than an hour before he sent Cole back with a letter. Spencer split the seals, flipped the single sheet of paper open, and read the contents.

To Captain Spencer, Commanding Flag of Truce

Captain: I am directed by the general commanding the district to inform you that all prisoners of war held by him were paroled on the seventh and were sent to the Federal lines.

P.D. Roddey, Colonel Commanding Cavalry.

Spencer stared at the note for several minutes, gathering his thoughts. This was not what he had expected. He looked up at Cole, then looked around what he could see of the town. It was bustling with locals, and with gray and butternut clad soldiers.

"Captain Cole," he said. "Am I not to meet with Colonel Roddey?"

"Er... no, Captain. The colonel said that as he did not have prisoners to exchange, there was no point in his meeting with you. He asked me to give you his respects, and to wish you well for your journey back to your own lines."

Spencer was nonplussed. He had come for information, and he did not have it. He was not inclined to return without it. He realized he had no choice but to turn about and make his way back the way he had come, or did he?

"Please convey my thanks to Colonel Roddey," he said, testily. "Inform him also that I will pass his note along to General Dodge."

Spencer saluted Cole, wheeled his horse, and, followed by his escort, set off at a gallop along the road toward Iuka. Cole smiled as he watched him go.

Spencer and his escort had slowed to a trot, and were some four miles from Tuscumbia when they came upon a couple, a middle-aged man and woman, walking toward them along the dirt road.

They were an indiscriminate pair to be sure. The man, perhaps in his early fifties, and the woman, some several years younger, were roughly dressed, not in rags, but their clothes had certainly seen better days. Both had sacks of something bulky slung over their backs. Both were obviously tired, and they were unarmed.

Spencer reined in his horse, and his escort closed up behind him.

"Who are you, sir, and what is your purpose?" Spencer said.

"And what might that be to you?" The man looked up at him defiantly. "I don't aff to tell yoh damn Yankees nothin'. Just get outa m' way and let me be about m' business."

"You're going nowhere until you tell me what you're about."

"Please, Mica," the woman said, pulling on the man's arm. "We don't mean no 'arm, sir," she continued, looking up at Spencer. We're just on our way to sell our produce and buy some salt an' flour. See?" She unslung the sack from her back, opened it, and held it up so that Spencer could see that it was full of small, round bread loaves.

"What about his?"

"Show him, Mica."

Reluctantly, Mica showed the inside of his sack; it was full of potatoes.

"Now, can we go?" the woman asked.

"Not so fast," Spencer said. "What do you know of the enemy troops in Tuscumbia?"

The man looked up at him incredulously. "What I know of the enemy," he growled, "is that they ain't no enemy, you blue-belly son of a..."

"No, Mica, stop," the woman quickly interrupted him. "He dint mean it, sir; he dint."

"By God, I did too mean it. And, if this son of a bitch wants to know 'bout the enemy, by God I'll tell 'im." He looked again at Spencer.

"They's more'n you kin 'andle. That's for sure. An' they's more comin', lots more."

"Mica, shut up." The woman was almost in tears.

"Shut up, my ass. These sons o' bitches come down 'ere throwin' they weight about, stealing our food an' our animals, an' I'm s'posed t' look tother way. NO SIR," he shouted. "Now get outa me goddamn way.

But Spencer didn't move. Instead, he drew his Colt Navy revolver from its holster at his hip, and pointed it at Mica.

"Now, old man," he said quietly, menacingly. "I am going to ask you once, and once only. If you don't tell me, I will shoot you in the leg. Now, what did you mean, there's more than I can handle. Just how many enemy troops are there in Tuscumbia?"

Mica looked up at him. His face had gone white. "I dunno," he said, "a lot."

Spencer drew back the hammer of the Colt and aimed the weapon at Mica's right leg.

"Stop, stop. I don' know how to say it. I ain't up on military terms, but they's a lot, more'n 3500, I'd guess, an' big guns too, more'n a dozen of 'em. Most of 'em come last week. That's it. That's all I knows. I don't know n'more. That's no lie."

Spencer looked long and hard at him, and at his wife. "You mentioned that there are more on the way. How many, and how do you know?"

"Just talk, that's all, just talk. We hears talk all the time."

"What talk?"

"Talk is that Gen'l Bragg's sending troops from Tullahoma, lots of 'em. How many, I don't know. It's all just talk."

Spencer released the hammer on the Colt and returned it to its holster.

"Off you go, then," he said, putting spurs to horse and riding around the two and away down the road, leaving them in a cloud of dust.

The couple stood for several moments, then they slowly walked after them. For several hundred yards, they followed the distant sounds of the Federal hoof beats on the dirt road. Finally, they stopped, listened and, with a nod of his head and smile, Sergeant Mica Hollister, 53rd Alabama Cavalry, and Mrs. Emily Rogers stepped off the dirt road, into the woods, and made their way to where they had tethered their horses. Less than an hour later, the two were in Colonel Roddey's field headquarters in Tuscumbia.

"How did it go, Sergeant?" Roddey asked.

"Just as you expected, Colonel. He swallowed it hook, line and sinker."

"Are you sure, Sergeant?"

"As sure as anyone can be, sir."

"How about it, Mrs. Rogers? Did he, do you think? Did he believe it?"

"I think he did, Colonel. I truly believe that awful man would have shot the sergeant if he hadn't."

Roddey nodded. "Let's hope you're both right."

"Mrs. Rogers. You, my good lady, are a treasure. I apologize for asking you to put yourself in such danger, but I had to be sure Spencer would believe you both. Only the presence of a woman could have persuaded him that you were what you were supposed to be. Your husband would have been proud of you. Thank you."

"There's no need to thank me, Colonel Roddey. It was little enough, and I was pleased to do it. Good day to you, Colonel. If you need me again, please don't hesitate to ask."

Captain Spencer did not arrive back in Iuka until well after midnight. General Dodge was asleep, and Spencer did not disturb him. Instead, he went to his tent, sat for a moment, scribbled some few words on a sheet of paper, then lay down to sleep. He was exhausted.

The following morning, the 18th, Spencer was up and about at first light. He was still dressed, except for his tunic, from the night before. He had an orderly bring a bucket of water from the nearby river, splashed his face, rubbed it dry, grabbed a large cup of steaming coffee, and then made his way quickly to see General Dodge.

"Welcome back, Captain," Dodge said, shaking his hand. "All went as planned, I presume?"

"Spencer looked down. "It did indeed, General. I estimate that Roddey has at least two brigades of cavalry, more than 6000 men, and as many as three batteries of artillery. And there are more on the way from Tullahoma." He did not mention how he had come by this information, nor did General Dodge ask. Instead, he assumed that, as always, Spencer had somehow come up with the required information. He merely nodded; knowing what he now knew, he was not at all surprised by such numbers.

"While you were away, Captain, I heard from General Hulbert. He informed me that Colonel Grierson and a full brigade of cavalry left LaGrange yesterday. Their target is Newton Station, Mississippi. Their objective is the same as Colonel Streight's, to destroy the railroad there and cut General Pemberton's supply line into Vicksburg.

"Both Grierson's and Streight's raids are of the utmost importance. General Hulbert fears the build-up of Confederate cavalry forces in this area is in direct response to Grierson's departure into Mississippi. We are to divert Roddey, to make sure that he does not pursue Grierson. The longer we can hold the enemy cavalry here, the better the chances will be for Grierson to succeed. The same for Colonel Streight; we must screen him from enemy cavalry, too. To achieve both objectives, we will move at once against Tuscumbia. Last night I gave the orders to ready the troops. We move out at seven o'clock this morning."

He paused for a moment, and then said, "I still have heard nothing from Colonel Streight, where he is, or when he will arrive, but I can wait no longer. To do so will allow Roddey to send troops after Colonel Grierson. That would not do, not do at all. Captain Spencer, you will take your company and ride upriver; find the fleet. We must find out what Colonel Streight is up to."

Spencer saluted and withdrew from the tent. Less than thirty minutes later, he and his escort were on the western shore of the river and heading north in search of the flotilla bearing Colonel Streight and his Mule Soldiers.

Chapter 13

April 18, 1863. Cherokee Bluffs, Alabama

General Dodge began his advance with the main body of his force of 4500 infantry toward Tuscumbia as planned at seven o'clock on the morning of the 18th; the 1600-man Federal cavalry brigade was already in the field.

In response to reports that Colonel Roddey and a large component of Confederate cavalry were on the east side of the Great Bear Creek, Colonel Cornyn and his cavalry brigade had left Iuka the previous day and had crossed the creek in pursuit of Roddey.

Colonel Roddey, having been informed that a large Federal force, estimated to be upward of 15000, was preparing to move east from Corinth, had been in the field for more than a week, and was well aware of everything that Dodge and Cornyn were up to, and he responded accordingly.

As Cornyn advanced, Roddey slowly withdrew eastward, leaving the way clear for Cornyn to continue on into the dense hinterland that was western Alabama.

Cornyn, encountering no resistance, was able to advance his brigade quickly eastward to and beyond Cherokee Bluffs, Alabama. Too quickly, in fact, and his regiments soon became strung out in the dense undergrowth. To the rear of the column, Cornyn had a short battery of artillery, two field pieces of Tamrath's Battery of the 1st Missouri Light Artillery. These and their accompanying caissons were being escorted by Lieutenant Edward Krebbs and two companies of the 9th Illinois Cavalry. The artillery was finding the going through the rough country to be extremely hard and the weather unseasonably hot. The heavy draft horses that pulled the weapons were exhausted and the small force soon became separated from the main body of Cornyn's brigade.

Roddey, his own force strung out over more than a mile, saw his chance and pounced on the stragglers, capturing both field pieces, both companies of cavalry under Krebbs' command, and Krebbs himself. But Krebbs did not go down easily. During the fracas, he managed to get one of the guns into action, and his few troopers fought valiantly, wounding several men and horses until they were overwhelmed by the superior Confederate force. Only a half-dozen of Krebbs' men managed to escape into the dense woodland. During the skirmish, several soldiers on both sides were wounded, but none were killed.

Colonel Cornyn, more than a mile away at the head of his column, heard the commotion and sent a rider to find out what was happening. The rider returned only minutes later with the news that Krebbs and his guns had been captured. Cornyn immediately turned his brigade around and ordered the 1st Alabama Cavalry Regiment to charge the Confederate positions.

The 1st Alabama was, unfortunately, almost all fresh recruits, many with little or no training at all. Upon reaching the enemy, instead of pushing forward with their overwhelming numbers, most stopped when they received the first volley from the much smaller Confederate force, and then retreated more than half a mile before their officers managed to rein them in and reverse direction. Thus, the Confederates took advantage of the situation and retreated into the woods with one of the guns and its caisson; the other gun was recovered. Cornyn was beside himself with rage at the lack of zeal of the 1st Alabama. Two men were killed in Cornyn's charge to recover his artillery, Captain Cameron of the 1st Alabama and a private of the 10th Missouri Cavalry. These two were the first fatal casualties of the campaign. They would not be the last.

General Dodge, still believing he was facing a Confederate force in excess of 6000 - as Captain Spencer had reported the previous evening - ordered Cornyn to fall back and draw Roddey's cavalry with him.

Dodge, himself, ordered his four brigades of infantry into cover along the Tuscumbia Road, there to wait for the enemy cavalry. He would not be disappointed.

Colonel Roddey, in hot pursuit of Cornyn's Federal cavalry brigade, ran slap into the lead elements of Dodge's ambush: the 3rd Brigade under the command of Colonel Moses Bane.

Unfortunately, Bane was a somewhat impetuous commander, and had he been a little more patient, the outcome of the ambush might have been the complete destruction of Roddey's force. As it was, Bane ordered his men to open fire on the leading elements of the Confederate force. The rate of fire from the hidden Federal infantry was devastating, and Roddey's men were halted and thrown back.

Knowing he now faced a vastly superior force, Roddey withdrew toward Tuscumbia. Dodge, still under the impression that Roddey was also in command of a very large force, was slow to respond to the Confederate rout.

By day's end, around four o'clock in the afternoon, Dodge had pushed Roddey back to within five miles of Tuscumbia, and there he stopped. Dodge was now in something of a quandary. His primary purpose was to provide a screen for both Streight and Grierson, to harass and distract the Confederate cavalry. He certainly had no intention of invading Alabama. Thus, still not knowing where Colonel Streight and his Mule Soldiers were, and, after much deliberation with his brigade commanders, he decided enough was enough. He ordered his forces to pull back to Great Bear Creek, giving up the thirteen miles he had won.

As General Grenville Dodge sat alone in his tent that night, he had but one thought in his mind. *Where in God's name is Colonel Streight?*

As darkness fell, Confederate Colonel Roddey, ever watchful of what General Dodge was about, and not pleased with his own performance that day - he had after all denied more than 6000 Federal troops their prime objective, Tuscumbia - set his own camp just two miles east of Great Bear Creek, and then settled down to await events.

As yet, the Confederate authorities - not Roddey, Van Dorn, Forrest, or even General Bragg - had any idea of the pending threat posed by Colonel Abel Streight and his Mule Soldiers.

Chapter 14

April 19, 1863. Columbia River at Savannah, Tennessee

Colonel Streight's fleet, now numbering nineteen vessels, having been joined overnight by two more gunboats, cast off from the docks at Savannah just after daybreak on the 19th of April. The day had dawned bright and sunny, the air crisp and chilly, and a light mist covered the waters of the Columbia. The birds were singing, the water gurgled and chuckled as it rolled along the hulls of the boats, the great paddle wheels thrashed, driving the great craft down river at a goodly clip. As far as anyone could tell, there was no enemy presence within a dozen miles. The troops aboard the transports were in fine fettle, having breakfasted well on thick, crispy bacon, beans, and strong black coffee. Life was good, at least for the present.

Five men of the 51st Indiana Infantry, now "mounted infantry," Sergeant Major O'Sullivan, Corporal Coffin, and the three privates who now seemed to have attached themselves permanently to the two NCOs, McHugh, Cassell and Doyle, were lounging on the upper deck of the *Hazel Dell.*

They leaned over the top rail and watched as the crews began to unhook the heavy ropes from the dock cleats. Just before the boat slipped its moorings, a dispatch rider in a hurry clattered down the gangplank and onto the dock, the horse's hooves slipping on the worn woodwork. Without as much as a break in the horse's stride, the rider galloped away along the west bank of the river, heading south, Sergeant Major O'Sullivan assumed, for the final destination in Eastport, Mississippi. It was but a passing thought because O'Sullivan was lovingly inspecting his new arsenal of weapons.

The two Colt Army revolvers were brand new and the thin sheen of light oil that covered them glistened in the early morning sunshine. O'Sullivan still wondered, though not with any real concern, how Coffin had managed to get his hands on such a pair, especially considering the price. They should have cost at least double what he paid for them.

The man's a bloody scoundrel. Beautiful guns, though. He hefted them, one in each hand, slipped them back into their holsters, then quickly drew them again, and spun them one time on his index fingers, reveling in the feel as the grips slapped back onto the heels of his palms. *Beautiful!* He returned them again to their holsters; they slipped easily into the fine leather. *Holsters are worth almost as much as the pistols.* He seemed unaware that Coffin and the others were watching him intently.

Next, he pulled the Richards ten-gauge shotgun from the bag, held it in both hands in front of him, arms out straight. He turned the gun end over end, held the muzzles of the barrels to his eye, leaving a gap for the sunlight to filter inside, nodding his head in approval as he did so. *Clean as new pin, so they are.* He flipped the gun over again, put it to his shoulder, sighted down the barrels, and across the river. They were short, very short, having been cut down to just three inches past the forestock. *They're no more than fourteen inches long, to be sure.* The ramrod had been cut down to suit. *I'd hate be on the receivin' end of this one. Cut a man in two, I'd be bound.* He held the gun in his right hand, at arm's length, pointed out across the river, and swung it back and forth, covering the riverbank. He nodded, satisfied with the feel and balance of the mutilated weapon.

"A fine gun, so it is, Coffin. Let's see what she can do." He reached into the bag, pulled out two large paper cartridges, inserted them, one into each barrel, and then rammed them down, seating them firmly. Next, he placed two percussion caps over the nipples and pressed them into place with his thumb.

O'Sullivan gazed out over the river, looking for a likely target. Seeing none, he eyed a slender tree some thirty yards away on the west bank of the river. Its trunk was about four inches in diameter. Feet apart, one behind the other, he put the weapon to his shoulder and... BAM!

The big gun kicked upward and dug deep into the soft flesh of his shoulder, almost spinning him around. On the riverbank, a section in the middle of the tree trunk disappeared in a cloud of fine splinters.

97

The top section dropped straight down to the ground, and then the whole tree fell over backward.

"God damn, that hurt," O'Sullivan said, ruefully rubbing his shoulder. "Here, Coffin. You try it."

"Oh no. Not me, Sergeant Major. That thing could do me some real damage. Let Cassell have a try. He'll try anything."

"You wanna give it a go, Cassell?" O'Sullivan said, leering at him.

Cassell, one of those over-confident, often foolhardy individuals who never came across a situation he didn't think he could handle, looked at O'Sullivan, then at the still smoking shotgun, and grinned. "Sure, why not?"

"Be sure you put the stock tight against your shoulder," O'Sullivan said.

Cassell smirked, stepped forward, took the heavy gun from the Sergeant Major, hefted it, and looked around as he heard his friends backing away on either side.

"Ain't no big deal," he said. "It's just a shotgun." Then he looked out across the river, threw the weapon up to his shoulder, and pulled the trigger. BAM. The big gun slammed hard into his shoulder, reared upward and backward over his head as he staggered back several steps, almost flying from his rapidly numbing fingers.

"Ow," he shouted, dropping the weapon on the deck. "I done broke me shoulder. Oh God that hurts." He sank to his knees on the wooden deck, rubbing his injured shoulder. His two friends were laughing fit to be tied; Coffin and O'Sullivan stood by; both were grinning.

"Well, now, Cassell. It does seem you might have met your match. Did I not tell you to hold it tight?" O'Sullivan said, stooping down to pick up the shotgun. "Anyone else like to try it?" he asked, looking at McHugh and Doyle. Both shook their heads and took another step backward.

"Fine! Well, that's enough of that then," he said, handing the gun to Coffin. "Clean it for me, will you, Corporal?"

Coffin took the gun from him, sat on a bench by the deck rail, and went about cleaning the weapon.

O'Sullivan sat down beside him and began to load his two new Colts. From inside the bag he took two boxes of six-paper cartridges manufactured by Johnston & Dow. These cartridges consisted of a pre-measured load of black powder and a conical bullet wrapped in nitrated paper (paper that had been soaked in potassium nitrate and then dried, to make it more flammable). One by one, he pushed the cartridges into the front of the revolving chambers, seating each one with the loading lever ram as he went. When each chamber was loaded, he placed a percussion cap onto each nipple, seating them firmly in place with a little pressure from his thumb. The whole process took less than a minute. When the first was loaded, he slipped it back into the holster and went through the process again with the second pistol.

Having loaded both guns, he stood, turned and faced the shore, drew both guns and fired them alternately until both were empty.

"My, but that's so much better," he said, sitting down again to reload. "Beautiful guns, so they are, Coffin. How many rounds did you get?"

"I got you four hundred, Sergeant Major, but they ain't hard to come by. You had ten packages of six rounds in the bag. The rest are with my gear. When those are done, I'll get more...." He would have continued, but he heard footsteps on the stairs, as did O'Sullivan and the three privates.

"Attention," O'Sullivan shouted, leaping to his feet as Colonel Streight appeared at the top of the stairs.

"As you were, men, Sergeant Major," Streight said as he ambled across the deck. "Target practice, Mr. O'Sullivan?"

"Er, no sir, well, sort of, sir. Just gettin' the feel o' my new guns."

"Can I see?" Streight held out his hand.

O'Sullivan handed one to him.

"Yes, Colt Army, fine weapon, I have one m'self. You have two I see. Not infantry issue are they, Sergeant Major?"

"No, sir. Indeed they are not. But as we are now a mounted brigade, I thought...."

"Yes, yes. I have no problem with it at all. Good idea, in fact. Now, Sergeant Major. What I want to know is this: how are the animals? The ones we have aboard the *Hazel Dell*, that is."

"Well, to tell the truth, Colonel, sir, they are a sorry lot. Sick as dogs, some of 'em, mangy, even. Weak and underfed, I shouldn't wonder."

Streight nodded his head and stared out across the river. "I'm sorry to hear that, O'Sullivan. I am counting on those animals to carry us more than two hundred miles across rough country."

"And I'm sorry to hear that, Colonel, so I am. They are not up to it, sir. Not at all."

"They have to be, Sergeant Major. They have to be. When we land at Eastport, sometime around mid-afternoon, there will be more mules waiting for us, so I understand. Weed out the sick and the weaklings. Have Sergeant Morgan feed the rest as best he can, good nourishing food, Sergeant Major, good nourishing food. Nothing but the best for them until we leave Eastport. Understood?

"Yes, sir. Nothin' but the best for the mules until we leave Eastport. I'll see to it. Er... Colonel, sir. Might I ask, where exactly is it that we're goin'?"

"No, Sergeant Major, you might not. Need to know, need to know. You, and the rest of the men, will know soon enough. Carry on with what you were doing." He saluted, turned, and walked slowly along the deck to the overlook at the bow, and there he stood, staring out over the river that stretched away into the distance, lost in thought.

O'Sullivan was not happy. *Need to know, indeed. If I don't need to know then who in hell does?*

"Coffin," he said, thoughtfully. "I have a feelin' we're in for a rough ride, an' I don't mean just on the bloody animals. Where the hell is the old man takin' us, I wonder?"

Coffin, enigmatic as ever, said nothing. He just shook his head.

"It has to be either Mississippi or Alabama, Sarge," McHugh said. "I really think the mules are a bad idea."

"Ain't for us to say, McHugh. Mississippi, could be, but Alabama is more likely. Grant has a whole bloody army all his own in Mississippi, so he don't need our lot. Has to be Alabama. Though I can't for the life of me figure out what for."

The *Hazel Dell's* steam whistle blasted its shrill note, long and loud, and then repeated the blast several times. They were less than three miles, about forty-five minutes, from Eastport, and the great riverboat came alive as dozens of crewmen began to ready the boat for docking.

O'Sullivan, Coffin, and the three privates took a last lingering look out over the river and headed down the stairs to gather their equipment and such limited personal belongings as they had been allowed to bring with them.

The time for idling was over. Streight's raid was about to begin.

Chapter 15

April 19, 1863. Eastport Mississippi

It was with more than a little relief that in the mid-morning hours of the 19th, the dispatch rider from General Ellet's marine brigade brought General Dodge the news that Streight expected to be in Eastport a little after noon that same afternoon.

Dodge seemed to take on new life and, immediately upon receiving Ellet's dispatch, sent a rider to meet the boats with a request that Streight join him at Great Bear Creek for a council of war.

Dodge's division, having been reinforced only the day before by the 7th Kansas Cavalry Regiment and 4th Ohio infantry regiment, was now more than 7500 strong. While he was waiting to receive Colonel Streight, now three days behind schedule, he gave orders to ready the division for departure.

The *Hazel Dell* steamed slowly dockside at around one-thirty in the afternoon. As the boat was secured at its mooring, Lieutenant Cole, the dispatch rider from General Dodge, ran up the gangplank and handed his missive to a somewhat surprised Colonel Streight.

Streight read the document and sent Cole away with a message that he would leave the *Hazel Dell* and make for Great Bear Creek as soon as his horse, and those of his escort, were disembarked. He left at the gallop and was, within two hours, in conference with the commanding general, a conference that lasted almost until midnight, when he returned to his command.

Streight left Lieutenant Colonel Lawson of the 3rd Ohio in charge of debarking the rest of the transports: men, animals, ordnance, wagons, and equipment. The fun was about to begin.

The men were unloaded first, then the mules, now down to slightly more than 1200. This took most of the rest of the afternoon and early evening. The rest of the equipment was on the dock shortly after ten o'clock.

The men pitched camp just outside of Eastport. The mules were loosely corralled some distance away to the south in an open field bounded on three sides by tall stands of trees and heavy undergrowth. And the mules, having been locked away below decks for some nine days were, to say the least, relieved to be out and about again. They let everyone who might be interested or not, within several miles in any direction, know about it by braying loudly and continuously.

And there were indeed some very interested parties within range of the non-stop braying. Colonel Roddey's Confederate cavalry had for several days been observing the goings on at the Federal encampments at Great Bear Creek, and at Eastport. He had known for almost a week that the great fleet of riverboats was on the way. He also knew of Colonel Streight's force thereon, and the mules, too. What he did not know was the mounted brigade's ultimate destination, the name of its commander or his objective, and he was eager to learn. Thus all through the day and long into the night of the 19th, Roddey's scouts and spies had been prowling the outlying limits of the Federal encampments, waiting and watching.

Roddey was the ultimate predator, as were most cavalrymen, on both sides. And so it was with great glee that his scouts watched as the huge pack of highly strung and extremely restless mules were debarked.

All of these proceedings were duly noted and reported to Roddey, who happened to be in a somewhat playful, or might it have been vicious, mood that evening. In any event, he called together several less than enchanting members of the 4th Alabama Cavalry. Messrs. Sergeant Jake Maxwell, Privates Rich and Clute Priestly, Chuck Horrocks, and Oscar Peck

"Now then, Sergeant," Roddey began. "It seems that the flotilla has indeed arrived from Nashville bearing, so I am told, almost twelve hundred mules." He looked at the gathered troopers. They were all grinning widely.

"It's the Jackass Brigade, Colonel, sir," Private Peck said, laughing.

Roddey smiled. "Clute, mules, as I understand it, are not fond of cats. Is that true?"

"You betcha, Colonel. Mules hates cats. Hate 'em wi' a passion," Clute Priestly answered, nodding enthusiastically.

"I thought so. Do you think we could round up a few, cats, that is?"

Clute looked at his brother, nodding. "That we can, Colonel. How many you want?"

"I have no idea. How many do you think it would take?"

"Take to scatter them beasts, you mean, Colonel?"

"That's what I mean, Private."

Clue thought for a moment, then said, "Don't rightly know, sir. A half-dozen should do it, I thinks." Again, he looked at his brother, who nodded but said nothing.

"Six, then, Colonel; six should do it."

"Well then. Off you go. Find as many as you can, then wait until they've all settled down for the night, around ten or eleven, I shouldn't wonder. Then turn 'em loose among the mules and get the hell out of there."

The five men left Roddey's tent, gathered together some hemp sacks, mounted their horses, and went into Tuscumbia looking for cats. They had some luck, but not enough. By seven o'clock that evening, they had managed to scrounge together only three strays. It seemed that the good citizens of Tuscumbia loved their little furry friends, and were keeping then safe indoors.

At a loss as to what to do next, the five sat down together under a large pine tree on the edge of the woods surrounding the town.

"Ain't enough," Clute said. "We needs more."

"That we do," Maxwell said. "But they ain't none. None we can steal, that is. An' folks ain't gonna wanna give up their kitties, that's for sure," he said, swiping at a yellow jacket with one of his gloves.

"So, whadda we gonna do?"

"Dunno." Maxwell swiped at another wasp, scowled up at it, then smiled. "I knows. Hell, I knows f'sure. I knows where there's a hornet's nest, an' I bet there are more aroun' ol' man Costamen's barn an' cowsheds. Let's go see."

Very carefully, they coaxed the huge hornet's nest from its anchor under the eaves at the rear of the livery stable and into one of the sacks; the nasty little critters were asleep for the night. From there, they went to Costamen's barn, but had no luck. At his cowsheds, however, they found another huge nest. This was duly deposited in a sack, and on they went. By eight o'clock, they were the proud owners of three somewhat scraggy feral cats and three alarmingly large hornet's nests. Not one of them had suffered a sting.

It took the five men with their arsenal of weapons of mass destruction until almost eleven-thirty that evening to reach the loosely constructed corral that was the temporary home to Colonel Streight's mules. There was still some isolated braying, but the mules were for the most part quiet. The night was clear and calm; the gently stirring pack of mules and the stockyards were lit by a brightly shining quarter moon.

Maxwell's Raiders found a dark place in the woodlands just to the south of the federal encampment and tied their horses to the trees. With inordinate care, they gently unloaded their sacks full of destruction and crept quietly around the perimeter of the woods until they could see the corrals where the mules were resting peacefully. The quiet of the night was broken only once in a while by the plaintive braying of a single mule that, for some reason or another, was unable to settle down. Soon, they arrived on the far west side of the corral, out of sight of any possible sentry or picket that might have been posted to lookout for such intrusions, but there were none. Such pickets that had been posted were on the east side of the encampment, and thus out of sight and sound of Maxwell's Raiders.

"Ready?" Sergeant Maxwell whispered, looking around at the four privates.

The four nodded.

Gingerly, Maxwell opened one of the sacks, reached inside and grabbed its occupant by the scruff of its neck. Then with a flip of his wrist, he tossed the struggling cat into the middle of the pack of mules. The cat howled, spun in the air, and with great dexterity landed with a squeal of rage, on all four feet, on the back of a startled mule. The cat dug its claws into the soft flesh of the mule's shoulders, causing it to bray loudly and buck wildly. The cat then dropped quickly to the ground and took off running between the legs of the drowsy mules. Another cat followed the first, and then the other. The mules were by now beginning to panic, but not enough.

Very carefully, Clute and Rich Priestly stripped away the sacks surrounding their highly volatile weapons then, with gloved hands, one on either side of their dangerous loads, they slowly bent over, lowered the hornet's nests between their knees, looked at each other and with a nod from Clute, together they heaved their nests up and away. The hang time could have been only a couple of seconds. To the watching five, however, it seemed like minutes that the nests were in the air. Then splat, splat. Each landed squarely on the back of a mule, one on a shoulder, while the other smacked down on a rump. The two nests exploded, and the air was immediately filled with angry hornets and the sound of buzzing so loud, so dense, it could almost be cut with a knife.

Only seconds later, the third nest landed on the rump of yet another startled mule. The panic among the pack was infectious, and complete. The corral was a whirlpool of spinning, braying, biting, and kicking mules, each trying to escape the stinging terror that surrounded them. Mule climbed on mule. Temporary fences, strong enough under normal circumstances, gave way like so much matchwood. And the animals stampeded. In every direction, they ran from the tiny buzzing fiends that were inflicting so much pain. And they ran, and they ran, taking down tents and anything else that might be in their way.

Maxwell and his happy little band of raiders were falling about laughing. Never, in almost three years of war, had any one of them done this much damage, caused this much chaos, with so little cost or effort. Maxwell's raid was a resounding success. For just a few minutes, they watched what they had wrought, then like ghosts, they disappeared into the night.

For fifteen minutes, chaos reigned, and then it was over. The mules were gone, and so were most of the tents.

Colonel Streight arrived back at the camp just before midnight. The ride back from Great Bear Creek had not been easy: it was dark and the road was a pitted track of destruction. The sure-footed horses had no trouble dodging the pitfalls, but that same sure-footedness made the going for Streight and his escort a nightmare that twisted back and forth with each switch of the horses' rear.

To say that Streight was not prepared for the chaos at Eastport would be an understatement. He had lost every mule he was issued, and some he was not. On entering the stockyard, he was beside himself with rage, and immediately began shouting orders to the already mobile members of his brigade.

Soldiers of every rank, in various states of dress and undress, were rushing back and forth in confusion. Those who owned or had been issued with horses were already in the saddle and heading out into the wild after the strays. Those on foot were quickly ordered to do the same. Within thirty minutes of Streight's return, the open fields and woodland around Eastport were seething with men desperately searching for their lost rides.

On top of a gentle rise, some five hundred yards or so to the east of the Federal encampment, a small group of shadowy figures watched as the entire Federal brigade, along with a large number of sundry dock personnel, scoured the woods for the errant animals. Finally, they turned eastward and headed back to Tuscumbia, not at all displeased with their night's work.

By two' o'clock it was all over. Of the 1200 mules that had disembarked from the *Hazel Dell*, just 927 were recovered, and those in a state of intense agitation. It was a blow that Abel Streight did not take lightly.

First, he rousted the guards for being less than vigilant, then he rousted the officers for not ensuring that the valuable animals were properly secured. Finally, he went to bed at a little after three o'clock in the morning, but sleep did not come easily to the Colonel. Tomorrow would be a long day indeed.

Chapter 16

April 20, 1863. Eastport Mississippi

Abel Streight awoke, after only three fitful hours of sleep, to the sounds of the bugle playing Reveille; it was six o'clock in the morning. He groaned, turned over in his cot and tried to sleep some more, but it was not to be. Within minutes, his orderly, a cow-faced corporal, was at the flap of his tent with a large tin cup of steaming coffee.

For more than ten minutes, Streight sat on the edge of the cot, nursing the hot tin cup. Although the weather during the day was mild, at five in the morning the air was decidedly chilly.

Finally, he stood, looked down at his crumpled uniform – he hadn't bothered to remove even his coat – and groaned again.

"TIMMS," he shouted. "Come here, now."

The cow-faced corporal was at the tent in an instant.

"I need a change of uniform, Timms. Please lay it out for me, and see that this one is freshly laundered and pressed as soon as possible."

Timms looked up at the colonel in obvious astonishment. Where in hell was he supposed to launder his colonel's uniform out here in the wilds of nowhere, Mississippi? But Timms was wise beyond his looks, and he could tell that the colonel was in no mood to debate the point. And so he went about sorting the spare uniform from the colonel's travel trunk. He laid it out carefully upon the cot, while Streight divested himself of the crumpled colonel's uniform of which he was so proud.

Less than an hour later, heartily breakfasted on three fried eggs, three strips of crispy bacon and two thick slices of fried bread, washed down with a second large cup of scalding hot black coffee, all supplied by Corporal Timms, the colonel was feeling like a new man. And so, well sluiced and shaved in steaming hot water, also supplied by the good corporal, Abel Streight, now garbed in his second best dress uniform, complete with frock coat and wide brimmed hat, stepped forth from his tent and out into the world. And what a world it was.

The stockyards were a heaving mass of excited and loudly braying mules, inexperienced handlers trying to control them, and a half-a-hundred infantrymen at the rails all either yelling advice or cat-calling and generally being as disruptive as possible.

Abel Streight strode from his tent onto the scene like an avenging angel. When he arrived at the stockyard with his escort trailing nervously behind him, the noise from the infantrymen died to a whisper. The braying subsided not a little.

"Where is Quartermaster Sergeant Morgan?" he demanded of an insignificant-looking private.

The private, tongue-tied, indicated a group of NCOs arguing together on the far side of the corral.

Streight took off around the corral at a fast pace, the junior officers of his staff almost running to keep up.

"Sergeant Morgan. What in God's name is going on here?"

"Not so much, I'm sorry to say, Colonel. We lost more'n 300 animals last night, and more'n fifty more are injured, too injured to walk more'n a few yards. We managed to round up some 900, or so, but that's about it."

"That, Sergeant, will not do. We have almost 1700 men. With only 900 mules and a handful of horses, we'll still have 600 men on foot. It won't do, Sergeant, not at all."

Morgan said nothing. There was nothing he could say. He simply shrugged his shoulders, gazed warily at the commanding colonel and waited for what was to come.

We have to recover more of the strays. YOU MEN," Streight shouted at the gathering at the rails. "Pay heed and stand ready. Sergeant Morgan; how many horses do you have to spare?"

"Not more than thirty-five, spare that is. We have more assigned, but spare... just thirty-five."

"How many of you men can ride?" Streight called out.

A dozen or so hands rose reluctantly.

"Good! The quartermaster sergeant will issue you with horses. You will go forth and round up the rest of the mules. See to it, Sergeant, at once. We cannot leave this place until we have mounts."

Morgan saluted, gathered the reluctant riders, and took them away to the stables on the east side of the town. There he equipped them with horses, saddles and ropes, and turned them loose, shaking his head as he watched them go. Of the seventeen men who claimed they could ride, he could see that at least ten of them had never sat a horse before in their lives. It was, he knew, not going to work. And so, with a deep sigh, he went in search of Sergeant Major O'Sullivan. He found him preparing for the day and lost no time in bringing him up to date as to the rapidly deteriorating situation at the corral and Colonel Streight.

O'Sullivan was well aware of the goings on of the night before, as he had been in charge of the nighttime roundup. What he did not know was the extent of the losses. He listened patiently to what Morgan had to say, nodding.

"The Old Man is in a terrible state, Ignatius. We lost more'n 300 mules, and he's of a mind that we can't leave until they are either found or replaced. He said the mission was doomed before it has even started. He laid it on me to get 'em all back, but hell, we have no one hardly who can ride, much less round up a passel of ornery mules. What the hell am I supposed to do?"

O'Sullivan thought for a moment, then said, "Come with me. We'll go have a word with Captain Ross of Company K."

"Ross? That son of a.... I never did get along with that man. Thinks he's better'n the rest of us mere mortals being that he's a cavalry officer, an all."

"True, that's true, Ransom, but the man can ride a horse, so he can. Does it for a living, and so do his men. Let's go see if we can wheedle a little help from the good captain."

They found Captain Phillip John Ross still in his tent. He was dressed but, as he had had little sleep the night before, he was in no mood to receive visitors.

"What is it, Sergeant Major?" he said, irritably.

"Well, sir. It seems the good colonel is in need of a little help, an' I was wondering if we might borrow a few of your troopers for the day, say twenty-five, or so."

Ross looked at O'Sullivan warily. "What the hell for?"

"Well, Captain. It's like this you see, sir. Last night, as you already know, we had visitors, and they did their level best to disrupt the good colonel's plans. They bolted the mules, the bloody lot of 'em."

"I know that. Hell the noise kept me up half the night, and most of my men were out on foot chasing them down. We got them all back, did we not?"

"Ah, but that's the point, Captain, sir. We did not. And the good colonel has asked, nay he has demanded that we go get the stragglers, all 300 of 'em."

"So, go get them. You have men aplenty. What do you need my men for?"

"Well now, Captain. Here's the rub. Ain't but a half-dozen in the whole bloody regiment who can ride worth a lick, not to mention we don't have horses for 'em anyway. Cain't send men out on mules. The bloody animals are barely broke. So, Captain. How about it... twenty-five, just for today? They ain't goin' anywhere anyway. The colonel said we're not leaving here until every man has a mount. So...?"

Ross heaved a heavy sigh, stared the sergeant major in the eye, then said, "Oh very well, but just for today. I'll give the word. Go to the corral and wait. I'll go tell Lieutenant Carvill what's required." And with that, he walked swiftly from his tent and began giving orders to a young second lieutenant who kept glancing over the captain's shoulder at O'Sullivan and Morgan as he listened.

"I never would have believed it," Morgan said to O'Sullivan as they walked to the corral where the cavalry horses were kept, a lot more securely than the mules.

"What? Believed what?"

"Ross! I never would have believed he would put himself out, not even for the colonel, at least without a direct order from the colonel himself."

"Ah, Ransom, you've a lot to learn. There were two things in play. First, the good captain owes me several favors; second, he knows well and good that he does, and that I have me own special ways of collecting. Captain he might be, but Top Soldier that I am, I carries a little more weight than does he. All I had to do was ask. I knew damn well he would comply. And why wouldn't he? It's not like I was askin' him to go a wranglin' himself, now was it?"

And so, with now more than sixty men in the field, twenty-five mounted cavalry troopers and the erstwhile members of Streight's infantry brigade who claimed they could ride, the hunt was on. It went on all through the rest of the day and well into the evening. By the time darkness had fallen, another 165 mules had been recovered; it was not enough. Colonel Streight ordered the men out again the following morning. By ten o'clock, however, with only seven more mules in hand, it was apparent that those that remained gone would have to be left to fend for themselves or, most likely, to the delighted Southern farmers who would, eventually, run across them.

And so it was, at just after twelve o'clock in the afternoon that day, the 21st of April, the Mule Soldiers, now more than four days behind schedule, mounted up, and set off to join up with General Dodge at Great Bear Creek, some thirty-three miles west of Tuscumbia. It was a sorry-looking procession that moved slowly out under a heavy rain that had turned the dirt road from Eastport to Tuscumbia into a veritable mud bath.

Colonel Abel Streight, closely followed by his regimental commanders and some dozen or so staff officers, was at the head the two-mile long column. Behind them, at the head of the 51st Indiana, rode Sergeant Major Ignatius O'Sullivan and Corporal Boone Coffin. O'Sullivan had packed away his kepi and was wearing a wide-brimmed cavalry Stetson, which drizzled a constant stream of water onto the vast horse soldier's oilskin that covered him from head to toe, and most of Lightning, too. The diminutive Corporal Coffin and Phoebe were no less protected from the weather than their "fearless leader." Together, the incongruous pair, hunched over their animals like two great, black sodden insects, rode slowly side-by-side, as the skies opened and the road turned into mush.

The head of the column made heavy going of the churning mud. For the rear of the column, the going was almost impossible. Those for whom there were no mules or horses trailed along at the rear, often knee-deep in the ooze. The wagons, each pulled by either six mules or six horses, were up to their axels before they had gone more than a mile: only twelve more to go.

At six o'clock, the head of the column was approaching General Dodge's encampment at Great Bear Creek. It was already dark, and it was still raining heavily. The column was now stretched out over four miles, and it would be after ten o'clock before the stragglers finally made it into camp.

The Federal soldiers of Dodge's small army turned out to greet them. They lined the road into camp, watching, and were quiet. There was little to be heard, except for the braying of several hundred mules that wanted to be fed. Hundreds of men lined the route as the first elements of Streight's brigade slunk into camp, sodden, miserable, and all in thoroughly bad tempers. Men hardened by three years of war, now astride mules or on foot in the mud, were prepared to answer the first snigger with gunfire. But there was no need. Whether or not it was sympathy or empathy, or both, not a chuckle or a laugh was uttered. And the Mule Soldiers pulled themselves together, sat up straight in the saddle, and swung silently into camp.

At six-thirty that evening, Abel Streight presented himself to Brigadier General Grenville Dodge. The two men were not strangers.

They had in fact spent time together during the campaign for Stones River at the turn of the New Year.

Streight had managed to dry himself off, at least a little, but he still presented a somewhat bedraggled appearance in front of the Commanding General of the District of Corinth.

"So, Colonel, your troops are here at last," Dodge said, with some rancor. "It would seem you have had quite a journey, quite a journey indeed. Please, sir, sit, if you will. Will you take a drink, Colonel? I have some very fine Scottish whiskey."

"I will indeed, General, and thank you."

"Not at all," Dodge said, opening the doors on a small wooden cabinet of a folding stand to reveal several bottles of scotch whiskey and several more of port, along with a half-dozen crystal glasses. He removed the cork from a bottle, already half-empty, and poured two generous measures of the amber liquid. He handed one to Streight, now seated on an unexpectedly comfortable folding chair, who took it gratefully and clasped both hands around the large, ornate glass. The other, Dodge kept for himself. And then he sat down in an identical folding chair.

For a moment, the two men sat quietly and sipped their drinks. At the first sip, Streight almost choked as the fiery, but oh so smooth liquid ran down his throat.

"By God, General, that's the real stuff. I thank you, sir. I needed it."

Dodge nodded and smiled. And for several pleasant moments the two men talked together of times gone bye, until finally, Dodge sat up a little straighter and said, "So, Colonel, tell me what went wrong."

Streight thought for a moment, hesitated, then said, "General, I must be honest with you. Everything that could possibly go wrong, did. From the moment we reached Nashville right up until this very moment, nothing has gone right."

Dodge looked hard at Streight, a deep frown upon his brow. He was not one for excuses, but somehow he did not think the colonel *was* making excuses. "Go on Colonel."

"General, my men are the best there is, totally dedicated. To date, every man has done his very best to ensure the success of this important enterprise.... No, sir, it is not the fault of my officers and men. If fault there is, then it is mine and mine alone. General, you know me, I am a loyal officer of the Union. Long have I espoused the need to destroy the Rebel enemy and reunite the Union. And, General, there is no one more loyal to the commanding general than am I, but..."

"Continue, Colonel," Dodge said, his voice hardening.

"It's the mules, sir. I had my doubts when General Rosecrans suggested such."

"Did you voice your concerns, Abel?" The use of Streight's first name was an indication of some amount of sympathy on Dodge's part.

"No sir, I did not. Perhaps I should have, but again I must take the blame for not making my concerns known to General Rosecrans, or General Garfield, for that matter. I was, I must state, most eager for the expedition to proceed. Now, I can only think that the mules were a bad idea, a very bad idea. That being said, General Dodge, we must make do with what we have.

"Do you know, General," Streight continued, "that I have more than 400 men still without mounts? We lost more than a 180 of them two nights ago to Rebel raiders, hence I was later arriving here than I intended to be, and I must apologize for that, too, General."

"Yes, Abel, I heard all about the cats and the hornets; very ingenious of them, if I may be permitted to say so. And no, Colonel, no apology is necessary. You are but a victim of the fortunes of war. Though I must agree that the choice of mules for such an expedition was... well..." He didn't finish, just shook his head, and stared up at the top of the tent pole.

The two men sat for several moments in silence. Then General Dodge seem to shrug off whatever thoughts were troubling him, looked at Streight and, rising to his feet, said, "More Scotch, Abel? I think we have time for just one more. Don't you?"

Streight nodded and handed his empty glass to Dodge who poured a goodly measure into both glasses and returned Streight's to him. Streight took it gratefully, raised it to his lips and took a deep swallow, smacked his lips in appreciation, and leaned back in his chair.

"So, Colonel, what of tomorrow?" Dodge asked. "How do you intend to proceed? Oh, by the way, I have appropriated for you from the 9th Illinois Cavalry 400 horses. I will also supply you with six wagons to transport your rations and ammunition."

Streight almost choked when he heard that. "Oh, thank God. And thank you, too, General. That will leave less than 200 without mounts. Surly I can forage afield and find that many over the next two days."

"Hmmm, perhaps you can. Now, sir. Your plans, if you please."

"Before we discuss my plans, General, might I be so bold as to enquire the enemy's strength?"

Dodge nodded. "My scout, Captain Spencer, visited Colonel Roddey's camp at Tuscumbia on the 16th, four days ago and believes that he might have as many as six thousand cavalry under his command. I tend to agree."

"What of General Van Dorn... and Forrest?"

"We've seen neither hide nor hair of either one, at least so far. My scouts report that both are at Van Dorn's headquarters at Spring Hill."

Streight nodded thoughtfully. "Six thousand, you say. That seems a great many. Is Spencer certain of the numbers?"

"As certain as he can be, I suppose. Spencer's a good man. Always gets the low down, and very rarely is he wrong."

"So, General," Streight said, "my plans are as follows. I am, as you now know, to make my way across Alabama, into Georgia as far as Rome. There I am to destroy the Western and Atlantic Railroad, and

117

all munitions, factories, warehouses, and supply depots I can find. I am also under the impression – I was, in fact told – that you would supply a diversion, a screen from the Rebel cavalry."

"That is true, Colonel, and so it will be. I plan to attack and take Tuscumbia."

"My plan is simple, General. I shall accompany you to Tuscumbia, then turn south to Russellville, then east again and head across country to Rome."

Dodge nodded in agreement. "Yes, Colonel, in fact, I suggest you position your brigade at the rear of my column for the march to Tuscumbia. If the Rebel scouts are on form, as they always are, they will assume that you are now a part of my command. We will leave this place at first light on the 23rd. Now, let us talk of your immediate needs."

It was well after eleven o'clock when the two men parted, Streight feeling a little more confident in the light of the four hundred extra mounts, Dodge with a deep feeling of impending doom.

The Mule Soldiers were, for better or worse, prepared. Streight's Raid was about to begin in earnest.

Chapter 17

April 23rd, 1863. Confederate Headquarters, Tullahoma, Tennessee.

General Braxton Bragg, Commanding General of the Army of Tennessee, was in a foul mood. He had been waiting most of the day for Brigadier General Nathan Bedford Forrest to arrive from Spring Hill. Never a patient man to begin with, by three-thirty in the afternoon of April 23, Bragg was pacing back and forth across his office, growling to himself as he went.

"Colonel Gault," Bragg called, stopping his pacing and returning to his desk.

"Yes, General," Gault said, peeking around the door.

"Come in, man. Come in. Have you heard from General Forrest?"

"Yes, sir. A dispatch rider arrived just a few minutes ago; I was on my way to inform you. General Forrest will be here within the hour. He was delayed at Columbia."

Bragg nodded, dismissed Gault, and sat at the desk, drumming his fingers on the desktop.

For days, he had been receiving reports from Colonel Roddey. On the 11th, Roddey had reported that a large fleet of gunboats and transports had left Palmyra with a large contingent of Federal infantry aboard. On the 19th, he reported the arrival of said gunboats and transports at Eastport, Mississippi, and this in and of itself was of great concern to General Bragg. But, as yet, he was holding his usual course of action, which was to wait and see.

On the 18th, Roddey reported the conflict at Cherokee Bluffs, and the visit by Federal Captain Spencer, a man not unknown to Bragg, thus there was even more cause for concern.

On the 20th, Roddey reported that, with the addition of the four Federal regiments from the riverboats, and several more from the west, Dodge's combined force now numbered more than ten thousand, and Roddey feared an invasion of Alabama was imminent. Thus, Bragg had finally sent for Forrest. Forrest arrived that evening at Bragg's headquarters at a little after eight o'clock in the evening.

"Where in God's name have you been, General?" Bragg asked angrily when Forrest walked confidently into his office.

"And good evening to you, General," Forrest replied, taking a seat, without being asked to sit, in front of the commanding general's desk. "I have," he continued amiably, "been on horse since before sunup this morning and, not having been gifted with wings, I have gotten here just as soon as possible. It's a very long way from west of Columbia, to Spring Hill to here, as I am sure you are well aware, General."

Bragg glared at Forrest. There was no love lost between them. Bragg considered Forrest to be an ignorant merchant-come-cavalry soldier, and he never hesitated to remind him of such. Forrest, on the other hand, regarded Bragg as both incompetent and ineffectual, a martinet wrapped up in minutia, and little, if any, use as a battlefield commander, owing his position of high command only to his close friendship with President Davis.

Bragg's face was gaunt and heavily lined. His hair and beard were almost entirely gray. He was a man rendered old beyond his fifty years by more than half a lifetime of military service, many months of ill health, the stress of high command, and the concerted efforts of some of his subordinates to have him removed from command of the army. The campaigns of Shiloh, Perryville, and Stones River had taken a terrible toll upon his frail body. Even so, his mind was sharp and quick, and he detested the man now seated in front of him with a passion.

Detest Forrest though he might, Bragg was not the fool most of his subordinates thought him to be. Forrest, he knew, was the one man under his command that could, and would, get the job done. Thus it was Forrest who now sat before him, rather than Forrest's superior, Major General Earl Van Dorn.

Forrest, at forty-two, was older than most cavalry commanders, Union or Confederate. He was a tall, well-built, muscular man with graying hair, a gaunt face, heavily tanned by a lifetime under the southern sun, and a neatly clipped Van Dyke beard. He was a restless man, short-tempered, impatient, full of vigor and vitality, and he did not suffer fools easily. He was an intuitive battlefield commander – some claimed he possessed second sight – and he could outguess, outthink, and outmaneuver his opponents, almost at will.

He was, as always, immaculately dressed, even after his long ride, having taken time to remove the inevitable linen duster coat that protected his uniform from the ravages of the great outdoors. His hat, along with his weapons, he had left with an orderly, more for his own comfort than respect for his commanding general. His lank hair was combed neatly back over his head, and he looked, as always, totally at ease. He was, in fact, more at ease than was Bragg, much to Bragg's irritation.

"General Forrest," Bragg began. "I am detaching you from General Van Dorn's command and sending you south to join with Colonel Roddey in Alabama, where you will take command."

Forrest raised his eyebrows, but said nothing. He knew well enough that Bragg would unlimber himself in his own good time.

"It would seem," Bragg continued, "that General Dodge has received a large number of reinforcements and is presently planning an invasion into Alabama. You, sir, are to oppose him, defeat him if you can, hold him until I can send reinforcements if you cannot."

"What forces does Dodge have, do you know?"

"Not for certain, but Colonel Roddey estimates them to number at least ten thousand, perhaps more, including a brigade of cavalry and two brigades of mounted infantry; one of them... one of them mounted on mules."

Forrest was incredulous. "On mules, you say? No, sir. Never could such a thing be. Mules?" He looked at Bragg, shaking his head.

"I can assure you, General Forrest, that is exactly how Colonel Roddey has reported it to me. The brigade in question fields some two thousand men, most of them mounted on mules."

Forrest frowned and nodded, considering what Bragg had just said. Then he simply shrugged his shoulders, seemingly unconcerned.

"Mules, then. And how many men does Roddey have?" Forrest asked, already knowing the answer but asking it anyway.

"He has a little more than 1800 officers and men."

"Hmmm, and I have just over 2600," Forrest said, and smiled grimly. "So, perhaps 4500 in all, then; more than enough, I shouldn't wonder."

"Well, General Forrest, that's as may be, but Dodge must not be allowed to take or hold any territory in Alabama."

Forrest nodded thoughtfully. "General, do we have any idea of the purpose of this... this mule brigade? Do we know who commands it?"

"We do not, General. I see no other purpose than to reinforce General Dodge for an invasion of Alabama."

Forrest shook his head in disagreement. "No, General. I do not think so. Why the mules? If Dodge's intention is to invade Alabama, he still does not have enough men to do it, and a brigade of infantry mounted on mules would be more hindrance than benefit. They would be better applied on foot. No, General, there's something going on here, something we don't know about. As you know, a large force of Federal Cavalry left LaGrange six days ago heading into Mississippi. I have a strong feeling that this mule business is more of the same."

"You may well be correct, General Forrest. All the more reason you should get yourself down there as soon as possible and find out exactly what is going on. I suggest you move quickly."

Forrest nodded in agreement. "I will send Colonel Edmonson and the 11th Tennessee on ahead, through Florence. If they leave at once, they should be there sometime on the 26th. I will follow as soon as I have taken care of some unfinished business at Spring Hill. I should be able to leave early tomorrow morning and join Roddey on the 27th."

"Good, very good, General. Please keep me informed daily."

Forrest stood, saluted his commanding general, and left the room, closing the door gently behind him, a first for Nathan Bedford Forrest.

Edmonson and the 11th Tennessee Cavalry left Spring Hill just before midnight. Forrest, true to his word, left at the head of the rest of his division a few minutes after nine o'clock the following morning.

Chapter 18
April 23rd, Great Bear Creek, General Dodge

As the sun rose above the treetops at Great Bear Creek on the morning of April 23rd, a ground fog covered the woods and fields, casting a mysterious light over the world as General Dodge stepped out of his tent. Reveille had sounded only minutes earlier, but Dodge, having slept little, was already dressed and ready for the day to come. He breakfasted lightly on one fried egg and two strips of crispy bacon washed down with two large cups of black coffee.

More than a mile away to the rear, Colonel Streight also was getting ready to face the day. Although he knew what was to come, he would not be involved in any of the action. His job, at this point, was to stay at the rear and pretend to be a part of General Dodge's force. Streight was happy to do just that, although he was impatient to be away and about his own objective – Rome, Georgia.

As for Streight's Mule Soldiers, they were to spend what time they had left before embarking on their great adventure breaking and getting used to their rides. Those on horseback would continue to go out foraging for mounts for those still without them.

It was just after six-thirty and still quite dark that morning when a dispatch rider arrived at Streight's tent with a request for him to join the general forthwith.

Five minutes later, having given strict instructions to Timms to pack and load his personal effects onto the senior officer's wagon, now under the charge of the erstwhile Private Doyle, he mounted his horse and rode at the gallop along the dirt road to Dodge's tent.

"Good morning, Colonel," Dodge greeted Streight. "I hope you are well rested and ready to move out within the hour."

"I slept hardly at all, General, but never mind, I am ready. What, sir, might I ask is your plan?"

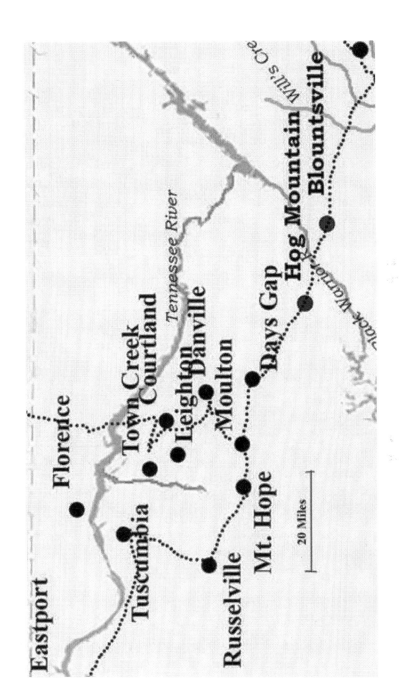

"My plan, Colonel, is to create a diversion so that you might escape southward, unobserved by our foes. I plan to invade and hold Tuscumbia." He pointed to a small map laid out on a folding table. "We are here, at Great Bear Creek. This is Little Bear Creek, some twenty-five miles west from here, where Colonel Roddey is encamped with a full brigade of Confederate cavalry. He has at least another brigade at Tuscumbia roughly six miles east of Little Bear, here. And here, to the north, so my scouts inform me, Forrest with a full division of cavalry, four brigades, is moving quickly to join Roddey. At the rate he is going, it will take him three days at the most. If Forrest joins Roddey before I can get to Tuscumbia, we will be in for the devil of a fight and you, my friend, will have little chance of success. Thus, we move out from here at seven o'clock. Do you have any questions, Abel?"

"How many men does Forrest have with him, Colonel?"

"Perhaps three thousand, maybe more. Roddey has at least six thousand. So, we face a combined force of at least nine thousand cavalry and perhaps six batteries of artillery, all battle-hardened, and with Forrest in command...well. I have some eight thousand effectives, including Cornyn's cavalry. You have seventeen hundred, but you will not be engaged. You must continue to make ready to move south at the first opportunity. Will you be ready, Abel?"

"The men are as ready as they ever will be, I think, although I still have some two hundred without mounts. I already have foragers abroad and hope to rectify that before we leave."

"All is as well as can be expected then. Go to your men, Abel. We move out within the hour."

"Coffin, you scallywag, where are you?" Sergeant Major O'Sullivan yelled from inside his tent.

"Here, Sergeant Major." Corporal Coffin ducked under the flap of the tent with coffee for them both.

"Bedad, Coffin, you do take liberties. Now it's coffee with the Sergeant Major each and every mornin', is it?"

Coffin shrugged. "I learned long ago that if I'm here, I'm in the way; if I'm not here, by God I'd better be and bloody quick, as so you say, Sergeant Major."

O'Sullivan grinned at the little corporal. "Well said, sonny, well said. Now, down to business. We'll be movin' out forthwith, I shouldn't wonder. In what sort o' condition is our transport?"

Your horse is saddled and ready; as is my... er, mule, Phoebe."

"Good. Now then, I have a feelin' that the old man is not goin' to be in the best of moods, what with the fiasco of last night, an' all.... What in the name of all that's holy is that?" he shouted as, right outside the flap of the tent, a bugler began sounding the call to mount up.

Coffin laughed aloud, a rare occurrence. "Boots and Saddles, Sergeant Major, Boots and Saddles. And that means 'mount up, now.'"

"I know that, you bloody moron, but Christ in..., do we get no warnin' then? He rushed around the tent, gathering his necessary belongings. "Get all this packed away an' on the wagon, Coffin, an' be quick about it. Where's me bloody horse?"

"He's awaitin' Sarge, over by the mess tent."

O'Sullivan ducked out through the flap of the tent, leaving Coffin to pack away the rest of his belongings. The camp was in an uproar. Few, if any, had any idea what the new bugle call meant, and those who did had little idea how to respond. Most of the Mule Soldiers were rushing this way and that, trying to find their assigned rides. O'Sullivan stood for a moment, looking around at the growing pandemonium.

"STOP! STAND STILL!" he shouted. But it went unheard. He pulled one of the Colts and fired a shot into the air.

127

"STOP AND STAND STILL, YA BLOODY IDIOTS. Now, orderly, like. Find your animals, saddle up and mount up, and forget the bloody bugle. TAKE YOUR BLOODY TIME AND DO IT RIGHT."

The mayhem turned slowly into organized chaos as hundreds of men crowded around the temporary corrals in search of their mounts.

More than a mile away to the east, the first elements of General Dodge's army were already on the road. Fortunately, for the Mule Soldiers, it would take more than an hour for the movement to trickle down the long column of infantry to them. Colonel Streight had been well aware of this when he gave the order to the bugler to sound the call to saddle. It had been a wise move on his part, he knew, as he watched from his tent the confusion and disorder as they went about becoming the mounted infantry they were now supposed to be. Finally, unable to watch any longer, he ducked back inside his tent and sat down to wait. Timms already had his horse saddled and waiting just outside.

But Boots and Saddles did not just cause chaos in the ranks. Private Doyle, the newest wagon master in Quartermaster Sergeant Ransom Morgan's commissary train, was having troubles of his own. Never in his life had he been forced to deal with more than one animal at a time. Now he was in charge of six, and a huge, canvas covered wagon to boot. He was so far out of his depth it would have been funny, had it not been for the urgency of the situation.

And so Doyle stood at the front of his wagon, looking over the ropes that formed the perimeter of the quartermaster's corral and stared at the mules therein.

"Take a deep breath, son," Sergeant Morgan said, clapping him on the shoulder. "You'll soon get used to it. Corporal Roark, get over here and show the new lad, Doyle, 'ow to 'itch the team."

Roark shambled over, grinning widely as he came. He was followed by two privates, also grinning.

"Show 'im how it's all done, Corporal. You'd better stay with him for a couple o' days, show 'im how to drive a wagon. He might look strange, 'im bein' so tall, an' all, but he's smart, an' he'll learn. Simpson can handle your team for a couple of days."

Roark nodded to Morgan, then turned to Doyle. "It takes more'n one man, sonny... by gad you's a big un," he said, looking up at him. "Anyways, we all teams up together and helps each other, like this. First, we has to gather 'em up and then harness 'em." This, with all four men working the team was quickly done and Roark and his companions began hitching the horses to the tongue of the wagon.

"The two nearest the wagon has to be the biggest and strongest, 'cause they's the ones that turns the front axle. They goes one on either side of the tongue. Then we take's the next two biggest and hitches them up, and then we does the same with the leaders. They ain't hitched either side of the tongue, but just to the end of it, cause it would get in they's way when they's turnin'. They leaders can be big or small, but they does have to be matched, an' they has to know each other, and they has to know how each other thinks. Hardly credible, ain' it? How two dumb animals like two mules could know how each other thinks, but leader animals does, they really does."

The first two mules were quickly attached to the wagon, followed by the center pair, followed by two more unlikely-looking animals, one a dirty gray, the other almost white, one was slightly larger than the other, but not inordinately so.

"They two are Sugar and Spice, an' they's two of the best. They can take this team all by themselves without no help from you, which is just what we wants with a new teamster, like youns. Now then, Master Doyle," Roark said, "up you jumps."

Doyle scrambled up onto the board, and Roark handed him three sets of reins.

"Now just you hold tight up there for jest a minute. I'll be with you directly." Roark walked around the team, checking each mule's harness as he went. Having satisfied himself that all was in order, he leaped lightly up beside Doyle. "Now then, give 'em a twitch of the reins and we'll take 'em roun' the corral."

Doyle did as he was asked. He twitched the reins... nothing. All six mules stood waiting patiently.

Roark grabbed the reins from Doyle and a long, slender whip from the side of the wagon. "Hah," he yelled and flipped the tail of the whip at the rear of the left hand lead mule. The tail landed gently on the rump of the mule, who started slightly then moved slowly forward. The other five mules walked obediently along with him. Doyle grinned happily as Roark handed the reins back to him.

By eight-thirty, Streight's Mule Soldiers were finally able to take their turn and join the end of General Dodge's long column, with Private Doyle and Corporal Jason Roark bringing up the rear.

By one-thirty in the afternoon, the head of the column had reached and crossed Caney Creek and then stopped to rest the men and the animals. The stop rippled slowly down the column until finally it reached Private Doyle, who was by now feeling no little pain. His buttocks were throbbing from the hard plank seat, and his forearms throbbed from heaving on the reins as the big wagon slewed this way and that along the deeply rutted dirt road.

At the head of Streight's column, O'Sullivan sat astride the great bay stallion now called Lightning, looking more like a cavalryman than did many of those who legitimately owned the title. Next to him, at a somewhat lower level, the diminutive Corporal Coffin sat astride the gray mule, Phoebe. They made an incongruous pair to say the least.

Just to the rear of O'Sullivan and Coffin, Privates Cassell and McHugh were not having an easy time with their rides. The mules Abel and Ignatius were not used to the saddle. Indeed, they were not used to control of any kind, having been broken only days before and, as obstreperous as they both were, they were not about to suffer the indignities of saddle and rider without putting up a fight or at least a protest. Thus, from time to time, as the mood took them, not only would they do their best to unseat their riders, they would lash out with their hind hooves and inflict pain and suffering upon those who might have been next in line and unwary enough to stray within range.

As the long column moved steadily eastward toward Tuscumbia, units of Roddey's Confederate cavalry shadowed it both to the north and to the south. For the most part, they stayed well out of range of the Federal sharpshooters and the Federal cavalry outriders. The main body of the Federal cavalry was under orders to make as much of a nuisance of themselves as possible, to create havoc and mayhem among the local populace, the idea being to draw attention away from the trailing Mule Soldiers. And create havoc they did. For more than twenty miles, as they shadowed their infantry counterparts, Federal Colonel Cornyn's troopers burned and pillaged farms, lumberyards, cotton gins, warehouses, and homes. The devastation they left along the way was terrible to behold. Once prosperous small farms and businesses and homes were burned to the ground. Animals and fowl were killed on the spot, or stolen for later consumption. Feed and lumber were burned without exception. And all day long, riders from the various Confederate units dashed back and forth to Tuscumbia, keeping Roddey up to date as to the status and deployment of Dodge's small army.

By mid-afternoon, the Federal column had reached the Little Bear Creek where General Dodge fully expected to be confronted by more than six thousand soldiers of Colonel Roddey's Confederate cavalry. He was disappointed; Roddey and his small force had withdrawn to Tuscumbia. By nightfall, all ten thousand Federals were within two miles of the town.

In Tuscumbia, all was quiet. Almost all of the town's populace had been evacuated. Those who remained, including Roddey, his staff, and several companies of troopers, watched as the sky to the west turned red from the glow of a half-a-hundred campfires.

Roddey himself was in an expansive mood. He was well aware of the fact that Dodge was under the impression that Roddey could field almost six thousand soldiers. The truth was, much to Roddey's amusement, that he had but eighteen hundred effectives. One sustained, concerted attack by Dodge would overwhelm him.

My grateful thanks to you, Sergeant Mica Holister, Roddey thought as he stared westward at the reddening sky. *You laid it on thick, and you laid it on well. How now, General Dodge? How now? What the hell are you up to? And what the hell do you intend to do with those Mules Soldiers?*

It was but a passing thought, but Roddey was in fact well pleased with himself, and with Holister. He was not, however, happy about the fact that he had been able to do little about the devastation wrought by the roving Federal cavalry; but he just did not have the numbers. But that was about to change, and soon. Late that afternoon, he had received a dispatch from General Bragg's headquarters in Tullahoma that General Forrest was on his way south with more than 2500 soldiers to join him.

But all that was yet to come. As of this moment, he could not afford an encounter with Dodge's overwhelming force. In the meantime, he would have to abandon Tuscumbia and hope the Federals would not do too much damage. Reluctantly, he trotted down the stairs from the upper floor of the large home. The lady of the house was long gone, had taken refuge at a friend's home in Decatur, as had most of the rest of the local folks. He walked through the front door and out into the dark and deserted street. His staff officers and a dozen or so troopers that served as his escort were waiting by the hitching rail where his horse was tethered. He stood for a moment, saying nothing, and staring again westward. Then he shook his head, gathered the reins in his left hand, put his left foot into the stirrup, and swung himself lightly into the saddle.

"So, gentlemen," he said, facing his men, "it begins. Is all clear, Major Julien?"

"All is clear. Only a few die-hards remain, Colonel. We tried to move them out, but they would have none of it," Julien replied. He commanded a battalion of cavalry that carried his name, and served as escort to Roddey and his staff.

"To hell with them then," Roddey shouted, wheeling his horse. "Let's get away from here." And with that, he spurred his horse and rode east through the town at a full gallop, closely followed by the rest of his retinue, leaving behind him a cloud of fine dust and no more than a dozen of Tuscumbia's residents.

Chapter 19

April 24, 1863. Confederate Column South of Spring Hill

The main body of Forrest's cavalry division – the 4th, 8th, 9th and 10th regiments – left Spring Hill, Tennessee and headed south. The division, battle hardened over more than two years of almost constant campaigning across Tennessee and Kentucky, was considered by General Bragg to be the best he had, although he would not have dreamed of saying as much to Forrest.

The Confederate horse soldiers, with General Forrest, his younger brother, Captain William Forrest, and his escort at their head, rode out of Spring Hill in column of threes. By the time the last regiment had cleared the town limits, the column was more than a mile long. Colonel Edmonson's brigade was now more than thirty miles ahead of the main column heading for Courtland, Alabama.

First in-column after Forrest's escort was Colonel George Dibrell commanding the 8th Tennessee Cavalry with Dibrell's escort and then Company A, commanded by Captain Windle, leading. Just to the rear of Windle rode the regiment's two senior NCOs, followed by a trio of the most nefarious-looking individuals Dibrell had ever laid eyes on. But looks, as they usually are, were deceiving. The trio were three of the toughest, and finest, scouts in Forrest's entire division, hence their exalted position, exceeded only by Sergeant Major Yancey Findel and Sergeant Jedidiah (Jed) Grimes, at the virtual head of the long column.

Will Steiner, Sam Corbett, Isaac Boggs, and indeed Findel and Grimes, were founding members of Captain William Forrest's company of scouts, the Forty Thieves. They had been together since the fiasco at Fort Donelson when the then Lieutenant Colonel Forrest had refused to surrender his force, along with the garrison of the fort, to General Grant. Instead, Forrest had led his men through the swamps at the dead of night to freedom. Each and every man that had been a part of the action on that wild and rainy night back in February 1882 was eternally grateful to their flamboyant commander. Each and every one of them would willingly die for Forrest, a fact of which he was well aware.

So, Steiner, Corbett, and Boggs jogged along together, talking among themselves as they went. None of the trio were the least bit bothered that they were heading out once again to face God only knew what. They had already survived countless battles and skirmishes, more than anyone had a right to expect, and they didn't anticipate anything different this time. They had every confidence in their commander's ability to get them through, no matter what. It was an attitude that instilled confidence and, very often, extreme recklessness.

Sam Corbett, the natural leader of the trio, had the appearance more of a pirate than a cavalryman. Instead of the short cavalry shell jacket, popular with the cavalry of both armies, Sam wore a knee-length uniform coat belted at the waist. Standard issue for Forrest's soldiers was a carbine, saber, and one hundred rounds of ammunition. Corbett and his companions took it upon themselves to supplement these basic requirements. Attached to Corbett's belt were two leather holsters, one on each hip; each held a gleaming, 36-caliber Colt Navy revolver. Also attached to the belt was a leather scabbard that held a Bowie knife with a 14-inch blade, honed razor sharp. At his back were two cartridge boxes. His feet and legs were cover by a pair of black leather, custom-made boots that came all the way up to just below the knee. On his head, Sam proudly wore a somewhat stained, cream-colored Stetson with the right side of the brim sewn up against the side of the crown of the hat. In the hatband he had sewn three eagle feathers, a gift from an Apache chief he had befriended before the outbreak of hostilities.

Strangely enough, the outfit was not out of tune with his looks. At six feet one inch, Sam Corbett was the tallest of the trio. Like all outdoorsmen, his face was the color of dark brown leather. A pair of pale blue eyes were set under hooded brows. His hair, the color of straw, hung like fine silk, over his collar and onward down his back for another six inches. A finely chiseled, aquiline nose topped a wild and wandering moustache that framed an incongruously thick pair of lips.

His chin was clean-shaven. His sense of humor was legendry, and he never missed a chance to exercise it. His mount Odin was a sturdy, high-strung chestnut stallion, small by some standards, but quick and intelligent.

If there had been a command structure between the three, Will Steiner would have played second to Corbett. Steiner, too, was a man of distinction. Not quite as tall as Corbett, he still cut an impressive figure. Heavier built, but with the same leathery skin, Steiner sported a bushy black beard and moustache that covered the lower half of his face. His apple-like cheeks and the tip of his bulbous nose were a dark red, ruddy color. Wide-set hazel eyes topped with a pair of bushy black eyebrows that matched his beard. His collar-length hair, too, was black, but long days under the southern sun had taken their toll: now it was interlaced with streaks of gray. His hat, a blue Stetson, was a Yankee souvenir, courtesy of a raid into southern Kentucky. He rode a rangy black stallion known as Lucifer.

The third member of the trio, Isaac Boggs, was a wild man, a product of the mountains of middle Tennessee. He was of medium build, five feet eleven inches tall, with dirty blond hair that he wore in a ponytail half way down his back and tied, for some reason known only to himself, with a yellow ribbon. His face was gaunt and deeply tanned and he wore the classic Van Dyke beard and moustache so popular with the officers of both armies. On his head, he wore a floppy, dirty yellow, version of a planter's hat. Like Corbett, Boggs had a great Bowie knife strapped to his waist. A single LeMat revolver was struck crosswise into a leather holster attached to his belt. Two sawn-off 12-guage shotguns were in holsters attached to his saddle, one on each side. He had no sense of humor at all, and was in fact a short tempered, dangerous individual known to go off at half cock for the slightest of reasons. Touchy as he was, Boggs was an indispensable part of the trio. He also rode a stallion, a very tough Apache-bred piebald by the name of Pig.

Together, the three men were a small but formidable fighting force in their own right.

Company A was followed in column by Captain John Morton's Tennessee Light Artillery, which included eight guns with caissons. Morton, lately promoted to Chief of Artillery to replace the deceased Captain Freeman, was something of an enigma. At twenty years of age, he still looked more of a kid than a senior artillery officer. Tall and slim, with a boyish face that only rarely wore a smile, he was a very serious young man who would have looked more at home behind the counter in a bank, rather than on horseback at the head of a column of artillery. Even so, Forrest trusted his judgment in all things implicitly.

And so it was that Forrest's Cavalry Division headed south from Spring Hill on a balmy morning in late April. Their destination was Decatur, Alabama, and from there to Courtland where he hoped to find Colonel Roddey. It was a journey of more than one hundred miles, and Forrest expected to arrive no later than early morning on the 28th, thus the pace that morning was a brisk one. The roads were in good condition and by late afternoon on the 26th, they had covered some ninety miles and had reached Brown's Ferry, Alabama, forty miles east of Florence, where they would board the ferry and cross the Tennessee River.

Nathan Bedford Forrest, an ex-slave trader and merchant, had no formal education or military training. He had joined the Tennessee Mounted Rifles as a private on July 14, 1861. His lack of military training did not, however, mean that Forrest was unable to see how badly equipped the CSA was. A wealthy man from his pre-war business dealings, Forrest offered to buy horses and equipment with his own money and raise a regiment of volunteer soldiers. This, as far as the Confederate hierarchy was concerned, was unprecedented, because wealthy merchants and planters were, at that time, exempted from military service. That someone of Forrest's wealth and prominence had enlisted as a private soldier was a little out of the ordinary, to say the least. Thus, a grateful Tennessee State Governor Isham Harris accepted his offer, commissioned him a lieutenant colonel, and authorized him to recruit and train a battalion of Confederate Mounted Rangers. This he set about with enthusiasm and, in October 1861, he was given command of a regiment, the beginnings of Forrest's Cavalry Corps, although that was to come much later in his career.

Although he did lack any military training, Forrest was an intuitive battlefield and cavalry commander. He had the innate ability to be able to outwit and outmaneuver his enemies, seemingly at will. Thus, upon his arrival at Brown's Ferry that balmy afternoon on the 26th of April, he divided his force. He sent Colonel George Dibrell with the 8th and 10th regiments and two sections of Morton's Battery – four guns under the command of Captain Mullins – west some forty miles along the north bank of the Tennessee River to Florence. Forrest himself boarded the remaining two regiments, the 4th and 9th, and rest of Morton's Battery, onto the ferry for the river crossing.

Forrest, a master of deception, had decided that Dibrell would take and hold Florence, and make as much noise while doing it as he possibly could. Once that objective had been achieved, he was to bombard South Florence on the other side of the river and do everything he could to make it appear that he was about to cross the river there and drive a wedge between General Dodge and his home base in Corinth, Mississippi. Meanwhile, Forrest would cross the river at Brown's Ferry and join with Colonel Roddey at Courtland early on the morning of the 28th. Together, Forrest and Roddey would then drive west and attack Dodge in Tuscumbia.

Chapter 20

April 24th, 1863. General Dodge, Tuscumbia, Alabama.

Friday, April 24th, dawned bright and clear. The sky was blue with not a cloud in sight. General Dodge also rose bright and clear, although he had something of a hollow pit in his stomach. Whether it was from lack of food – he had not yet eaten breakfast – or from a deep feeling of impending doom, he did not know. He had, as he usually did, awoken early, well before dawn, and was now standing on the eastern edge of his camp, accompanied by Brigadier General Tom Sweeny, commanding his First Brigade, and Colonel August Mersey, commanding the Second. They were soon joined by Colonel Bane of the Third Brigade and Colonel Fuller of the Fourth. All five of them stood together, staring down the dusty road toward Tuscumbia. Only a few houses were visible and, as far as they could tell, little was stirring inside the town.

"It looks quiet," Sweeny said, thoughtfully.

"Too quiet," Dodge agreed. "I don't like it."

"Ambush, General?" Colonel Mersey asked.

"Probably."

"How do you want to proceed, General?" Sweeny asked.

"There's only one way to proceed," Dodge replied. "We know he has at least six thousand effectives, so we hit 'em hard and fast. We hit 'em with everything we've got, and then some. If we don't drive them out with the first blow, we'll be in for a protracted, house-to-house fight, and that would be costly, very costly. We must avoid that, if we can.

"Colonel Mersey, you will have the right flank and deploy the Second Brigade to the south in line of battle and, on my command, will advance upon the town from that direction. You, General Sweeny, will have the center; Colonel Bane, you will be to the left and will advance from the north; Colonel Fuller, the Fourth Brigade will be held in reserve."

139

"Artillery, General?" Sweeny asked.

"Of course. Please have Captain Chapman's battery brought up and deployed in line here, from north to south." He reached into his vest pocket and withdrew a silver pocket watch, flipped it open, looked at it and noted the time – just after seven-fifteen. He closed the watch and replaced it in the pocket from whence it came.

"Let's see if we can stir things up a little. Captain Chapman may not open fire before all three brigades are in line and ready to move forward. Understood? Good, go to it, then, gentlemen. Time is not on our side."

By nine o'clock, all four brigades were in position; the town was surrounded on three sides. Chapman's Battery, four Parrott Rifles and two twelve-pounder Napoleons, was deployed in a line facing east, with some fifteen yards between each gun. All was ready. All was quiet, both in the Federal ranks and in the town. Not a sound was to be heard anywhere as the long ranks of Federal soldiers waited. And they waited.

For almost a half-hour, the men of the three Federal brigades stood in line of battle, awaiting the command to move. At the center of the line, just to the rear of the First Brigade, General Dodge sat astride his horse, surrounded by his staff and escort. He watched, staring into the distance at the silent town. He just could not understand it. Surely they knew he was there. Hell, he was damned sure they knew. *What the hell are they up to?*

Finally, he looked down, over the heads of the First, to where General Sweeny was standing, facing him, awaiting the command to move out.

"Advance the colors!" Dodge said it quietly, but it was easily heard by General Sweeny, who repeated the order loud enough for all to hear.

Regiment by regiment, the color guards stepped forward, their flags and banners snapping in the breeze. And again, all was quiet.

Dodge looked to the left and the right and, finally, he looked at Captain Chapman, who was also awaiting Dodge's command. Then, with a sigh, mentally accepting the inevitable, he raised his hand, pointed at Chapman, and nodded.

Chapman spun on his heel and shouted, "By section, Fire."

BAMBAM... BAMBAM... BAMBAM. Two at a time, the six guns of Chapman's battery fired, and Dodge watched as the six Hotchkiss shells arched up and away toward the town. As the last gun fired, Dodge swept his hand down, giving the order for all three brigades to advance.

"GUIDE CENTER, FORWAAARD," General Sweeny shouted the order to advance. And General Dodge watched the shells as they arched down into the center of the town, followed by the dull CRUMP, CRUMP, CRUMP... as each shell slammed into wooden building or dirt street. He could see the splintered shards and planks of wood as they cartwheeled high into the air.

His soldiers advanced on the town, slowly at first, then at the trot, and then in a full-blown charge. Men rushed into the town from every direction. But all was quiet. Not a shot was fired. The town was deserted. Running men skidded to a halt, swinging their weapons wildly from side to side, expecting at any second to be on the receiving end of a volley of gunfire, but it never came. General Dodge had taken Tuscumbia without a shot being fired, except by Captain Chapman's artillery, which had on inspection, done only minor damage to one home and a small shop.

On the top of a rise, just to the northeast of the town, Confederate Cavalry Colonel Cornyn, too, was sat astride his horse, watching. He had a slight smile on his lips, a grim smile. He did not like giving up without a fight, but he was also a good battlefield commander and he knew when the odds were against him. Thus, in this case, he was sure that retreat was the better part of valor. He sat for but a few moments, then wheeled his horse and nodded for his staff to follow, then rode away at the canter toward Courtland and, so he hoped, reinforcements.

Chapter 21

April 24th, 1863. General Dodge Field Headquarters, Tuscumbia, Alabama.

By mid-afternoon, General Dodge's forces had settled into the town of Tuscumbia. Most of his men, and many of Streight's Mule Soldiers, had found shelter in the abandoned homes and various commercial buildings. General Dodge. along with Colonel Streight and several senior officers, had taken rooms in a large, two-story home on the main street that belonged to one of Tuscumbia's most affluent citizens, a man by the name of Thomas Rodman. Rodman and his family had left the previous day to take refuge in Decatur, taking with them only what they needed to sustain them for the few days, hoping that the rumors of General Forrest's imminent arrival were true, and that they would be home again within the week.

It was a large house, two stories with several outbuildings, including a kitchen, two outhouses, and what might once have been slave quarters. There were five bedrooms on the upper floor and a single bathroom. At ground level, the ceilings were ten feet high. Each room had a fireplace with a rustic wooden mantle. There was a large dining room, a parlor, living room, a small library and a pantry.

By noon, General Dodge had called a meeting of his senior officers, along with those of Colonel Streight. The officers were assembled in the dining room. Dodge, his five brigade commanders and Colonel Streight were seated around the large dining table upon which was spread a map of Northern Alabama. Dodge sat at the head of the table. Streight's four regimental commanders, his surgeon, Major Peck, and Major Vananda were standing with their backs to the walls.

"The time has come, gentlemen," Dodge began, "for us to talk this thing through. Before we do, however, Colonel Cornyn, you must to horse and pursue the enemy cavalry. We need to know exactly where they are and what they are doing. I want no surprises. Is that clear?"

Cornyn rose from his place at the table and, with a salute to the commanding general, but without saying a word, walked quickly from the room.

"Now then, gentlemen," Dodge continued. "Our mission and situation is as follows: Our orders are to provide a diversion, a screen if you will, for Colonel Dodge and his Provisional Brigade as they head west to Rome. This, I think, is a simple enough task. We now hold Tuscumbia and Florence and, when you are ready to leave, Colonel, we will move to the east and demonstrate against Leighton and Courtland. That should give you plenty of time and cover to make your exit to the south.

"Now, as I understand it, "Dodge continued, rising to his feet and leaning over the map, "you intend to move south from here, first to Russellville, and then westward through Newburg, Moulton, and then on through Days Gap. Is that not correct, Colonel?"

"It is, General, but I will not be able to leave for at least two more days. I am still short of three hundred mounts. My men are foraging far afield but, I regret to say, with little success. The farmers, so it seems, have turned all of their stock loose and there are very few animals to be found."

"You are already almost a week behind schedule, Colonel. You cannot delay your departure for much longer. All reports indicate that Forrest is moving quickly and will be here within forty-eight hours. I can hold him, but for how long... well, and as of now, I do not know if he knows what we are doing. If he does not already know that will be to the good. If he figures it out, there will be no stopping him."

"True, General. By day's end, I will have at least some idea of the shortfall and will make the necessary adjustments to my brigade. Every one of my men must have a mount. If necessary, I will leave some of them behind with you, General."

"Good, good. So, here we have it, Colonel Streight. You and your provisional Brigade will leave Tuscumbia no later than the early morning of Monday, the 27th. In the meantime, Colonel, I suggest you get what rest you can. I think you may be in for something of a wild ride.

"Colonel Sheets," Dodge continued. "Have Captain Spencer report to me as soon as possible. Colonel Phillips, you must take your regiment and go to Florence. I need to know the situation there. That's it then, gentlemen. Go about your business and report back to me as soon as possible. I want no surprises."

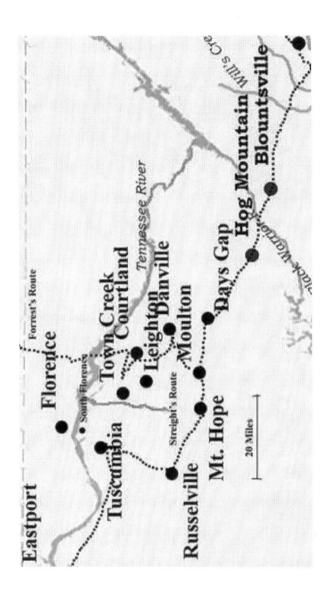

Captain George Spencer arrived at the house just a few moments after the last senior officer had retired to his room on the second floor. Dodge ushered him into the dining room and together the two men began to study the map.

"George," Dodge said, "I'm not at all happy with this cockamamie scheme we are involved in. It has the makings of disaster written all over it. Streight seems to be in no hurry to get started, his men have little to no cavalry experience, and then there's the mules. Whoever came up with that idea should be discharged with ignominy. I have never heard of such an ill-advised idea. Nevertheless, we must, Captain, make it work. Before anything else, however, I need to know exactly what I'm facing. How many men do you have at your disposal?"

"No more than twelve, General. But they are all good men and I trust each one of them implicitly."

"Good. Now, I want you to take the lead. Colonel Cornyn is out chasing the enemy cavalry, I hope, somewhere in this area, here." He indicated a large area on the map just to the west of Leighton. "Colonel Phillips is on his way to Florence. That leaves these two areas, here and here." He pointed out two areas to the north and south along the west banks of the Town Creek River, midway between Tuscumbia and Courtland.

"Go immediately to Town Creek and deploy your men north and south. Have them keep a sharp lookout for enemy activity to the east. You, Captain, must go to Courtland. Keep out of sight. I want to know the minute Forrest arrives. Any questions?"

"No, General. We will leave within the hour."

"Excellent, and good luck to you, Captain. As soon as you know something...."

Spencer nodded, stood to attention, saluted, and left the room. Forty-five minutes later, he and his small troop left Tuscumbia, heading east at full gallop.

Sergeant Major Ignatius O'Sullivan and Corporal Coffin were likewise housed in one of the homes, one almost as large as that now occupied by the senior command staff. It was the home of one of

Tuscumbia's finest, but this one had not been abandoned, and their reception was not one of welcome.

"Who the hell are you?" The man stood in the living room doorway, holding a shotgun.

"Well now, is that any way to treat a poor traveler?" O'Sullivan said with a grin.

"You're no damned traveler. You're a damned Yankee; that's what you are," he said, raising the shotgun until it was level with O'Sullivan's chest.

"'Tis true, so it is," O'Sullivan said, amiably. "But come now, that's no reason to hold a gun on a man. We mean you no harm. In fact, we're here to protect you, so we are."

The man took a step forward; the gun was now less than two feet from O'Sullivan's chest. O'Sullivan moved like a striking snake. With a single fluid motion, his left hand swept forward, grabbed the barrel of the shotgun, and swept it away, leaving the old man open handed, and open-mouthed.

"Now then, sir, that's a whole lot better. Is it not?"

The man just looked at him, then his shoulders slumped and he turned away and walked into what O'Sullivan supposed must be the kitchen. O'Sullivan followed him. Coffin tagged along behind.

The man sat down at the kitchen table, a long trestle made from southern yellow pine. It gleamed in the light shining in through the windows, the surface worked and pocked by many years of use.

O'Sullivan stood in the doorway and looked down at him, waiting.

The man looked up at him. "What do you want? We have nothing here: no money or jewels. There's nothing for you to steal. Why don't you just leave? You're not wanted here."

O'Sullivan nodded. "We're not here to steal from you, sir. All we want is shelter for the night, food and drink, and a warm place to sleep. In return, I'll see that no one else bothers you. Are you here alone?"

147

The man looked sharply at him and said, a little too quickly, "Yes, alone. There's no one here but me."

O'Sullivan smiled sideways at him. "Alone, do you say? And why, then, are you so nervous? Coffin, search the house, if you will."

The man glanced down at a section of the floor on the far side of the kitchen. O'Sullivan smiled. "And I would start with the cellar, if I were you."

"Cellar? What cellar?" Coffin asked.

"Over there." He pointed to a gaily-colored throw rug on the far side of the table.

Coffin pulled the rug aside and, sure enough, there was a large square trapdoor with a large iron ring.

"Please, Sergeant," the old man said, his head in his hands. "It's just my wife and daughter and a little one. They'll do you no harm. I promise."

"Bring 'em up, Coffin."

Coffin lifted the door and called down, "Come on up. You've nothing to fear."

A second later, a female head appeared in the opening, and a small woman with graying hair climbed unsteadily out from the cellar below. She was followed a moment later by a much younger woman. She stood with her head and shoulders above the level of the floor and handed a small child, a little girl no more than three years old, to her mother, then she, too, climbed out of the cellar, and the two of them stood quietly, heads bowed, in front of the two Federal soldiers.

"And a fine lookin' family you are, I must say," O'Sullivan said. "Do you, by any chance, have names?"

"My name, Sergeant, is William Blount, and this is my wife, Sadie, our daughter, Constance Brooks, and our granddaughter, Julia."

"And where might your husband be, young lady?"

She looked at him, defiantly, eyes watering, glittering. "He will be here shortly."

"Oh will he now? Then we'd best be prepared to greet the fine young man that he must be."

"Oh, you won't be needing to greet him. He'll be greeting you and the rest of your savages. He's with General Forrest and is expected here momentarily."

"Ah, so he is, then. Well, I don't think that momentarily is the correct word, young miss. As I am led to understand, the good general is at least two days' ride from here. We will, I think, either be long gone when he arrives, or standing ready to meet him, in line of battle. But who knows about such things? I am but a poor Sergeant Major, so I am, and I does what I'm told; well, mostly.

"Now then, no one here is going to hurt you. We are not savages, although you say that we are. Me an' Coffin here just want a dry, warm place to lay our heads, an' a nice hot meal, or two. For that, no one else will bother you, I promise, and we'll leave you when the brigade moves out no worse than you were when we arrived. What do you say, Mr. Blount?"

"You'll leave us alone, all of us?" Blount asked, looking pointedly at his daughter. The girl's face colored up, but she said nothing.

O'Sullivan heaved a big sigh. "You really do believe we be bad folks, don't you? We are not, I assure you. You have my word on it, sir," he said, handing the now empty shotgun to Blount. Then he changed his mind and tucked the weapon under his arm. "But I will say this: if you even think of doing either one of us harm..." He opened the flaps on the twin holsters at his hips. "Well, let's say no more about it. Where would you have us bed down?"

"We have only one spare room, Sergeant Major, and it has only one bed. There are beds in the cellar...."

"Good enough, Mr. Blount, good enough. I'll take the spare room. You, Coffin, will bed down in the cellar."

Coffin looked at him, a wounded look on his face. "Er... I don't like dark places, Sarge."

"It won't be dark, Corporal. The good lady will have lamps enough, I'm sure. Isn't that right, Mrs. Blount?"

The lady nodded and looked at her daughter, questioningly.

She was no more than twenty-four years old, slim, tall, perhaps five feet nine inches, with dark red hair that hung around her neck and shoulders and framed a face that was not quite beautiful, but attractive nonetheless, with large eyes the color of pale jade. She was not a full-figured girl, but shapely in a gentle sort of way. She wore a light blue gingham dress with a white lace collar. The dress was drawn in at the waist by a length of dark blue silk cord tied in a bow at the front.

"If you'll look after Julia for a moment, I'll show the Sergeant Major to the spare room. If you'll follow me," she said to O'Sullivan, walking quickly to the foot of the stairs where she stopped and turned to wait for him.

"Down there, then, Corporal," O'Sullivan said, as he followed Constance Roark. "I'm sure you'll do fine."

"The hell with that.... Pardon me language, ma'am, sir, miss, but I ain't sleepin' in no hole in the ground. I'll sleep outside, and thank *you*, Sergeant Major." And he spun on his heel and marched out of the front door, leaving a grinning O'Sullivan standing at the foot of the stairs.

"Well, now," he said, chuckling, "ain't he the one, though? Never mind, me dear. Up you go; show me where to lay my poor old head, and I'll be grateful to you, so I will. Oh, and my good lady Blount, if you will, ma'am, please give me a call when dinner is ready and, while you're at it, give that no good corporal of mine a shout, too. You'll find him skulkin' in his tent round by the stable, I shouldn't wonder. He'll be alookin' after the animals." Then he followed the young Mrs. Brooks up the stairs.

He dumped his bag on the bed and looked around the cozy little room. The small bed, too small for O'Sullivan's large frame, was bedecked with a hand-sewn floral quilt. Other than the bed, there was only a couple of small pieces of furniture: a rocking chair and a washstand with a bowl and jug. He lay down on the bed and went almost immediately to sleep.

It was a little after seven o'clock that evening when Constance roused him from his reverie. At her call, he awoke with a start, feeling like death had taken him. His mouth was thick, his head ached, and his backside felt as if it had been beaten with a hammer. The pain from the long hours in the saddle, unused to horseback as he was, was unlike anything he'd ever felt before. His joints were so stiff from the ride he could barely raise himself from the bed, but he did so, swilled his face with cold water from the jug, changed his shirt, and went downstairs to find a rather raggedy Corporal Coffin standing self-consciously at the open door. Outside, the weather was cool, but the sky was clear and looked like it would be a pleasant evening.

Together, the two Federal soldiers entered the dining room to find the family already gathered around the table; two extra places had been set for O'Sullivan and Coffin.

To say that they were not welcome would be an understatement. No one spoke as they entered the room. Blount was already eating. He looked up at them, waved his fork in the general direction of the two empty chairs, and continued eating.

"Good evening to you all," O'Sullivan said, sitting down at the table.

No one answered him.

"Is no one going to give thanks, then?" he said.

Again, there was no answer.

"Well, now," he said, as Constance placed a large bowl of stew in front of him. "That looks mighty fine. Thank you, ma'am."

Coffin looked up as she placed a similar bowl if front of him, but he said nothing.

"Does anyone...." O'Sullivan began.

151

"Enough." Blount slammed his fork down on the table. "It's bad enough we have to put up with enemy soldiers at our table. I will put up with that, but I will not put up with you prattling on like a friend of the family. You are not. You are at my table under sufferance. Kindly keep your remarks to yourself; eat the food we provide, and then get the hell out of my sight."

Coffin cringed down in his seat, put down his fork, rose from the table, and walked quickly out of the house. O'Sullivan looked long and hard at his reluctant host.

"It's right you are, sir, and I can't say that I blame you. I will say this, however: if not me, then someone else. Someone else who might not be so caring about you and your family, especially the young lady here. I could leave you to the tender mercies of others, so I could. But I will not. Nor will I eat the food you so obviously begrudge. I will use your spare room only to sleep. I will spend as little time in your home as possible. I have no doubt we will be gone by Monday. Good evening to you, sir, and to yours. I will be back before ten." And with that, he, too, rose from the table and walked out of the house, leaving the Blount family staring after him, open-mouthed.

Minutes later, he joined Coffin, now sitting miserably at a nearby campfire, gnawing on a hunk of roast pork cut from a small pig rotating on a makeshift wooden spit above the fire.

"Now then, old son," he said. "Looks like we outwore our welcome even before we arrived. But never mind, me dear. Slice your old sergeant a nice piece o' that pork." He looked around at the gathered soldiers; Cassell, Doyle, and McHugh, along with a half-dozen others of various ranks, were also gathered around the fire, which crackled and spat as the pork fat dripped into the flames, sending showers of sparks up into the cool night air. It had, after all, turned into a pleasant evening.

Federal Lieutenant Colonel Jesse Phillips, with the 7th and 9th Illinois, and two companies of the 15th Illinois Cavalry, arrived in

South Florence around four o'clock that afternoon to no resistance from the townsfolk. Across the river, Florence itself was quiet, though he could see people seemingly going about their daily business and several Confederate cavalrymen seated around a campfire.

"YOU MEN OVER THERE," he shouted. "Would you be so good as to send a boat? I would like to send a courier over under flag of truce."

"Why don't you go straight to hell, Blue Belly?"

"ONE LAST CHANCE, SERGEANT. SEND A BOAT, NOW!"

"Or you'll do what? Swim on over an' get your ass shot off, why don't ya?"

"Captain Muldrow," Phillips said quietly to his artillery officer. "Let's see if we can get them to change their attitude. Please range your guns on the large house just to the right of the campfire and lay a couple of rounds on it."

It took Muldrow less than five minutes to unlimber the two three-inch Parrott rifles, load them with Hotchkiss shells, and range them on the white house across the river.

"Whenever you're ready, Captain."

BAM, BAM. The two shells arched across the river. The hang time at this close range was only about two seconds, and then both shells slammed down into the house, exploding on impact, sending showers of wood cartwheeling high into the air. The house was demolished; only a pile of broken, smoldering wood remained. The men at the campfire had, on seeing the guns being unlimbered, fled into the relative safety of the town itself. Within minutes of the two explosions, a dozen or more civilians came running from the town to the riverbank, waving their arms and shouting. One of them was wildly waving something white tied to a stick.

"Now then," Phillips said to Muldrow. "That's better, much better, don't you think, Captain?"

153

Phillips cupped his hands around his mouth and shouted, "SEND A BOAT OVER. I WISH TO PARLAY."

It was not long before a small boat rowed by two men was heading across the river toward them. Five minutes later, Phillips and two of his men were standing on the riverbank in Florence itself. The Confederate cavalrymen were nowhere to be seen.

"Who is in charge here?" he asked, looking around the group of men and women now standing in front of him.

"I am," said a tall, surly-looking man dressed for business. "My name is Wood, sir. I am the mayor of Florence, and I own the bank. Why are you firing on us, Colonel? We can do you no harm."

"You, Mr. Mayor? Perhaps not, but those Reb soldiers... also maybe not. How many of them do you have here, sir?"

"Ten, perhaps twelve, no more than that. They arrived this morning. I know no more about them than that, Colonel."

"What unit are they with, do you know?"

"They said they were with Julian's Battalion. Though what that might mean, I have no idea, sir. And, I might add, they have already left, and at the gallop."

"Julian's Battalion is part of Cornyn's brigade. Is it not?"

I have no idea, Colonel. Florence is a quiet town. We have no military presence here. At least not before now, and they seem to have gone. So, Colonel, why don't you do the same? There's nothing for you here."

Phillips nodded, staring hard at the mayor. "Perhaps you are right, sir. But then again.... Hmmm. Very well, sir, I have no desire to spend any more time in this God-forsaken place than I have to. That being so, if your men would be so good as to row me back across the river, I will leave a company of cavalry there, and be on my way. Be assured, however, that they will report instantly to me any enemy activity. If that happens, I will return and lay waste to your little town. Is that understood, Mr. Mayor?

The mayor gritted his teeth, and then indicated with a wave of his hand for the two men to row the colonel and his men back across the river.

Only minutes later, Phillips was on the road back to Tuscumbia, leaving Company B of the 9th Illinois in South Florence to keep an eye on the goings on across the river. By nightfall, he was back in Tuscumbia and had reported to General Dodge that Florence posed no threat. Little did he know that that would soon change.

Far away to the east, beyond Tuscumbia, Colonel Cornyn with a force of eleven hundred men of the 7th Kansas and 10th Missouri Cavalry was in hot pursuit of Confederate Colonel Roddey. They had left the main Federal force in Tuscumbia a little after eleven o'clock that morning, the 24th, and quickly found the trail. The tracks left by Roddey's horsemen were deep and well defined, thus Cornyn was able to push forward almost at the gallop, resting only a few minutes every half hour.

By three o'clock in the afternoon, Roddey knew he was in trouble. Spotting a line of trees to the east, he urged his men to the gallop and, on reaching the trees, called a halt and ordered his men to dismount. General Forrest had taught all of his units that the horse was no more than a mode of rapid transportation from one skirmish to the next, that the cavalryman was, in fact, no more than a rapid response infantry soldier. Thus, Roddey ordered the horses to be taken well to the rear, out of harm's way, and his artillery to be unlimbered and placed at the center of his line of battle.

For some twenty minutes, Roddey's brigade waited in silence, listening to the sounds of shouting and yelling in the distance as the Federal cavalry drew closer. Roddey stood at the ready, between the two twelve-pounder Napoleon guns, each one double-loaded with canister.

Then, at the western edge of the open field in front of them, the first Federal horsemen burst from the scrubland.

"FIRE!" Roddey shouted.

BAM, BAM. Both guns roared together, sending a hail of one-inch iron balls screaming across the open field. Unfortunately – fortunately for the Federal cavalry – the distance was short, less than three hundred yards, and the guns were ranged just a little too high. Most of the canister balls went over the heads of the riders. The volley from the more than eight hundred Sharps rifles, however, did not. The air was alive with the buzz of incoming Confederate Minnie balls and the crackle and twitter of wood shattering as the canister balls tore chunks of wood, branches, and splinters from the trunks of the trees. It seemed to be raining twigs, leaves, and wooden debris of all shapes and sizes.

More than twenty Federal horses went down, screaming in pain. Several men were wounded and two were killed outright.

Instantly, Cornyn shouted the recall and the bugles echoed across the field. He might as well have not bothered, because his men, totally surprised, turned on instinct and dashed back into the cover of the scrub they had left only a moment earlier.

Cornyn was now at a loss as to what to do next. He was, so he thought, heavily outnumbered, and outnumbered he was, but not by as many as he thought.

Roddey had only nine hundred men in line of battle – two hundred more were at the rear, looking after the horses; Cornyn had slightly more than eight hundred. It would have been an even match, had it not been for the two Confederate field pieces. As it was, Cornyn, thought he was outnumbered at least two-to-one, maybe more – this thanks to the erstwhile Captain Spencer's encounter with the good farmer, Sergeant Mica Hollister.

For several moments, Cornyn was lost in a state of indecision. He looked east across the open field, wondering.... He knew he could not mount a frontal attack. Those cannons, even though he couldn't see them for the trees, put paid to that idea, even if his own lack of numbers did not. He had, he realized, little choice but to hunker down under cover of the trees and wait.

For more than an hour, the two sides exchanged fire across the field, but to little effect. Several more Federal soldiers were wounded, as they were on the Confederate side, but all more by luck than design. Slowly, the rate of fire dwindled away to nothing, on both sides.

Across the clearing, Roddey stood between the two great guns, smiling grimly. He was, as always, supremely calm. His men were quiet. Not a sound could be heard from the long lines of gray-clad soldiers as they waited; even the birds were silent. The vast cloud of white gun smoke drifted slowly upward through the trees and dispersed in the gentle breeze above the treetops.

He took out his field glasses, put them to his eyes, and scoured the line of trees and scrub on the far side of the field. He couldn't see much, just the flitting of blue figures dashing this way and that, looking for a safer place to take cover. Then, right at the center of the Federal line, he spotted an officer. He, too had field glasses to his eyes. Even at that distance, he could see that the officer was a colonel, and that he had been spotted; the Federal colonel was watching him, too.

Roddey, something of a pragmatist, could see the irony of the situation, and he smiled to himself. Then, without really thinking about it, he raised his gloved hand and waved at his counterpart and was surprised when he received a wave in return.

He lowered his glasses, turned and walked to the rear of the two cannon, out of sight of the Federal colonel. *No point in making myself a target.*

Unlike Cornyn, Roddey was not indecisive. He knew that they were at a standoff. Better, he knew that although he did indeed outnumber the Federal cavalry force, it was not by much. There would, he decided, be no standing fight. He would wait until dark, then retreat beyond Leighton, just a mile away to the east, back to Courtland, and await the reinforcements that were already on the way.

On the far side of the field, Cornyn had watched his adversary walk back into the cover of the trees, and he settled down to wait.

As darkness fell, the Confederate forces quietly limbered the two guns, and the entire brigade silently moved out of line, through the trees to the waiting horses, mounted, and then disappeared like ghosts in the night.

It was not until after dawn the next morning that Cornyn realized that Roddey was gone, and he was not in the least upset to learn about it. He was, in fact, more than a little relieved. He had, after all, lost two good men, more than twenty horses, and now had a dozen wounded men to care for. Thus, he determined not to pursue Roddey, but to return to Tuscumbia.

Chapter 22

April 26, 1863, General Dodge's Field Headquarters, Tuscumbia

"So, Colonel," Dodge said, as Abel Streight entered the dining room he was using as his office. "How goes the foraging. Do you have enough mounts and, more to the point, are you ready to leave this place and pursue your mission?"

"I have enough animals, mules and horses, to mount all but about 200 of my men, General. I have ordered my surgeon, Major Peck and his assistant surgeon, Captain Spencer, to conduct a thorough examination of the entire brigade. That examination is already under way and should be completed no later than five o'clock this afternoon. I have instructed Peck to weed out the weaklings, the sick, and those he feels are incapable of traveling. It is my intention to leave for Russellville sometime in the early evening."

Dodge nodded, looked hard at him and said, "I hope your plan works, Colonel, really I do. You have a long and difficult road ahead. I do not envy you, sir. At first light tomorrow, I will move east toward Courtland and, God willing, will engage the enemy. You, Colonel, must make your best pace to Russellville. You must put as much distance as you can between your brigade and any possible pursuit."

"Well then, General, with your permission, I will be about my business. There's a lot I need to do before I can leave."

"God be with you, Colonel." Dodge rose from his seat and the two men saluted each other. Streight turned and left the room, leaving General Dodge staring after him, slowly shaking his head.

Earlier that morning at the Blount home, Sergeant Major O'Sullivan had carried his equipment down the stairs and was ready to leave. He was met at the bottom of the stairs by Constance Brooks and William Blount.

"You are leaving us, then, Sergeant Major." It was more of a statement than a question, and it was said with no little hint of pleasure.

"That I am, and I thank you for your hospitality."

"There's nothing to thank us for," Blount said. "You took what you wanted. It wasn't given willingly. Just be on your way and bother us no more."

O'Sullivan nodded, his eyes narrowed. "What you say is true, Mr. Blount, but we are at war, and you are the enemy. That being so, I think I treated you with more respect and consideration than you deserve." He looked then at Constance and continued, "Mrs. Brooks, I wish you well, and I hope no harm comes to that husband of yours. If you see him, tell him to stay out of our way." Then he turned once more and walked down the four steps and away.

By four o'clock that afternoon, Doctors Peck and Spencer had given almost two-thirds, some 1100 men of the Provisional Brigade, a very quick and cursory medical examination, an examination that was little more than a couple of questions, a hand on the forehead, a look down the throat, and an assessment of the overall demeanor of the individual. Upon that alone, either they passed the individual as fit for duty, or they removed him from the roster. Both doctors were exhausted. Never before had they seen so many men in a single day, and they still had almost 700 more to go.

It wasn't until after nine o'clock that Peck sent the last man back to his unit and made his way to Colonel Streight to report. He had removed 217 men from the duty roster. Streight could now mount his entire brigade, 1614 men, including the officers. He was ready to leave.

And so it was that after a long and tiring day, Colonel Abel D. Streight mounted his horse and moved to the head of the long column. His staff officers were in line just behind him, followed by the ever-present Sergeant Major Ignatius O'Sullivan and his sidekick,

160

Corporal Boone Coffin. Next in line came the six great wagons, each hauled by either a team of six mules or six horses. The first of those wagons was in the hands of Corporal Roark and Private Cullen Doyle.

The wagons were followed in line by the artillery, two Mountain Howitzers, and their caissons. The heavy wagons and artillery had been placed in a forward position in the column to take advantage of what Streight hoped would be firm conditions under foot and wheel, rather than having them dragged through feet-deep mud at the rear of the column; mud churned by the hooves of the more than 1600 animals. It was sound thinking.

Almost a quarter-mile to the rear of the artillery, Privates Silas Cassell and Andrew McHugh were, despite being covered from head to toe in oilskins, already soaked to the skin. The rain, driving in almost horizontal, seemed to find every small opening or crevice, and turned the already uncomfortable wool uniforms into instruments of torture. The stiff wool cloth turned into soggy wet constraints that scratched and rubbed the skin raw. The McClellan saddles beneath them were even worse. The barely-minimal twin strips of rawhide that covered the frame of the open seat, one for each buttock, slammed like hammers at the said buttocks and that, combined with the sodden rags that their woolen britches had become, made for a painful ride, to say the least.

The two men, riding side-by-side in the rain, were almost beyond despair at the prospect of the long night that lay ahead. Two of the most outgoing, ever chattering, members of the brigade, they now had little to say to each other and nothing at all to their comrades in hell.

It was exactly eleven o'clock that night when Streight gave the order to move out. He could not have picked a worse time; the night was black, the sky unseen and a driving rain came down in torrents. That coupled with the chill wind made life in the saddle, especially for those new to it, almost unbearable, and they had not yet traveled more than a few hundred yards. It was going to be a long night.

For better or for worse, Streight's raid was at last under way.

And it was to get worse, much worse.

Barely had the head of the column left the camp than it was plain for all to see that a night march was a mistake, and particularly so under the prevailing conditions.

The road was narrow, deeply scored and scarred by the traffic of many years, muddy, and overhung on either side by tree branches bowed almost to the ground under the weight of the water. The night was almost pitch black, and the road underfoot could not be seen without the aid of a lamp. One hundred yards beyond the perimeter of the camp, Streight had no option but to call for point men bearing oil lamps to ride a few feet ahead of the column to light the way for Streight and his escort. As more and more wagons and riders left the camp, a string of flickering lights could be seen jiggling slowly along the dark road. Each wagon was equipped with two lamps. The leaders of each company also carried lamps, fixed on poles and inserted into makeshift leather pockets.

The rain continued unabated through the night, bitterly cold, soaking rider, animal, and equipment alike. The surrounding woodland was a dank, dark, and sinister nightmare, and through it all, the column plodded unsteadily forward. The two point men, reluctant at first about their assignment, soon realized that they were in the best position. The road underfoot, though wet and streaming with water, was still relatively firm, as it was for Streight, his escort, and the few soldiers who were in the column ahead of the wagons, including O'Sullivan and Coffin.

As the column progressed, however, the state of the road deteriorated to little more than an oozing quagmire that sucked and dragged upon wheel, hoof, and foot. By one o'clock in the morning, the head of the column had slowed to less than a walking pace and had traveled little more than a mile. Most of the brigade had not yet left the encampment. Most of the men already on the road had been forced to dismount. So deep and thick was the mud that man and mule could barely make headway alone, much less together. Each man was struggling knee deep in liquid ooze, dragging his mule as best he could. In many places, the road was cut by fast-running water that had to be forded. The wagons slowed to barely moving, their wheels axel-deep, the teams struggling even to make headway. On it went, the long column fighting its way through the dark and the driving rain toward Russellville.

At two o'clock, Colonel Streight called a halt. From the front to the rear it took more than fifteen minutes for the order to trickle, company by company all the way to the rear,

Halt… Halt… Halt… Halt!

Cassell and McHugh, side by side, on foot, knee deep in mud, drenched and bedraggled, stood together with their heads close to those of their respective mules, equally drenched and even more bedraggled. Men and mules were exhausted and miserable beyond endurance. For three hours they had staggered through the mud, dragging their mounts, staggering, falling, and the animals had done little better. The darkness was palpable, the rain descending in sheets from an invisible sky. The soldiers could see only dimly by the flickering light of the oil lamps, and then only for a yard or two.

"I wanna die," Cassell yelled, over the wind and rain.

"I'm already dead," McHugh yelled back. "How much longer? I don't think I can stand much more of this. My pants are heavier than this goddamn animal."

Cassell staggered through the mud the few yards to the sodden grass bank and the roadside, dragging Abel the mule along with him. Still hanging onto the leather thongs that served as reins, he collapsed to the ground, lay back, stared up into the invisible foliage, and let the downpour wash the mud from his face. McHugh joined him. The two mules stood together, heads down, ears flattened against the wind and rain. All around them, front and rear, hundreds of men and mules stood and waited.

"Oh my god. Oh my god," Cassell gasped. "We're all gonna die out here. Forget the goddamn Rebs, we'll all drown. The skin on me knees an' the inside o' me thighs is gone, rubbed off, goddamn raw."

163

"Oh shit," McHugh forced out, through chattering teeth. "Oh shit. Shit, shit, shit. I musta pissed on a gypsy." He looked at Cassell, startled. The man was giggling, then laughing, then choking wildly, coughing and spluttering. He was close to hysteria.

"Geeze, Silas. Get a hold o' yerself."

Cassell rose onto his elbows, tilted his head back as far as it would go, and coughed as if trying to get rid of his lungs. His kepi fell off, his hair hung in strands to the sodden ground, then he rolled over onto his belly and threw up, retching, heaving the remains of the salt pork and beans he had eaten just a few hours earlier into the mud.

"Oh god," he said. "I'm gonna die. I know I am."

"No y'ain't," McHugh yelled. He grabbed Cassell by the collar of his oilskin and shook him violently. "I done told yo to get a hold o' yerself. NOW DO IT!"

Cassell, elbows in the mud, face in his hands, coughed, hawked deep in his throat, spat, then rolled over onto his back.

"All right, all right," he gasped. "Gimme just a minute." He coughed again, sat up, looked at his friend, and with water running down his face, he smiled grimly. "Hell, Andy, life gets tedious, don't it?"

McHugh grinned back at him and nodded. "Ha. Ya think this is bad. Did I ever tell ya 'bout—"

"Yeh, ya did," Cassell interrupted him, putting his hands over his ears. "Just gimme a minute, Andy, just a minute, please."

McHugh nodded and lay back, letting the rain wash over his face.

The regulation ten-minute halt was soon over and the men, those who had managed to lie down, were called back to their feet, and the mud. Slowly, company by company, the march, if it could be called that, resumed.

Streight had hoped to reach Moulton, some forty miles out of Tuscumbia, by the end of the next day. But by daylight, after more

164

than seven hours on the road, they'd covered only five miles, and the rain continued to fall, whipped and driven by the wind.

By five o'clock that afternoon, the 27th, the head of the column, after covering more than thirty miles over some of the most wild and unforgiving terrain, under the most appalling conditions imaginable, had passed through Russellville. They turned east and were approaching the tiny mountain settlement of Mount Hope, and there Colonel Streight called a halt. After almost twenty hours in the saddle and on foot, the Mule Soldiers had traveled only thirty-four miles; Moulton was still ten miles away to the east.

The rain continued to fall. It was more than twelve hours later that the last of the Federal soldiers struggled into camp, man and beast soaked to the skin, exhausted and hungry.

It had been a night and a day to remember, or perhaps to forget, and it was not yet over. The animals had to be fed and cared for, the camp had to be set, fires had to be lit, and food had to be cooked. There was not a dry stick of wood to be found anywhere. Foragers were sent out to find what they could, and what little they did find was usually inside barns: old and not so old furniture, the walls of wooden stalls, and the like. And so the nightmare continued.

The senior officers all found beds in local homes, much to their owners' fury. Abel Streight found accommodations at the home of Dr. L. N. Templeton, a wealthy planter whose plantation consisted of almost a thousand acres. Templeton was, fortunately, not at home, being away fighting for the Confederacy. His daughter, Jenny, however was at home, and was a Union sympathizer to boot. At least she made it known to Streight, and to anyone else who might enquire, that she was, but... who knew, really? Nevertheless, the good lady went out of her way to make sure that Streight had everything he needed to relax and recover from his ordeal.

There was no such welcome for the enlisted men. As the rain continued to fall, they pitched their pup tents in the muddy fields, wrapped themselves in their oilskins, and did their best to stay dry and rest. It was a forlorn hope.

165

For Doyle, however, the wagon master's job came with an unexpected bonus. He and his friends, Cassell and McHugh, were able to bed down among the various barrels and boxes inside the wagon; not the best accommodations in camp, but far better than most. The three of them, having been among the first to arrive in Mount Hope, were able to dry off, eat a good meal, and sleep, though fitfully, through the night.

O'Sullivan also found a billet inside a wagon. He bedded down among great sacks of feed. The waterproof coverings that he and Coffin had worn during the ride from Tuscumbia had, for the most part, kept them and their mounts reasonably dry. Their mounts, apart from those of the senior officers, were stronger and fitter than any the rest the brigade were riding. Thus, O'Sullivan, warm and content under a thick woolen blanket, was fast asleep long before the last of the stragglers wandered into the camp.

Coffin also found a warm spot to spend the night. After more than an hour of searching, he had found a barn on the southern side of the town. He led O'Sullivan's great horse, Lightning, and Phoebe the mule inside, pulled the barn door closed behind him, and tethered the two animals to a post in the center of the building. He pitched his small tent in a dry corner and spread a thick layer of straw on the dirt floor inside. Next, he cleaned and groomed the two animals, talking soothingly to them as he went about it. Finally, he went inside the tent, wrapped himself tightly in two thick, woolen blankets, laid himself down on the straw, and was, within minutes, in a deep sleep, the horse and mule munching contentedly on a vast pile of hay.

Neither O'Sullivan nor Coffin awoke until Reveille at six the following morning.

The journey from Tuscumbia to Mount Hope had been costly. The sickest of the mules, those that had started out with the beginnings of distemper, had one by one throughout the long night and day fallen by the wayside. By the time the brigade reached Mount Hope, Streight had lost forty-three of his precious animals and

166

seventeen of his soldiers had collapsed, twelve of them with hypothermia; two had died in route.

At seven o'clock that evening, the 27th, Streight called a meeting with his senior officers. They gathered in the kitchen of the farmhouse. Of the farmer's daughter, there was no sign.

"Not an auspicious beginning to our enterprise, gentlemen." Streight was seated at the head of a large, pine table, big enough to seat a dozen or more. He was exhausted, his voice was tired, and he slumped forward in his chair, shoulders rounded.

"What a terrible journey." Streight continued. "We should have waited until the rain stopped. The men... the men are exhausted, worn out, and we have barely begun." He shook his head, staring at the bare tabletop in front of him.

"We couldn't wait, sir," Colonel Sheets said. "The enemy will be well aware of us by now. We had to put as much distance between them and us as we could. In fact, Colonel, we need to be back on the road again as soon as possible."

Streight shook his head, tiredly. "No. We'll wait. The men are exhausted and in no condition for a fight. The animals, too, must have rest. We'll wait until morning. Perhaps the rain will stop by then. Let the men rest until six o'clock, and then make sure that all of the animals are inspected and properly fed. Those that are unfit to travel must be left behind. Colonel Hathaway, tomorrow morning, as soon as your men have eaten breakfast, send out foragers. We must replenish our food supplies and, more important, we must replace the dead animals, and those we will have to leave behind."

He paused for a moment, staring down at his hands. Then he looked up again and around the tabled at his officers. "I am tired, sirs. I had not contemplated this, the weather and all. Let's get some rest. We will leave here no later than noon tomorrow."

Chapter 23

April 27, 1863. Confederate Force at Florence Alabama

Confederate Colonel George Dibrell arrived on the eastern approaches to the small town of Florence a little before mid-day on April 27. The river crossing at Brown's Ferry was more than forty miles away to the east. Forrest had crossed the river there late in the afternoon the previous day and made camp for the night. By eight o'clock, he was on the road south to Courtland where he would join with Colonel Roddey.

In the meantime, Colonel George Dibrell, along with several of his staff officers, had found a vantage point on a low ridge just to the north of the town. It was a beautiful day; there was not a cloud in the sky. From where he was sitting, still on horseback, brass-bound binoculars to his eyes, he could see the sleepy little town, the river, the small settlement of South Florence beyond the river, the tents with the guidons of Company B of the 9th Illinois fluttering the light breeze, and forty or more horses corralled some distance away beyond. The main body of his own brigade was just to the northeast, hidden from the town by the ridge upon which Dibrell was now standing.

All was quiet. As far as Dibrell could tell, Florence was a ghost town. Even among the tents of Federal Company B in South Florence, there was little movement. Company B, so it seemed, was at rest.

Dibrell stared thoughtfully down upon the vista laid out below, tapping the rim of the binoculars on the pommel of his saddle.

"Captain Mullins," he said, to his chief of artillery seated beside him. "What do you think would be the range of those tents?"

Mullins did the math in his head. "Nine hundred yards, perhaps nine-fifty."

"Bring up one of the Rodmans, if you would, Captain, and have the brigade move forward onto the ridge. Let's make a show for the boys in blue, shall we?"

168

Mullins turned his horse and galloped away to the main body of the brigade, gave the necessary orders, and within minutes a three-inch, rifled Rodman gun was being unlimbered atop the ridge beside the little gathering of Confederate officers. The rest of the brigade was forming up in a line more than a half-mile long on the crest of the ridge.

"Solid shot, if you please, Mr. Mullins. We want to scare them away, not necessarily kill them. When you are ready, one round."

Mullins dismounted, went to the gun, sighted it on a tent on the right side of the encampment, turned the elevating screw a half-turn, then stepped back away from the gun, lanyard in hand. He looked questioningly up at Dibrell.

Dibrell looked once more across the river at the small group of tents and nodded.

Mullins yanked the lanyard and BAM. At nine hundred yards, the hang time for the solid shot was a little less than five seconds; the small group of Confederate officers watched as the conical solid iron shot arched into the air, over the town and the river, to the encampment beyond. The shot fell a little short of the tent, the intended target, but it had the desired effect. Almost instantly, the men of Company B were out of the tents, in various stages of dress, looking north at the long line of Confederate cavalry assembled on the ridge.

Dibrell could see that an officer was shouting orders and waving his arms, but he could not hear what he was shouting. Dibrell smiled at the obvious panic in the Federal encampment.

"Now, gentlemen," he said, quietly. "All we have to do is wait."

They did not have to wait very long. The Federal cavalrymen quickly gathered up their belongings, saddled their horses, mounted, and rode away at the gallop, leaving their tents behind them. The Confederate brigade on the ridge howled with laughter.

As they watched, a small group of civilians rode out of Florence toward them.

"Good morning, Colonel. My name is Wood. I am the mayor of Florence. To whom do I have the pleasure of speaking?"

"Colonel George Dibrell, Forrest's Division, Confederate States Cavalry. It's good to see you, Mr. Mayor. We did not disturb you too much, I hope," Dibrell said, with a wide grin.

"Not at all, Colonel, not at all. They arrived two days ago, destroyed one of our homes, but other than that, they kept themselves to the south side of the river. Thank you for driving them away, sir."

"My pleasure, Mr. Mayor. Is there anything more we can do for you?"

"Not a thing, Colonel, not a thing. How, might I ask, is the good General Forrest?

"Always the same, sir. In good spirits and itching to get at the Rebs."

"That's good to hear, Colonel. My wife and I would be pleased to host you and your staff for dinner this evening. What may I tell her, sir?"

"As much as I would like to accept your kind invitation, I must decline. I am awaiting the arrival of General Van Dorn. He is already on his way south from Spring Hill and should be here directly." This was, of course, a lie. General Van Dorn was indeed in Spring Hill, but he had no intention of joining Dibrell. But the mayor did not know that and was, unwittingly, the messenger who would send the good news to General Dodge in Tuscumbia.

"Then I will thank you for your good offices and let you be about your business. Please convey my best regards to General Forrest, and tell him that we are ever grateful for his efforts on our behalf."

Wood sat tall in his saddle, saluted Dibrell, then turned and rode back to Florence to deliver the news that Van Dorn was on his way. Dibrell, a slight smile on his face, watched him go, then gave orders for the brigade to make camp on the north side of the river. There was work yet to do.

Late that same afternoon, Captain Rice of Company B, arrived back in Tuscumbia and was immediately ushered into General Dodge's headquarters. There he joined Captain Spencer, who had arrived back in Tuscumbia only moments before Rice.

Spencer listened as Rice described what had happened at Florence, and the presence there of a large force of Confederate cavalry. He nodded as he listened, all the while switching his gaze back and forth between Rice and General Dodge. Rice, having completed his report, left the room, leaving Spencer alone with a now visibly concerned General Dodge.

""General, sir," Spencer said. The two men were seated together at one end of the dining table. "I think that there is little at Florence to concern you. General Forrest has already made the river crossing at Browns Ferry and will be in Courtland by morning. It is my considered opinion that what Captain Rice observed at Florence is no more than a ruse. A feint to distract you until Forrest joins with Roddey."

"What makes you think that, Captain?"

"Two things, General. First, such a feint is typical of Forrest. He has built his career and reputation upon deception. It makes sense, then, that he would try to lead us to believe he intends a river crossing at Florence, but we know, General, that there are no boats capable of making such a crossing there; therefore, it must be a ruse.

"Second, whoever it was at Florence, made no attempt to kill or capture Rice and his men. Rice stated that they fired but a single shot at them, and it fell short. As large a force as Rice described would have crossed at least a small force and bombarded the hell out of Rice's company. No, General. What happened at Florence was no more than a diversion. In fact, I would bet my soul that there are no longer any Confederate forces anywhere close to Florence. They will, by now, be on their way to rejoin Forrest and Roddey."

171

"You may well be right, Captain Spencer, but what if you are not? If that Reb force is still at Florence, and if they do manage a crossing there, we will be trapped between two large forces. We already know from your previous visit to the Rebel stronghold that there is already a considerable number of the enemy there, and now we also know that Forrest himself is about to join them. We could, Spencer, find ourselves outnumbered to the east, and cut off from retreat to the rear. That, sir, would not be acceptable. We need to know what the situation is in Florence. You must go at once. Take two men with you and make all possible speed. Once there, determine the situation and then return at once. If you leave now, you can be in South Florence within the hour. Go, sir, and go quickly."

Spencer was indeed in Florence within the hour, and it took him less than ten minutes to figure out that his surmise had been wrong, and that it was a good thing that he had not, after all, put his soul at risk. On the far side of the river, the terrain was ablaze with dozens of campfires. Hundreds of tents had been pitched along the riverbank and across the fields to the north. There were gray uniforms everywhere.

Spencer was astounded, but it took him only minutes to find a somewhat friendly face, an old man, a farmer sitting on the porch of a small shack, smoking an old clay pipe.

"Good evening, sir," Spencer said, dismounting and flipping the reins over a post just in front of the shack.

"Good ev'nin' yerself."

"Lots of company you folks have," Spencer said, nodding his head in the direction of the river.

"Yep, and more to come, so they sez."

"Who says?"

"Why Mayor Wood sez, that's who."

Do you know who they are, by chance?"

"Nope. Some of Forrest's people, I s'pose."

"You say there's more to come?"

"Ha!"

"Well. Tell me, man. I need to know."

"I bet you do, but you'll not be hearin' it from me."

Spencer looked hard at him, and drew and cocked his Colt, "You might want to reconsider that, old man. How would you be able to look after your folks with your knee shot away?" He let the pistol dangle from his finger by the trigger guard.

The old man stared at the weapon, then said, without looking up, "Mayor Wood sez that General Van Dorn is on his way south. With how many, nobody knows, an' that's all I knows, so be off with you and leave me the hell alone."

Spencer nodded, holstered the gun, turned and rode away. An hour later, he was back in Tuscumbia and had reported his findings to General Dodge. Dodge was not happy to receive the news, but was more concerned about the strength of the enemy forces gathering at Courtland, to the east.

Spencer, from his previous fact-finding expedition of the 23rd, was still convinced that Roddey was in command of at least 5000, possibly more, and would soon be joined by 2500 more under the command of General Forrest.

By the numbers, General Dodge felt he still might have a small advantage, but he also felt that the Confederate forces held the high ground – figuratively speaking. They were mobile where he was not. And Forrest was an army unto himself, if only by reputation. And now Van Dorn.... Well, that he would have to deal with later. For now, he had a job to do.

Dodge, not an indecisive man, quickly made up his mind and sent for his senior commanders. The meeting lasted no more than ten minutes.

"We must move quickly, gentlemen. Colonel Streight is, I hope, well on the road to Russellville. As far as we know, from Captain

Spencer's reports, there is a large enemy force at Florence, but they have no way of crossing the river. All other Confederate forces in this area are concentrated in and around Courtland. General Forrest will, so I am told, arrive in Courtland early tomorrow morning. They must not be allowed to break out.

"We will leave here no later than nine o'clock this evening and head east to Courtland. There, or somewhere along the way, we will bring Forrest to battle. If we can defeat him, so much the better, if not, we must delay him, at least through tomorrow. If we can do that, gentlemen, our job will be done and we can return to Corinth. That's it, gentlemen. Go to your brigades and prepare to move out on my command."

Chapter 24

April 28th, 1863 - The Battle of Town Creek

It had rained most of the night and when Forrest arrived in Courtland in the early hours of Tuesday morning, the 28th, it was still raining. He was wet, muddy, and more than a little miserable. Colonel Roddey was waiting for him, dressed and ready to travel.

"General Forrest, sir." Roddey snapped a salute as Forrest reined in his sweating horse. "And mighty good it is to see you. Maybe now we can give them damn Yankees what they deserve."

Forrest swung down from the saddle, flipped Roddey a casual salute, and looked around the bustling encampment. "It would seem, Colonel, that you are making ready to break camp."

"Indeed I am, General. The enemy is less than four miles away, on the west bank of Town Creek. We need to move out, at once, sir."

Forrest nodded. "All in good time, Colonel. I need a change of uniform and a fresh horse. Where, sir, may I ask, is your tent?"

"This way, General," Roddey said, leading the way.

Thirty minutes later, refreshed, shaved, and dressed in an immaculately laundered and pressed fresh uniform, Forrest was seated with Roddey at a small folding table, a cup of steaming, black coffee in hand.

"How many of them are there, Colonel?" he asked.

In total, General, they number slightly more than 10,000, including Cornyn's Cavalry Brigade, some 1800, and there's a mounted brigade of, perhaps 1700. The mounted brigade, General is on... er, they are on mules, sir."

"Mules, yes I know. They left Nashville by river on the 10th and arrived in Eastport on the 19th. What, do you think can that be about?"

"I have no idea, General. As far as I can tell, they are reinforcements for Dodge's command. They are certainly still with him."

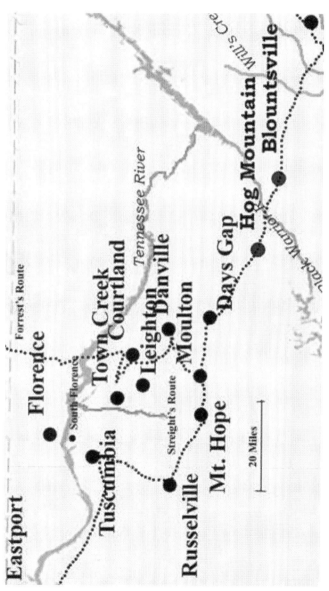

"And Dodge is camped to the west of Town Creek, here, you say?" Forrest said, looking down at Roddey's small map spread out on the table before them.

"Yes, sir. We gave ground before them all day yesterday, harried them constantly, slowed them down until dark when they halted for the night. Then we retired here to Courtland to rest the horses and await your arrival. My scouts report that, except for the rain that flooded the river, all is as it was when we left Town Creek last night."

Forrest nodded, stared at the map, sipping on the scalding hot coffee and thinking. "What artillery does Dodge have with him, Colonel?" he asked absently, not taking his eyes from the map.

"Three batteries, General. Eighteen guns, most of them Parrotts or ordnance rifles."

"Eighteen, eh," Forrest said, thoughtfully. "We cannot allow them to get them guns across the river. Is all ready, Colonel?"

"It is, sir, and has been since before you arrived."

"Yes, well," Forrest said, drily. "Good for you, Colonel. Let's away then, and give these Blue Bellies a taste of Southern hospitality."

By five o'clock that morning, Forrest was back in the saddle, covered from head to toe in a black oilskin, on a fresh and very high-strung white stallion. Accompanied by Colonel Roddey, Forrest was at the head of his division, some 3800 hundred officers and men, in columns of fours, heading west out of Cortland at the canter toward Tuscumbia.

An hour later, with the exception of Dibrell's brigade, which was still at Florence, Forrest's Cavalry Division, was enroute to Town Creek some ten miles west of Courtland.

General Dodge had arrived on the west bank of Town Creek at midnight and had camped his army several hundred yards to the west of the river. In the early hours of the morning, he had received reports from several of his scouts that Forrest was approaching with a large

177

force of cavalry, but was not expected to arrive at Town Creek before seven-thirty, thus he had roused his army before first light.

By the time Forrest arrived, the Federal brigades were already in line of battle some three hundred yards west of the river. General Dodge and his staff were on horseback on top of a high ridge just to the rear of the battle line, waiting, watching, and making ready to cross the river.

But Forrest, typically, was early. His philosophy had long been that *victory goes to the one that gets there first with the most,* and this encounter would be no exception to the rule. Thus, by six o'clock, Forrest's division was less than a mile to the east of Town Creek and could see the smoke of the Federal campfires spiraling upward over the trees in the distance. Forrest's force was hidden from the enemy by vast stands of scrub and pine trees that lay between them and the river.

Forrest ordered the division into line, by file – line abreast – and to move slowly forward through the trees and scrub. This effectively put his division into line of battle, but still mounted. Forrest and Roddey, together with Forrest's staff forward of the line, walked their horses through the forest. For ten minutes they breasted their way through the undergrowth, until, finally, they reached the edge of the woodland, a half-mile from the riverbank. Forrest quickly raised his arm, a silent order to halt. Twenty yards to the rear, the Confederate brigades halted, and they waited.

Forrest reached down, lifted the lid of a stiff leather pouch fixed to his saddle and pulled forth a large pair of field glasses. For a moment, he ranged them back and forth over the seemingly sleeping Federal encampment. Then, just behind the enemy camp, and to the right, on top of a high ridge, he spotted a small gathering of Federal officers. They, too, were scanning the opposite side of the river, Forrest's side.

Forrest grinned, banged Roddey's left arm with his glasses, then indicated the small group on the hill a little more than a mile away and well beyond the river.

"General Dodge, I fancy," he whispered, handing the glasses to Roddey.

Roddey peered through the glasses, handed them back to Forrest, nodding his agreement as he did so.

"So, quietly, now, move back, dismount the men, and have Mr. Morton bring up his guns, as quietly as possible."

Captain John Morton, Forrest's Chief of Artillery, at twenty years old, was young for a captain, much less for a captain of artillery, and he looked even younger. Those who didn't know would swear that he looked no more than fifteen years old. It was a look that belied an insightful military commander, and a brain that could compute distance, range, and trajectory accurately, and almost instantaneously. He was tall, slim, weighed no more than 140 pounds, clean-shaven with wavy fair hair that framed a thin, boyish face. His uniform hung loosely about him, the red kepi was set jauntily upon his head, and if he was ever excited, he rarely showed it. He was a master of self-control, and did not suffer fools lightly.

By six-thirty that morning, all eight of Morton's guns were in line fifteen feet back from the edge of the line of trees, hidden from the enemy.

Forrest, now dismounted, field glasses in hand, walked to the edge of the trees, and again scoured the far side of the river and the ridge upon which the Federal officers were still grouped. He pulled a large silver pocket watch from an inside pocket of his coat, flipped it open and noted the time. It was six-forty, the rain had stopped, the sky was clearing and, to the east, a watery sun was about to lift itself above the treetops.

He returned to where Morton was standing beside one of the steel, three-inch Rodman rifles. "John," he said, quietly, "do you see that group on the hill?"

Morton nodded.

"Good. Now, John, see if you can put a Hotchkiss among them."

179

Morton had his gun crew load the designated exploding shell into the gun. It was done with hardly a word spoken among the crew. Morton adjusted the alignment slightly, turned the elevating wheel a full turn, took a firm grasp on the lanyard, then stepped back, satisfied. He looked up at Forrest, an unspoken question.

Forrest, a grim smile on his face, nodded, and Morton pulled the lanyard, BAM!

The range was a little more than a mile to the top of the hill, some 2100 yards. Morton had estimated the elevation at 5.3 degrees. The shot was good. The hang time was almost seven seconds, and the Confederate officers watched as the shell arched up and over the river, then down again into the midst of the already scattering officers. Unfortunately – fortunately for the Federal officers – the shell did not explode. Instead, it slammed into the earth, already made soft by the overnight rain, pitched a fountain of dirt skyward, and buried itself.

"They are here, then," Dodge said to no one in particular, stating the obvious, and more than a little disconcerted at Forrest's early arrival.

With the arrival of Morton's shell, Dodge and his staff had ridden quickly from the hill and away to the rear, to higher ground west of his encampment, well out of range of Forrest's artillery. Still on horseback, he scoured the distant line of trees for signs of the enemy. He could see none; visibility was poor and Forrest's force was well hidden.

All four of Dodge's brigades were already in line of battle, one behind the other, and had been making ready to attempt a river crossing. No easy task due to the state of the river, but now with the enemy already present on the opposite side, it would take some rethinking.

"Colonel Sheets," Dodge said, never taking his eyes from his glasses. "Have Major Booth bring up the artillery, all three batteries, and put them in position, forward of the rise, over there." He pointed, indicating a depression some 300 yards west of the river, and almost

1200 yards from the line of trees that still hid Forrest and his division. The trees themselves were almost hidden by a light ground mist. The river was a raging torrent, almost ten feet above flood level, swollen by the downpour of the past two days. Dodge had to get his troops across if he was to do Forrest any real damage. It took Booth less than ten minutes to get his guns unlimbered, in line, and ready for the commanding general's next order.

"We must get across the river," Dodge said, thoughtfully. "How far away is the railroad bridge?" he asked Colonel Cornyn.

The Federal cavalry commander rose up in the saddle and tried to look to the north, but the view was hidden from him by the terrain. "Perhaps a half-mile, General, maybe a little more."

"Send a small party to take a look at it, if you please, Colonel, and have them report back soonest."

Second Lieutenant Jonas Carvill and five troopers were duly dispatched to the Memphis and Charleston Railroad Bridge. They arrived there within minutes, walked their horses across the bridge, encountered no resistance, and observed no enemy presence. But enemy presence there certainly was. Forrest was well aware of the railroad bridge and, upon arrival at Town Creek, the first thing he had done was deploy Colonel Edmonson and his 11th Tennessee Calvary to guard the bridge, but with strict orders to lie low under cover of the trees east of the bridge, and under no circumstances was he to open fire unless the enemy attempted a crossing in force. Thus, Edmonson and his men watched as the six Federal troopers crossed over the bridge, stood for a moment, looking up and down the line of trees, then turning again to re-cross the bridge and ride away to the southwest and General Dodge.

As soon as the Federal troopers were out of sight, Edmonson sent a courier to Forrest to inform him of the situation. Thirty minutes later, the courier returned with orders for Edmonson to stay in position and make ready to receive the enemy as they attempted a crossing, upon which he was to defend the bridge against all hazards, and that a section of Morton's battery, two twelve-pounder Napoleon guns, was

181

on its way to support him. He was also told to expect the enemy within the hour.

"The bridge is clear, General," Carvill said upon his arrival back on the hill. "We found no sign of enemy activity on either side."

"Good, very good, but that, I am very much afraid, will not be the case for very long. Lieutenant Carvill, please ride to Mr. Booth and convey to him my orders. Quickly, now!" He handed Carvill a folded sheet of paper. Carvill took it from him, opened his tunic, shoved the paper inside, saluted Dodge, spun his horse, and rode away at a gallop.

On the far side of the river, Forrest and Roddey watched as Carvill rode quickly down the hill and into the depression where Booth was at his guns.

"Not long now, Colonel," Forrest said to Roddey.

"Mr. Morton, you may open fire, sir. The targets are the enemy artill–"

KABAM! An enemy solid shot slammed into one of Morton's bronze Napoleon guns, smashing its carriage and sending the barrel cartwheeling into the air, and its crew scattering in all directions. Other than putting the gun out of action, and a shard of spinning wood from the gun carriage inflicting a nasty face wound to the gun sergeant, no one was hurt.

"Go to it, Mr. Morton," Forrest shouted.

BAM, BAM, BAM, BAM, BAM. All five remaining guns of Morton's battery opened fire, one after the other. Two seconds later, Booth's battery was on the receiving end of five exploding Hotchkiss shells. Due to Booth's battery being out of plain sight of the Confederate battery, they did little harm; the same was true for Booth's artillery – they, too, could not see the enemy. The artillery battle that now commenced was one where each side was firing blindly at the other, with little serious effect, other than to keep the heads of both sides down, and under cover. And they did. For now, at least, both commanders realized that, with the distances involved, there was no point in expending small arms ammunition, especially the Confederate cavalry carbines. This was an artillery duel, pure and simple.

For more than two hours, the two sides hurled barrage after barrage at one another, all to little or no effect. From solid shot to exploding shells, and even bar and grape shot, though at a range of more than a thousand yards the bar and grape were of little use.

Slowly, the trees behind which the Confederate cavalry had taken cover were stripped of their foliage. They were forced to draw back fifty yards more, giving General Dodge the opportunity to move some of his infantry forward toward the riverbank.

General Dodge was adamant that his forces must cross the river, and soon.

"General Sweeny," Dodge said to the commander of the Federal First Brigade. "We cannot delay any longer. We must get the division and the artillery across the river as quickly as possible. You will move the First north and cross over at the railroad bridge, which is certain by now to be defended. If all goes well there, you will send word back to me immediately."

To say that Dodge and Sweeny did not get along would be an understatement. Sweeny, a career military officer, had little respect for what he called 'part-time soldiers,' nor was he impressed with political appointees, which Dodge was. He made no attempt to hide his dislike for his commanding general, or his lack of respect. And so, on hearing that he was assigned to what Dodge considered the most difficult task he could assign him, he simply snorted and walked away, leaving Dodge, teeth clamped together, staring after him.

"Colonel Bane," Dodge said to the commander of the Federal Third Brigade. "You will immediately move into the position left open by General Sweeny. You will then have one of your regiments move to the riverbank and begin felling trees to form two, no three, footbridges; Major Booth will provide artillery cover. As soon as the bridges are complete, you will move the Third across the river and engage the enemy.

"Colonels Mersey and Fuller, as soon as the First and Third Brigades are across the river, you will follow in quick time with the Second and Fourth. Colonel Cornyn, you will ready yourself to provide cavalry support wherever it might be needed, and to assist Major Booth with his crossing. Questions, gentlemen?" There were none. "Good luck, then, and may God be with you."

Brigadier General Sweeny was not a big man, a little over five feet nine inches tall with a full head of black hair and a luxurious full beard. At forty-three, he was somewhat older than Dodge's other three brigade commanders, and he looked it, but that was not really surprising considering his checkered military career.

Sweeny was an expatriate Irishman, born in Cork on Christmas Day in 1820. He came to the United States in 1833 and, during the voyage across the Atlantic, he managed to get himself washed overboard. After more than a half-hour in the frigid waters, he was hauled back aboard, little the worse for the experience.

In 1846, the restless Irishman enlisted as a second lieutenant in Burnett's New York Volunteers. He fought in the Mexican War under General Winfield Scott and was wounded in the groin at the Battle of Cerro Gordo. He was wounded again in the Battle of Churubusco, this time in the right arm, so severely that the arm had to be amputated. For his heroism, he was nicknamed "Fighting Tom." Despite his debilitating injuries, he continued serving with the 2nd US Infantry until the outbreak of the Civil War. In 1861, he was commissioned Brigadier General and given command of the 52nd Illinois. He commanded the 52nd at Fort Donelson. At Shiloh, in command of a full brigade, he was wounded three times more, twice in his remaining arm and once in the leg. As roughly as his military career had treated him, he had lost none of his enthusiasm or ardor. When the time came for him to fight, his Irish blood rose, and he took on an air of invincibility.

And so it was that, at ten o'clock that morning, Sweeny, quietly whistling Gary Owen as he marched, arrived at the head of his brigade on the western side of the Memphis and Charleston Railroad Bridge. They were not alone.

Just beyond the line of trees on the far side of the Bridge, Colonel Edmonson's Confederate brigade, dismounted, in line of battle, with two artillery pieces loaded with canisters and ready to fire, was waiting.

No sooner had General Sweeny's leading regiment crested the rise, than Edmonson gave orders for the gun crews to fire.

BAM, BAM. The two great guns reared upward and backward, then slammed down again on their wheels, the two gun crews already moving quickly to reload.

Across the bridge, the Federal infantry, not expecting opposition, was thrown into a panic as more than a hundred one-inch iron balls, hurtled over the bridge and, fortunately, just over their heads. No one was hurt, but the blue-clad column dispersed right and left on either side of the railroad, and dropped flat on the ground, taking what cover they could from fallen trees and rocks. Sweeny, no longer whistling, stood his ground, glaring at nothing he could see beyond the far end of the bridge. And there he continued to stand, seemingly oblivious of the hail of Confederate Minnie balls howling around him like a swarm of angry hornets, until one of his officers jumped on his back and threw him to the ground, growling and swearing as only an Irishman can.

For more than an hour, Sweeny's brigade swapped fire across the river, the Confederate forces holding the advantage of two field guns and their hidden positions in the tree.

Sweeny's men were effectively pinned down, but that did not stop them hurling thousands of rounds at the unseen enemy. Miraculously, casualties on either side were minimal. Sweeny's brigade, up until eleven o'clock, had suffered less than a dozen men wounded, the Confederates only six. All that, however, was about to change.

No self-respecting, hot-blooded Irishman could suffer being pinned down like Sweeny was. His brigade consisted of three regiments: the 52nd Illinois, the 66th Indiana, and the 2nd Ohio. These were commanded respectively by Lieutenant Colonel John Wilcox, Colonel DeWitt Anthony, and Colonel James Weaver, and together they included some 1300 men.

Under covering fire from his front lines, Sweeny and four staff officers ran, heads down, zigzagging through the long grass to a small depression one hundred yards to the rear. The weather was cool and damp, but Sweeny was sweating profusely when finally he sat down on the grassy slope, out of sight and danger from the Confederate enemy.

"Captain Cranmer," he said, gesturing for the officer to join him. "Go to Colonels Wilcox, Anthony, and Weaver, and have them join me here as quick as they can. And keep your bloody head down, *boyo*."

And then he waited, head back against the slope, breathing hard, sweating. He opened two of the top buttons of his frock coat and pulled the collar open, revealing the neck of his bright red undershirt. When Cranmer returned at the run, with the three colonels in tow, he was agitatedly mopping his brow and neck with an emerald green square of silk, a gift from a lady friend.

"Ah, so there you are," he shouted, as the four men breasted the top of the depression. "Sit down and rest a moment and listen to me.

"This standoff is bloody ridiculous. Those rascals over there have us nicely pinned down. We must get our people across the bridge, so here's what we'll do.

"Colonel Wilcox, you will move the 52nd to the north of the bridge and form a line of three ranks. You, Colonel Weaver, will close the gap left by Colonel Wilcox and form your men up in line to the south of the bridge, also in three ranks. Colonel Anthony, you an' the 66th are with me. We are going to bust across that bridge and capture those bloody guns."

He looked at his three regimental commanders, eyes wide in question. "Nothin' to say, have yeh? Good, now then, we know roughly where those bloody guns are, so, when me and Colonel Anthony here charge the bridge, you two will open fire by rank and you will keep on firing until the last man of the 66th clears the end of the bridge. At that point, you will form your regiments and follow me, post haste, over the water, right?"

Again, the three officers had nothing to say; they were well aware of Sweeny's military acumen, and that he was an aficionado of British military tactics, one of which he had just ordered. All three men and their respective regiments were fully conversant with and well-practiced in the tactic of Volley Fire.

"So, then," Sweeny continued. "Go, gentlemen, to your commands. When all is ready, send word, but DO NOT open fire until you hear me shout the word, NOW! Understood? Good, away you go then, and be quick about it; time's a wastin'."

While Weaver and Wilcox were moving their regiments, Sweeny was also on the move. He and Colonel Anthony spent several minutes going from company to company, explaining what was about to happen. By eleven-thirty, Sweeny was in position with Anthony at the head of the 66th, under cover, just thirty yards or so to the west of the bridge. He had received word that Weaver and Wilcox were ready and waiting.

BAM, BAM. The two Confederate guns roared, and Sweeny waited until the canister balls had screamed over, head high, then he jumped to his feet and shouted, "NOW," at the top of his lungs, and then charged onto the bridge.

As Sweeny and Anthony, followed by more than five hundred screaming infantrymen, charged onto the bridge, Colonels Weaver and Wilcox stood, stepped forward, then turned and faced their men.

"FRONT RANK... FIRE!"

To the north and south of the bridge, some three hundred men in the front rank fired their rifles together. It was a horrendous noise, not the usual ripple of fire, but a single huge explosion as they pulled their triggers together.

"MIDDLE RANK... FIRE!"

"REAR RANK... FIRE!"

"FRONT RANK ... FIRE!"

As soon as the front rank fired, they dropped to the ground and reloaded their rifles. As they were doing so, the middle rank fired, and then they too dropped and began to reload. And then the rear rank did the same. As they did so, the front rank, having completed their loading, rose to their feet and the cycle began again. A well-trained rifleman could load and fire his Springfield rifle three times per minute. Thus a brigade, firing by rank, could fire a volley every six seconds. The overall effect of this was an almost continuous volley of Minnie balls howling across the river, into the Confederate positions. So concentrated was the rate of fire that neither the gun crews nor the dismounted cavalry could return fire. It was now their turn to be pinned down.

General Sweeny and the 66th charged across the bridge, howling and screaming as they went. As they ran off the bridge, they split and charged the trees in line. Back on the western side of the bridge, Colonels Weaver and Wilcox gave the order to cease firing and ordered their regiments to form up in column of fours and follow the 66th across the bridge.

Confederate Colonel Edmonson was no coward, but he immediately grasped the situation. Sweeny's leading elements were closing rapidly on his artillery. He quickly ordered them to limber the guns and get them out of danger. As they went to work, Edmonson had his troopers concentrate their fire to protect them. At the same time, he ordered the bugler to sound the retreat. It was over, at least for him.

By noon, Sweeny was in command of the bridge on both sides of the river, Confederate Colonel Edmondson having conducted an orderly, fighting retreat. He had denied General Sweeny the capture of his two guns, something he would not, under any circumstances, have wanted to report to General Forrest.

"Now then, Captain Cranmer," Sweeny said, as he sat down on top of one of the wooden pilings that supported the bridge, a little breathless from his exertions. "Go you to General Dodge, offer him my compliments, and inform him that the railroad bridge is taken, and that the way is open should he wish to take advantage of it."

Cranmer saluted Sweeny and ran back across the bridge, turned south, and went in search of General Dodge.

Dodge, however, was not pleased to see Cranmer, though he did grudgingly acknowledge the capture of the bridge. He was not about to give Sweeny the pleasure of providing the way across the river. All morning long, Bane's brigade had been felling trees so that they fell to lie across the raging waters of the river. By eleven-thirty, they had managed to build three tenuous bridges at the narrowest points, and Dodge's three remaining brigades were preparing to attempt a crossing.

"Captain Cranmer, you will return to General Sweeny with my compliments and inform him that we now have no need of the bridge and that we are preparing to make the crossing. Tell him also that he is to advance along the riverbank and attempt to turn the enemy's flank and drive him southward. You may go, Captain." Then Dodge turned away and left Cranmer staring after him.

When Captain Cranmer returned, General Sweeny was already assembling his brigade on the eastern shore of the river. He laughed aloud when the captain told him what Dodge had said and slapped him on the shoulder. "And why am I not surprised, do you think? No, never mind, Captain, don't answer that, someone might hear you."

Sweeney listened intently to the rest of what Cranmer had to say, and then gave the necessary orders to his regimental commanders to ready the brigade for the advance southward toward Forrest's right flank.

To the west, General Forrest and Colonel Roddey had been joined by Colonel Edmonson. Forrest was not pleased with the way things were going. Already he knew that Sweeny was across the river and preparing to move south. And he could see that Dodge, too, was ready to attempt a crossing. That in itself would not have been a problem, had it not been for the fact that if Sweeny were to suddenly appear on his right flank, he would be caught between two fires, and that, Forrest would never allow to happen. He was, in fact, preparing to withdraw to the east.

It was a few minutes after noon when a rider, James Mahoon, one of Roddey's scouts, came skidding to a halt behind Forrest. His horse was lathered and breathing hard, its rider disheveled.

"General Forrest, sir," the rider gasped between breaths.

Forrest was directing fire from a section of Morton's battery, and was himself in a state of agitation and in no mood for trivial matters.

"Yes, Mahoon, what is it?" Forrest shouted, impatiently, recognizing the trooper as one he had sent earlier to keep watch on the enemy situation across the river to the southwest.

"Sir, a large force of mounted infantry has separated from the rear of the enemy column and is heading southeast toward Moulton."

"How many is a large force, Mahoon?"

"It's hard to say, General, at least 1500, maybe more."

"Southeast, you say?"

"Yes, General, and, sir, they are on mules."

Forrest thought for a moment. *What the hell is going on? Those damn mules again. Are they trying to flank me, I wonder? Well, no matter. For now, I need to get out of this mess. Then I can worry about the goddam mule soldiers.*

"Thank you, Mahoon. You may rejoin your regiment," he said, turning once more to watch the two gun crews as they fired load after load of canister across the river. The Federal artillery was maintaining a withering fire from the west, and men were already streaming across the hastily constructed bridges.

"Colonel Roddey. Colonel Edmonson, to me," Forrest shouted.

The Confederate commanders arrived at the run.

"It's time, I think, for us to leave this place. General Sweeny has crossed the river to the north and soon will be upon our right flank. Pull your men back; the enemy has the river."

It took only minutes for the Confederate commanders to begin a fighting withdrawal. The eight guns of Morton's battery were swiftly limbered and withdrawn. Slowly, rank by rank, the gray-clad regiments slipped away through the trees, firing as they went. By one o'clock, General Dodge was in command of both sides of the river. By two o'clock, his brigades were marching resolutely eastward in pursuit of Forrest. By four o'clock, Dodge had decided that enough was enough. He was now within three miles of Courtland and, from reports sent to him by Captain Spencer, he was under the impression that Forrest was retreating toward Decatur, some twenty miles to the east of Courtland. He was, however, still worried about the large Confederate force at Florence. If they were indeed planning a river crossing there, he would be caught between two fires, cut off from his headquarters in Mississippi. With that in mind, he ordered the pursuit to be called off. It was time, he thought, to return to Corinth.

Upon hearing that Dodge had ordered the pursuit to be called off, General Sweeny lost no time in riding to meet with the commanding general.

"Good God, General," Sweeny shouted, exasperated. "They are done, sir! Why in the name of all that's holy are we not going to finish them off? We outnumber 'em two-to-one."

"That, General Sweeny, is not why we are here. My orders were to provide a screen for Colonel Streight and delay any perceived enemy pursuit of the colonel's brigade. This I have done; the expedition has been a complete success, and I now propose to return to Corinth. I have other fish to fry, General. You are dismissed, sir."

Sweeny was astounded. As a career officer, he knew good and well that when you had the advantage of your enemy, you pressed it to its logical conclusion. You destroyed your enemy in total; you did not let him go to fight another day, a fight that might not go quite so well.

He also knew, however, that there was no point arguing with the general. The man was a buffoon with little to no military training or experience. Outranked by Dodge as he was, he had little option but to follow orders and, in true military fashion, that's exactly what he did. He saluted Dodge, and without bothering to wait for him to answer it, wheeled his horse and galloped away. He returned to his brigade, knowing full well that Dodge had made a monumental mistake and had misread Forrest completely.

By seven o'clock that evening, most of Dodge's force had re-crossed the river and had gone into camp, leaving only two regiments to guard the eastern approaches to the river.

General Forrest, however, far from retreating toward Decatur was in fact back at his headquarters in Courtland, in conference with Colonel Roddey.

Chapter 25

April 28, 1863. Confederate Headquarters, Courtland Alabama - 6pm

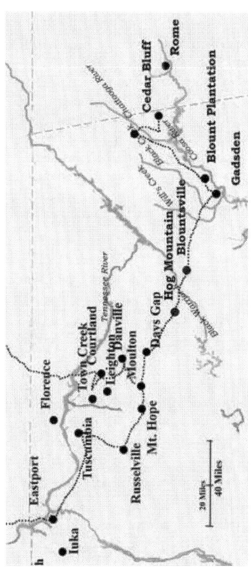

"What the hell are they up to?" Forrest said, quietly, more to himself than to Roddey. He looked up from the map, glanced sideways at him, and said, "What Dodge has been doing makes no sense. Why would he leave Corinth and come all this way? There's nothin' of value here. This is farm country. There has to be more to it."

He stared at the map and shook his head. "And why didn't Dodge press home his advantage? Instead, he followed us almost to Courtland, then turned around and headed back the way he'd come. And what the hell is that mounted brigade all about? They are certainly not on their way here, and Dodge doesn't need 'em anyways. He already has us outnumbered almost two-to-one."

Forrest stared thoughtfully down at the map. "They've traveled all the way from Nashville, more than eight hundred miles by river and land, but for what purpose.... And mules, too...." He shook his head, and then looked again at Roddey. "Any thoughts, Colonel?"

Roddey, too, stared down at the map, then said, "No, General, as you say, none of it makes any sense."

Together, they stood by the table in silence, heads bowed, staring at the map, their arms folded across their chests.

"It has to be about those Mule Soldiers, Phillip," Forrest said, thoughtfully. "If we can figure out what they are all about, we'll have an answer."

Roddey said nothing. Forrest unfolded his arms, placed both hands on the table, one on each side of the map and stared down at it, concentrating all his thoughts. With the forefinger of his left hand, he pointed to a spot on the map just west of Town Creek. "They are here, right?"

"Yes, General, they are now, but they were in Tuscumbia for almost three days."

"And what of the Mule Soldiers? Where are they?"

"I don't know exactly where they are, General. We now know that they parted from Dodge when he left Tuscumbia, and headed south, but.... Well, there have been no reports since Mahoon returned early this afternoon. He was sure that they were heading east toward Mount Hope and Moulton, but that makes no sense. Moulton is more than twenty miles to the south and, as far as I know, there's no good way to get here from there."

Forrest nodded his head, said nothing. For several minutes, he studied the map, then began tracing on it with his finger.

"Got it!" Forrest said, excitedly. "Rome, Phillip! It's Rome they're after. Dodge is just a diversion, look. Look at this whole area. There are absolutely no targets of value, anywhere, nothin'. But Rome. There's the railroad, the warehouses, the factories, even the bridge. That blasted mounted brigade is going after Rome. I'd bet my life on it. Have the regimental commanders report to me here for briefing, Colonel, and quickly. We have little time to waste. The longer we delay, the harder it will be to catch 'em."

The first to arrive was Colonel Edmonson.

Forrest began, "I do not trust what we are hearing, but I cannot discount it. I cannot believe that Dodge would come this far, more than a hundred miles, only to return to Corinth, achieving nothing. Take with you the 4th Alabama, Colonel Edmondson with the 11th, and Julian's battalion. You will cross the Bear Branch here." He pointed to a spot on the map. "There you will wait until morning. Should whosoever is in command of that mounted brigade turn north again, you will hold them there until I can reinforce you.

"As to Dodge," Forrest continued. "You, Colonel Hannon, will take the 53rd and return to Town Creek and find out what he's really about. If he is indeed on his way to Corinth, you will return here, soonest.

"That's all, gentlemen, at least for now. I expect to see you all back here before first light with news. I need to know exactly the disposition of all enemy forces.

195

"The rest of us need sleep. We have been on the road for five days and the men are exhausted. Get something to eat and settle down. We ride early in the morning."

By four-thirty on the morning of the 29th, the bugles were sounding Reveille. Men were rushing hither and thither, stirring campfire embers into life, making coffee, fixing breakfast, and preparing for what promised to be a long day. Forrest himself had risen at four and had already eaten and consumed two vast tin mugs of scalding hot coffee. By four-thirty he was washed, dressed, and had personally undertaken the supervision of the preparations for the pursuit of the Mule Soldiers.

The artillery was cleaned and inspected, caissons were replenished, horses were inspected and serviced as necessary, rations were issued for both men and horses, and by nine o'clock the division was ready to move out.

Chapter 26

April 28, 1863. Moulton, Alabama - Colonel Streight

The morning of the 28th dawned bleak, wet, and cold. Colonel Streight's hope that the rain would stop was a forlorn one not as heavy as it had been the day before, it made for a miserable beginning to the day. By first light, just after six-thirty, the men of Colonel Hathaway's regiment, the 73rd Indiana, were mounted and spread far and wide across the countryside around Mount Hope, searching for food and fresh mounts. The rest of the Mule Soldiers spent the morning preparing the brigade to move east.

At eight o'clock, Colonel Streight, having been provided with a good breakfast of eggs and ham by Dr. Templeton's daughter, left the house to make his rounds of the troops and their mounts. He stood for a moment on the front porch of the house and stared across the farmyard at the vast array of tents spread out across the farmer's fields. The campsite was a bustling hive of activity. Men were tending campfires, cooking breakfast, and grooming mounts. The aroma of cooking bacon and hot coffee wafted enticingly across the sodden acres. Leatherwork was being inspected and oiled, artillery was being cleaned and readied for action. Wagons were also being inspected; nuts and bolts were tightened, axels greased, and leathers oiled and replaced as needed. He took note of the acres of mud, shook his head, and glanced up at the still invisible, overcast sky; a light rain was falling steadily. He shuddered, pulled the collar of his oilskins up around his ears, settled his wide-brimmed hat a little more tightly upon his head, then stepped down from the porch and splashed through the muddy water toward the edge of the encampment.

For more than an hour, Streight wandered back and forth, inspecting men, horses, mules, wagons, and artillery, offering a greeting here, and a word or two of encouragement there. The men, for all the bad weather they had so far endured, and that they knew was yet to come, were in good spirits. Streight felt his own spirits begin to rise as he made his rounds.

By ten o'clock, the first of the foragers were beginning to return. The results of their expeditions were mixed. Some patrols had had no luck at all, but some, like that of Lieutenant Wade of Company G did well enough to compensate for those that didn't.

At around eight-thirty that morning, Wade had happened upon a plantation some six or seven miles to the south of Mount Hope. At first, the plantation appeared to be deserted. Upon searching the grounds, however, his men discovered two small houses and a large barn set together some distance from the main house, and out of sight behind a small rise. It was a fortuitous find: the houses were the refuge of the women of the big house. Between them, they had spirited away the horses, mules and a number of cattle. At the back of one of the houses, Wade discovered two large, flatbed wagons, each loaded with cured meat hidden under canvas covers.

Ignoring the protests of the women, Wade had his men round up the cattle, liberate the animals from the barn, hitch the mules to the two wagons. By nine-thirty, his small group was wending its way through the hills and dales back to the Templeton Plantation.

And they were not alone. In all, Streight's raiders made off with more than a hundred mules, forty-two horses, three wagon loads of animal feed, and enough meat to keep the brigade in food for several days. The local populace was devastated by their losses. Those who were able to prove their Union sympathies, and there were more than one might think, were compensated for their losses by Streight's quartermaster in Yankee greenbacks. Those with Confederate sympathies, well... they received nothing, their contributions to the Federal brigade being deemed the "fortunes of war."

By noon, Streight and his Mules Soldiers were back in the saddle and on the way east toward Moulton. The light rain made the going difficult, but not as bad as it had been the day before. They arrived in Moulton at four o'clock that afternoon, the 28th.

Streight called a halt and had his men bed down for the night. He gave orders that the animals were to be fed first, and then the men. Then he went off to find a place for himself.

Again, he found comfortable accommodations in the home of a local farmer and his family. Unlike Dr. Templeton's daughter, the farmer was not a Northern sympathizer, and he made it clear to Streight that he was not welcome. Streight smiled gently at the farmer, his wife and two small children, and tried to assure them that he meant them no harm, that he simply required a place to rest and a good meal.

The members of the family said nothing. The lady of the house stood behind her husband with her arms folded and a grim look on her face. The farmer, blocking the entrance into the house, stood with his arms straight down by his sides, fists clenched, and refused to move.

"Sir, madam," Streight said, quietly. "You have no choice. If you will not accommodate me, I will have my men turn you out and I will accommodate myself. As I have already assured you, I mean you no harm, and I will disturb you and your family as little as possible. Now, sir, if you will be so good as to show me where I might lie down and rest for a while...."

Reluctantly, the farmer nodded, then moved to one side and allowed Streight to pass through the door and into what obviously was the main room of the small house. The lady of the house glared angrily at him, unfolded her arms and gestured with a switch of her head that Streight was to follow her. She showed him through to the back of the house and into a small room. It was, he could tell, the bedroom for at least two of the children. There were two beds, a small table, chest of drawers, children's clothes lying about, and several wooden toys on the floor. Quickly she gathered up the clothes and kicked the toys out of the way, then turned and flounced out of the room, leaving Streight behind, somewhat amused.

Amused he might have been, a fool he was not. He did not trust the farmer even a little, and he trusted his wife even less. And so, fearing for his life, he had a chair positioned outside the door of the bedroom, and had his adjutant detail four men to take turns, two hours each, to sit on guard outside the door. This made the farmer and his wife even angrier.

"You, sir," the farmer growled through gritted teeth, "are a scoundrel and a thief. Rest here, if you must, but I will not allow my wife to cook for you."

Streight nodded, then shouted for his aid. "Corporal Timms. To me, if you please."

The corporal entered the room and saluted.

"Timms, have one of the cooks report to me here as soon as possible. Then ask my senior officers to report here as soon as they have eaten. Oh, yes, and designate six men to escort these nice people off the property and to friends of their choosing."

The corporal saluted Streight and left. Streight turned and smiled gently at the farmer and his wife, then said, quietly, "I think you will be happier elsewhere. You need not worry. Your home is safe in my hands, and we will be gone at first light tomorrow, at which time you may return to your home. I wish you both a good night." Then he turned and walked into the bedroom, quietly closing the door behind him.

At seven-thirty that evening, a courier arrived from General Dodge with news of the situation to the north; it was not good news, at least as far as Streight was concerned.

The dispatch stated first that Dodge had driven the Confederate forces from Town Creek all the way to Courtland. At this, Streight smiled. The missive then went on to say that Dodge now considered his duty done, and that he was returning to Corinth. This piece of news wiped the smile from his face. Even worse was the news that Colonel Roddey had been joined by General Forrest, and that Streight would be well advised to make all speed toward his objective.

Streight sat very still on the small bed, staring into space, his mind a whirlpool of disconnected thoughts. Try as he might, he could not pull them together into any sort of order that made sense.

He took out his pocket watch, noted the time, then rose from the bed and walked to the front door where he found a private on guard outside. He dispatched the guard to find his senior officers and request that they join him immediately.

Ten minutes later, all six men and Streight were crammed into the small living room. Streight, Colonels Sheets and Hathaway were seated; Colonels Lawson, Rogers, Captain Smith and Major Vananda stood with their backs to the walls.

"So, gentlemen," Streight began. "I have only moments ago received a dispatch from General Dodge. It seems we have been abandoned, left on our own to face whatever the enemy may throw at us."

He then went on to relay to them the contents of the dispatch. When he had finished, he looked at them, each in turn, and asked, "Your thoughts, gentlemen?" It was a question that no one wanted to answer.

"Well then," he said, "let me give you mine. We, sirs, are in trouble; a great deal of trouble. General Dodge has left too quickly, and we are now a full day more behind schedule. Look here." He pointed to a point on the map already spread out on the table before him.

"This is Courtland, Roddey's field headquarters. This is Moulton, where we are. From there to here is no more than fifteen miles as the crow flies; twenty, perhaps twenty-two, by road, and there is now nothing to stop them coming after us. As far as we know, they could already be just beyond the next hill. We must leave here as soon as possible. Colonel Hathaway, send scouts to Courtland. We need to know the disposition of the enemy. If they are already on the road, I want to know who and how many. I have no doubt that it will be General Forrest himself.

"Colonel Sheets, gentlemen, prepare your commands to move out immediately. We leave as soon as you are ready. No delays, gentlemen; no delays." He stood, saluted his officers, then spun on his heel and left the room to prepare himself for the coming journey and the perils that he was now sure lay ahead.

By ten o'clock that evening, Hathaway's scouts, one by one, were returning, all with good news. One had even managed to penetrate the enemy lines at Courtland itself and was able to report that, although the Confederate camp was a hive of activity, there was no sign that the enemy was on the move, at least not yet. Streight, somewhat relieved by the good news, continued with the preparations to leave Moulton.

By eleven o'clock, the preparations were complete, and the long column was again on the road eastward, and it was still raining. By late afternoon the following day, the 29th, they had covered slightly more than sixteen miles and had camped for the night in a shallow gorge five miles to the west of Sand Mountain.

Chapter 27

April 29, 1863. Confederate Column - Pursuit Begins

The morning of the 29th dawned bright and clear; the rain had stopped and the pale blue skies were a tapestry of scudding white clouds.

Brigadier General Nathan Bedford Forrest slept later than usual that morning. He awoke to the sound of his orderly pouring water into the basin on the table at the side of his cot.

"Good morning, General," the orderly said, ducking quickly out through the flap of the tent.

"Umph." Forrest stretched, threw back the covers, and reached for his pocket watch; it was a few minutes after six o'clock. For a moment he lay back on the cot, relaxed, rested, listening to the sounds of the camp already busy preparing for the business of the day ahead. As always, Forrest had slept well. Very little ever bothered him enough to cause him loss of sleep.

He stretched once more, rubbed his eyes, and rose from the cot. His morning preparations were carried out on a strict routine. First, he washed his face with a soft cloth and small piece of lightly scented soap and shaved. Then, he cleaned his teeth on a piece of damp cloth dipped in salt. Next, he combed his hair and beard, and then he began to dress. First, a clean white shirt, a black ribbon tie, gray uniform britches, black suspenders and black, knee-length leather boots. He'd barely pulled them on when his orderly returned with a heaping plate of bacon, eggs and fried bread, and a tin cup full of steaming coffee.

He laid the tray on the cot, removed the bowl of water from the small side table, and placed the tray with food upon it.

The orderly ducked out through the flap, leaving Forrest eating hungrily. He finished the meal quickly, put the plate aside, downed a swallow of the coffee, and stepped out of the tent.

It would be a fine day. The air was crisp and cold, the dew glittered on the deep green grass, and a slight mist hung in the trees still wet from the night rain. The sun was already visible, a watery, yellow disc in the eastern sky peeking above the line of the trees.

A good day for a fight, Forrest thought, taking several deep breaths.

He turned and went back into the tent, letting the flap fall back into place behind him. He raised the mug to his lips and drained the last of the coffee, grounds and all. Then he took his knee-length, uniform frock coat from its hangar, slipped into it, and buttoned it almost to the throat. He turned down the collar, fingered the embroidered gold stars and wreath that were the symbols of his rank, then turned and reached for his leather belt. He strapped the belt around his waist, adjusted the position of the LeMat revolver at his right side, and shrugged his shoulders several times to adjust the fit of the heavy uniform coat. Finally, he looked again at his reflection in the mirror that hung on the tent pole, teased the beard, nodded to himself, pleased with his appearance. He was now ready for the day ahead. He looked again at his watch, noted the time – a little after seven – took his hat from its peg, and ducked out through the flap of the tent.

The remaining brigades of the Confederate cavalry, twelve hundred troopers in column of threes, cantered out of the camp at Courtland a little after nine o'clock on the morning of the 29th, heading toward Moulton, some twenty miles away to the south. Forrest, little knowing that the Mule Soldiers had left Moulton before midnight the previous evening, was in a particularly good mood. This was what he lived for. He turned in the saddle and looked back. The banners and guidons of his escort and regiments fluttered and snapped in the breeze. The long column of troopers stretched away into the far distance, so long its end was hidden, out of sight beyond a low hill to the north. It was a grand sight and one that never failed to stir his blood.

By late afternoon, they were in Danville, four miles north of Moulton. It was already growing dark, so Forrest decided to bivouac for the night and rest the men and horses. A little after seven o'clock, Colonels Roddey and Edmondson rejoined the column, bringing its strength to just over two thousand.

Forrest already knew from his scouts that the Mule Soldiers had left Moulton and were on their way west into the mountainous country around Days Gap and Sand Mountain but, ever wary, he sent scouts to reconnoiter all possible routes the Federal raiders might take.

Like everything else about Forrest's command, his company of scouts was something of an anomaly. Led by his younger brother, Captain William (Bill) Forrest, they were a band at company-strength of forty (give or take, depending upon the situation) of unpaid mercenaries known throughout the Western Department of the Confederacy as the "Forty Thieves." Although the younger Forrest was a commissioned Confederate officer, his scouts were not part of the military. Unpaid though they might be, these erstwhile raiders rarely went short of anything and were, in fact, experts in the art of the forage, and its associated trading. The Forty Thieves were given free license, officially, to forage for and keep whatever they could find and confiscate. They were moderately wealthy men, and they loved both Bill and General Forrest unconditionally.

On reaching Danville, the Forty Thieves were given time only to feed and water their mounts and themselves before they were dispatched in pursuit of the Mule Soldiers.

Captain Bill Forrest, with Will Steiner on one side, and Sam Corbett and Isaac Bogs on the other, followed by the rest of his company of scouts, left Danville around seven o'clock that evening. By ten, they were approaching the perimeter of the Federal encampment.

Although the night was clear, there was no moon. Forrest could tell, however, from the glow of a half-a-hundred campfires that they were approaching a sizable encampment. They were several hundred yards out and the company had already slowed their horses to a slow walk, when he called a halt.

In whispers, Forrest discussed the options with his three lead scouts. A course of action was quickly decided upon, and the company was split into two sections with Forrest and Steiner at the head of one section. Corbett, with Boggs, would lead the other.

Quietly, the section led by Corbett and Boggs split away and rode at the walk to the west. The plan was that Forrest and twenty men would stay where they were and wait for twenty minutes, time enough they had all agreed for Corbett and Boggs' men to circle to the rear of the encampment and come up on the south side of it.

While they waited for the second group to get into position, Forrest had his men dismount and tether their horses; they would travel the rest of the way on foot. Meanwhile, they stood and waited, under cover of darkness and the surrounding scrubland.

At approximately ten-thirty, Forrest, assuming that the second group were by now in position on the far side of the Federal encampment, signaled for his men to follow him. Like ghosts, they crept toward the flickering campfires.

The Federals had camped at the bottom of a shallow gorge. Hundreds of small tents were scattered across the bottom of the depression. All was quiet. Many of the fires had burned low, most of the Federals were already abed. Only a dozen men were still awake, sitting beside the fires, smoking or cooking.

All around the encampment, in every direction, on the high ground, were mounted sentries. These were quickly and quietly overpowered, hog-tied and gagged, and then left lying on the damp forest floor.

Captain Bill Forrest made a quick and approximate assessment of the Federal numbers, then sent a rider back to Danville to inform General Forrest of the situation and disposition of the enemy. Then, the Forty Thieves wrapped themselves in blankets and settled down under the trees to await the morning. Most of them slept fitfully in the cold night air, some slept not at all, simply dozing as the night hours slipped by. Then, at around four-thirty in the morning, it began. A raucous, cacophonous din echoed out of the gorge and around the forest beyond. It was the most ungodly sound, a sound like none any of them had ever heard before.

Forrest's men rose up out of their blankets, eyes and mouths wide open, bordering on sheer terror. As they listened, the noise continued unabated. Forrest pulled himself together, signaled for his men to follow him and all twenty-one men crept to the edge of the gorge and stared down into the melee below. Some thirteen hundred mules were demanding their breakfast, milling about inside their temporary compound, and each and every one of them was braying loudly for their food.

Forrest collapsed backward onto the damp grass, laughing silently, holding his side with one hand, the other clasped tightly over his mouth, He was not alone; every man of them was rolling about on the forest floor, trying hard not to make a sound, but it was impossible. Soon they were all hooting, hollering and cackling so hard they were in tears. Fortunately, the noise of their mirth was drowned out by the cacophony in the gorge below.

Forrest and his men watched for several more minutes as hundreds of Federal soldiers burst from their tents in various states of dress. Officers were running this way and that, trying to bring order to the uproarious situation. But it was no good; the mules insisted on being fed. Only after thirty minutes and many hundreds of buckets of feed later did the noise subside to natural levels. By then, Bill Forrest and the Forty Thieves were once again in the saddle and heading back to Danville.

By eight o'clock that morning, the 30th of April, the long column of Mule Soldiers, by some miracle, was also on the road heading east toward Days Gap, leaving only a rearguard of the 1st Alabama Cavalry under the command of Captain David Smith. Smith and men lingered in the gorge, cooking breakfast and generally taking it easy, totally unaware that their position was now known to the enemy, and that they were already on the way toward them.

Chapter 28

April 30, 1863. Streight on the Road to Days Gap

Thursday, April 30, dawned bright and clear, with no sign of the rain that had dogged Streight for almost a week. The call of the hungry mules came as no real surprise to any of the members of the Provisional Brigade. They were all used to it and, for as long as they could remember it seemed, they had treated the early morning cacophony as a wakeup call with no need at all for Reveille.

Colonel Streight also woke to the sound of the mules and, as he took note of the clear sky, he was feeling a little more optimistic about his chances of success. And Streight was no man's fool. He was a skilled and experienced commander, and he knew beyond a doubt that his pursuers could not be far behind him. Thus, at the earliest opportunity, he got his brigade back on the road, heading east to Sand Mountain, leaving Captain Smith and the 1st Alabama Cavalry in command of the camp. They had orders to bring up the rear, keeping a sharp eye out for enemy activity and, should they observe any, delay it as best they could to allow Streight time to prepare. Smith did not have to wait long.

Streight's column, now moving quickly and easily along the dry road, was tightly grouped, though it stretched back for more than a mile. The tail end of it had barely cleared the perimeter of the gorge when the leading elements of General Forrest's cavalry arrived.

Forrest was also in an optimistic mood. The men were up and ready to move out at a moment's notice. His brother William and his scouts had arrived back in Danville just after seven o'clock in the morning and had immediately reported. He found the general already dressed and was in conference with his senior officers, a large map spread out before them on top of two small folding tables.

Forrest, along with Roddey, Edmondson and Colonels McLemore, Biffle and DeMoss (commanding the 4th, 9th and 10th Tennessee

Cavalry Regiments, respectively) each listened intently as Forrest the younger described the events of the night and morning. Each of them broke into a smile as he related the story of the "Mule Call."

"The gorge is here, General," Captain Forrest said, pointing to a spot on the map. "The enemy's strength is at least sixteen hundred effectives, maybe a few more, but not less."

"Do we know who is leading them?" Forrest asked, looking at his brother.

"No, sir."

"Well then, we must proceed assuming that whoever it might be is a competent commander. That being so, gentlemen, were it me in his position, I would assume that pursuit must be close at hand. Whoever it is knows that our scouts must soon discover his whereabouts.

"You say that you left the pickets bound and gagged." He looked at his brother, who nodded in return. "Then he already knows. I warrant, sirs, that he is by now long gone."

He looked down at the map, thought for a moment, then said, "Colonel Roddey. You, sir, along with Colonel McLemore, will take this northerly route." He traced the route on the map with his finger. "If they are taking the route I think they are taking, you will be riding parallel with them, almost side-by-side, in fact," he said with a grin. "You must make the best time you can, Colonel, and try to get in front of them, here, where the two roads join and become one. If you can do that, and we are behind them, we will have them, and this adventure will soon be over.

"The rest of you are with me. Captain Forrest, you and your scouts will lead the column. Away with you all, then, and God speed and God bless."

By eight o'clock that morning, General Forrest and 1200 of his troopers were on the road; the pursuit had begun in earnest.

By the time the Confederate column arrived at the gorge where the Mule Soldiers had camped for the night, only Streight's rearguard remained in the camp, some two hundred men. They were, it seemed, in no hurry to follow the brigade. Instead, they were eating a late breakfast.

Forrest, his brother William, Captain John Morton, Forrest's artillery chief, and several members of the Forty Thieves, including Will Steiner, Sam Corbett and Isaac Bogs, all still in the saddle, stood together under cover of the trees close to the rim of the gorge.

It seems," Forrest said, to no one in particular, "that we are too late; the chickens have left the coop."

There's no way we can get down there without them knowing... Hmmm... Who, I wonder, is running this farce?

"Mr. Morton, bring up two of the howitzers. Let's see if we can stir things up a little. Will," he continued, twisting in the saddle to look back at Steiner. "Go that way," he pointed east, "to the entrance of the canyon. Stay hidden, but when they run outta there, and run they surely will. I want you to grab one or two of them and bring 'em back here. I want to know who is in command of these fools."

Steiner and his two cohorts, accompanied by three more of Bill Forrest's scouts, slipped quietly away through the trees.

"Two rounds, Hotchkiss, Mr. Morton," Forrest said, as the artillerist supervised the positioning of the two, short-barreled bronze artillery pieces. "Over their heads, Mr. Morton, over their heads. You may fire when you're ready."

Morton gave the order to load, computed the range and adjusted the elevation of the two guns to ten degrees of elevation. Then he looked up at Forrest, who nodded his head once.

"FIRE!" Morton shouted.

BAM, BAM. The two explosive shells arched high into the air and then down again, slamming into the bank on the far side of the gorge where they exploded on contact, sending fountains of dirt and rock twenty feet into the air. Startled Federal soldiers raced to grab their equipment and mounts. Captain Smith and the 1st Alabama were mounted and galloping out of the gorge in just moments. Unfortunately, some of them were not quite as quick off the mark as they might have been. The leaders, tightly bunched, hurtled past Will Steiner's small party, who were well hidden behind a large patch of blackthorn and scrub. But then the numbers of retreating Federals thinned and Cobb, waiting a hundred yards closer to the canyon, watching the stragglers, yelled, "NOW!" And the five Confederate scouts in the forward position, dashed from the trees, just in time to confront three luckless Federals, a corporal and two privates.

On spotting Steiner, the three men hauled their horses to a long skidding stop, wrenched their heads around, kicked hard, and galloped furiously back into the canyon: bad mistake.

The three men galloped their horses to the end of the canyon, skittered to a stop, wheeled, and then tried without much success to control them. The horses, skittish, nervous, high-stepping back and forth, spinning, first this way and then that. All the while, their riders were pulling their carbines from their holsters, trying to hold their mounts still enough to be able to draw a bead on the six scouts, now spread out in a wide semi-circle, boxing them in, carbines at the ready.

"I seriously wouldn't do that," Steiner yelled, dropping his reins and bringing his carbine to his shoulder and aiming it at the corporal.

"Throw down your weapons, NOW!"

For a moment, the three Federals hesitated then did as they were told; the three brand new, Smith carbines fell to the dirt floor and three sets of hands rose slowly above three grim-faced heads.

"Well, now," Steiner said, walking his horse slowly forward. "Ain't that nice? Hope you boys 'preciate what we just did fo' y'all. War's over fo' yous. Nice quiet prison camp. Libby, I shouldn't wonder. But first, y'all have a meetin' to attend. Come now, boys. Gen'l Forrest is awaitin'."

211

The small party, three of the scouts to the front of the three Federals, and three to the rear, trotted out of the mouth of the canyon, turned left, and rode at the trot, through the trees to where General Forrest and his escort were waiting.

Forrest had decided to take advantage of the stop. The horses were hot and lathered, so he ordered a sixty-minute break so that the saddles could be removed and the horses cooled. He also ordered the rest of Bill Forrest's scouts into the canyon to gather whatever hot food and coffee they could find among the still smoldering camp fires and bring it back to be shared among as many of his troopers as possible. He was, by now, of the opinion that time was not as of the essence as he had thought it to be. Mounted or not, the Federal brigade was close at hand. He had time to plan his next move.

Forrest was seated, out in the open, under a tall shade tree on one side of a small clearing, drinking coffee with several of his officers when Steiner and his crew returned.

Quickly, the six scouts dismounted and dragged the three Federals from their saddles, tied their hands behind them with leather straps, then led them to where Forrest was talking quietly with his regimental commanders.

"Here you be, Gen'l Forrest," Steiner said, dragging the corporal forward.

Forrest simply nodded and looked over the rim of his tin cup at the corporal, who was shivering nervously.

"You cold, boy?" Forrest asked.

"No, sir."

"Then what you shakin' for?"

The corporal didn't answer. He simply shrugged his shoulders and looked away. In return, he received a kick to the back of his knees from Steiner, and almost fell.

"That'll do, Steiner," Forrest said, sharply. "You an' the rest of you boys go see to your horses. Be ready to mount up in thirty minutes, no more. Understood?"

The six men backed away, leaving the three Federals standing sheepishly in front of the general.

"Lieutenant Clarke," Forrest said to one of his aids. "Go bring up a seat for Corporal...?" He looked in askance at the now raggedy-looking man standing in front of him.

"Flint, sir. Corporal Flint.

"Sit you down then, Corporal Flint. Let's you an' me parlay a little, if you don't mind." It was said quietly, but there was no mistaking the mean-looking glint in Forrest's eyes as he stared intently at the Federal corporal.

The man sat down as ordered, his hands tied together and resting in his lap.

"So, Corporal Flint, and think hard before yo' answer. Who is in command of that Jackass Brigade yo're a part of?"

The question brought a loud snigger from the officers standing in a semi-circle around the two of them.

Corporal Flint tightened his lips, and Forrest thought that the man was not going to answer.

"Colonel Streight. Colonel Abel D. Streight is in command, sir."

"Streight, eh? I've heard of him. Good man, so I'm told. And how many men, exactly, does the good colonel command, and where are they going?"

"That, General, sir, I'm not 'quired to tell." And he clenched his teeth tightly together, turned his face slightly to the left, dropped his chin a little, narrowed his eyes, and waited for the shoe to drop.

It didn't; Forrest leaned back in his seat and smiled. "How about I tell you the answer, Corporal? Rome?" He watched the corporal's face, and then grinned at his reaction. "Thought so. I don't have the time

213

for anymore such foolishness. Take these three fools away. Boots and Saddles, Mr. Clarke. Boots and Saddles."

It was noon when the Confederate column took to the road, following Colonel Streight and his Mule Soldiers along the narrow dirt and rocky road that led through Days Gap and on upward toward the top of Sand Mountain.

Colonel Streight, at the head of the Federal column, was already on top of the Sand Mountain plateau, about a mile-and-a-half out from the gorge, when he heard the two cannon blasts that announced the enemy's arrival at his late campground. The column stretched back for almost a mile and a half, but tightened up appreciably at the sound of the Confederate guns.

Now he was seriously concerned, but not for the first time. From the moment he had learned from General Garfield that his men were to be mounted on mules, he had been concerned. He knew his animals, and he knew how stubborn and unruly they could be, and he had been right. Not only were they stubborn and unruly, they kept his men up half the night and more with their constant braying and need for attention. But more than that, since first setting eyes upon them, when he noted their poor condition, he was concerned that they would not be able to make the long and strenuous journey. To date, he had lost almost two hundred of his mules to distemper and poor condition. True, the foraging had gone well, and he had been able to replace most of them, but still....

Now he was concerned about the men. After more than a week in the saddle, and none of them used to it, they were sore, tired, and irritable. The McClellan saddles had taken their toll on man and beast. The constant rain, the heavy wet woolen clothing, and the hard leather had worn the skin from buttocks and thighs, and the hair from the backs of the mules. Men and mules were covered in raw, weeping sores that were irritated, first from the rough and wet material, and now from the sand that inevitably infiltrated the men's clothing, exacerbating an already bad situation. And the wet sand had worked its

214

way under the saddles to scour away what little skin might have been left, leaving raw patches of flesh, weeping and suppurating.

At almost the same moment that he heard the blasts of Confederate cannon fire, scouts arrived with news that, not only was Confederate General Nathan Bedford Forrest in close pursuit, Colonel Roddey was taking a parallel route just to the north. If things continued as they were, Roddy would flank the Federal column at the junction of the two roads some three miles or so to the east.

Streight was not surprised to hear that Forrest was on his tail; nor was he particularly alarmed by it. What did alarm him was the news that he was about to be flanked.

Streight had no desire for a pitched battle though he had little doubt that he could successfully mount one if he had to. His overriding orders were, however, to cut the Confederate supply lines at Rome, and that's exactly what he intended to do.

Weighing all of his options, Streight opted to run at least to a point where the danger of his being flanked was nullified. He was also fortunate in that he personally knew the area and the terrain quite well, having spent several months in 1862 recruiting from the heavily Union populace in the greater Sand Mountain area.

With his escort in close support, he stood to the side and from the saddle pushed his regiments to their best speed. Soon the mules were trotting quickly by most loudly braying their protest as they went.

Once they were all up on the plateau, the going became relatively easy. The terrain was open, almost treeless, and windswept, broken only by sandy dunes that lay parallel to the road in gentle ridges. And it worked, they passed by the junction of the two roads long before the enemy came even close to it.

For more than an hour, Streight kept the Mule Soldiers moving quickly eastward, all the time looking for strong defensive position to fight the battle he now knew was inevitable. He found the perfect spot.

All the while Streight had been running eastward, the terrain had slowly been rising. Now, at an elevation of a little more than a

215

thousand feet, the road widened and leveled out, running in a straight line, eastward across the center of a flat, open plain that was studded with rocky outcrops. The plain was bordered to the north by a deep ravine with walls steep and inaccessible, and to the south by a sodden and almost impassable swamp. The distance from the road to the edge of the ravine was approximately 175 yards, from the road to the swamp it was about a 150 yards.

Streight smiled grimly as he inspected the site, and immediately gave orders for the brigade to dismount. The wagons, horses and mules were taken further east and then down an easy slope into the ravine, out of sight and out of the line of fire.

Cutting across the plain form north to south, from ravine to swamp, the terrain rose more than a dozen feet to form a ridge that Streight realized would provide excellent cover. The ridge had a gap roughly at its center through which the road ran west to east. From the ridge back to where the road narrowed and sloped away down the mountain, the distance was a little more than 400 yards.

As soon as the animals and wagons had been disposed of, Streight formed his brigade into line of battle to the east of the ridge and then settled down to wait.

216

Chapter 29

April 30, 1863. The Battle of Days Gap

To the west, Captain Smith was doing stalwart work delaying the
Confederate pursuit. He was, in fact, fighting a running battle with the
lead elements of General Forrest's division, namely Captain William
Forrest and his scouts who had pulled well ahead of the main
Confederate column.

Smith had divided his small command into two sections, each to
take turns to face the enemy. The first section would lie in wait, horses
to the rear, and when the enemy came into view would fire upon
them, forcing them to take cover. They would hold their position for
as long as possible, then run quickly to the rear, mount up, and ride
east, past the second section, already under cover and awaiting the
enemy. They continued this turn-about action until they were in
danger of being flanked, then they all galloped furiously east to the gap
where Streight's entire division was now in line of battle behind the
ridge.

High on the Sand Mountain Plateau, Colonel Streight had taken
advantage of the terrain and had placed his four brigades in a line some
three hundred yards long from north to south, effectively blocking the
entire mountain pass. His own regiment, the 52nd Indiana, was to the
left of the road, behind the ridge, with Hathaway's 73rd Indiana on his
left, extending all the way to the edge of the swamp. Colonel Lawson
was deployed to the right of the road with Colonel Rogers and the 3rd
Ohio on his right, extending the line of battle all the way to the ravine.
Streight's artillery, two bronze mountain howitzers under the
command of Major James Vananda, was deployed at the center of the
line, to the right of the road and the left of the 3rd Ohio. Only the
road was left open, this to allow Captain Smith through when he
rejoined the main force.

From his position on top of the ridge, just to the left of center,
Colonel Streight looked along the line, first across the road to his right,
then left to the swamp, well pleased with what he saw. Some fifteen

hundred Federal soldiers in three ranks, the front rank at the crest of the ridge with a clear view to the west, the rear ranks just below them, waiting for the command to advance. All along the line, all was quiet, the bayonets glittered in the sunshine, the banners and guidons of the four regiments snapped in the light breeze that wafted across the plateau, the two gun crews stood at the ready, their pieces double-loaded with canister. It was an inspiring sight, and Streight was almost overcome by the feeling of great pride that stirred within him.

"Boone," O'Sullivan said to Corporal Coffin, swinging down from the saddle. "I think we're in for a fight. I want you out of here. Take my horse and go with the animals and the wagons. Stay with them until you hear from me. If anyone asks, you're there under my specific orders."

"But...."

"No buts, son. For once in your life, just do as you're told. You never was cut out for combat, an' this ain't no time to start. Here." He handed Lightning's reins to Coffin, who was mounted on his mule. "Look after him for me. I'll see you shortly."

"What about this?" the corporal asked, pulling the Richards from its scabbard.

"No. It's too slow to load, an' it will just get in the way. You keep it safe. I'll make do with these." He pulled the two big revolvers from their holster, checked the loads, and returned them.

"Go now, and stay out o' trouble. Do not leave the ravine until I come for you. D'you hear?"

Coffin nodded, looking worried. "What if...." He didn't finished the question, just looked down at the smiling O'Sullivan.

"Ha! Don't you worry none. Ain't nothin' going to happen to me. The luck o' the Irish will see me through; always has, always will. Go now; go on."

Reluctantly, Coffin rode east after the wagons, down into the ravine, with Lightning walking sedately behind.

O'Sullivan watched him go. He did not turn away until the little corporal had disappeared around the bend. Then he pulled the two revolvers from their holsters, rechecked the loads, nodded his head, satisfied, then flipped them over on his forefingers, and slid them smoothly back where they had come from. Then he turned and walked quickly to the ridge to join Colonel Sheets and the rest of the 52nd Indiana.

Barely fifteen minutes later, Captain Smith and his rearguard cam galloping furiously up the rise toward them. The troops guarding the road moved aside to allow them through then quickly closed the gap behind them. As they did so, Captain William Forrest and a troop of yelling and hollering Confederate scouts, galloping at breakneck speed, hurtled around the bend and up the rise after Smith's rearguard.

General Forrest had for the past two hours been steadily closing the gap between the two forces. By noon, he was at the junction of the two mountain roads, a mile west of where Streight had formed his battle line. There, he was joined by Colonel Roddey. McLemore and Biffle were still on the road more than a mile to the rear. His brother, Captain Bill Forrest, was a half-mile out in front of the main force, chasing the now fleeing Federal rearguard.

William Forrest, closely followed by Steiner, Corbett and Bogs, now less than five hundred yards behind the tail end of the Federal rearguard was out front. He held a Colt Army revolver in one hand, reins in the other, hat flying behind him on its cord, kicking the horse, urging it forward, faster and faster, the rocks and dirt of the mountain road flying from its hooves. The horse plunged on up the slope, then round the bend, its hooves flying sideways on the loose dirt as it fought to keep its footing.

As they rounded the bend, some 400 yards to the west of the Federal positions, and turned up the slope toward the ridge and the gap, they had no idea what awaited them.

Like a great clap of rolling thunder, 600 Federal Smith carbines opened fire.

Then, BAM, BAM. Major Vananda's two howitzers hurled more than 150, one-inch iron balls down the slope toward the galloping Confederate scouts. The effect of the volley was devastating. Almost a thousand Minnie and canister balls howled across the gap, many overhead, some wide to the left and right. Horses went down screaming, men were flung from their mounts down onto the rocky surface of the road to be trampled by those behind and unable to stop in time. Many of the balls that went wide slammed into the rocks at the side of the road. Those made of lead flattened under the impact then went spinning wildly back into the air, some of them inflicting grievous wounds to man and horse.

William Forrest, several yards out in front, was the first to go down, hit in the thigh by a Minnie ball. Isaac Boggs was killed instantly, hit in the center of his chest by a canister ball that would likely have gone completely through him, had it not slammed into his spine, tearing it apart. His horse raced onward as its rider tumbled head over heels backward over its rump and to the ground.

Steiner lost the little finger of his right hand to a Minnie ball, something he didn't even notice as he dragged his horse to a long skidding halt, then leapt from the saddle to go to Forrest's aid. Of the three, only Corbett was unscathed, though his clothing was torn in two places by the passing of Minnie balls. His horse had a long, deep crease that ran for more than a foot along its left buttock, the result of a close encounter with a canister ball. The horse had by instinct reared, almost throwing Corbett, then spun on its hind hooves, and careered headlong back down the slope with Corbett heaving on the reins in a vain effort to halt its headlong flight.

Despite the casualties at the front of the column of scouts, those at the rear escaped relatively unharmed. Before the Federals could loose a second volley, most of them were able to retreat back down the road and around the bend, leaving behind only those that had gone to the aid of Bill Forrest. They, too, were able to take cover behind the rocky outcrops at the side of the road.

It was but a few minutes later that General Forrest and the rest of the Confederate force arrived. He was met by the retreating scouts, who quickly informed him of the situation up ahead and of the plight of his younger brother.

Forrest, as always, was quick to assess the situation. From the top of a mound on the edge of the swamp, some six hundred yards to the west of the Federals on the ridge, he surveyed the enemy positions. Through his glasses, he could see the Federal flags and banners fluttering all along the ridge. He quickly decided that the swamp was not an option. To attempt that, would to have the men bogged down, making easy targets of them. Likewise, the ravine was too steep. His only option was a frontal attack.

Behind the ridge the Federal regiments waited, but not for long. No sooner had the ranks closed behind Captain Smith than they heard the thundering of hooves and the loud yells of the advancing Confederate scouts. And then, they saw them.

"FIRE, FIRE, FIRE, FIRE, FIRE!"

BAM, BAM, and the rolling, thunderous roar of the rifles and artillery echoed and reverberated across the top of the mountain. Vast clouds of gray-white smoke billowed out and upward from the cannons and rifles, obscuring the view and providing temporary cover for the unfortunate Confederate scouts. When the smoke cleared, several seconds later, carried away by the breeze, the road ahead and the open space to either side, was clear; not a soul was stirring. The wounded men had been dragged to cover. Only Boggs' dead body, lying spread eagled on its face, gave any evidence of what had just happened.

Colonel Streight climbed once more to his vantage point at the top of the ridge, raised his glasses to his eyes, and scoured the terrain to the west. Nothing, except.... On top of a similar ridge, more than 500 yards away to the left at the edge of the swamp, a like figure, glasses to his eyes, seemed to be looking at him across the void.

For a second, the two continued to watch each other. Then, with a sweep of his hat and a bow, General Nathan Bedford Forrest greeted his opponent. Colonel Streight smiled slightly, stood to attention, and saluted. The game was on!

On the ridge to the west, General Forrest also smiled when he saw the Yankee colonel salute him. Forrest was an old school Southern gentleman and, formally uneducated though he was, he respected all of the finer traditions of the Old South, chivalry being one of the most important. And he appreciated the seemingly good humor of his opponent even though he was about to do his damnedest to kill him.

But Forrest, already aware that his brother had been severely wounded, but was in no immediate danger, was in something of a quandary. The rigors of the past seven days, the long march from Spring Hill and the hectic pace from Danville to Days Gap had taken their toll. More than nine hundred of his troopers had dropped by the wayside. The horses, exhausted by seven days of virtually non-stop, fast-paced travel, almost half of his force had, one small group after another, been left behind, to recover as best they could. That, and the fact that he had split his force, had left Forrest with only slightly more than eleven hundred effectives, but he and his remaining troopers pressed on, knowing that he was outnumbered and could afford no mistakes.

"Colonel Roddey," Forrest called, as he strode down from the ridge. "Colonel Edmondson, Major Julien, Captain Morton, to me, if you please, sirs."

The three men formed a small semi-circle around Forrest as he crouched down and, with a small stick, outlined the enemy positions.

222

"They have the advantage. This here's a low ridge." He drew a squiggly line in the sand. "It stretches from one side of the pass to the other. There ain't no way around them. There's a canyon on the north side, here." He drew a cross at one end of the squiggly line. "The land drops away almost a hundred feet, I guess. On the south side, it's all swamp; no ways through it." He looked up at them.

"There are two guns, here and here. Infantry is all along the ridge, from canyon to swamp. We either stop right here and wait for 'em to move out, or we hit 'em hard here in the goddamn front, here, here and here." He scraped three deep lines in the sand. "Sirs, I propose we hits 'em right now."

"Phillip," he said to Roddey. "You an' Major Julien will charge hard and fast up the right side, alongside the edge of the swamp, this way. You, Colonel," he said to Edmondson," will dismount your men and move into line of battle, here at the center. Me an' my escort an' what's left of the scouts will take the left flank along the edge of the canyon.

"Mr. Morton," he said, looking up at his artillery chief. "You will bring up your battery, all eight guns, an' put 'em here, here, here, and here an' fire by section. You'll go before we do, an' you must be quick about it. It's about 350 yards, give or take, to the ridge, an' they'll let loose as soon as they sets eyes on you. Get them guns into action fast; don't wait for me. Double-shot 'em with canister, open fire, an' keep 'em boiling. You have to keep their heads down until we can get movin'. The rest of the men will provide you with cover until you can open fire. Got it?" He looked up at them, each in turn, they all nodded, and then he rose to his feet. "Let's get started, then."

Edmondson's men deployed quickly to the north side of the road, taking cover behind whatever rocky outcrops they could. As soon as they were in position, they began an almost continuous fire at the Federals on the ridge. Each man was armed with a .52 caliber, model 1860 Sharps carbine. The Sharps was popular with cavalry units for several reasons, not least of which was its rate of fire. Even though it was a single-shot weapon, its breach-loading, falling block action

223

enabled a well-trained rifleman to maintain a rate of fire between eight and ten rounds per minute. And every member of Edmonson's battle-hardened brigade was a master of the Sharps.

The range was a little under four hundred yards; the Sharps was deadly accurate to five hundred yards, and the Federals under a hail of Minnie balls had little option but to keep their heads down.

Under cover of Edmondson's continuous fire, just to the right of his positions, Captain John Morton soon had all eight of his guns – two three-inch, rifled Rodmans, two twelve-pounder mountain howitzers, and four twelve-pounder bronze Napoleons – unlimbered and ready for action. They were a little closer together than he would normally have placed them and that worried him, but space was tight and he had to make the best of what was available. All eight were double-loaded with canister. Quickly, he sighted the guns, adjusted an elevating screw here and there, then stepped back and yelled, "FIRE!"

BAM, BAM... BAM, BAM... BAM, BAM... BAM, BAM. One pair after another, the eight great guns leapt into the air, reared backward under the force of the recoil, then slammed back down onto their wheels. More than six hundred one-inch iron balls howled across the plain, rising slowly as they went until they slammed into crest of the ridge. Some of them screamed only inches above the heads of the Federals lying face down, out of sight, just below the crest.

No sooner had the last gun roared than the crews swung into action, reloading the pieces: sponge, charge, ram, shot, ram, primer, lanyard, ready, "FIRE!"

An experienced gun crew could maintain a rate of fire of close to three rounds per minute, and Morton's crew was among the best. For several minutes, as Roddey's cavalry brigade readied themselves to charge the southern end of the ridge, they hurled load after load of canister toward the Federal positions.

Roddey, already at the head of his troops, his horse excited, stamping and rearing, turning and twisting, awaited Forrest's command.

Forrest was dismounted and had joined Morton just to the rear of the eight guns.

"MR. MORTON," he shouted in the artillery chief's ear. "Have two of the Napoleons moved forward two hundred yards to give Colonel Roddey close support."

Undercover of fire from Edmondson's riflemen and Morton's remaining six guns, the two cannon to the right of the battery were moved quickly forward to a point less than 150 yards from the ridge, a wide open, highly exposed position.

"Mr. Edmondson," Forrest shouted. "As soon as those two guns are in action, you will charge the ridge. I will support you on your left flank. Colonel Roddey will charge the left flank," he shouted, waving his arm in Roddey's direction.

Unfortunately, Roddey mistook the gesture for the order for him to charge and, with a great yell, he kicked his horse into action and charged forward along the perimeter of the swamp, his brigade streaming behind him, screaming and yelling.

"GODDAMN!" Forrest shouted, as he spun round and saw what was happening.

"COLONEL EDMONDSON, CHARGE! NOW!"

Edmondson and his men leapt to their feet and headed at the run across the open plain. Forrest, running hard, cut to the left behind him, shouting and waving his arms in the air for his own small force to charge. By the time Forrest's men were able to get moving, they were already fifty yards behind Edmondson. Forrest was almost beside himself with rage.

Morton's forward battery opened fire just as Roddey swept past. The rest of Morton's guns could not fire for fear of hitting their own men. It was all now up to Roddey, Edmondson, and Forrest.

Only moments before Edmondson's brigade had opened up its covering fire for Captain Morton, Colonel Streight, now fully aware of

225

what was happening in the Confederate positions to the west, had ridden the lines behind the ridge. He talked to his regimental commanders, discussing and planning the coming action. He was already certain how events would unfold; the enemy had few options to consider. Streight knew he was in a strong position and even planned should the opportunity arise to take the offensive.

Colonel Hathaway of the 73rd Indiana and Colonel Sheets commanding the 52nd, were standing together at the center of Streight's left flank, their respective regiments to the right and left just below the crest of the ridge.

"Colonel Hathaway," Streight said, "I do believe the enemy is making ready to charge our positions. What do you think of charging them when they reach the top of the hill?"

Hathaway looked at Streight, not quite sure of what he was hearing. Then, with some hesitation, he said. "Your orders, Colonel, whatever they might be, will be carried out, sir."

Streight looked hard at him. "I know that, Colonel, but what I want to know is what you think of making such a charge."

Hathaway straightened himself a little. "I think, Colonel, that it would be a good move."

Streight nodded, satisfied with the answer. "Good. Very good. It will be done on my command, and when the order is given, it must be a grand charge with the men making as much noise as they can."

Hathaway looked at Colonel Sheets and both men nodded their agreement. The two regimental commanders then walked the line from south to north, making the rest of the battle line aware of Streight's plan.

Colonel Sheets, now back in line, readied himself, looked skyward and muttered a silent prayer; Sergeant Major Ignatius O'Sullivan, standing next to him, heard the muttered prayer, and looked at him. Sheets looked back at him, pursed his lips, tilted his head to one side, shrugged his shoulders, and said with a tight grin, "Just in case, Sergeant Major, just in case."

O'Sullivan simply nodded, looked to his right, spotted Cassell and McHugh in the third rank some dozen yards away. They were sitting together, talking quietly.

It was at that moment, some 350 yards away to the west, that Confederate Colonel Edmondson's brigade opened fire on the ridge.

Every man in the Federal line threw themselves to the ground as hundreds of Minnie balls thudded into the face of the ridge or went whirring over their heads. It was strange sound, a loud humming, buzzing noise, a combined and continuous droning sound that seemed to set the air to vibrating and, for some, it even grated upon the teeth.

Few men dared to look over the top of the ridge. Those who did, including Streight and his officers, watched as the Confederate batteries were unlimbered and then went into action. The howl of the Minnie balls flying overhead was joined by that of hundreds of canister balls. Then, in the distance, they heard a great yell and the noise of the Minnie balls and canister abated. Peering over the top of the ridge, the Federal officers could see the Confederate cavalry already streaming toward them, and the ranks of Confederate soldiers to the center of the line beginning their charge.

Almost immediately, Streight could see that something in the Confederate ranks was amiss. The cavalry was hugging the perimeter of the swamp that curved to the enemy's right, thus a gap between the Confederate right and center was beginning to appear. As they advanced, it widened, leaving two of their artillery pieces dangerously exposed.

"Here they come," Streight shouted. "Prepare to receive the charge."

The entire Federal line, all three ranks stood and advanced to the crest of the ridge, leveled their rifles, and waited, as did the crews of Major Vananda's two howitzers. O'Sullivan, still at Colonel Sheets' side, drew his pistols and cocked the actions.

"FIRE!"

More than sixteen hundred rifles roared together, joined by the two great explosions as Vananda's guns hurled their deadly loads of canister toward the oncoming Confederate ranks. The Confederate onslaught seemed to stagger under the blow, slow down, then speed up again.

Quickly, the Federal riflemen reloaded their weapons.

"FIRE!"

And another volley of Minnie balls swept across the diminishing gap between the ridge and the advancing enemy. This time, there was no doubt about it. Roddey's cavalry brigade, without slowing, swept to its left in a great circle. At its head, Roddy galloped back the way they had come, leaving the two artillery pieces now totally exposed.

"CHARGE!" Streight shouted.

As the bugles called the charge, the entire Federal brigade leaped to its feet and stormed over the crest of the ridge, yelling and screaming, firing their carbines as they went, stopping only momentarily to reload. Then they were off again, running, staggering over the rocky terrain, tripping, falling, rising again, firing, reloading and running.

Colonel Sheets did not hesitate. With his sword in one hand, a Colt Navy revolver in the other, he charged forward and, with three giant steps, was over the top of the ridge, running and stumbling. O'Sullivan was just as quick. The two men at the head of the 52nd Indiana charged, screaming and yelling, toward the dismounted Confederate brigade, its banners and guidons streaming out behind them.

The two forward Confederate howitzers were quickly overrun. Most of the twenty-four horses that served the limbers and caissons were either killed or severely wounded. The gun crews and the gun captain had fled as soon as they saw the blue-clad horde appear over the crest of the ridge.

Colonel Edmondson's dismounted brigade had advanced to within two hundred yards of the ridge, and there they dropped to their knees and continued firing across the now rapidly closing gap between them and the charging Federals. It was a forlorn effort. Edmondson's brigade was outnumbered almost three-to-one. The Confederate line broke; his men turned their backs to the hail of lead that howled in on them. Slowly, they started back the way they had come, first walking backward, firing and loading as they went. Forrest's escort and the scouts were doing the same, and then they were all running. The Confederate charge had turned into a rout.

Within seconds, so it seemed, the entire Confederate division was on the run, breaking to the rear. Roddey and his men were already on their way down the slope to the west.

Forrest was in an uncontrollable rage. Try as he might, he could not stem what had in mere seconds become a total rout of his division, something he was not used to nor would he tolerate.

And then they were gone, leaving the Federal forces, the Jackass Brigade, in charge of the field, yelling and hooting with joy and pride.

Streight, on top of the ridge, was grinning like a fool. After his long and arduous trek, he had at last proved that his was a credible force, capable of pressing its mission to a successful conclusion. As he watched his men returning, and the Confederate guns and caissons being dragged along the road and through the gap in the ridge, he was very happy indeed.

"Where is Colonel Sheets?" he asked as Colonel Hathaway ran up to him and saluted.

Hathaway's face turned from smiling to grim as he replied, "Over there, Colonel."

Streight looked to where he was pointing. Sergeant Major O'Sullivan crested the ridge, carrying the colonel in his arms.

"Wounded, Colonel," Hathaway continued. "His wound is mortal; he is dying, shot through the gut, and there are more, sir. Many more."

Streight's joy slipped away. Colonel Sheets was a close friend, and it had been to him that he had turned over command of his own regiment, the 52nd, Indiana, when he had taken command of the Provisional Brigade, the Mule Soldiers.

Sadly, Streight nodded. "That's too bad, Colonel, entirely too bad. Jim was a good man, and I shall miss him. Sergeant Major, please have Colonel Sheets placed in one of the wagons with the rest of the wounded. Colonel Hathaway, please have Doctor Peck do all he can for him, make him as comfortable as possible."

He was quiet for a moment, contemplating his options.

"They are gone, Colonel Hathaway, at least for now, but they will return, we can count on that. We must leave this place," He looked around, over the plain to the west, and then along the road to the east.

"We must leave this place, now, Colonel. We must continue our mission. Prepare your regiment to move out immediately. I will send orders to the others to do likewise." He saluted Hathaway then turned sadly away.

O'Sullivan did as he was asked. He carried the dying colonel down the road into the canyon where he was met by Boone Coffin and, together, they lifted him into the back of the wagon driven by Private Doyle.

Five minutes later, just before one o'clock that afternoon, the Federal column was again on the road heading east over the top of the plateau toward Hog Mountain and relatively friendly territory. Many members of Streight's Federal 1st Alabama Cavalry Regiment had been recruited from among the heavily Union sympathetic area around Sand Mountain. Not only was it friendly territory, the men of Streight's cavalry regiment were intimately familiar with it, which would soon prove to be an advantage for Colonel Streight and his Mule Soldiers.

Streight again ordered Captain Smith and his now reinforced rearguard, some 220 cavalrymen, to harry and delay the Confederates as much as possible. It was a task that Smith was eminently suited for, and he was not more than a mile east of the ridge at Days Gap when he split his small force into two groups and deployed them north and south of the road behind a series of rocky outcroppings. Then, with the horses tethered, close by and out of sight, he settled down to wait.

By five o'clock that afternoon, the brigade had covered slightly more than ten miles and was crossing Crooked Creek, just two miles from Hog Mountain.

General Forrest was in a rage, not just at his defeat. He was furious at the loss of his two Napoleon guns, a loss he blamed entirely upon Lieutenant Willis Gould who had been in charge of them. He yelled at Gould, at Morton, and at everyone around him. He vowed that no matter what it took, even if every one of his men died in the attempt, he would have them back.

Forrest berated Roddey for his premature charge, for leaving a gap in the line, for retreating in the face of the enemy, and for a whole litany of offences that spewed and spluttered from his lips, some not even the slightest bit related to the events of only moments ago. Though they all cringed under Forrest's onslaught, they were not too affected by it. Roddey had seen it all before, and not just once. Forrest was, after all, Forrest, and they all took the bad with the good and were, for the most part, grateful for it.

Forrest gathered his forces, including those of McLemore and Biffle, who had arrived late to the battle, and prepared again to assault the enemy and, perhaps, regain his guns.

With every man back in the saddle, Forrest decided that now was not the time for caution and tactics. He decided upon an all-out cavalry charge that would, so he hoped, sweep all before it.

Whooping and yelling, the Confederate brigades charged across the plain. Fire from the ridge was light. As they swept along the road and through the gap, the division splitting in two, each section wheeling either to the left or the right, Forrest realized that only a few Federal pickets had been left behind, and even those were now hightailing it away to the east. The Mule Soldiers were gone, along with their dead and wounded, and so were his guns. The Battle of Days Gap was over.

231

Over the next several hours, Forrest rested his troops and took stock of his situation. The battle had cost him dearly. His already depleted numbers had been reduced even further. His losses included thirty-three killed and ninety-two wounded, including his Brother William, and at least forty more who were taken prisoner by the Federals, 165 in all.

Forrest, ever resilient, shrugged of his losses and prepared to continue the pursuit. He looked at his pocket watch and was surprised to see that it was only a little after one o'clock in the afternoon. The battle had lasted for less than an hour.

Chapter 30

April 30, 1863. Crooked Creek to Hog Mountain

General Forrest, still smoldering from his defeat at Days Gap and the loss of his guns, was now worried that Colonel Streight might receive reinforcements from the north from General Dodge, although he didn't think it very likely. His scouts had informed him that Dodge was still enroute west toward Corinth, *Still, ya never can tell. Better to be sure than suffer another beatin'.*

Most of his regiments had by now returned to the main force. Forrest took a rough count and figured he had close to 1700 men at his disposal. He looked, no, he glared around the group of officers now assembled just to the east of the ridge.

"Colonel Edmonson," he said. "You, sir, will take the 11th and go north to the river. You will scour the river for crossings, for boats, rafts, craft of any sort and shape, and you will destroy them all. Dodge is apparently heading west. And so he might be, but we cannot be sure that he has not sent aid to Colonel Streight. There must be none. Is that clear, Colonel?

"Yes, General."

"Go now, and quickly."

Edmondson left the group and went to his brigade, swung quickly into the saddle and, with a wave of his hand, they galloped away to the west; they would turn north at the next road junction.

"And you, Colonel Roddey...." Forrest stared at him. Roddey stared back unafraid.

"Your performance, Colonel, back there was unacceptable." Forrest looked around the assembly. He was not one to mince words and never was he bothered about chastising an officer in front of that officer's peers or subordinates. Roddey had been expecting no less.

"What in God's name were you thinking?"

"You gave the order, General, and I obeyed."

"I gave the order? I GAVE THE ORDER? I did not give the order, goddamn it. You took off like a scalded rat, leaving the rest of us standing there like a bunch of dicks swingin' in the breeze. You, Colonel, are responsible for the deaths of thirty good men." He glared at Roddey, his chest heaving, his temper barely in check. "Colonel Roddey, I do not want you here. You will take the 4th and escort the prisoners and the wounded back to Decatur, and there you will stay. You may go, sir."

Roddey, tight-lipped, came to attention, saluted Forrest, then spun on his heel and walked quickly away. Forrest and the rest of the officers stared after him.

"Colonel McLemore, Colonel Biffle, you are with me," Forrest said. "This Colonel Streight is no fool, and he has us outnumbered. He will be difficult to apprehend, but apprehend him we must."

He glanced over to where Roddey, already mounted and at the head of his regiment, was preparing to leave. Roddey looked back at him, flipped him a somewhat casual salute and, without waiting for Forrest to return it, wheeled his horse and galloped away down the road toward the west.

Streight did have the advantage of numbers, though not by quite as many as Forrest thought. The battle of Days Gap had cost him almost a hundred men, killed, wounded, or missing. And, by the same token, Streight was equally convinced that Forrest had him outnumbered three-to-one. Forrest, however, with the departure of Roddey and Edmondson, was down to slightly less than one thousand troopers. It was, at least at this point, almost an equal match.

Forrest ordered his two remaining regiments, along with his escort and scouts, to mount up and move out. It was almost two-thirty when Forrest, his small force streaming behind him, galloped eastward along the road, away from the ridge at Days Gap in pursuit of Colonel Streight.

They had been on the road no more than ten minutes when they ran into Captain Smith's Federal rearguard.

234

Smith, a veteran cavalry commander, had chosen his position well. Hidden behind a series of large rocks and boulders with a wide-open, windswept plain to the east, over which he and his men had a commanding field of fire, he waited, but not for long.

All was quiet, not a sound was to be heard other than the whisper of the wind through the grass. Then he heard it, very faint at first, the thunder of hooves, then louder and louder as the galloping Confederates drew closer.

"READY, BOYS," Smith shouted, and 220 men pulled back the hammers of their carbines.

To the west, the head of the Confederate cavalry column rounded the bend, Forrest at their head.

"FIRE!" Smith shouted, and all 220 rifles exploded together, hurling their deadly loads of 50-caliber Minnie balls across the open grassland at the Confederate cavalry.

Forrest was taken completely by surprise, but his reactions were instantaneous. First, he saw the clouds of white smoke spurt from the muzzles of the Federal rifles, then the explosion of gunfire, then the shriek of the spinning Minnie balls. It all happened in an instant, but to Forrest it seemed to happen in slow motion. Many of the shots went wild, some overhead, some wide, but some found their marks. More than a dozen men went down, some were wounded, some thrown to the ground as their horses collapsed beneath them.

Forrest threw himself out of the saddle; the rest of his men did likewise. The horses were left to fend for themselves. Most of them ran back the way they had come, some scattered north and south on either side of the road.

To the west, Captain Smith grinned in delight. "Give 'em another volley, boys, and then we're away."

Again, the rifles roared and clouds of white smoke billowed out and upward to be quickly dispersed by the quickening breeze.

Forrest's men, now flat on the ground, stayed low, as the balls whined like angry hornets over their heads. They stayed down, waiting....

For several minutes, the Confederate cavalry lay with their faces pressed into the earth then, cautiously, one by one, they ventured to raise up and look around them.

"GODDAMNIT!" Forrest shouted, jumping to his feet. "They've gone. Go catch them goddamn horses, quickly now."

And gone they had, not a shot had been fired at them in return. Smith and his men road east at the gallop. A mile father on, they again dismounted, took cover and waited.

But Forrest was not to be taken by surprise again. It took his men almost an hour to round up the scattered horses and resume the pursuit. This time he sent scouts on ahead. He followed at the canter, rather than at the gallop. Even so, he was not quite prepared for what happened next.

Smith, instead of deploying his men across the road from north to south, placed his men in ambush. Roughly one hundred men were ranged two hundred yards from and on either side of the road. The positions were elevated, the road itself in a slight depression.

As Forrest, at the head of his column, approached the divide – four of his scouts some three hundred yards out front – he felt his horse tense underneath him.

"HALT!" Forrest shouted, throwing up his right hand, and pulling his horse to a stop.

As he did so....

"FIRE!" Captain Smith shouted.

Two of the scouts went down, the others raced back to the column; the range was extreme. Forrest's horse's finely-tuned instincts had saved him. Even so, he had no option but order the dismount and scatter his troopers left and right into cover. By the time they had dismounted, Smith and his rearguard were back in the saddle and heading east again.

And so it went on, a running battle that Forrest, try as he might, could neither win nor control. By the time they had traveled six miles, he'd had to dismount his men five times and he was becoming angrier as the miles rolled by. His adversary was a master of the game, and he was playing to win.

By five o'clock, however, Smith had done all that he could, and he rejoined the 3rd Ohio at the tail end of the brigade at Crooked Creek. Forrest was only minutes behind him. Smith urged Colonel Lawson to complete the crossing, relaying to him that Forrest was but a moment or two away. Lawson could in fact hear the Rebels yelling as they hammered along the road toward him.

Unfortunately, there was little he could do to hurry the last of his regiment across the creek. His mules were thirsty, and insisted on stopping to drink. Indeed, the entire brigade had suffered delay after delay as the thousand-plus mules ambled slowly through the swift-running water, stopped to drink along the way.

Streight, now knowing that Forrest's arrival was imminent, had no other option but to put Colonel Hathaway's regiment into line of battle on the eastern shore of the creek. As Forrest's brigades hurtled around the bend, and onward to the creek, Hathaway gave the order to fire, and again, and again.

Under heavy fire, Forrest's cavalry had no option but to dismount and take cover. They were not, however, in the best of positions, and Hathaway was able to hold them back until the 3rd Ohio had completed its crossing.

By now, however, Colonel Streight knew he was once again in deep trouble and, with his escort, rode east by himself, leaving the brigade to follow on behind. He had not gone more than a mile, however, when he found exactly what he was looking for: a rugged ridge that stretched along the top of Hog Mountain. To the right, left and rear, the position was bounded by vast stands of tall pine trees. To the front was a steep slope up which the narrow road meandered, this way and that until it reached the top and crested the ridge. It was, he decided, a strong and easily defended position. He sent a rider back down the road to hurry the brigade forward, while he himself continued to reconnoiter the position.

He looked from the top of the ridge, down toward Crooked Creek. The valley stretched out before him, the long column of his brigade stretched for more than a mile as they climbed from the creek to the ridge. In less than an hour, he had deployed the brigade in line of battle along the crest of the ridge. Only Captain Smith and the 1st Alabama remained on the road, fighting a fierce rearguard action just east of the crossing. Before long, they, too, had rejoined the rest of the brigade on the ridge.

With the horses, mules and wagons safely to the rear, Streight placed his regiments in line along the crest of the ridge. His four guns – his own two mountain howitzers and the two Napoleons he had captured from Forrest, were placed at the center of the battle line, and they commanded the valley to the river crossing some two miles away and several hundreds of yards below. He was pleased with what he saw, confident even. He pulled his pocket watch from inside his coat, flipped it open, noted the time, closed it, and put it away. He glanced up at the sky; there was still an hour of daylight left. He waited.

Some distance away to Streight's right, high on top of the ridge, Sergeant Major O'Sullivan, now in command of the remaining sixty men of Company A, 52nd Indiana, had found what he was looking for, a natural wall of jagged rock that stretched some twenty yards, north and south, on Streight's extreme right flank. To the front, the face of the ridge fell steeply away, a precipitous drop of more than forty feet; on the crest, the rocks varied in size from a few feet to more than ten. He had found the natural equivalent of the walls and battlements of a medieval English castle. It was the perfect defensive position.

As he stood on top of one of the rocks, he could see the crossing at Crooked Creek in the valley below. And he watched as Captain Smith withdrew his men and led them up the hill toward him. He stepped down from the rock to face the men of Company A, now standing in a group around him. The rest of the brigade was stretched away to the left in a line some two hundred yards long. He looked to the left and nodded. *This is as good as it gets. There's no way around us. I would not want to be on that slope, bloody suicide, so it would be.*

Company A included a color sergeant, two corporals and fifty-six privates, including Silas Cassell and Andy McHugh. Boone Coffin was, once again, out of sight, on the downslope two hundred yards to the east with the wagons, horses, mules and thirty-one wounded officers and men, looking after O'Sullivan's horse, and his own mule, Phoebe.

O'Sullivan looked up at the darkening sky, then at the men of Company A. *Not long now.*

"This is the spot, boys. Spread yourselves out along these rocks and take a peek over the top, an' keep you're bloody heads down. Cassell, McHugh, you are there." He pointed to a spot where there was a gap in the wall, two low-lying boulders flanked on either side by high, jagged rocks. "That's it, right where I can keep an eye on ya. All right, then. Go to it, boys. Sergeant Henry. You keep them colors furled for now. The rest of you, prepare your weapons, make yourselves comfortable, and then we wait. When they come, and come they will, I want those Smiths hot, hot, hot. Until then, you will not, I repeat NOT, fire a shot until you get the order from me, then you fire, an' keep right on firin' until you either run out of ammo, or I tell ye to stop. GOT IT?"

Meanwhile, Forrest, now well aware of what was going on up ahead, also began to prepare for battle. Although the road up the mountain was steep, it was smooth and easily negotiated. To the right and left of the road was scrubland, low-lying vegetation over rock and sand.

239

He placed his escort, about a hundred men, at the far right with Colonel McLemore and the 4th on their left; Colonel Biffle and the 9th were at the center, the scouts on the far left. Behind Biffle, he placed two bronze, twelve-pounder Napoleon guns.

When all was ready, he surveyed the top of the mountain and the ridge through his glasses, but the light was failing quickly and the Federals were well hidden.

"Captain Morton," Forrest said to his artillery chief. "On my command, you will throw two rounds at that rocky outcrop, on the ridge, there, to the left." He pointed to where he wanted Morton to aim.

Morton made the necessary adjustments, nodded to Forrest, and stood back.

"On my mark, Mr. McLemore, Mr. Biffle. Fire at anything that moves up there."

He looked around, then looked at Morton, and nodded his head.

"FIRE!" Morton screamed.

BAM, BAM. The two great guns roared; the noise and the shock waves reverberated and echoed across the face of the mountain. The two Hotchkiss shells screamed upward then down again to slam into the face of the ridge, explode, and send showers of dirt and rocks high into the air. At the same time, the two Confederate regiments opened fire with their Sharps carbines. Even though they were both breach loaders, the Sharps was easier and faster to load than the Smith carbine the Federal brigade had been issued with, and the Confederate line was able to maintain a rate of fire in excess of seven rounds per minute.

The top of the ridge became a flaming inferno. Morton continued to hurl round after round of explosive shells against the top of the ridge, which began to crumble and fall under the onslaught. The air above the Federal defenders was alive with Minnie balls that whirred overhead like swarms of angry wasps. But Streight's men had plenty of cover, and the Confederate assault had little effect other than to make them keep their heads low.

Seeing that he now had an advantage, at least he thought he had, Forrest ordered his escort and McLemore's regiment to charge the enemy's right flank.

KABAM, KABAM. Two Confederate shells slammed into the rock face behind which O'Sullivan and Company A were waiting. Both shells exploded, sending shock waves through the rocks and enormous fountains of dirt, rocks, and scrub high into the air. Overhead, the air was filled with the shriek of a thousand angry hornets. Minnie balls, canister, and shrapnel tore through the trees beyond the crest of the ridge, shattering the branches, smashing and tearing at their trunks.

Company A, on Streight's extreme right flank, carbines at the ready, peered over the top of the ridge and watched.

Darkness was falling fast, and the rate of Confederate fire slowed. Then, faintly at first, O'Sullivan heard it: a warbling wail that echoed and grew as more than six hundred gray-clad soldiers several hundred yards away, down the mountain to the west, rose to their feet and charged up the slope toward them.

It was what Streight had been waiting for.

"FIRE!"

BAM, BAM, BAM, BAM. Major Vananda's guns fired, and so did the more than 1400 riflemen all along the ridge, all except those of Company A.

O'Sullivan stood, oblivious to the hailstorm around him, his right hand in the air, the ten-gauge Richards shotgun tucked under his left arm, watched and waited.

On and on, up the slope they came; the charging Confederates seemed oblivious of the hail of lead and canister that tore into them from above. They were less than seventy yards from the crest of the hill when O'Sullivan dropped his right hand, giving the order for his men to fire.

BOOM, BOOM, the recoil from the Richards slammed the stock of the heavy gun hard into his shoulder, but he didn't seem to notice. Swiftly, he dropped to one knee, laid the shotgun to one side, drew the two Colt revolvers and emptied both weapons into the lead elements of the Confederate attack.

As he fired, he glanced to his left where Cassell and McHugh were steadily working their carbines. He grinned; his boys were doing him proud.

Cassell and McHugh were veterans of several major battles and more than a dozen skirmishes. Though both were able to maintain a rate of fire of almost three rounds per minute with their trusty, 1861 Springfield rifles, they no longer had them. The heavy, muzzle-loading long rifles had been replaced by the shorter, lighter, breach-loading Smith carbine. Both men, and indeed the rest of Streight's brigade, had soon become adept at loading and firing the weapon. And, though not quite as quick and simple to fire as the Sharps carbine, favored by cavalry units, Federal and Confederate, they could easily get a shot off every ten seconds.

The effect of Company A's barrage was devastating. McLemore and Forrest's escort were thrown back in confusion and were soon running headlong back down the slope.

As his retreating regiments streamed past him, Forrest realized that what he faced was no rookie Federal force. His enemy held the high ground and he had no option but to play Streight's game. He stood at the foot of the slope, out of sight under the cover of a rapidly darkening sky. With his fists clenched on his hips, his feet apart, he stared upward into the night at the firestorm exploding on the ridge above.

As darkness descended on Hog Mountain, the battle continued. The noise could be heard for miles in every direction, the flashes of the gunfire lit up the top of the mountain and could be seen all across the valley. As the night closed in, the rate of fire on both sides dwindled only a little, each side firing at the other with only the muzzle flashes to guide their aim. It was a losing situation for both sides. Of the two sides, Streight held the advantage of the high ground and was easily able to keep the enemy at bay.

Forrest regrouped and for the second time in less than an hour, he led the charge toward the ridge, McLemore's men streaming behind him. The great white horse leapt and scrambled its way up the loose rocky slope. He was less than a hundred yards from the top when the horse faltered, then staggered. Its forelegs buckled and it crashed to the ground screaming. The horse had been hit in the chest by a Minnie ball. Forrest was thrown over its head, and he fell crashing to the rocky hillside, the breath driven from his body, the side of his head crashing into a rock. For several moments, he lay there, hovering between consciousness and oblivion, unseen by his men. Then he staggered to his feet and down the rocky slope to rejoin his escort, who were about to go in search of him. But it was not yet over. Forrest, blood streaming from a cut on the right side of his forehead, ignoring pleas for him to retire to the rear, grabbed another horse and mounted. Yelling for all he was worth, he led his escort in another wild and futile charge up the hill.

High on the ridge, on the extreme right flank of the Federal brigade, O'Sullivan was taking a break. It was almost nine o'clock and the fighting had been raging on the slopes of Hog Mountain for more than three hours.

Sitting on the dirt floor with his back to the rock wall, he leaned his head back against the stone, eyes closed, seemingly oblivious of the din going on around him. To the left and right, Company A was heavily engaged. Three times they had faced Forrest's cavalry as it charged almost to the top of the ridge, but each time the gray-clad horde had been thrown back. The slopes below were littered with dead and wounded men and horses. By the light of the flickering fires on the mountainside and the flash of gunfire, they could see them, and still Forrest continued to assault the ridge.

The night air echoed with screams of pain, the rolling ripple of rifle fire, and the continuing blasts of the great guns of either side. The rocky face below the position occupied by Company A was slowly being demolished. As each Confederate shell slammed into its face, great chunks of rock and stone were torn away. On either side, and to the rear, O'Sullivan could hear the crackle of Minnie and canister balls tearing chunks of wood from the trunks of the trees, sending huge splinters spinning into the air. It seemed to be raining twigs, leaves, and wooden debris of all shapes and sizes.

As the third Confederate charge slowed, then stopped, then slowly began backing away down the slope, firing as they went, Private McHugh jumped to his feet, yelling and waving his arms in victory.

"GO, GO, GO, ya goddamn Rebs."

Cassell, also kneeling, dropped his carbine and threw both of his arms around McHugh's legs, trying to pull him back down. Too late. A 52-caliber Minnie ball from a Confederate sharpshooter more than three hundred yards away down the mountain, slammed into McHugh's upper arm just above the elbow, spinning him round and throwing him sideways to the ground.

Cassell jumped to his feet, grabbed him, and pulled him backward away from the wall, and settled him down on his back among the rocks. McHugh's face was white. He was already in shock, barely conscious. The wound was devastating; the arm hung limp, useless from the shoulder, and blood pumped out of the sleeve of his jacket in spurts.

O'Sullivan, seeing McHugh go down, dashed to their side, and quickly assessed the wound.

"Holy Mother of God," he said. "That's a bloody bad one. Hold him tight, Cassell."

O'Sullivan took the Bowie knife from his belt and quickly cut away McHugh's sleeve at the shoulder, leaving the arm bare. The arm just above the elbow was a bloody mess: flesh torn away from the bone, the bone itself shattered into three or four pieces that O'Sullivan could see, and maybe more hidden by the pumping blood and torn flesh.

"Hold him tight, now," he said, stripping McHugh's belt from his britches. "Don't let him move."

He wrapped the belt tightly around the upper arm three times, then slipped the end through the buckle and pulled it tight; McHugh screamed with pain. The blood stopped flowing, and McHugh passed out.

"That arm will have to come off," O'Sullivan said, not looking at Cassell. "Can you carry him?"

Cassell looked down at his wounded friend then up at O'Sullivan, his face grim and nodded.

"Good, take him to the rear to Doctor Spencer. He will know what to do with him. Here, let me help ya."

Together the two men lifted McHugh's limp body to his feet. Cassell put his shoulder to McHugh's belly while O'Sullivan held him upright, then gently draped him over Cassell's shoulder, and then steadied him as he stood upright. O'Sullivan clapped him gently on the shoulder and he walked, staggering slightly under the weight away down the slope to the rear where Doctors Spencer, King, and Peck and six aids were tending the wounded.

At nine o'clock, as the battle raged on, Forrest's men continued to assault the ridge, only to be repulsed each time with heavy casualties. The mountain became a hellish place, echoing with the screams of the wounded and the dying. Still Forrest assaulted the hill, leading every charge himself.

For more than three hours, the two batteries, Confederate and Federal, had kept up an almost continuous bombardment, one against the other. Both were now dangerously low on ammunition. Casualties on both sides were heavy. Forrest had suffered more than three hundred killed and wounded, including several officers and countless horses. Streight's brigade was doing somewhat better having the advantage of the high ground and the rock wall. Even so, he knew it was all but over. His men were exhausted. As the fires burned out, it became more and more difficult to see the enemy; both sides were firing blindly at the muzzle flashes.

As the fighting slowly abated, and the night drew in, Colonel Streight decided it was time to leave. He walked the line from one end to the other, offering words of encouragement to the men, and orders to the officers to prepare to pull back.

Having taken stock of his remaining supplies of ammunition, he ordered the two Confederate guns spiked and their carriages smashed, rendering them useless to the enemy. He had enough ammunition left only for his two howitzers.

At nine-thirty, he walked the hundred yards to the rear to confer with Doctors Peck, King and Spencer. He found Spencer and his aids working feverishly, surrounded by wounded and dying soldiers.

Spencer had just finished removing the leg of a wounded private when he looked up and saw Streight approaching. As he inserted the final two sutures into the flap of skin that covered the end of the bone, he sighed, clipped the twine, and stood upright. From the look on the colonel's face, he knew that the news was bad.

"Mr. Spencer," Streight began. "How are things going?"

"Not well, Colonel. At the last count, we have more than eighty wounded, including those we brought with us from Days Gap."

Streight nodded thoughtfully. "Doctor, it is time for us to leave. We cannot take the wounded with us. We do not have wagons enough to carry them." He pulled a wry face, then continued, "You, I am afraid, and your aids, must stay with them. Doctors Peck and King will stay with the brigade; there no doubt will be work for them later."

Spencer dropped his chin and stared at the floor, then lifted his head, looked Streight in the eyes, and said, "It will be my honor to stay, Colonel."

Streight nodded. "You need have no fear of the enemy, Doctor. Forrest is not an animal and, I have no doubt, will himself have need of your services. May God be with you, Doctor."

Streight came to attention in front of the doctor, saluted, then spun on his heel and walked quickly back toward the ridge.

One by one, in column of fours, the Federal brigade pulled back from the ridge and marched down the slope to where the wagons, horses, and mules were waiting. This time it was Colonel Hathaway and the 72nd Indiana that was to act as the rearguard. He would take advantage of the night, and whatever cover he could find along the way, attack any pursuers, and provide time and cover for Streight and his Mule Soldiers to make their getaway. It was ten o'clock.

Several hundred yards away, down the mountain to the west, General Forrest was once again regrouping his men for yet another charge up the hill.

"STOP," he shouted. "Listen!" The horses and men milling around stopped in their tracks.

Nothing! All was quiet. The battery on the ridge was silent. The muzzle flashes had died away to nothing. Only the crackling of small fires and the cries of the wounded on the hillside broke the eerie silence that had descended over the battlefield.

"GODDAMN IT," he yelled. "They've done it again; they're gone. AFTER THEM! Come on, come on," he shouted, putting spurs to horse and galloping off up the hill, his men following.

Forrest crested the ridge and reined in his horse, not a shot was fired. The enemy had, indeed, gone, leaving only the detritus of the savage battle behind them. Dead Federal soldiers lay here and there among the rocks. More than a hundred dead Confederate cavalrymen lay dead on the hillside; double that number lay wounded, some dying, some unconscious, some moaning softly, some screaming in pain. Forrest noted, savagely, the remains of his two guns.

Forrest looked down the slope to the east. More than a hundred yards away he could see the flickering light of a half-a-hundred oil lamps, and several campfires. Warily, pistol in hand, he walked his horse forward, toward the flickering lights. Doctor Spencer was waiting for him at the side of the road.

"General Forrest," he said, as Forrest reined in his horse in front of him. "Doctor William Spencer, United States Army, at your service. I wish you good evening, sir." He flipped the general a casual salute, very much at ease

Forrest was silent for a moment, and then he returned Spencer's salute, though not quite so casually.

"Good evening to you, Doctor," he said, dryly. "You and your aids may consider yourselves my prisoners. Please continue with your work. I, too, have many wounded men. They will be brought to you forthwith. You will, Doctor, treat them as you would treat your own.

"Colonel Biffle," he said, turning in the saddle, "Please organize burial details. Bury them all, ours and theirs. Treat them all honorably." Then, without another word, he walked his horse slowly eastward, staring into the distance, thoughtful, but seething with anger.

Spencer returned to work. He had his hands full. He was now the only qualified doctor on site, and it would take days to see to the numbers that lay on makeshift cots and stretchers before him. He would, of course, treat the most severely wounded first.

Dr. William Spencer had graduated from Geneva Medical College in New York at the age of twenty-five in 1859. Now, more than four years later, he found himself on a lonely and desolate mountain top in Northern Alabama, surrounded by the dead and wounded of two armies. It was a daunting situation. His enemy was, so he had heard, savage, ignorant and cruel. He was twenty-nine years old, had worked almost non-stop for more than ten days, and he was tired, bone tired. But he was a good and conscientious doctor, and now went to work with a will.

Slowly he worked his way through one procedure after another. The wounds were horrendous: head wounds, stomach, legs, arms.... Gashes, missing fingers and hands, feet dangling by tendons, arms and legs shattered. One by one, the most serious first, he cut, sawed and stitched away on a makeshift table – several wagon boards on two roughly-built trestles – until he came at last to Private Andrew McHugh.

Spencer looked down at the shattered arm, shook his head, and went to work.

First, he administered chloroform, then, without removing the belt that had stemmed the flow of blood, he cut partway through the skin and flesh just above the wound with a large, thin knife, already crusted in blood, and trimmed away the flesh to reveal more of the bone. Next, with a small saw, he cut through the humerus bone, just below the shoulder, until it was severed. He trimmed away the rest of the flesh, leaving a large flap of skin, freed the severed arm, and handed it to an aid, who threw onto a growing pile of limbs just to one side of the table.

Spencer then tied off the arteries with horsehair, removed the leather belt, and filed the end and edges of the bone smooth so that it would not work through the skin. Finally, he pulled the flap of skin all the way over the wound and sewed it closed, leaving a small drainage hole. One of his aids then covered the stump with plaster and bandaged it. McHugh was removed from the table and laid on one of the cots until he would awake or not.

Spencer watched as they carted him away. Then he gathered up his instruments, swilled them off in a barrel of bloody water, and turned to his next patient. And so it went on, hour after hour, one poor soul after another was laid upon the table, operated on, and then moved quickly onward. By eight o'clock the following morning, Spencer had, over the past nine hours, performed more than one hundred procedures, large and small, one of them on a Confederate Captain, a certain William Forrest. Spencer was exhausted.

It was earlier, at around midnight, when he received word that Forrest wanted to speak with him. He was reluctant to go, already having more than a hundred patients to still tend and care for, and they were still bringing in Confederate wounded from the lover slopes of Hog Mountain, but he had no choice. He arrived at General Forrest's tent and was ushered in by his orderly.

"General Forrest, sir," he began, nervously. "I must protest, sir. I have no time to parlay with you, nor am I at liberty to discuss the particulars of our force."

Forrest, seated on a small folding chair, smiled up at him. "Please, Doctor, be seated. How are your patients this morning?"

"They are numerous and many of them are in peril for their lives. I should be with them, sir," he answered, still on his feet.

"And so you will be. But first, you will do as I say and be seated," he said, mildly, indicating the chair in front of him.

"Good. Now we can talk eye-to-eye, man-to-man." He smiled at Spencer. "First, I must ask you, how is my brother?"

"He does well, General. I have removed the ball from his thigh and stitched the wound closed. He is stiff and will not be able to travel for several days, at least, but he will recover."

"Good. I thank you, Doctor. Now to that Colonel Streight of yours: he is quite a soldier. He does have the will to fight, and he fights dammed well. I would that we had more like him on our side. But his cause is doomed. It is just a matter of time before I have him. His numbers must be dwindling significantly, would you not say so?" he asked, his head on one side, his eyes fixed on Spencer's.

"I have nothing to say, General, about my Colonel, the disposition of his troops, or his objectives."

Forrest smiled and nodded. "Well said, Doctor. Unfortunately, I have to leave and chase him down, and now must leave you to the tender mercies of my rearguard. I have given orders that you and your aids are to be well treated and given every assistance possible, but.... Well, my men are somewhat rough and ready, and I will not be here to keep them entirely in check, and you, sir, and what has been left here by your superiors are all subject to the spoils of war." He looked at Spencer, but Spencer only stared unblinkingly back at him.

"Very well. Go back to your duties, Doctor. I will see you again when this is all over. But be careful, very careful how you deal with my men, wounded or not. You may go now."

Even before Forrest left in pursuit of Streight, around two o'clock in the morning, the 1st of May, the men of his division went about robbing the bodies of those few Federal dead that had not yet been buried, and the wounded Federal lying abed, and Spencer and his aids. They took Spencer's horse, his Colt Navy revolver, and most of his food. They did, however, allow him to keep his medical supplies. Then, leaving only a few men to guard the prisoners, the Confederate rearguard moved out, following Forrest's main force westward toward Blountsville.

Chapter 31

May 1st, 1863. The Road to Blountsville

General Forrest, at the head of his division which was now significantly depleted, rode away from Hog Mountain in the early hours of the morning under a bright, moonlit sky.

The mistakes of the pursuit from Days Gap to Crooked Creek and Hog Mountain would not be repeated. Colonel Streight was a master of the art of the ambush, and Forrest would not allow himself to be so badly treated again. Thus, he sent a party of scouts on ahead of the column to find the enemy and assess his disposition. They were ordered to ride carelessly, to be ever alert and, if possible, to draw the enemy's fire; every man in the party was a volunteer.

The volunteers rode at the canter about a half-mile ahead of the main column. They were less than an hour out from Hog Mountain, at around one-thirty, when one of them noticed steel glinting in the light of the moon.

"Blue Bellies, boys," he yelled. "Over there, to the right."

The volunteers wheeled their horses, lay low in their saddles, and spurred their horses back the way they had come. Hathaway's men fired wildly after them, but to no effect.

Within minutes, the scouts were back with the main Confederate column and had reported the enemy's positions to Forrest.

Forrest grinned. *Now, m' fine boys. Let's see how you like a taste of your own medicine.*

Quietly he ordered Colonel McLemore to advance slowly, taking with him a section of artillery, each of the two guns drawn by hand under the cover of darkness. Then....

BAM, BAM! The range was close, almost point blank. Unfortunately, due to the darkness, both guns fired high, followed by an equally poorly aimed volley of rifle fire, and the resulting swarm of canister and Minnie balls flew harmlessly over the Federal's heads. But it was enough. Hathaway and his men, all mounted on mules, with the exception of Hathaway himself, who was mounted on a horse, galloped sedately away under cover of darkness, to rejoin the tail end of Streight's brigade.

The next encounter came just after two-o'clock; as before, Colonel Hathaway had his Federal brigade deployed among the heavy undergrowth thirty yards or more to either side of the route. The full moon cast dark shadows over the dense tangle of scrub oak, pine trees, cedars, dogwood, honeysuckle, trumpet vine, poison oak, briar, and blackthorn. It was as difficult to see out of it as it was to see in, and Hathaway's were well-hidden, too well-hidden.

But Hathaway, too, had learned from past mistakes. This time he let Forrest's scouts pass unchallenged, and it was only because of a deeply felt sense of foreboding that Forrest slowed his column to a walk.

Fearing that he had been discovered, Hathaway gave the order for his men to fire. Again, the darkness played a pivotal role in what happened next.

At the outburst of gunfire, the party of Confederate scouts, now well beyond the Federal positions, spurred their horses. They turned to the right in a wide sweeping circle that took them to the rear of Hathaway's positions, and back toward the point where Forrest's troops, already dismounted, were hastily forming a line of battle. Forrest had his two mountain howitzers brought up and quickly put into action. The night was rent with the rolling crackle of rifle fire and steady BAM, BAM of the two big guns. From a distance, the battlefield appeared to be suffering under a wild, but isolated thunderstorm. The sky was lit up by the muzzle flashes of both sides, the roar of gunfire rolled and reverberated through the night, and the light of the full moon shone down on the rolling clouds of smoke. The muzzle flashes appeared as bolts of red lightning flashing inside the swirling white clouds.

For almost an hour, the battle raged back and forth. Both sides took casualties, but the night, even under the light of the full moon, was equally kind to the combatants of both sides, neither one could see the other. The gun crews and riflemen fired blindly across a gap more than two hundred yards wide, with only muzzle flashes to aim at. As ferocious as the battle raged, casualties were low. Slowly, as both commanders realized the futility of the situation, the rate of fire on both sides dwindled almost to nothing.

Finally, Hathaway, knowing he had done all he could to delay Forrest, mounted his brigade and they crept quietly into the night, leaving only a small rearguard of a dozen men with orders to continue firing sporadically at anything that moved.

By three o'clock, Hathaway was on his way east, following Streight's main force toward Blountsville

Even Forrest had had enough, at least for this night and, receiving a report from one of his scouts that Hathaway was gone, he gave orders for his men to camp for the night where they were, feed the horses and get some rest. The remainder of Hathaway's rearguard crept silently into the night.

Meanwhile, ten miles away to the east, Colonel Streight and his Mule Soldiers, men and animals exhausted to the point of collapse, struggled onward. Every hour along the way, they stopped for ten minutes to rest, and provide the starving and thirsty mules with what little sustenance they could scrape together. It was little enough. They had by now been on the move from Eastport to Hog Mountain for nine days, almost without respite. The poor quality of the mules they had received at Nashville was taking a heavy toll; from Tuscumbia to Hog Mountain alone they had lost more than three hundred of them, many of them to the ravages of distemper, most of them to sheer exhaustion. Silas Cassell's mule, Abel, was just one of them. Even so, the number of men on foot had not increased significantly. Diligent foraging by Captain Smith and the 1st Alabama Cavalry had replaced perhaps fifty percent of the lost animals and battlefield attrition among his men accounted for the rest of the discrepancy.

But Colonel Streight was now an extremely worried man, deeply concerned for the outcome of his enterprise and the welfare of his men. Morale among the men was low and many of them were abandoning personal items and pieces of equipment they decided would no longer be needed, fearing they would slow them down. Not so for O'Sullivan and Coffin; both of their animals carried almost all of the necessities they had started out with, but then again, both of their animals had been, and still were, in prime condition, though both were tired and sluggish.

The road from Hog Mountain to Blountsville was easy going. It ran downhill, dropping more than six hundred feet, across wide-open terrain where vegetation grew only in sparse patches, a wind-swept desert, largely uninhabited and with little opportunity to forage for food.

As he rode on through the night, Streight noted the unforgiving landscape and, as badly as he needed forage, he knew that Forrest must need it more. Thus, his idea was to press on, to find a place where he could feed his brigade, animals and men, and then deny Forrest access to the supplies he needed. If he could do that, it would give his men and animals time to rest and recover. He required at least twenty-four hours respite.

And so, the Provisional Brigade struggled onward through the night. They reached Blountsville a little after eight o'clock in the morning, the 1st of May. The ride from Days Gap had been a tortuous forty-three miles, a ride that had been little more than a running battle.

Chapter 32

May 1, 1863. Streight - Blountsville, Alabama

Colonel Abel D. Streight was a worried man. What lay before him to the east was largely unknown. True, his scouts a scoured the terrain ahead as far as the city limits of Blountsville, but beyond that...

To his rear, the Confederate Wizard of the Saddle was, so he thought, in hot pursuit and had him out numbered more than two-to-one. Neither was true. Forrest had bedded his division down for the night more than fifteen miles to the west of Blountsville and, in fact, Streight had Forrest outnumbered. Streight still had slightly more than fourteen hundred men; Forrest was down to less than nine hundred.

Be that is it may, Streight was deeply concerned about his tenuous situation. His animals were in poor condition, he needed more of them, food was short, and men and animals were exhausted. Even so, there was no stopping. By seven o'clock that morning, the march had become almost a mad dash to Blountsville, and at eight o'clock his leading elements, including himself, his escort, his regimental commanders, followed by Company A, 52nd Indiana, Sergeant Major O'Sullivan, Corporal Coffin, and the newly promoted Corporal Silas Cassell, galloped into the small city.

Friday morning, May 1st, was a time for celebration in Blountsville. The townspeople had risen early to prepare for the May Day festivities. The town square was alive with gaily-dressed women and children, along many of the more sedately-dressed male members of the small population. And so it was with no little surprise and a certain amount of horror that everyone stopped what they were doing, turned and stared, open-mouthed as the wild-looking band of Federal soldiers, most of them mounted on mules, clattered into the town center. For many, at least for the members of the small crowd that now gathered at the roadside to watch them arrive, they were the source of much amusement. They laughed, hooted, and jeered the bedraggled, scruffy, dirty, unshaven band of raiders mounted on an equally bedraggled band of bony, pathetic-looking animals that brayed constantly. The mules were hungry and thirsty after more than twenty-eight hours without rest, having been fed only whenever their riders could spare a moment to fish whatever small morsel of food they could find from within their haversacks.

It was not that the brigade lacked feed for the animals, they didn't, although, in an effort to speed the brigade onward, Streight had had most it transferred from the wagons to pack mules. The five wagons were then abandoned and burned. There simply had been no time to stop and feed them, until now.

As soon as O'Sullivan and Company A entered the town square, without waiting for orders, he set about securing the town.

"Cassell," he shouted to his brand new corporal. "Take fifteen men and picket the western approach. At the first sign of enemy riders, you get back here as fast as you can. Now go!"

Cassell, at the head of his small company, mounted on a replacement for the mule he had called Abel, clattered west the way they had come. About a mile-and-a-half outside of town, he halted the group and ordered them spread out in a wide semi-circle with a view that commanded any and all approaches from the west. There, they all dismounted, and each man settled down to wait, hand-feeding and watering their animals from leather buckets brought to each man by riders from the town.

"Colonel Hathaway, Mr. Rogers, Colonel Lawson, Captain Smith, Sergeant Major," Streight called, as Cassell and his men galloped away. "To me, if you please."

The five men, still on horseback, gathered around Streight, ready for what they were sure must come next.

"I have no idea how much time we have," he began. "I suspect not long at all, a few hours at most. I was hoping we could rest a while. Unfortunately, I fear that will not be so.

"Captain Smith." Streight looked at the cavalry commander. "We have to secure the approaches to the west. We cannot allow the enemy to surprise us; pickets are not enough. As soon as you have fed and watered your horses, and your men, you will ride west in support of the pickets. Lie back a half-mile and wait. If the enemy appears, engage him and hold him, if you can. You must provide me with time to move the rest of the brigade. As soon as you can, Captain, and thank you." He saluted Smith, and then turned to the rest of his command.

"Gentlemen, have the men scour the town for food and animals, and have them do it quickly. I have no doubt, no doubt at all, sirs, that Forrest is no more than a couple of hours behind us. We must grasp every opportunity and then be ready. Have the saddles removed, the animals fed and watered, and get what little rest you can. I fear, gentlemen, that it will not be very much. Go now, all of you."

Streight sat upright, rigid, in the saddle, and looked around the silent crowd of grim-faced townsfolk.

"Ladies and Gentlemen of Blountsville," he called out. "My name is Colonel Abel Streight. I am in command of these forces. We are in sore need of food, supplies, and fresh mounts. My men are searching your town for those supplies. They mean you no harm, nor will any of you come to any provided you do NOT interfere with them and their labors. You will be fairly compensated for what we take, in United States dollars and by the tired animals we must leave behind." He looked sternly around the quiet gathering.

"I understand how you feel, but this is war and war breeds necessity, and necessity cannot be denied. Once we have what we need, I intend to rest my command for an hour or two, and then we will be on our way. Now, I suggest you go about whatever it was you were doing when we arrived. Thank you all."

The crowd did not move. They simply stood and watched. Streight simply nodded once, shrugged his shoulders and rode slowly through the town in search of Sergeant Major O'Sullivan. He found him on the western edge of the town with Corporal Coffin.

"Sergeant Major."

O'Sullivan turned, came to attention, and saluted. "Sir!"

"At ease, O'Sullivan. Corporal Coffin, give us a minute, if you don't mind."

Coffin took the reins of O'Sullivan's horse, and those of Phoebe the mule, and led them away to a drinking trough where he allowed them to get their fill.

Streight dismounted, took a step closer to O'Sullivan, placed a hand on his shoulder and looked him in the eye. "A couple of things, Sergeant Major. First, I want to thank you for what you did for Colonel Sheets."

"Ah, 'twas nothin' Colonel, sir. He was a good man, one of the best, so he was."

"Yes, he was, and I thank you all the same. Now then, you, O'Sullivan, are the most experienced soldier I have in this command. I need advice. I need an objective opinion. In short, I want your thoughts, your honest and true thoughts."

O'Sullivan looked him in the eye, frowning. "Errrr, I'm not sure what you're meanin', Colonel."

"Sergeant Major O'Sullivan. You have been in this man's army longer than any among us. You fought in the Mexican War under General Winfield Scott. You've been with me since this war began, at Shiloh, Stones River, now here, and all without receiving so much as a scratch. You are the most knowledgeable man in the brigade. Now then, you know what we are about. Can we reach our objective? Can we win?"

"Oh, sir. That's not for me to say. I'm not trained to know such things."

"What you are, O'Sullivan, is the most experienced professional soldier I have ever met, generals and all. We are all volunteers; I am colonel only by virtue of my position in society. Now, speak up, man."

O'Sullivan thought for a moment, hesitated, then straightened his back and said, very quietly, "Not a hope, sir. Pardon me. Not a hope in hell."

259

Streight's face, already pale, went white. He dropped his chin, slightly, and shook his head. "You are indeed forthright, sir. Explain, please, Sergeant Major."

"Ah, sir. Where to begin? First, Rome is still almost a hundred miles away. Second, the men, mules, and horses are knackered, so they are. Third, we have one of the most feared, tenacious, an' able cavalry commanders in the entire Confederacy only an hour or so away, an' closing fast upon us, I shouldn't wonder. Finally, if what I'm hearin' is true, he has us outnumbered more'n two-t'-one. It's on'y a matter a time before he catches up to us. Can we beat him? We can, but on'y if we find the right field, like that one back there at Hog Mountain. We could a had him there, Colonel. There was no way he could a driven us off that mountain, but...."

He looked at Streight; the man was deathly pale.

"I suggest, Colonel, not that it's my place to suggest anythin', that you get the men back in the saddle and get us outa here, to some place we can hold."

It was at that point that, some mile-and-a-half away to the west, they heard the distant rattle of rifle fire.

"Boots and Saddles, O'Sullivan, NOW!" Streight turned, swept himself up into the saddle and rode back to the town square, where his men were already climbing aboard their mounts, watched by the now grinning crowd.

A mile away to the west, Silas Cassell and the rest of the pickets were riding hell-for-leather through the lines of the now dismounted 1st Alabama Cavalry, where Captain Smith was preparing to receive the enemy. Fortunately for him, it was not Forrest's full force that was heading rapidly toward him, just a group of perhaps forty Confederate scouts. A single volley from Smith's men and they were soon heading back the way they'd come.

Smith remounted his men, stood for a while looking east and then, seeing nothing, galloped his force back into Blountsville where he joined the trailing elements of Streight's brigade now preparing to leave. Smith watched as they rode away to the east, then at a distance of about a mile, he followed them, looking for a place where, with as little danger as possible, he might engage the enemy and perhaps slow him down. Even as he left, riding at the rear of his small column, the first Confederate riders entered the town at the gallop. Smith spurred his horse into life and galloped away as a half dozen of Forrest's men rode out after him in hot pursuit. And then, in a cloud of dust, he was gone, and his pursuers, slowed, halted, looked after him, then turned and cantered back into Blountsville.

General Forrest, at the head of his main force, now less than nine hundred men, rode into Blountsville to the sound of cheers. The gathered townsfolk, some now so much the richer, having been well paid by the Federal foragers, were glad to see their famous general, and they made him welcome.

But Forrest did not stay long in Blountsville. He rested his men and horses for just a couple of hours, making sure all were fed and watered, before he was again on the road.

Colonel Streight, now realizing that all that O'Sullivan had said was probably true, shrugged off the reality of it all and persuaded himself that he could indeed achieve his objective; he could win.

For an hour, he rode on in silence, thinking, plotting, and scheming. What O'Sullivan had said about the Fortress Hog Mountain was correct. Had he made a stand there... well, he hadn't, and now was not the time to dwell upon the past. But later, perhaps, somewhere....

Chapter 33

May 1, 1863. Black Warrior River, Alabama

Tired and weary as the men of Colonel Streight's brigade were, General Forrest's men were equally so. Thus, he decided to take advantage of the friendly people of Blountsville and allow them a couple of hours to rest, and look to the welfare of the horses. It was a welcome break, one Forrest himself appreciated more than he would have thought. He ate a full breakfast of eggs, bacon, and beans, supplied by one of the townsfolk, and then he was up and about again, checking equipment, artillery, horses, etc. Above all, Forrest was an angry man.

Since his arrival at Courland on April 27th – *was it only five days ago?* – he had fought three major engagements at Towns Creek, Days Gap, and Hog Mountain, not to mention a half dozen costly skirmishes with Streight's rearguard along the way. He had been defeated in each and every one of them. He was also steadily losing men and horses, as much to exhaustion as to gunfire. It was something to which Forrest was unaccustomed, and it grated upon his very soul. But the pursuit, he knew, must be nearing its end.

From now on, he knew that there would be no rest for Streight and his brigade, or for his own force. And he knew that the longer the chase continued, the more tired and discouraged the Yankees would become.

Forrest let his men rest in Blountsville until mid-morning. It was a little after eleven o'clock when they resumed the pursuit. Streight, his pace slowed by the weary animals, was less than two hours ahead; Gadsden lay twenty miles away to the southeast.

Ten miles out from Blountsville, the Black Warrior River posed the next obstacle for Streight. The river was swollen, the ford was deep, the water a fast-running torrent. It would take time for the Federal brigade to cross, time Streight did not think he had, especially since almost every yard they had traveled had been contested by Forrest's scouts.

The scouts, more than fifty of them, had quickly caught up with the ever-vigilant Captain David Smith and the Federal rearguard. Mile after mile, the two small forces fought it out. Smith made a mad dash, finding whatever likely cover he could, quickly dismounting his men, then lying in wait for the pursuers, unleashing several deadly volleys, then leaping again onto their horses and away to repeat the action.

And all the while, the men of Streight's brigade could hear the almost constant sound of gunfire in the distance.

When they reached the banks of the Black Warrior River, Streight knew he was once again in trouble, that Forrest was less than an hour away. He determined that if he could get his men across before Forrest arrived, he would be able to leave a small force on the eastern shore, and that they would be able to hold Forrest long enough for the main body of the brigade to escape.

But Colonel Streight was in a somber mood. His grand enterprise was little more than a fading dream. He ordered Colonel Hathaway to deploy his 73rd Indiana in line of battle two hundred yards to the west of the Black Warrior. They were to hold the enemy at bay while the rest of the brigade crossed the river. Then he asked all of his regimental commanders and their immediate subordinates to join him for a conference on the eastern shore of the river.

"I am sad to have to admit, gentlemen, that we are in dire trouble," he said, to the small gathering, all still mounted, watching the slow-moving column negotiate the rushing waters of the ford. He looked at them each in turn. When he saw O'Sullivan, he sadly gave him a slight nod of his head. O'Sullivan nodded his head in return. He knew what was coming.

"We are still some ninety miles away from Rome," Streight continued. "The enemy is all but upon us. We cannot prevail. They out-number us by at least two-to-one."

The officers looked at each other but said nothing. It was not news to them. Each one of them had been wondering how much longer they could keep on going.

Then Streight seemed to pull himself together.

"BUT WE ARE NOT DEFEATED!" he shouted. "Three times we have defeated the best the Confederacy has to offer, and we can and will continue to do so. Yonder lies Gadsden." He pointed toward the east. "There we can deny the enemy goods and supplies aplenty, and beyond that, who knows? We will keep going, gentlemen, and we will fight until we can fight no more."

The sentiment earned him a small cheer, not just from his officers, but also from a small crowd of soldiers that had gathered to hear what the colonel had to say.

"Major Vananda, you will deploy your howitzers on the rise, there." He pointed to a spot on a small hill some one hundred yards from the river bank. "Immediately you clap eyes on the enemy, you will open fire and you will continue to fire until I send word for you to rejoin the column.

"Colonel Hathaway, as soon as the last company has crossed the river, you will withdraw under covering fire from Captain Smith and Major Vananda. You will join Major Vananda on the hill and cover Captain Smith's withdrawal. Both of you will remain with the artillery and stop the enemy from crossing. You will hold, sirs, until you receive word from me to rejoin the column. Go to it, gentlemen, and may God be with you."

The officers wheeled their horses and rode away. Streight remained where he was. O'Sullivan walked his horse ahead a couple of steps and joined him.

"Well, O'Sullivan, how long can we continue, do you think?"

O'Sullivan smiled wryly. "Your guess is as good as mine, Colonel. For sure, we're not done for yet. Tired though they may be, there's still fight aplenty in 'em and fight they will."

"I agree, Sergeant Major. But I do wonder if it's worth it, the deaths that are surely yet to come."

"War is war, Colonel. It's what we do, it's what you must do. It's your bound duty to continue the fight to the bitter end, whatever the cost."

Streight nodded, said nothing, and the two men watched as the brigade struggled across the river.

BAM, BAM! On the crest of the hill, Major Vananda opened fire as, far away in the distance, the first gray-clad horsemen burst into sight. The range – almost two-thirds of a mile – was extreme for the two mountain howitzers. But Vananda's aim was good and, almost seven seconds later, KABAM, KABAM. The two explosive shells slammed into the hard-packed road among the lead elements of Forrest's scouts. The effect was devastating: two great plumes of dirt, rocks and shrapnel flew among them, inflicting terrible wounds to horses and men.

Three horses went down immediately, great chunks of flesh gouged from the chests and flanks by spinning, fist-sized pieces of iron. Two men were also hit by shards of iron, several more were knocked out of the saddle by jagged chunks of rock. The rest of the scouts, even as a second pair of shells came hurtling inward, wheeled their frightened animals and made a mad dash back down the road.

KABAM, KABAM! Again the showers of rock, dirt and iron, but the scouts had gone, leaving the struggling men and horses to fend for themselves. On the hill to the east of the river, Vananda's guns were quiet, waiting.

To the west, some mile-and-a-half from the Black Warrior River, General Forrest heard the two explosions on the road ahead and called for the column to halt. Minutes later, the company of scouts came galloping around the bend. While most of them galloped on by to join the rest of the column, the leader hauled his horse to a halt in front of Forrest.

"General, sir," he shouted, "The Yankees are holed up at the river, trying to get across. They got guns on a hill the far side, an' most o' 'em is already acrost."

"How many guns, Sergeant?"

"Two, sir, that I knows of. We got five men an' hosses down back there."

Forrest, twitched his head to the side, indicating for the scout to go to the rear. "MR. MORTON. TO ME, IF YOU PLEASE."

Captain John Morton rode forward to join Forrest and Colonels Edmondson, Biffle and McLemore at the head of the column and, together, the five men rode slowly forward until they could see the distant hill where the two Federal guns were mounted.

"Mr. Morton, bring up the Rodmans. Place 'em on the road, back there," Forrest twisted in the saddle and pointed, "out of sight and range of those two Yankee howitzers. Then see what you can do about knocking 'em out."

Morton rode away to the rear to fetch up the two three-inch, rifled cannon. Forrest and his three regimental commanders stayed where they were, looking out over the plain toward the river.

"They have the river," Forrest said, "and they can have it. To try to stop them would indeed be costly. We'll let 'em go, for now, at least. They are already ours; it's only a matter of time, a matter of where and when. This time it will be at a place of my choosing. I will not expend any more lives than I have to; we have lost enough men already to this man's crazy dream. But we will turn that dream of his into a nightmare."

He turned and, followed by Biffle, Edmondson, and McLemore, walked his horse a few yards back down the road to where Captain Morton was readying his two guns.

"Whenever you're ready, Mr. Morton."

Morton nodded, walked the fifty yards forward to a point where he could see the target, estimated the range, then walked back again.

"Four degrees, twelve hundred yards. FIRE!"

BAM, BAM. The two great steel guns roared, reared almost three feet into the air, then slammed down again. Two three-inch Hotchkiss shells arched a low trajectory reaching an apex of less than one hundred feet, then arched down again, over the river, and slammed into the slope of the hillside twenty feet below Vananda's two howitzers.

On top of the hill on the east side of the Black Warrior, Major Vananda first saw the clouds of white smoke from Morton's guns, and then, a second later, heard the two explosions and the scream of the incoming shells.

KABAM, KABAM. One after the other the two shells smashed into the hillside below his two guns. The ground shook under the two explosions, his men ducked under the shower of dirt, but no one was hurt.

"Move them back," he shouted, as two more shells hurtled overhead to explode more than a hundred yards to his rear. The two guns were quickly rolled back off the crest of the hill, out of sight of the enemy, under cover of the ridge.

Vananda walked up the gentle slope to the crest, peered over the top and made a mental note of the range and direction. He returned to his guns, made several adjustments to direction and elevation, scrambled back up the hill, looked forward, then back at the two guns, then forward again, then scrambled back down the hill, made slight adjustments to both elevating screws, then went back up the slope, and yelled, "FIRE!"

Both guns roared together. The trajectory was extreme, as was the range for the two small guns. High into the air the two shells arched and, slowly, as Vananda watched and counted under his breath, they arched downward again. As Vananda's count reached nine, he saw two small puffs just beyond the line of trees then, a second later, he heard the two explosions. Although he could not see it, he knew that his fire was on target, and so did Morton as the two shells exploded within twenty feet of his two guns.

For more than an hour, the two sides exchanged shells, neither one doing more than superficial damage to the other. What few injuries there were, were inflicted by flying rocks and shrapnel, but as neither side could see the other, the gunfire served only to keep the heads on both sides down and the Confederate cavalry away from the river crossing.

Progress at the ford was slow, even by normal standards. The river over the stony floor of the ford was running more than four feet deep, and very fast. The pack mules, heavily laden with ammunition and food suffered the worst. They had to carry an almost impossible load and withstand the pressure of the rushing waters. For two of them, heavily laden with dry food for the animals, it was too much, and they were swept away into the deeper waters beyond the ford. The weight of their packs dragged them down and they disappeared never to be seen again.

Finally, by midafternoon, the tail end of Streight's column crossed the river and made its way slowly along the winding road, eastward toward Gadsden. Thirty-minutes later, Vananda and Hathaway received word from Streight that they were to rejoin the column; Captain Smith would again provide the rearguard.

It was close to five o'clock in the afternoon when Forrest completed his crossing of the Black Warrior River, and he was, for once, in a good mood. Having decided that all he had to do was follow and harass the Federal column, and that the natural attrition of their numbers would work their toll on Streight's men and morale, he could now take his time. Time, he decided, was now on his side.

And so, as Forrest followed the last of his men across the rushing waters of the Black Warrior, he called a halt and ordered his men to water their horses in the river and feed them and tend to their needs. Saddles were removed, sores on the horses' backs were slathered with salve, and the men settled down to eat and rest.

Chapter 34

May 2, 1863, Gadsden, Alabama

As darkness fell over the Black Warrior River, and while most of Forrest's men were able to rest for a few hours on its eastern shore, Forrest himself was wide-awake, restless, and unable to remain still for more than a moment or two. He walked back and forth along the riverbank, his hands clasped behind him, deep in thought. He stopped here and there, sat for a while on the edge of the river, staring into the dark, fast-moving water, and then he was on his feet again. He sat down again, this time beneath an ancient willow tree where he closed his eyes, listened to the sounds of the rushing waters, and tried once more to rest, but sleep wouldn't come. Finally, he gave it up and walked resolutely back to the main body of his men where he found Colonel Biffle, seated by himself on a cracker barrel beside a small campfire, staring into the embers; he, too, was unable to rest.

Biffle turned away from the fire when he heard Forrest approaching, and made as if to rise.

"No, Colonel," Forrest said. "Please, remain seated."

He grabbed another barrel moved it closer to the colonel, and then sat down beside him.

"We have them, Colonel," Forrest said, after a moment. "I'm sure of it. No more pitched battles if we can avoid it. We must wear them down, give them no time to rest."

Biffle nodded. "We are not doing so well ourselves, General. The men have been in the saddle almost constantly for the past seven days. We are losing men and horses, especially horses, at a worrying rate and because the Yankees are grabbing every horse or mule they can find, we are unable to replace them. We are leaving more able-bodied men behind because of the lack of mounts than we are losing to the enemy. I would guess that they have us outnumbered at least two-to-one, maybe more."

"True, you are indeed correct, Colonel, which is why we must avoid any further costly engagements if we can."

Forrest pulled out his pocket watch, flipped it open, and noted the time; it was just after ten o'clock in the evening.

"How are your men, Colonel?" he asked, knowing full well what the answer would be.

"They are exhausted, General, as are we all."

Forrest nodded, sat quietly for a moment, staring into the fire, listening to the crackle and snap of damp wood burning, throwing showers of sparks into the air.

"We have to keep at 'em, Jacob. One more day, two at the most, and it will be over." He leaned forward, extended the palms of his hands to the fire, warmed them, rubbed them together, and then turned his head to look at Biffle. "They can't be too far ahead, even now. What do you think? Six, perhaps seven miles? Two hour's ride, at most."

Biffle continued to stare into the flames. "If that, General," he said, without looking up. "If I leave now, I should be able to catch them by midnight."

Forrest grinned wryly. "You always could read my mind, Jacob. Catch 'em, yes. Nip at their heels, but stay out of direct contact. Let 'em know you're there. Do not engage them." Forrest took a small folded map from an inside pocket of his coat, opened it, and held it for Biffle to see.

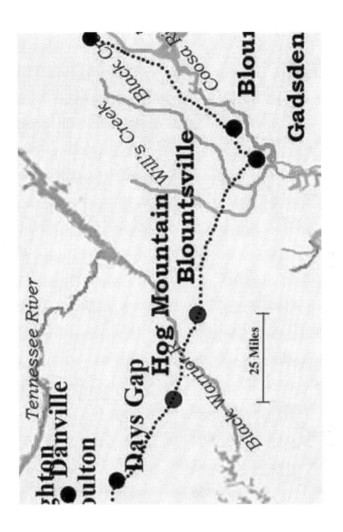

"When they leave Gadsden, they will take this road, the Gadsden-Centre Road. It's a good track, quite smooth, and they will make good headway. You should take this road here, to the north, Owl's Hollow Road; it runs parallel to the Gadsden-Centre road. Let them see you, Jacob; let them see you.

"I will let the men rest a while longer, then follow you. When I catch up, you can rest your men and horses. Go now, Jacob, and quietly."

The two men stood, shook hands, and parted, Colonel Biffle to rouse what was left of his regiment, General Forrest to sit down again by the fire and resume staring into the flames.

Less than thirty minutes later, Biffle's regiment rode quietly away from the Black Warrior River. As the tail end of his column cleared the camp, the lead elements increased their pace to a fast canter. Both he and Forrest were wrong about the time and distance. Colonel Streight was ten miles away and, because of the dark and moonless night, was now more than five hours ahead.

Forrest looked again at his watch; it was exactly ten-thirty.

At just before midnight, eleven miles out from the Black Warrior River, Colonel Streight called a halt and ordered his brigades to rest. Men and animals fell asleep almost where they stood, but it was an uneasy sleep. Forrest and his cavalry were, as well they knew, only a few hours away at best.

At first light they were again on the road, moving east toward Gadsden, now only a few miles away. They rode on at their best pace for two more miles to Will's Creek, where Streight again called a halt, this time to eat breakfast. It was as good a meal as any of them had tasted in almost a month. The foragers had done stalwart work over the past ten miles, sweeping vast areas in every direction, confiscating farm animals, horses and mules wherever they could find them, paying for them or not as they determined the sympathies of the farmer in question. Some were paid in Yankee greenbacks, some with IOUs, and many more with worn out mules that would take many months of nursing back to good health.

And so, breakfast that morning consisted of fresh ham for all – bounty from the foragers – beans, crackers and coffee. It was a grand meal, only the second real meal in two days, and everyone felt the better for it.

As the men and animals, company by company, finished eating, so they remounted and began to cross the creek. Though not as wide as the Black Warrior, Will's Creek, also swollen by the incessant rains of the past several days, it was a formidable obstacle. Again, mules and horses had to fight the raging current but, because of the shorter distance, the crossing proceeded at a good pace without incident. By eight o'clock that morning, the entire brigade with the exception of the rearguard had made it across and were making good time toward Gadsden.

Unfortunately, Captain Smith and his rearguard had to forego breakfast. No sooner had they rejoined the brigade than Forrest and his escort came clattering along the road and over a slight rise toward them.

Streight, sitting astride his horse on the far bank of the creek, watched as Smith dismounted his cavalry and prepared to defend the crossing.

"Hold them as long as you can, Captain," Streight shouted, then wheeled his horse and galloped after the tail end of his brigade, and he didn't stop until he reached the head of the column. Once there, he ordered the column to the gallop, and the lumbering brigade surged sloppily forward, each and every mule protesting loudly.

For almost an hour, Captain David Smith and his 1st Alabama Cavalry held Forrest at bay. Then, with a whoop and a yell, he and his men leapt into the saddle, oblivious of the Minnie balls whirring around them, and plunged into the surging waters of Will's Creek and away. Smith's men were all better mounted than the rest of Streight's brigade, having been given the pick of what horses the foragers were able to find. Thus, their horses were, for the most part, fresh, and Smith soon caught up with the column, now approaching Black Creek and within four miles of Gadsden.

Black Creek, however, was no creek at all; it was a raging river more than a hundred feet wide. The only way across, as far as Streight could tell, was a single-span wooden bridge, and that filled Streight with joy. *At last. Lady luck is smiling down upon us.*

273

He called a halt in front of the bridge, sent scouts north and south along the riverbank to find out if there were any other river crossings that might be of use to the enemy. With his escort, he clattered across the bridge, noting its condition as he went, then returned again to the western side of the river.

"GET THEM ACROSS, NOW," Streight shouted, over the noise of the water rushing past the wooden pilings. Then he turned and galloped back to the far side, turned, watched, waited, and signaled each regimental commander to join him. Before the last man, Captain Smith, (well, he thought he was the last man) cleared the bridge, Streight was already issuing orders.

"Major Vananda, place your guns over there and open fire as soon as the enemy appears. Colonel Hathaway, deploy your regiment to the north and south on either side of Major Vananda. Sergeant Major O'Sullivan, take A company and burn the bridge. NOW, O'SULLIVAN, NOW!"

Ten minutes later, after a wild gallop along the riverbanks, the scouts returned with the news that, other than a narrow, rickety wooden bridge, wide enough only for a single person walking, more than a mile downstream, there was no other way across the river. That second bridge was in a state of disrepair. The boards had been stripped from the deck, exposing the waters rushing by below, and the entrance on both sides had been blocked by planks of wood nailed to the uprights, closing it off from traffic; it was impassable. There were no fords either; the bridge now before them was the only way to cross Black Creek.

Even before the last of Smith's men and the four scouts Streight had sent to look for alternate river crossings had cleared the bridge, it was burning. O'Sullivan's men had found a dismantled barn only yards away and had piled wood siding onto the bridge and set it afire. The fire burned slowly at first, then took on a life of its own, spluttering and coughing, until it finally exploded into a raging inferno. In less than fifteen minutes, the bridge became impassable.

And then, at full gallop, a blue-clad horseman came haring down the road toward the bridge with General Forrest himself at the head of his escort close behind him.

As he neared the bridge, the man, a private of Captain Smith's cavalry, saw the raging fire, realized he was lost. He reined in his horse, wheeled him around to face the oncoming riders, raised his hands and, with a wide grin on his face, awaited his fate.

He was, in fact, a very fortunate man. Forrest himself ordered the man to the rear, and then paroled him. In less than an hour, the private had been labeled a non-combatant and set free, Forrest having no available men to keep prisoners. For him, the war was, at least until he could be exchanged, over.

On the far side of the Black Creek, Vananda and Hathaway's men opened fire, but they did little damage, staying only long enough to make sure the bridge was down and impassable.

As Forrest and his escort watched, the flaming timbers of the bridge slowly collapsed into the raging waters of the river and were swept downstream, leaving only the ends of the blackened, smoldering pilings sticking up above the water.

General Forrest sat astride his horse and watched as the last few burning planks from the bridge over Black Creek fell hissing into the water, and he smiled. *Well done, Colonel. You are an adversary to be reckoned with. We will meet again and soon, I think.*

Then he turned and, followed by his escort, walked his horse slowly back down the road along which he had so recently come. As he did so, he noticed a small house just a few yards from the road and perhaps two hundred yards from what now remained of the bridge.

Forrest walked his horse to the gate of the white picket fence that surrounded the home and, before he could dismount, was greeted by a petite, sixteen-year-old young lady.

"Good morning, ma'am," Forrest said, sweeping his hat from his head, "and what might be your name and who lives here with you?"

"Good morning, General," the girl said with downcast eyes and a shy smile. "My name is Emma Sansom and I live here with my little sister, Jennie, and my mother. Our brother, Rufus, is away fighting for the cause with the 19th Alabama Cavalry."

"Would you like some lemonade, General?" The girl's mother had joined her in the doorway.

"Er... no thank you, madam, but I do need some help, if you might be so inclined as to provide it."

"Anything, General. Anything at all."

"As you can see, our Yankee friends have destroyed the bridge and, as far as I know, there ain't no other way across the river, an' it will take the best part of a day, maybe two, for us to raise another bridge. Do you know if there's another way across the river?"

"I do, General," Emma said, excitedly. "There is a trail just to the north over that way. We use it to drive our cows across the river to town. I could show you...." She cast her eyes down embarrassed. "At least I could if you'd have one of your men saddle my pony."

"There's no time for that. Here, run over here, quick now, and jump up behind me."

The girl did as she was asked. She ran to a low embankment to the left of the house, holding her skirts as she went, skipped up on it, grasped Forrest's extended arm, and he swung her up onto the horse's back behind him.

"Emma Sansom." Her mother's voice was raised in mock concern. "Just what do you think you're about? That ain't no way for a lady to act. You get down from there right now."

Forrest laughed. "You need have no fear, Mrs. Sansom. She will show me the way across the river, and I will return her forthwith. Now, young lady. Which way do we go?"

"That way." She pointed over his shoulder. "Through the trees, over there."

Forrest put spur to horse, and the animal leapt forward. Emma Sansom had her arms clasped tightly around the general's waist, and the left side of her face squeezed tight against his back.

For several hundred yards, Forrest and Emma Sansom cantered through the woodland, twisting this way and that, ducking under one low branch and then another until at last they arrived at the river bank. As far as Forrest could tell, it was no different from any other section of the river; it looked deep, and the water was rushing by at a fast pace.

"Are you sure?" he asked.

"As sure as anything, General, sir. It's a little deeper than usual, but it's shallow enough for you to get your men across."

Forrest nodded. "Hold on," he said, walking his horse slowly forward into the rushing water. Step-by-step, he urged the horse forward. The water rose up around the horse's legs, swirling, eddying, but the horse remained steady and stepped quietly onward. Now the water was up to the horse's belly, and Forrest was about to stop him, but the horse took several quick, leaping steps and scrambled up the bank on the far side.

"Good work, old fella." Forrest patted the horse's withers. It shook its head, whinnied, swung its head around, and tried to nip Forrest's knee.

"And good work to you, too, young lady. You may just have saved the city of Rome in Georgia a terrible fate."

For a moment, he surveyed the river crossing and the terrain to the north and south, then he once again urged the horse back into the water and across the river. Five minutes later, they were back at the Sansom's front gate, where he offered her his arm, and then gently lowered her to the ground, much to the relief of her anxiously waiting mother.

"Emma, Mrs. Sansom," Forrest said, looking down at them. "I thank you kindly for your help, but we must be away from here as soon as possible. My compliments to you, ladies." He swept off his hat, bowed deeply in the saddle, and then led his senior officers through the trees to the river crossing, leaving Emma and Mrs. Sansom smiling as they watched him go.

The Confederate cavalry, led by Colonel McLemore and the 4th Tennessee, began crossing the river immediately. The long column, in single file, wended its way through the trees at the rear of the Sansom home to the riverbank. Once there, the horses plunged into the water and breasted their way quickly to the other side.

Captain Morton's artillery, however, was not so easy to get across the river. The guns had to be double-teamed; it took twelve horses per gun to haul them over the rocky river bottom and up the muddy river bank. The ammunition had to be broken down into small packs, and then taken over on horseback to avoid getting the powder wet.

The river crossing cost Forrest only a couple of hours. As soon as the crossing was completed, Forrest, once again at the head of his column, set out in pursuit of the Federal raiders.

Colonel Streight and his Mule Soldiers covered the four miles from the Black Creek to Gadsden in just over an hour; they arrived on the outskirts of the city at ten o'clock in the morning, much to the consternation of the townsfolk. They were at this point some three hours ahead of Forrest, but Streight knew that the gap would soon be closing. Scouts had reported that Forrest had found a ford and his forces were already crossing the river.

Gadsden was a large and busy community and, for some reason, the residents had not been warned of the Yankee's approach. Thus, the ever-important foraging went well: fresh horses and mules were traded for Streight's broken down animals, and food supplies were replenished. By the time the Federal brigade was ready to leave, little was left for Forrest's cavalry.

Foraging was not just a way for Streight to keep his own force going, he also used it as a tactic of war. From Tuscumbia to Gadsden, every fit horse or mule his foragers could find, every morsel of feed for men or horses, had either been assimilated or destroyed, which accounted for Forrest's ever-decreasing numbers.

This time, Colonel Streight was able to stay ahead of his pursuers, thanks to the burning of the Black Creek Bridge. He spent only enough time in Gadsden to replenish his animals and supplies, and then he set his men to destroying anything they could find that might be of aid to the enemy.

Thousands of pounds of flour were destroyed, as were almost two thousand guns of every type and caliber, including muskets, rifles, and pistols. The bridge over the Coosa River was burned, along with several ferry boats, another delay for Forrest's troops, or so Colonel Streight hoped. He knew, however, that the tenacious Confederate general would not be delayed for long. It was time for him to speak frankly.

"Corporal Timms," he said, with a deep sigh. Timms, his orderly, had just appeared with coffee for the colonel. Streight was sitting on the front porch of a small store on the main street. "Thank you." He took a sip of the hot, strong liquid and smacked his lips in appreciation. "Timms, I need you to find Colonels Hathaway, Lawson and Rogers, also Major Vananda, Captain Smith... and Sergeant Major O'Sullivan. Go quickly, Timms. Have them meet me here as soon as possible."

It was eleven o'clock when the last of the group, Colonel Rogers, arrived.

"Good, we are all here. Sit down, please, gentlemen." He waited until they were all seated. "First, I must compliment and thank each and every one of you for your support over the past three weeks. Your conduct, all of you has been exemplary."

The five stared at him, and then glanced at each other. This was not like Streight at all.

279

"The time has come, I believe, for us to face facts. Rome is yet some seventy miles away. Our scouts have discovered a large enemy force is two miles to the north and moving east, parallel to ours. Forrest himself, having come upon a passable ford on the Black Creek, can be no more than three hours to our rear. I was hoping the downed bridge would hold him for at least a day, even longer, but it was not to be. The men and animals are very tired, and I now fear our enterprise is in great danger." He paused for a moment, lost in thought. His officers were grim-faced, silent. He took a sip of coffee, and then continued, "But I will not give up. My plan is to carry out my orders, and continue on to Rome and destroy the railroad.

"Our only hope, as I see it, is to reach Rome before the enemy does, and destroy the bridge, and that means that we must march through the night. The Coosa River is no Black Creek. If we can destroy the bridge, the river will hold Forrest for two days, at least. For now, however, the men and their mounts cannot keep up this murderous pace. They need time to be fed, and to rest for an hour, or two, at least. And that, sirs, can mean only one thing: we shall be caught. It is inevitable, and we will be faced with another major confrontation.... This is not the place for such a conflict. We must away from here and pick the locale with care."

There was no arguing with his logic. Gadsden was no place for a pitched battle.

"Captain Smith. Once again, you must protect our rear. The rest of us will be away from here within the hour. Major Vananda, see to your weapons. They will soon be needed. Any questions, sirs?"

Captain Smith cleared his throat. "As you say, Colonel, both men and horses are fatigued unbearably, and although mine have been better served than most with fresh horses. My men have been almost constantly engaged with the enemy for almost a week; they are tired, sir, tired out of mind and body, and are falling asleep in the saddle. I do not exaggerate, Colonel. I have seen men fall off their mounts. The enemy has taken many stragglers. My numbers are dwindling. Can you supply me with replacements from your regiments?"

Streight nodded. "No one, Captain Smith, has served this brigade better than you. I will do what I can to see to your needs. But we must move on, gentlemen, and quickly. The enemy is nipping at our heels."

By noon, the Federal column was again on the road and headed northeast, skirting the Chattooga River, toward Rome, still more than seventy miles away.

Map: Gadsden to Cedar Bluff

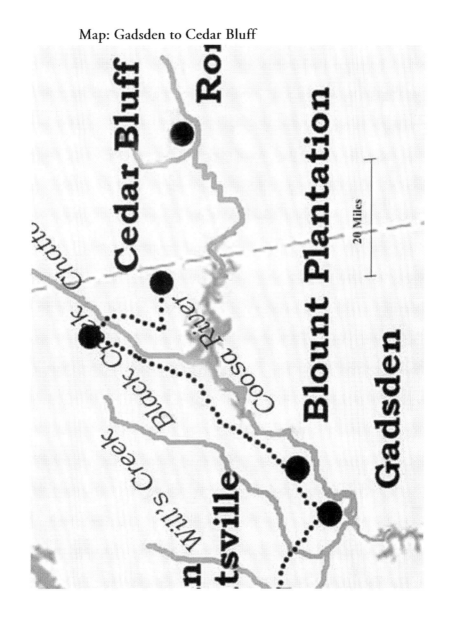

Chapter 35

May 2, 1863 Blount's Plantation

Forrest arrived in Gadsden a little after three o'clock in the afternoon and found, as he expected, that the enemy brigade had left three hours earlier. The town was in a state of devastation. All of the buildings were intact, but what little had not been plundered – food, hardware, weapons, and supplies – had been burned or despoiled; the only animals to be found were the worn out beasts left behind by the Yankees. Gadsden was a wasteland. He turned in the saddle, one hand on the reins, the other on his horse's rump.

"Steiner, Corbett, to me," he called.

The two scouts rode forward and joined Forrest at the head of the column.

"Go to Rome, and quickly. Warn them that the Yankees are coming, and will be there, if I don't stop them, by Sunday mornin'. Tell them they must hold the bridge at all hazards; destroy it if they have to. If the enemy crosses the river, they will destroy the bridge and deny me the crossing. We will lose the town, the railroad, the factories, the warehouses, and God knows what else. Take the northern route. You should pass the Yankees before morning. Go now. Stop only to change horses."

The two scouts saluted Forrest, spurred their horses, and rode away out of Gadsden at the gallop.

The Mule Soldiers made good speed along the Gadsden-Rome Road. By three-thirty in the afternoon, they had covered more than eleven miles, and Streight decided the time had come to keep his promise, to rest and feed the men and animals.

As he surveyed the terrain, Streight considered that he might just have found the perfect spot to confront Forrest. Blount's plantation was set more than two hundred yards to the south of the Gadsden road, on a long ridge that offered open views to the west, south and north. The Gadsden road could be seen stretching away into the distant west for several miles. From Gadsden, it meandered across an open plain toward the plantation. Then, some two hundred yards out, it made a sharp turn to the left, continued on for another hundred yards, then turned sharply right again and continued on past the farm toward Rome. The road was bordered on either side by dense undergrowth, twenty yards deep, tightly-packed stands of tall pines, old-growth cedars, scrub oak, briar and blackthorn, all set back from the road about twenty feet. Beyond the thickets, to the north and south, lay wide-open fields, meadows, and grasslands.

Streight sat astride his horse, flanked by his escort and regimental officers and, with his glasses, searched the road and fields to the west for any signs of movement.

"Nothing," he said, to no one in particular, still with his glasses to his eyes, "but they are there. I can feel it. It will not be long. We must prepare." He lowered the glasses and rested them on the pommel of his saddle.

"Sergeant Major O'Sullivan." Streight turned in the saddle, twisting to look behind him. "Detail a section to feed the animals and prepare hot food for the men." He nodded to O'Sullivan and turned again in the saddle to face the west. O'Sullivan wheeled his horse and left to do as he was bid.

"Captain Smith," Streight said, staring out over the Gadsden road, "Place skirmishers down there." He pointed to the road where it ran parallel to the ridge upon which they were sitting. "Set them back among the undergrowth, out of sight. Tear down those fences." Again, he pointed. "And use them to barricade the road there, where it turns to the left. Pick ten men, the best riflemen in the brigade and post them as sharpshooters, there, there, there ... and there. If we can stop them at the turn, and drive them out into the open fields beyond the road... well, we'll see."

Streight looked to his left where Hathaway was sweeping his glasses back and forth, searching the terrain.

"There, Colonel," Hathaway informed him. "There's movement, on the road. I can just make them out."

Streight raised his glasses. At first, he didn't see them. Then, no more than a shimmer of light on the horizon, made tiny by the distance, he could just make out the low cloud of dust at the head of a column. They were still almost three miles away, but even at that distance, he could tell they were moving quickly.

"Colonel Hathaway," Streight's voice was terse. "Deploy the 51st and 73rd along the top of this ridge, set them back a pace or two, keep a low profile.

"Major Vananda, place your howitzers at the center of the ridge, and set them back also.

"Colonel Lawson, you will place the 3rd Ohio on the left flank and hold the end of the ridge. You, Mr. Rogers will place the 80th Illinois on the right flank.

"We have good position, gentlemen. Let's go to it."

As Forrest crested the rise almost three miles from the Blount plantation, he had one of those feelings he could never quite understand: a slight prickling of the skin at the back of the neck, a hollow feeling in the pit of his stomach, a tightening of his chest muscles. Individually, he counted them as nothing; together, he never ignored them. *Now, is no time to begin.*

"Whoa...." He threw up his right hand and drew in the reins with his left. The command echoed back down the column, from one company commander to the next.

He withdrew his glasses from the leather pouch on his saddle, raised them to his eyes and surveyed the landscape ahead.

The wide, dusty road stretched endlessly away to the east. In the distance, he could make out the low-lying thickets that flanked the road, and beyond them the ridge, and... something, glittering on top of the ridge. *Field glasses?* He smiled.

"There they are, on the ridge. Now we have them.

"Colonel McLemore, take your regiment and go that way." He pointed to the north, where the road turned again to the right, though it was hidden by the trees and scrub. "Make a wide sweep and converge on the northern end of the ridge. Colonel Edmondson, Colonel DeMoss, you are with me."

He sat for a moment, glasses to his eyes, made up his mind, replaced the glasses in their pouch, and raised his right hand.

"UNFURL THE BANNERS.... FOWAAARD."

He put spurs to his horse's flanks and sped off down the road toward the ridge at the canter, the long column streaming out behind him. A mile out, Forrest ordered the charge. The Confederate buglers played the call, the horses leapt forward, streaming left and right into line abreast, banners and guidons flying in the breeze.

They were a little more than a half-mile out from the Federal positions on the ridge when, KABAM, KABAM, two shells exploded fifty feet above their heads, showering the leading group with sharp, spinning shards of iron. KABAM, KABAM, two more followed in quick succession, but these exploded yards behind the fast-moving troopers.

Forrest and the leading group leapt over or smashed through the makeshift Federal barricades at the roadside. They were now within two hundred yards of the Federal line of battle on top of the ridge, and there they ran into a firestorm of canister and Minnie balls.

A dozen horses went down, screaming, throwing their riders into the dirt. On the ridge, however, things were not going quite as well as Colonel Streight might have hoped. Only moments earlier he had learned that much of his ammunition had been ruined, soaked in the rushing waters of the Black Warrior. The supply of useable ammunition was down by a third. Some of it appeared to be dry but was, in fact damp, and for a time the rate of fire from the ridge was sporadic; misfires were prevalent all along the battle line.

Forrest's regiments hit the center of Streight's line hard, but it held, and the Confederates were driven back beyond the road to regroup and try again. Twice more, supported by Morton's artillery, they hit the Federal center, and twice more the line held. Forrest, once again was being sorely used by his Yankee counterpart.

At the Federal center, Major Vananda's two howitzers hurled load after load of canister down from the ridge, some at full velocity, some, because of the damp powder, barely making it out of the muzzles of the guns.

A half-mile away, in the open fields beyond the road, Captain Morton had deployed his six guns in a line fifty yards wide. From there, he kept up a steady rate of fire of two rounds per gun per minute. But Streight had deployed his men with sagacity. He had set his battle line back a few feet from the crest of the ridge, thus they were out of Morton's line of sight and Morton could do little more than pound the face of the ridge or fly his missiles close to the crest. The result was that most of the shot and shell that cleared the ridge flew harmlessly over the defender's heads with a few exceptions.

Here and there, an exploding shell would rain shrapnel down on the blue-clad soldiers and, occasionally, a shot would hit with devastating effect.

Major Vananda's two small guns were set back several feet from the crest of the ridge, which meant that he was virtually firing blind. He kept running to and from the guns, making adjustments to line and trajectory. This he kept up for the best part of an hour. Finally, tired, grimy and almost blind from the caustic gun smoke and debris, he sent Private McWilliams forward to direct his fire.

McWilliams crept to the edge of the crest, stood upright and peered over it. Vananda fired his guns, McWilliams watched the effect and, with a series of hand signals, gave the gun captains corrections either for direction, elevation, or both. It was a system that seemed to be working quite well, until a Confederate solid shot from one of Morton's Rodmans smashed into the center of his face. The three-inch iron ball, the size of a small man's fist, hit him squarely on his upper

287

lip, between nose and mouth. McWilliams' head exploded in a fountain of blood, brains, and bone. For a moment, his headless body stood upright, then slowly toppled over to the left in front of one of the two mountain howitzers.

Only moments after McWilliams' horrific end, Colonel Hathaway became the victim of a Confederate sharpshooter. Armed with a 52-caliber Sharps long-rifle, the man had climbed a large cedar and from that elevated position had a clear view over the top of the lowest part of the ridge. Hathaway was walking the section of the line held by the 73rd Indiana, offering words of encouragement to the men when he was spotted by the sniper. It was a shot of more than 250 yards. The sniper's aim was true, and Hathaway was hit in the chest. He went down and was dead within a few minutes. Colonel Streight, on hearing of Hathaway's death, was devastated.

Just before dark, at around five-thirty, a strange silence settled over the battlefield. Forrest had pulled his men back beyond the trees to the west of the road, out of sight of the ridge. Streight, taking advantage of the sudden stop in the Confederate attack, ordered food and water to be brought to the front line. It was right about then that Sergeant Major O'Sullivan and four privates approached the colonel, who was on foot, close to the end of his right flank, discussing the death of Colonel Hathaway with Colonel Rogers.

Streight and Rogers turned when they heard the men approaching; they were frog-marching a ragged-looking Confederate soldier with them.

"We found him over there, Colonel," O'Sullivan said. "He was creeping about in the trees. He had this with him," he held out a Sharps carbine for the two officers to see, "but no ammo. Seems they are running low. Says his name is Haynes, Colonel, William Haynes of the 4th Tennessee Cavalry. Thought you'd want to talk to him, sir."

Streight looked at the man. "Well, what do you have to say for yourself, man?"

"Not a durned thing, Yankee, 'sept that we're gonna whup yuh, and whup yuh good."

"I need to know, Private Haynes, how many men Forrest has with him."

The man let out a loud and bitter laugh; there was no humor in it. "I bet yuh does, Colonel. I jest bet yuh does. But you'll get nothin' from me."

"One more chance, Private. How many men does General Forrest have with him?"

Haynes took a deep breath, straightened himself up, stuck out his chest, looked Streight in the eye, and said nothing.

"Sergeant Major O'Sullivan. Take this man to the rear... and... shoot him."

O'Sullivan looked at Streight, incredulous, but grabbed Haynes' arm nonetheless.

"WAIT, WAIT," Haynes screeched. "Yuh cain't do that. I'm a prisoner o' war. Yuh cain't shoot me."

"Look around you, Private Haynes. Does it look like I have the time or the resources to take prisoners? I can shoot you, and I will shoot you. Take him away, Sergeant Major."

Again, O'Sullivan pulled roughly on the man's arm, and again Haynes yelled, "WAIT," then said, "All right, all right, I'll tell, but yuh cain't kill me, yuh just cain't."

"Very well." Streight looked Haynes sternly in the eye. "How many men does General Forrest have with him? What units?"

"Roddey, Sir, Colonel Roddey. Colonel Dibrell, an' Biffle, Starnes, an'... Armstrong... yeah, Armstrong an' McLemore an' Colonel Whitfield, an' I don' know who the hell else, Colonel, an' that's the truth. They's spread out acrost the way to the north and south. Gonna get 'round yur flanks." The man was shaking, scared; he was also lying. It was not what Streight wanted to hear, but he believed him. He

289

already knew about the large force marching parallel to him to the north and was not surprised to hear that there were more.

"Take him away, Serg–"

"WAIT," Haynes screamed. "Yuh said yuh wouldn't kill me."

Streight shook his head, frustrated. "Take him away, Sergeant Major, give him some food and then parole him; turn him loose."

O'Sullivan, grinning widely, steered Haynes away to the rear, leaving Colonels Streight and Rogers staring after him.

"We're done, Colonel. They have us," Streight said to Rogers. "Forrest must have more than 2500 men out there. Corporal," he beckoned, and the man ran to him.

"Go to Captain Russell with the 51st and ask him to report to me, here. Quickly now."

Some five minutes later, Captain Milton Russell was standing before him. The man looked tired, very tired. His uniform was filthy, covered in mud and grime. His leather gloves, once a pale shade of yellow, were muddy with holes worn into the finger ends, through which his fingers poked. For some reason, Streight noted that his finger nails were bitten and ragged.

"Captain, I want you to take two hundred of the best mounted men and ride to Rome. Get your men across the Chattooga and the post guards to secure the ferry for the rest of the brigade to follow and then carry on to Rome. There, you will secure the Coosa River bridge and hold it until we can join you. The city is well to the south of the Confederate lines at Chattanooga and so you should encounter little resistance, unless... well, unless Forrest's men get there before you. Go quickly, Captain. There is no time to lose. If Rome gets word we are on the way, they will burn the bridge."

Russell left in a hurry to select and ready his new command. He was on the road less than an hour later.

The battle of Blount's Plantation continued on, sporadically, for another two hours. As darkness fell, Streight decided that enough was enough, and that it was time to move out. He had two of the farm's outbuildings set afire to provide light for his men as they worked to get the brigade moving again. He deployed his rearguard under Captain Smith along the crest of the ridge with orders to bluff the Confederates into thinking that the Mule Soldiers were still there. Smith was to have his men to keep firing, sporadically, into the darkness, and only to withdraw from the ridge under pressure.

Streight and his brigade left the Blount Plantation a little after ten o'clock, quietly, under cover of darkness, and resumed the trek east toward Rome. It was a sad-looking collection. What animals remained were exhausted and barely fit to travel. Many of the men were now on foot, their mounts having given out or died along the wayside. Ammunition was dangerously low, and morale was lower still. In his heart, Streight knew that the end was near, but still he kept going, a slave to his orders until the last.

Chapter 36
May 3, 1863. - The Road to Cedar Bluff

As darkness fell over the Blount Plantation, General Forrest withdrew his men a mile back down the road toward Gadsden. He was by now certain that it was just a matter of time before they reached the end of the chase. Through his glasses, he scrutinized the distant ridge, shimmering in the light of the burning buildings, and he smiled, grimly.

He's on the move again. I have to put a stop to it. This crazy Colonel is out to kill us all, himself included, but not tonight. He has to keep going; I don't. There's time for us to rest, get something to eat, and some sleep. But not for you, Colonel Streight. Tired as you and your men and animals must be, you have to keep going because you know that I am right behind you. Go, Colonel Streight. Go. We'll meet soon, perhaps tomorrow.

Forrest made up his mind and ordered his men to stand down for the night. This time there would be no catnapping, no choking down a quick meal of dry crackers and cheese. Tonight it would be a proper meal. They would use up whatever remained of their rations, leaving only enough for breakfast.

Fires were lit, bacon, beans, even cornbread, were cooked. The men were in a riotous good mood. Even they could tell that the end was near, and that to them would go the victory. By ten-thirty that evening, most of them were fast asleep. Forrest would get his first real sleep in more than a week.

It was a little after four o'clock in the morning, May 3rd, when Forrest's orderly shook him awake and placed a cup of scalding black coffee on the ground beside him.

Hour after hour, the long Federal column, now down to less than twelve hundred men, struggled on through the night. All along the way the roadside was littered with dead and dying mules, and the detritus of an exhausted army: packs, personal items, cooking pots and pans, anything the tired men thought they could do without, even water canteens.

By four-thirty in the morning, they had covered the nineteen miles to the Chattooga River ferry where they expected to find Captain Russell's men guarding boats and the crossing, but the bad dream turned into a nightmare of momentous proportions. Russell's men were not there, nor were the boats. Contrary to his orders, Russell had crossed the river and continued on toward Rome, leaving the ferry and boats unguarded. Confederate scouts had destroyed the ferry and sunk the boats.

Streight was now at loss as to what to do next. It was still well before dawn and he was trapped on the wrong side of the river. He sent scouts up river to see if they could find another place to cross the Chattooga. They returned less than an hour later with news that there was indeed another crossing, at Dyke's Bridge, just a couple of miles or so farther upstream.

The Mule Soldiers were now in unfamiliar territory. The road turned into a rutted dirt track and, in almost total darkness, the brigade lost its way, first turning one way and then another. The only bright spot, literally, was the burning of a small iron works, the light from which gave them at least a little, if temporary, respite from their floundering around in the dark.

By five o'clock in the morning, the 3rd of May, Streight's brigade was in a state of total devastation. The men were in crisis, disoriented in the blackness, cold, hungry, distraught, panicky, confused, and the animals, most of them, were on their last legs. But still they pressed on through the darkness.

It was just after dawn when, by the early morning light of a watery sun, the lead elements of the column, Colonel Streight at its head, arrived at Dyke's Bridge. The colonel felt an overwhelming sense of relief when he saw that the bridge was intact. The eleven hundred-odd men, what few animals were left, the single wagon, and the two howitzers were soon across the bridge, which Streight immediately ordered burned, in hopes that it would delay the dogged Confederate general he knew could not be far behind. But Forrest was not as close as he imagined. Indeed, he did not leave Blount's Plantation until just after first light, and was now more than five hours behind Streight and his brigade.

Now, safely across the river, Streight ordered the brigade to stop. There was time, he hoped, to feed the men and animals, and for them to rest for a short while.

Still on horseback, Streight watched as the last man crossed the bridge and slid down from his exhausted mule. Of the eight hundred mules he had received in Nashville, less than two dozen now remained on their feet. He looked out over the brigade spread out over an open field. They were indeed a sad-looking lot, filthy, unbathed for almost two weeks, unshaven – beards uncombed and matted with dried mud – uniforms ragged and torn, feet blistered inside of soggy boots. It was a sight that saddened him greatly, but he was also filled with an inordinate sense of pride. Never for a moment, to his knowledge, had a single one of them complained or deserted. Those they had left behind were either dead or too badly injured to travel. His men were the stuff of legend. Tired and bedraggled as they were, they were still a formidable fighting force with plenty of fight still left in them. A good rest and they would be on their feet again, ready to face whatever the future had to offer, and Rome was less than forty miles away. He did not intend to let them down.

It was just after midnight when Confederate scouts, Will Steiner and Sam Corbett, arrived in Rome. By one o'clock, the word had spread around the town that "The Yankees are comin'," and then, the two scouts dropped like dead men into the first two beds they could find. The warning was given, but most of their story was left untold. Only a few people knew that General Forrest was on his way.

Most of the able-bodied men of Rome were away fighting for the Confederacy. Those who remained were an eclectic assortment of older men and boys loosely organized into what they proudly claimed was a militia; the said militia was under the command of General George

Black, retired, now the local hotelier. It was not much of a force, but Black was determined to protect the city and that meant the city's two bridges on the Coosa River.

Within minutes of the scouts' arrival, the town was awake and preparing to defend itself. Church bells were ringing the alarm, men and women were running around in every direction. Some of them were armed with whatever weapons they could find, including modern military rifles, muzzle-loading shotguns, Revolutionary War flintlock muskets, swords, knives, hatchets, whatever they could lay their hands on.

Three riverboats at the town docks cut their moorings and steamed upriver, a railroad train fired up its boilers and by two o'clock was chuffing slowly northward toward Chattanooga. Two ancient cannon were set up behind barricades of earth-filled flour bags on the riverbank facing west, one on either side of the main covered bridge.

As luck would have it, there was at least one professional Confederate soldier in Rome that morning. Lieutenant C. W. Hooper of Stonewall Jackson's brigade was there to recruit for that famous general's command, and it was to him that General Black turned for assistance. There was not much the young lieutenant could do with what had by now turned into an unruly mob of yelling and wildly enthusiastic defenders. Still, he did his best to organize the more than two hundred men and boys into some sort of cohesive force, and deployed them on the riverbank to await the arrival of the raiders.

All of this activity was going on with most of the townsfolk under the impression that they were on their own. They were unaware that Forrest was hot on the heels of the Yankee army, as they thought it to be. Scouts were sent across the bridge to search the countryside for signs of the enemy force while the townsfolk prepared for battle.

Federal Captain Milton Russell had crossed the Chattooga ferry around midnight and had ridden throughout the night to arrive at the Shorter farm a little before nine o'clock in the morning.

295

Russell had not had an easy journey from Dyke's Ferry. The pace had been slow; he had lost men, mules, and horses steadily throughout the night. When he finally arrived at the Shorter place, he was running more than four hours behind schedule and was down to almost one hundred men. That four-hour delay cost him dearly, the more so Colonel Streight.

The Shorter farm was just a couple of miles west of Rome and within sight of the main Coosa River bridge. As he advanced his tiny force toward the bridge, he could see that it was heavily defended and that there was little chance that he could prevail in an all-out assault. Thus, he decided to wait for the main force to arrive. He wrote a quick note to Colonel Streight, outlining the situation, the defenses, and offering his own opinion that the bridge could not be taken by his own small force alone. He was further convinced of this during a conversation with one of the townsfolk who happened along the road past the farm.

Russell questioned her at some length, and she managed to convince the somewhat gullible captain that the town was occupied by a large force of Confederate infantry. Had he been able to arrive on time in the early hours of the morning, and had he been able to reconnoiter the approaches to the town and its bridges, he would have known better. But he was in sight of the now fortified main bridge and could see the two heavy guns and the men milling around them. And so, as tired as he and his men were, he was only too willing to believe the old woman's rambling story, and he settled down to wait, under the watchful eyes of Confederate Lieutenant Hooper and his ragtag army of defenders.

Colonel Streight's Provisional Brigade, now down to less than eleven hundred men, had crossed the Chattooga River at Dyke's Bridge at first light and had rested there for an hour before moving on toward Rome, now only thirty miles away. They traveled slowly, first for about four miles to the south of the bridge, then turned east and traveled on for five more miles. As they struggled onward, the pace slowed almost to a stop, and Streight knew it was time to rest yet again. It was now nine o'clock, and they were close to the junction of the Gaylesville-Gadsden road when they came across a small farm, just beyond Cedar Bluff.

They rode on past the farm, and the road junction, and Streight called for the column to halt, then gave the order for the horses and mules to be unsaddled and fed. The men were to feed themselves as best they could.

They hadn't been at rest many minutes when Captain Russell's courier arrived at the gallop, and he was bearing the worst possible news, that the defenses on the bridge over the Coosa were impregnable. Hearing that, and knowing that General Forrest with a vastly superior force was on his way to intercept him, Streight was devastated.

Streight dismounted, handed his horse off to a junior officer, and sat down on a large rock to think. His regimental commanders, Colonels Lawson and Rogers, along with Major Walker, now in command of the 73rd Indiana, Major Vananda and the ever attentive Captain Smith, respectfully stood back and waited.

For a few moments he sat with his elbows on his knees, his head bowed, his chin resting in his hands, his eyes closed. Then, abruptly, he rose to his feet, turned and faced his officers.

"It is over, gentlemen, but we shall give a good account of ourselves. Deploy the men in line of battle, over there, behind that low ridge in the field," he said, pointing the way. "Set them across the road that they may defend the approaches. Major Vananda, place your howitzers on the road at the center of the line—"

"Colonel, Sir," Vananda interrupted, "I am afraid we have little ammunition left, not enough for more than a few minutes, at best."

Streight merely nodded. "Captain Smith, go to the rear with the horses and what is left of the mules, and see that they are fed, sir. When that is done, see that they are secured, and then return here, and find your men a place in the line. In the meantime, sirs, we will wait."

They did not have to wait for long.

General Forrest had awoken early that morning at the Blount Plantation, and he was in a fine mood. He had had rested well, as had his men and their mounts and, by five o'clock, he was on the road following the Mule Soldiers at a fast pace. His men, now bright, bushy and ready for anything were laughing and shouting as they went. The ride to Dyke's Bridge took just over three hours, the trail being well marked by the passage of the Federal column.

The burned bridge posed no real delay for the Confederate force. The water was relatively shallow, though the bottom of the river was rocky and uneven.

"DISMOUNT! Unload those packs and strip off your clothes. We're gonna tote it all across the river on our backs." When he said *our* backs, he really meant *their* backs. Still, no sooner was the order given than the entire division, now down to only 520 men and officers, stripped down to their underwear, bundled up their clothes and, holding them above their heads, plunged into the swift-running waters of the Chattooga.

Once on the other side, they set their clothes in piles on the ground, then rushed back across the river for another load, frolicking in the chilly, yet refreshing, water.

"Get the horses across first," Forrest shouted. "Unlimber the guns, Mr. Morton. Put ropes on 'em and have the horses haul 'em across, quickly now. An' the caissons." He looked around. "You men, you over there, to me.

"Start totin' the ammunition across. That's it, up high on your shoulders. Higher, go on, right up high as you can. Now go, go, go."

One by one, the heavy packs were hand-carried across the river. Then they carried the food. In less than an hour, everything was on the east side of the river; the men were shivering, but laughing and joking as they struggled into their clothing. The horses were quickly reattached to the guns and caissons, the men mounted, and the column was moving eastward again at a fast clip; the river crossing had taken less than an hour.

At nine forty-five, the Federal brigade had been in line of battle behind the low ridge, no more than a grassy knoll perhaps three feet high, for just over an hour. Most of the men were lying on their backs, asleep.

To the west, out of sight behind a small hill, they heard them coming. At first, it was no more than a dull thrumming sound way off in the distance. Then as it grew louder, they recognized it for what it was, the sound of hundreds of horses' hooves thudding on the dirt road.

"ON YOUR FEET, MEN. Advance the colors." Less than a third of the men staggered to their feet and turned to face the enemy. The colors lay, still furled, beside their bearers.

Less than half of Streight's men were now alert and lying on their bellies, aiming their Smith carbines toward the sound of the galloping hooves. The rest were still dead to the world, their officers trying hard to kick some life into them. Then, as the forward elements of Forrest's division hammered at full gallop around the hill and into sight, they opened fire.

Forrest's lead elements, on rounding the hill, immediately spotted the Federal line of battle that stretched across the road and fields some five hundred yards away to the east and, with a hail of Minnie balls and canister flying over and around them, they hauled their horses to a long, skidding stop. Then they wheeled them and quickly rode back the way they had come, disappearing around the hill to the west, leaving two men dead on the road, several more wounded, and a half-dozen rider-less horses running panic away to the south, two of them streaming blood from wounds to their flanks.

Forrest, on hearing the burst of gunfire up ahead, called the column to a halt, then leaped down out of the saddle and ran, field glasses in hand, to the top of the hill. For several minutes he took stock

299

of the situation up ahead, looked around him, contemplating, and then, with a wide grin on his face, he ran back down the hill to rejoin his men.

"We have 'em, by God. We have 'em," he shouted excitedly. "Colonel McLemore, take your regiment and swing out to the left; Colonel Biffle, you go to the right. The rest of you with me."

Forrest's small force advanced slowly, on foot, to a point where they could see the Federal battle line, and then they dropped to the ground and opened fire.

From what he had seen from the top of the hill, Forrest knew that even with his numbers severely depleted, Streight still had him outnumbered by two-to-one, and that a frontal assault on Streight's line of battle would be extremely costly, to both sides, and with an uncertain outcome. But he had also noted that the hill was an almost perfectly round circle, a low, grass-covered pyramid some two hundred yards, or so, in diameter, perfect for what he had in mind.

"Colonel McLemore, pull your regiment back to the rear of the hill and remount.

"Captain Pointer. To me, sir."

Pointer ran, head down, to join Forrest

"Flag o' truce, Captain. Get their attention and ride on over. Tell their colonel that I demand their surrender and give him this." He handed the captain a scrap of rumpled paper.

The flag of truce was duly produced and Captain Pointer, with a small escort, rode slowly along the road toward the Federal positions.

The note was given to one of Streight's officers who handed it to Streight himself. He quickly scanned the content of the note, then turned to Colonel Lawson.

"He is demanding our surrender, 'to halt the useless further and useless effusion of blood.' Captain Jackson, please go to all of the senior officers and have them join me here, immediately."

Captain Pointer waited patiently.

The senior officers arrived one by one, Colonel Rogers first, Major Vananda last.

Streight looked at them each in turn, Forrest's paper in hand.

"He is demanding that we surrender, gentlemen... and that I cannot do unless certain conditions have been met. First, we must all agree that there is no other alternative, and second that we are facing a superior force.

"As you now know, Rome is forbidden to us; the bridges there are heavily defended and General Forrest is just a few hundred yards away. Without our being able to continue on to Rome, if the enemy is indeed superior, we do not so I believe, have any alternative but to concede to his demands. Your thoughts, sirs?"

Colonel Lawson cleared his throat. "Colonel, we have discussed this probability several times over the past several days. We do not, in my opinion, have any other option but to accede to the General's demands. We could fight on here, but the outcome would be inevitable. We would, in the end, have to surrender. It makes sense, as General Forrest has suggested to stop any further and unnecessary effusion of blood."

Streight nodded, then turned and walked the few yards to where Captain Pointer was waiting.

"Please tell the general that I would like to meet with him, face-to-face, to discuss the terms of our possible surrender."

Sergeant Major O'Sullivan, who had been listening to the conversation, slipped quietly away to the rear.

Pointer saluted, then wheeled his horse and galloped back to his own lines, and General Forrest.

Forrest listened to what Pointer had to say, then sent him back again to tell Streight that he would meet with him halfway between the two opposing sides at eleven o'clock.

Then he turned to his regimental commanders. "As soon as we meet, you begin moving the men and artillery, as I have laid out. Understood?"

They all nodded their agreement. Forrest looked at his watch; it was just after ten-thirty. He had time to clean up before his meeting with the Federal commander.

At precisely eleven o'clock that morning, General Nathan Bedford Forrest, dressed immaculately in a fresh shirt and uniform, and accompanied by a small escort of four junior officers, rode out to meet Colonel Streight.

"Good morning to you, Colonel," he said, returning Streight's stiff salute. "Are you ready to meet my terms, sir?"

"Before I can do that, General Forrest, I wish to enquire of your entire company strength...." He leaned sideways a little, looking over Forrest's shoulders. He could see Confederate troops in column of threes, circling to the right around the hill.

"Sir," he said, "it is not proper that you move troops while under a flag of truce. Please have them stop."

Forrest turned in the saddle and smiled as he saw his troopers trotting around the hill, each company separated by a section of artillery, two guns.

"I must apologize, Colonel. My officers had no orders to move their regiments. Captain Pointer, please ride to Colonel McLemore and ask him to hold for a while."

The captain rode away, the long column did not stop. It was, in fact, not a column at all, but just one regiment and two sections of artillery, each separated by a company of cavalry, all circling the small hill. What the Federals were seeing was no more than Forrest's bluff; he had effectively turned five hundred men into more than two thousand, and four guns into..., and he was inwardly smiling that his bluff appeared to be working. Streight's face was white.

"How... just how many guns do you have, General? I have already counted fourteen."

"Fourteen? I thought there were twenty. The rest must be still coming. Now, Colonel. Your surrender, if you please."

"Your terms, sir?"

"Your regiments will be allowed to retain their colors," Forrest began. "The officers will retain their side arms, the men their personal belongings, packs and so forth. Your men will be paroled and sent north within ten days. You and your senior officers will be held until you can be exchanged. Is that acceptable to you, Colonel?"

"For me, it is, but I would first like to confer with my officers before I formally accept you terms. Do you agree, sir?"

Forrest nodded. "We will meet again here in thirty minutes. In the meantime, I will have the terms written out for you."

The two men saluted and each returned to his respective side.

The two men met again at just after noon and both signed the articles of surrender. Colonel Abel D. Streight's grand enterprise was at an end; he was just twenty miles from his goal. But the ceremony was not yet over, nor for Forrest was the danger. If Streight should somehow discover the true strength of his force, Streight would be well within his rights to rescind the agreement and force Forrest into a battle that he might not win. It was imperative that the Federal brigade lay down its arms as soon as possible. And so, when Streight requested that they move off the road and into the open field for the laying down of arms, Forrest was alarmed but had no other choice than to agree.

But all went well. The Federal arms were stacked in the field and Forrest's men took charge of them. They also took charge of the remains of Colonel Streight's Provisional Brigade, now prisoners of war. The raid was now well and truly over.

The commanders at together, watching as the ceremony came to its conclusion. Forrest looked at Streight and offered him his hand.

"You, Colonel Streight, have no need for feelings of failure. You have led me on a merry chase, and you are a most valiant foe. You have fought the good fight until you could fight no more. No man could ask for more. You have my respect and my admiration, sir."

Streight looked him in the eye. "I thank you for your kind words, General, and...." Something in the look on Forrest's face filled him with dread.

"General Forrest, tell me, sir, and please tell me true. Exactly how many men did you have opposing me?"

"Now, Colonel. You know I can't tell you that nor would I if I could. Let's just say that it would not be quite as many as it appeared."

"That, sir," Abel Streight said, through gritted teeth, "is ungentlemanly, and I demand that you return our weapons and provide me with a fair fight."

"Colonel, never have I professed to be a gentleman. As to returning your weapons...." Forrest seemed to think about it, then said, "No! I cannot do that. You were duped, Colonel, an' well an' truly so. And... as I'm sure you well know," he said with a wide grin on his face, "all is fair in love an' war, Colonel; all is fair in love an' war."

High on a rise, several hundred yards away to the north, two men sat, watching, one on a large horse, the other on a mule. For several moments they sat, silhouetted against the bright sky, as the events unfolded before them. Then they turned and disappeared. From their place among the prisoners, Corporal Silas Cassell and Private Cullen Doyle watched them go. Cassell and Doyle and the rest of the enlisted men were held in Rome for almost two weeks before they were paroled and sent north to be exchanged.

Nine days later, Sergeant Major Ignatius O'Sullivan and Corporal Boone Coffin rode into the Federal encampment at Murfreesboro, tired, but in good spirits.

Author's Note:

Much credit must be given to Robert L. Willett who wrote what I consider to be THE definitive work on this subject: *The Lightning Mule Brigade*. I used it extensively during my research, along with various other historical accounts and reports of Streight's Raid. You can read *The Lightning Mule Brigade* for yourself. It's available in paperback on Amazon.

Everything you have read here actually happened. Yes, even the incident of the cats and hornets. The words the characters spoke are mine. The timeline is accurate. There are no available maps, so I had to build my own. They, too, are as accurate as I could make them.

There are many versions of Emma Sansom's story, many of them sensationalized and embellished by the press of the day. Most of what was reported about the incident at the time makes little sense, knowing what we know today. What you read here is my own version of the way I think it probably happened.

The story of Federal Private McWilliams losing his head? Yes, it actually happened.

Colonel Streight and his officers were sent to Libby prison where they were held until the end of the war with the exception of Colonel Streight, who, along with more than a hundred more Federal officers, escaped via a tunnel dug from the cellars... but that's another story. Streight and Captain W. Scearce made their way across many miles of Confederate territory and arrived in Washington on March 1, 1864. He rejoined his regiment and was promoted to Brigadier General in March 1865. He retired one week later and died at his home in 1892 aged sixty-three.

Streight's Raid took place at the same time as, and was loosely coordinated with, the more famous Grierson's Raid (the inspiration for the book, *The Horse Soldiers* by Harold Sinclair, and the movie of the same name starring John Wayne and William Holden).

I had a lot of fun creating the fictional characters. My inspiration for Sergeant Major O'Sullivan was the cavalryman you see on the front cover of the book. Silas Cassell was created for one of my friends, Ken Cassell.

Thank you.

If you liked this book, I really would appreciate it if you would take just a minute write a brief review on Amazon (just a sentence will do). It really does help. If you have comments or questions, you can contact me by email at blair@blairhoward.com, and you can visit my website http://www.blairhoward.com to view my blog, and for a complete list of my books. So, I thank you for purchasing the book. I hope you enjoyed reading it as much as I did writing it. If so, you may also enjoy my novels of the Civil War:

Comanche

A Novel of the Old West

On a dark day in April 1865, only days after the Civil War had ended, a band of former Confederate guerillas slaughtered more than forty Comanches, most of them women and children. Thus began a six-month reign of terror along the Santa Fe Trail as Comanche chief, White Eagle, took his revenge. The U.S. Cavalry was assigned the task of tracking White Eagle and his warriors down. Lieutenant Colonel Ignatius O'Sullivan's orders were to either bring them in or kill them. O'Sullivan, with two companies of cavalry tracked the Comanches through the mountains for more than six weeks, until....

O'Sullivan took to the trail in July of 1865, and followed them into the mountains along the northern border of Comanche lands. Can he bring the wily chief and his well-armed warriors to bay? Can his soldiers fight the Comanche on their own ground?

You can grab your copy here on Amazon for just $3.99. It's free to read for Kindle Unlimited members. Here's the actual link: http://www.amazon.com/dp/B00XLX9OSC

The Chase

A Novel of the American Civil War

During the last few days of the Civil War, a company of Confederate raiders rode into the small Kansas town of Elbow. There they raped, pillaged and murdered among the local populace, thus triggering a chain of events and a chase that extended for more than a thousand miles across the grasslands and mountains of Kansas and the deserts of New Mexico.

Along the way, Confederate Lieutenant Jesse Quintana, a ruthless, cold-blooded killer without a conscience, and his men massacred a band of Comanche women and children, fought two battles with Comanche War Chief, White Eagle, and murdered and plundered his way southwest along the Santa Fe Trail.

Quintana had a nine-day start over his pursuers, Captain Ignatius O'Sullivan and Sergeant Major Boone Coffin, along with an Osage Indian scout and a small company of Federal cavalry. The climactic end to the chase came among the mountains on the Mexican border six weeks after it began.

You will remember O'Sullivan and Coffin from the author's previous novel, *The Mule Soldiers*. Their adventures continue.

You can grab your copy on Amazon. It's free to read for Kindle Unlimited members. Here's the link:

http://www.amazon.com/dp/B00V0VZ8ZK

Chickamauga
A Novel of the American Civil War

Just after first light on the morning of September 18, 1863, in the deep woods on the banks of Chickamauga Creek, a single brigade of Federal infantry stumbled into a full division of Confederate cavalry, and so began one of the bloodiest conflicts of the American Civil War.

Chickamauga is the true story–fictionalized–of that momentous conflict. For two days, the Confederate Army of Tennessee, under the command of General Braxton Bragg, and the Federal Army of the

Cumberland led by Major General William Rosecrans, tore at one another during a battle that ebbed and flowed, favoring first one side and then the other. But, the Devil is in the details, and a single, inaccurate battlefield report led to a glorious Confederate charge and the total and devastating defeat of the Federal army. Chickamauga is the story of heroism, desperate deeds, and death and destruction on a scale which had never been seen before.

The story of the Battle of Chickamauga is told through the eyes of the Generals who planned the grand strategies, and the soldiers who fought, often hand-to-hand, one of the bloodiest conflicts in American History.

Chickamauga is the intense story of the young men–the everyday soldiers, who must fight, not only the enemy, but also their own fears and inner doubts to find the courage to face seemingly insurmountable odds. It's also the story of their superior officers, and the generals who control their fates–men who are determined to charge into Hell itself to achieve victory. You'll stand side-by-side with them as they contest one disordered, ear splitting, ground shaking battle after another.

The author weaves unbelievable, but true, tales of breakdowns in communication, insubordinate commanders, and strategies that falter and fail in the heat of total war. You'll learn of the iron bonds forged between friends and companions on the battlefield, and morals and ideals brought into question. You will become a part of a victory achieved through pure grit and dogged determination, split-second decisions, and total dedication to the cause. Chickamauga is the story of ordinary people in extraordinary times.

This 1863 battle–on the banks of Chickamauga Creek, the River of Death–cost the armies of both sides more than 37,000 casualties; it was the bloodiest two days of the entire Civil War.

You can grab your copy on Amazon. It's free to read for Kindle Unlimited members. Here's the link: http://www.amazon.com/dp/B00MBU78HK

A Little More Than Kin

A Short Story of the Supernatural

This short story of the supernatural came from an idea I had many years ago when I was wandering around a grand old house turned hotel on Jeykll Island on the coast of Georgia. To be honest, I was being nosy. I was where I shouldn't have been. Anyway, I went into one of the rooms. It was bare except for a single piece of furniture and an old wooden washstand with a porcelain bowl and jug thereon. Even though it was the middle of summer, it was cold in that room and I had a weird feeling that I was being watched. I stayed only a couple of minutes and then left. No, nothing happened but that experience did provide the inspiration for this story, A Little More Than Kin. You can grab your copy here on Amazon. It's free for Kindle Unlimited members. Here's the actual link: www.amazon.com/gp/product/B00YSDG6B2

25601039R00175

Made in the USA
San Bernardino, CA
13 February 2019